P9-DDF-817

**HERITAGE
VILLAGE
LIBRARY**

THIS BOOK DONATED BY

HERITAGE VILLAGE LIBRARY FUND

Acclaim for the Work of DONALD E. WESTLAKE!

"Dark and delicious."
— *New York Times*

"[A] book by this guy is cause for happiness."
— *Stephen King*

"Donald Westlake must be one of the best craftsmen now crafting stories."
— *George F. Will*

"Westlake is a national literary treasure."
— *Booklist*

"Westlake knows precisely how to grab a reader, draw him or her into the story, and then slowly tighten his grip until escape is impossible."
— *Washington Post Book World*

"Brilliant."
— *GQ*

"A wonderful read."
— *Playboy*

"Marvelous."
— *Entertainment Weekly*

"Tantalizing."
— *Wall Street Journal*

"A brilliant invention."
— *New York Review of Books*

"A tremendously skillful, smart writer."
— *Time Out New York*

"Suspenseful...As always, [Westlake] writes like the
consummate pro he is."
— *Cleveland Plain Dealer*

"Westlake remains in perfect command; there's not a
word...out of place."
— *San Diego Union-Tribune*

"Westlake is one of the best."
— *Los Angeles Times*

Curtis couldn't stop staring at the island, as they moved out away from the Mallory.

Mud. Soup, as Manville had predicted, in which every mark of man had sunk and crumbled and disappeared. And when he was ready, the same thing, the same sudden stripping away and finality, would happen again, on a much vaster scale. The buildings that fell then, when he was ready, the buildings that would crumble and melt away into the sudden soup, would not be low half-rotted barracks, but skyscrapers, concrete and metal and glass, some of which he himself had built, or helped to build.

I gave them, he thought, I'll take them away. And with just as much pleasure, just as much skill, just as much efficiency, the buildings he had helped put up he would knock down again...

HARD CASE CRIME BOOKS
BY DONALD E. WESTLAKE:

361
THE COMEDY IS FINISHED
THE CUTIE
FOREVER AND A DEATH
LEMONS NEVER LIE (writing as Richard Stark)
MEMORY
SOMEBODY OWES ME MONEY

SOME OTHER HARD CASE CRIME BOOKS
YOU WILL ENJOY:

JOYLAND by Stephen King
THE COCKTAIL WAITRESS by James M. Cain
THE TWENTY-YEAR DEATH by Ariel S. Winter
ODDS ON by Michael Crichton writing as John Lange
BRAINQUAKE by Samuel Fuller
EASY DEATH by Daniel Boyd
THIEVES FALL OUT by Gore Vidal
SO NUDE, SO DEAD by Ed McBain
THE GIRL WITH THE DEEP BLUE EYES
by Lawrence Block
QUARRY by Max Allan Collins
PIMP by Ken Bruen and Jason Starr
SOHO SINS by Richard Vine
THE KNIFE SLIPPED by Erle Stanley Gardner
SNATCH by Gregory Mcdonald

FOREVER
and a
DEATH

by **Donald E. Westlake**

A HARD CASE CRIME NOVEL

7/17

A HARD CASE CRIME BOOK
(HCC-129)
First Hard Case Crime edition: June 2017

Published by
Titan Books
A division of Titan Publishing Group Ltd
144 Southwark Street
London SE1 0UP

in collaboration with Winterfall LLC

Copyright © 2017 by the Estate of Donald E. Westlake

Cover painting copyright © 2017 by Paul Mann

All rights reserved. No part of this book may be reproduced or transmitted in any form or by any electronic or mechanical means, including photocopying, recording or by any information storage and retrieval system, without the written permission of the publisher, except where permitted by law.

This book is a work of fiction. Names, characters, places, and incidents either are the products of the author's imagination or are used fictitiously, and any resemblance to actual events or persons, living or dead, is entirely coincidental.

Print edition ISBN 978-1-78565-423-7
E-book ISBN 978-1-78565-424-4

Design direction by Max Phillips
www.maxphillips.net

Typeset by Swordsmith Productions

The name "Hard Case Crime" and the Hard Case Crime logo are trademarks of Winterfall LLC. Hard Case Crime books are selected and edited by Charles Ardai.

Printed in the United States of America

Visit us on the web at www.HardCaseCrime.com

ONE

I

The helicopter sped eastward under a clear blue sky, low over the Coral Sea. Its flattened footprint scudded beneath it, rolling out the slate-gray waves, then immediately gone, and the waves leaped up again.

Inside, the copter had been custom refitted with light blue industrial carpet over a plywood floor on which stood eight broad swivel chairs in two rows of four, upholstered in a darker blue vinyl. A gray bulkhead up front with a curtain in its doorway separated this main cabin from a small galley, with the pilot's compartment beyond that. On the bulkhead wall, next to the doorway, was imprinted a large symbol of an entwined RC, in dark red, looking vaguely snakelike or like an espaliered tree.

Richard Curtis, owner of the initials and the helicopter and almost everything else he could see, occupied the rear seat on the right. The other three passengers, two men and a woman, all venture capitalists with whom Curtis had had dealings in the past, were his guests, seated where he could look at them, consider them. There was too much noise inside here from engine and wind to make conversation possible, but Curtis didn't need conversation, not now. What these three knew of his business and the reason for this flight was what they needed to know, and what they didn't know was everything that mattered.

They had flown out here from Townsville, on Australia's northeast coast, into the clear morning air, crossing over the southern part of the Great Barrier Reef, past Tregosse Island and Diamond Island and the Lihou Cays, and now Curtis felt the craft veer slightly to the right, which must mean the pilot had found the *Mallory*.

Yes, tugging gently at its sea anchor in the modest ocean swell, the yacht *Mallory*, named for Curtis's father and with the entwined RC next to the name on both sides of the bow, stood offshore from Kanowit Island, where the final preparations were underway. George Manville, the engineer, would be over there on the island; this experiment was his baby. But he'd return to the *Mallory* when he saw the chopper arrive.

The circular white landing pad was aft, above and just forward of the observation area at the fantail. The helicopter lowered slowly, delicately, toward that constantly shifting white circle, then at last gently touched it and immediately seemed to sag, as though to clutch and hold onto the moving ship.

Even before the rotor blades had stopped turning, two groups of men ran forward, crouched, converging on the copter. The four men in gray work jumpers secured the craft to guy cables fixed in the deck, while the two in white steward uniforms slid open the side door, lowered the metal stairs, and stood by to offer a helping hand.

Curtis debarked first, nodding at the stewards, needing no help. An ocean breeze ruffled his thin gray hair as he crossed the pad, and he patted it down. He looked toward Kanowit and yes, the launch was coming this way, almost invisible against the gray sea except for its white wake.

Glass doors slid automatically open as Curtis entered the lounge, where a third steward waited, smiling a greeting, saying, "Morning, Mr. Curtis. Good flight?"

Curtis never thought about journeys, only destinations. What was a good flight? One where you weren't killed? He ignored the question, saying, "Tell Manville to come see me in my cabin as soon as possible." Turning to his three guests, who had followed him in here, he said, "The stewards will show you your cabins. You'll have time to freshen up before the show starts."

"A beautiful boat," Bill Hardy said, smiling as he looked around in honest envy. An Australian, he was both the most candid and the shrewdest of the three.

"Thank you," Curtis said, returning Hardy's smile, though not with as much candor. "I like the *Mallory*, it relaxes me." In fact nothing relaxed him.

Then he nodded to them all, and went away to his cabin, forward, just behind the bridge, where he could be alone until Manville arrived. He was consumed with so much anger, so much hatred, that he found it hard to be around other people for very long. The snarl beneath the surface kept wanting to break through.

And of course, everybody knew about it, which only made things worse. Everybody knew they'd driven Richard Curtis out of Hong Kong, those mainland bastards, once they'd taken over. Everybody knew they'd cheated him, and robbed him, and driven him out of his home, his industry, his *life*. Everybody knew Richard Curtis's great humiliation. But what nobody knew was that the game wasn't over.

Binoculars were kept in the drawer of the table by the large picture window in the parlor of his two-room cabin suite. Looking through them, Curtis saw Manville's launch almost here, and far away—brought much closer through the lenses— Kanowit Island, a round low hillock of scrub in the sea, with the rotten bent shapes of the Japanese army's barracks and sheds, nearly sixty years old, standing here and there on the island like the ghost town remnants they were.

Curtis watched the island through the binoculars. Manville's people were still at work over there, just visible, scurrying like ants, completing the preparations.

In how long—two hours?—Kanowit Island would be changed completely from what it now was, wrenched into a new existence. If Manville were right, it would change into something good and useful; if he were wrong, it would become something destroyed and irreparable. But Manville had to be right, Curtis needed him to be right.

In how long—two hours?—step one.

2

Kim Baldur stepped out of her jeans, lost her balance, and grabbed the upright post of the bunkbed beside her to keep her feet. The *Planetwatch III* had been steaming serenely forward through the sea, at a regular and pleasing rhythm, and had made that one little faltering jounce at just the wrong second.

Kim decided, to be on the safe side, she should sit down on the lower bunk—it belonged to Angela, her bunkmate, already up on deck—while she finished removing the jeans and then pushed her feet down into the legs of the wetsuit. The neoprene felt, as always, a little slick and slimy when she first put it on, but her body would slowly warm it, and later, if she was in the water, it would be the most comfortable thing you could imagine.

Would she go into the water? She wanted to, she always did, but who knew what would happen today, when they finally got to the island? Something, I hope, she thought. Let *something* happen.

This was her first run on *Planetwatch III*, the first time she'd volunteered with this ecological guardian group, and she was reluctant to admit to herself that so far it had been mostly boring. She was 23, she had nothing behind her but college and a few discarded boyfriends, and it had seemed to her, before she would have to settle down into an ordinary career, that she should put her time and her intelligence and her enthusiasm to work somehow, for some greater good. To join the volunteers of Planetwatch, to use the SCUBA-diving skills she'd learned as a teenager in the Caribbean, to sail the high seas on a mission to save the world, had seemed beforehand the height of adventure. But it was strange how the days on the ship were merely drudgery, and stranger still how indifferent to her heroism the world remained.

Dressed, and with her flippers tucked under her left arm, Kim left the small metal-walled cabin. Outside, the narrow corridor was empty, and echoed as usual with some faint distant clang; something to do with the engine room.

As she moved along the corridor toward the ladder, which was merely a series of metal rungs bolted into the side wall and leading up to a round hatch always kept open except in heavy weather, Kim unconsciously brushed her right knuckles along the cool wall, a habit she had learned early on because of the sometimes unpredictable movements of the ship.

A small freighter that for years, under the name *Nyota*, had plied the Indian Ocean out of Djibouti, this vessel had been bought cheap by supporters of Planetwatch after *Planetwatch II* had been sunk by an underwater explosive off a French atoll. She was a solid ship, refitted for passengers but still retaining a bluntness and a tendency to plunge hard into the waves that was a leftover from her freighter days.

Kim climbed the ladder one-handed, lithe as a monkey, the flippers still under her left arm. At the top, she turned to the open doorway in the metal wall just beside her and stepped out onto the deck.

Here she stood at the prow, one deck below the bridge, her ears full of the rushing hiss of the ship as it cleaved its way through the water. The sense of motion this far forward was mostly vertical, short hard slaps up and down as *Planetwatch III* sliced northward toward Kanowit.

She looked first at the sea; she always did. Today it was a pebbly mid-gray, with darker tones beneath and tiny whitecaps popping here and there. A three-foot sea, at most; bliss to dive in.

And the sky was almost completely clear, a gleaming acrylic

blue, except for a bundle of gray clouds along the western horizon, toward Australia. They'd be having a beautiful sunset over there, some hours from now.

It had at first astonished Kim that there were no real sunsets in mid-ocean, not what was meant by the phrase 'a beautiful sunset.' The sun did often go down behind the waves in a variegated display of color, pale shades of pink and blue and green darkening toward night, but all in a neat and controlled manner, without that bruised sky, those blazing reds and oranges, that lush riot of purple exclamation points. "What you're looking at when you look at a sunset ashore," Jerry had explained, early in the trip, "is pollution. What you see out here is the natural sunset. What people ooh and aah over back home is just rotten air, clouds of toxic waste, streams of acid rain. When the sunset you see off the coast of Malibu looks like that one out there, we'll know we've done our job."

Jerry Diedrich was Planetwatch's leader aboard, and Kim was coming to the belief that he knew everything about everything. A lean and weathered man in his early forties, he had a starving poet's good looks, and Kim sheepishly knew she would have developed a schoolgirl crush on him weeks ago if he hadn't made his homosexuality so open and unquestionable. (He and Luther Rickendorf were the only couple on the ship.)

Turning away from sea and sky, Kim looked up toward the recessed deck next above her, where Angela stood, in faded cut-offs and a dark green halter, shielding her eyes from the sun with both cupped hands as she stared out at the sea.

"Kanowit Island," Angela said, and pointed out toward the horizon, northward. "Dead ahead. Jerry says we'll be there in fifteen minutes."

"Good," Kim said. She moved away down the narrow port deck toward the SCUBA tanks.

3

"This is George Manville, our genius engineer," Curtis said. "George, this is Bill Hardy, from Australia, Abdullah Wayarabo from Indonesia, Madame Zilah Graca deCastro from Brazil."

They all greeted each other, Curtis smiling on them with what seemed like paternal indulgence, seeing the contrasts among them. Manville, for instance, was an engineer, and nothing but an engineer, who had made no accommodation to the fact that he was presently quartered on a ship. He still wore the same workboots, the same chinos, the same button-down work shirt with the ballpoint pen in his breast pocket, as though he were on some construction site in Chicago. He was a simple creature, George Manville, but brilliant, usefully brilliant.

The venture capitalists were as unlike one another as they were unlike George Manville. Bill Hardy, the Australian, was open and hearty, a glad-hander, everybody's pal, who hid his icy shrewdness as though it were a fault, rather than his greatest strength. Abdullah Wayarabo, connected through various marriages to the Indonesian royal family, had a courtier's smile and smoothness mixed with the arrogant assurance of the extremely rich; he could command while seeming to be obsequious, and almost always get his way. Madame deCastro, the Brazilian widow of a major construction figure in South America, was a heavyset severe woman in her sixties, who had never been noticed during her husband's life; since his death, it had become clear she'd been the brains of the company all along.

These three, plus Manville and Curtis, were gathered in the

aft lounge for the explanations that would precede the event on the island. Manville had set up two easels with charts and drawings stacked on them, and now stood to one side while Curtis began: "The history of Kanowit Island is brief. I bought it, two years ago, from Australia. They retained mineral rights, but it's a coral atoll, there's nothing under it except porous rock and salt water. Australia got it in 1946, at the end of the war, from the Japanese, who had occupied it in 1937. Before that it had been nominally Spanish, having been claimed for the Spanish throne in the eighteenth century, but Spain never occupied the island in any way and no longer contests ownership. The title is skimpy, but it's clean. The island is mine."

Wayarabo said, "Does Australia claim legal jurisdiction?"

"Yes." Curtis spread his hands. "Every dry inch of the planet must be under the legal and political control of *some* nation, and for us Australia's not a bad jurisdiction at all. There's nothing we mean to do on the island that breaks any of their laws."

Hardy said, "Gambling?"

"My lawyers already cleared that," Curtis told him. "We're considered offshore, as though we were a ship. We can operate a casino, but we must pay taxes to Australia. They understand and approve that what we want to do here is create a new destination resort. A championship-level golf course, tennis courts, a casino, a first-class hotel, conference rooms. Kanowit Island stands at the southern tip of the Great Barrier Reef, longest barrier reef in the world, where the best snorkeling on Earth can be found. We've already made arrangements with the appropriate airlines for flights, when we're ready, from Australia, the Philippines and Hawaii."

Madame deCastro said, "Club Med?"

"More up-market than that," Curtis told her. "Think Rock Resorts, only international. We've done customer projections, we'll give you all of that. But the point today is the demonstration. George?"

Manville stepped forward as though he were about to run them through a routine of calisthenics. He said, "Kanowit Island is an irregular oval, almost a circle, roughly two miles across. The island was smaller when the Japanese took over in the thirties; they built a very thick concrete ring wall, then did landfill into it from the surrounding ocean floor. The island is really just a bit of coral that sticks above the surface of the sea, and it's very shallow for almost half a mile out from it in all directions, so no large boats can go in, unless we were to cut a channel in the coral, and that we wouldn't be permitted to do."

Wayarabo, with a faint smile, said, "You'd have environmentalists all over you."

"We may have anyway," Curtis told him, and nodded to Manville: "Go on, George."

"Having enlarged the island," Manville said, "the Japanese installed structures and equipment to make it a listening post, to track cargo convoys or military fleets. Most of the equipment was in a honeycomb of tunnels cut into the landfill. At the end of the war, most of the equipment was removed. The rest, and the buildings, were abandoned and are now a ruin."

"Normally," Curtis said, "what we would have to do, with such a place as that, is bring in bulldozers, heavy equipment, barge them all in and living accommodations for the crews, and painstakingly reconfigure the whole island to our needs."

"Expensive," Madame deCastro said.

"Even impractical," Wayarabo suggested.

"Which is why," Curtis said, "we're trying this experiment."

Manville said, "What we're going to use today is a wave, sea water itself, a very special kind of oscillating wave called a soliton. The soliton is usually created deep in the ocean, caused by a seismic shift in the ocean floor, and it's the root cause of the tsunami, the huge destructive wave that every once in a while marches across the Pacific."

"But not around here," Curtis hastened to add. "The tsunami normally hits farther north, sometimes gets all the way to Japan."

Manville said, "The soliton has been recreated in laboratory conditions, by scientists who want to study it, possibly learn how to control it. They've written papers on their work. We're adapting those papers to our own needs. What we're doing here, we've flooded the tunnels the Japanese dug, we've sealed off all the exits, we've placed small dynamite charges at specific spots in the tunnels, radio-controlled, and they'll discharge serially, just about ten minutes from now. If we've done our job right—" Manville shrugged, while Curtis looked grim "—the charges will create a laboratory-style soliton, an oscillating wave."

Wayarabo said, "Which will do what?"

Curtis said, "The Japanese increased the size of the island with landfill. The tunnels are in the landfill, because the coral beneath is too porous and the sea would come in. Landfill, no matter how well done, is unstable. In the Los Angeles earthquake a few years ago, several pieces of elevated freeway collapsed, and every one of them was built on landfill. One of the most serious collapses was at a place called La Cienega Boulevard, and in Spanish 'la cienega' means 'the swamp.' "

Hardy said, "You mean to break up the landfill with this wave?"

"We mean to turn it into soup," Curtis told him.

Manville said, "The soliton, once it gets started, feeds itself, builds its own energy for quite a long time. That oscillating wave will break down the tunnel walls and spread through the landfill, breaking it up, so that when it finally wears itself out, the entire island, if our projections are right, will be nothing but a lake of mud, held in by the concrete retaining wall."

Hardy said, "If the wall doesn't go."

"We've tested the wall," Manville assured him, "and it should stand firm."

Madame deCastro said, "If the wave keeps generating its own force, won't it eventually push down into the coral, start breaking *that* up? Then at the end you wouldn't have any island at all, and possibly some damage to the reef."

"That's what some of the environmentalists are bleating about," Curtis told her, "and they're wrong."

Manville said, "The power has exits, through the landfill and eventually upward. Force always takes the easiest route, and the coral isn't the easiest route."

Curtis said, "What's going to happen is, the buildings will break up and sink into the mud. The tunnels will fill in. Nothing will be left but mud, which we think will dry in five to six weeks, draining downward through the coral, to leave a clean, flat, absolutely empty island. Then we come in with our own soil, our plantings, our construction crews. As a way to clear a site—"

"If it works," Manville said. He had to express that engineer's caution, he had to keep doing it.

"Yes," Curtis said, irritated. "If it works, and in my heart I know it will, it can save us millions, not only on this project, but on other projects in the future."

A steward had appeared in the doorway while Curtis was speaking, and had waited for Curtis to be done. Now he said, "Sir, the captain asks me to inform you, a ship is moving toward the island."

4

Jerry Diedrich stood beside Captain Cousseran on the bridge of *Planetwatch III* and looked out at Kanowit Island, so near and yet so far. It seemed deserted, but with some new low metal structures among the crumbling barracks buildings; controls for the explosion? Well off from the island to port waited the yacht, *Mallory*, solid, starkly white, hardly moving in the small sea. To Jerry, the yacht looked mostly like a dove, impossibly large, resting in the water, wings folded; and what a wrong image *that* was!

Captain Cousseran, a heavyset Belgian, a man who'd captained Dutch cargo ships until his retirement, when he'd volunteered to join Planetwatch, probably most out of boredom, spoke in French to his steersman, then said to Jerry, "This is as close as we can go."

"We'll send a launch ashore," Jerry said, and the radioman, at his desk behind the others, said, "Captain, the *Mallory* is calling us."

Jerry grinned. "I thought he might. Full of threats, I suppose."

"I'll take it," Captain Cousseran said, reaching for his microphone.

Jerry said, "Put it on the loudhailer, let the whole ship hear it."

"Yes, good."

When next he spoke, Captain Cousseran's voice echoed outside the bridge, loud and distorted, but plain enough to be heard and understood anywhere on the ship. The sound, so strong here, would fade away almost to nothing long before it reached the *Mallory*. *"This is Captain Cousseran."*

"This is Captain Zhang Yung-tsien of the Mallory. *I am asked to inform you that you are too close to Kanowit Island for safety."*

"It is the intention of some members of our party to go ashore."

"You cannot approach any closer, the sea is too shallow."

"They will go by launch."

"I am asked to inform you that a series of explosions will shortly take place on the island, and it will not be safe there, or anywhere close by. There will be a considerable shock wave."

"Since my party is determined to go ashore, Captain Zhang, I would ask you to delay the explosion until we can have a face-to-face meeting."

"I am asked to inform you that that is impossible. The timing devices on the island have been set, and it is too late to change or stop them."

Jerry, angry, feeling the old frustration, clenched his fists. "He's lying!"

"Surely, Captain Zhang, there is a fail-safe mechanism to permit you to abort the explosion."

"There is not. I am asked to inform you that the timing equipment for the explosions is on the island, that they are set to begin the operation in under four minutes from now, and that it would be impossible at this point to get to the island in time to stop them. Anyone who tries to approach the island now is in very grave danger."

"Lying, lying." Jerry gritted his teeth, partly because he was afraid Captain Zhang was telling the truth. He needed to stop Richard Curtis, stop him now, stop him for good.

"Captain Zhang. I can't believe your employer would create such a dangerous situation, leaving himself open to serious con- sequences if anyone should be harmed. Our launch will be ready to leave in two minutes. Again. I ask you—"

"This is Richard Curtis."

Jerry's shoulders hunched at the sound of the voice, the sound of the name. So arrogant, so sure of his power, so sure he's *unassailable*. We'll see.

And the hated voice went on:

"This is my ship and that is my island, and you are trespassing. I have explosives over there on my island that will kill anybody who gets too close to it. You have been warned, repeatedly, and if any harm happens to the sentimental idiots who are your passengers it is on their—"

Jerry couldn't stand it anymore, and grabbed the mike away from Captain Cousseran. When he spoke, he knew his voice trembled with passion, but he couldn't help it, and he didn't care:

"And if harm happens to the reef? Irreparable harm to the coral?"

"Who is that?"

"This is Jerry Diedrich, leader of the sentimental idiots. I will personally be in that—"

Out of the corner of his eye he saw it; an orange-suited figure rolled backwards over the rail and down into the sea.

He was so startled the words faltered in his mouth.

Who was that? He held the mike, but he couldn't speak.

Kim! It had to be, he knew it, that goddam eager stupid Kim. What was she doing? Did she think he *wanted* her to kill herself?

Hand trembling, Jerry held the mike against his lips, so that his chattering teeth hit the metal:

"You saw that. You have to stop it now. You have no choice."

5

"Who *is* that?"

Curtis stared through his binoculars, held in his left hand with the mike in his right, but the diver had disappeared the instant he hit the water. Into the mike, with impatient sincerity, Curtis said, "Diedrich, don't be a fool. Get that man back."

The voice over the radio sounded scared, as well it should: "I can't. I didn't— It wasn't my order."

Was the diver moving toward the island? Or would he stay by the ship, waiting to be told what to do next? Curtis said, "If that idiot gets too close to the island, he's dead. I'm telling you, Diedrich, and it's true. We're not talking one explosion here, we're talking half a dozen in a rolling pattern, each with its own shock wave. If that man's going toward the island, you've killed one of your own people. And I will pursue you in the Australian courts."

"Then *stop* it!"

"I *can't*, you bloody fool! You've been told and told. It's too late."

The silence from Diedrich sounded shocked, but there was nothing to be done about it, not now. Handing the mike to Captain Zhang, Curtis said, "There's nothing more to say to them." Turning away, carrying the binoculars, he stepped out onto the wing, the small open area to the right of the bridge. He leaned on the rail there and, through the glasses, he looked toward Kanowit, empty and silent.

Diedrich. It was him again, Jerry Diedrich. The other environmental groups, and even other arms of Planetwatch, spent most of their time on the government polluters, the bomb-testers and radioactive-waste dumpers. Only Diedrich was always there, every single time, when the Curtis Construction Company was doing anything that impinged even slightly on environmental concerns.

Curtis Construction was large, not as large as it used to be, but still big enough to be a player in most of the major construction work around the globe, the dams, the widening of rivers, deepening of ports, construction of harbors. And every time, sooner or later, Diedrich would appear, a plague, a pest.

Would he show up later, in Hong Kong, when it really mattered? Was there no way to stop him?

Holding the binoculars, Curtis scanned the water between the island and the environmentalists' ship, but could see nothing. The diver would stay underwater, to move faster, but couldn't be very deep, not amidst all that coral. If he was out there now, near the island, and if the shock waves didn't kill him, then being battered repeatedly against razor-edge outcroppings of coral surely would.

He hadn't meant anyone to die, not this time. Later, when the real thing happened, a whole lot of people would die, but *they* would deserve it. These environmentalists were merely well-meaning ignoramuses, minor irritations; all except Diedrich. There was no need, as the French had once done, to kill them.

But if the diver *did* die, could that be used to hamper Diedrich, tie him up, keep him away when it was important for Curtis to be unobserved? There were recordings of the ship-to-ship conversation, there would be proof of the repeated warnings, and of Diedrich's refusal to heed them. When he got back to Sydney, Curtis would turn it all over to the lawyers, let them harry Diedrich for a while, see how he enjoyed it,

Curtis scanned the ocean through the binoculars, seeing

nothing, only the wavelets, the constant shifting movement of the sea. And then the ocean trembled, it flattened into hobnails, and the binoculars shuddered, punching painfully against Curtis's face.

6

At first the sea seemed to shrink, to turn a darker gray, as though it had grown suddenly cold, with goosebumps. There was a silence then, a pregnant silence, like the cottony absence of sound just before a thunderstorm. The island seemed to rise slightly from the sea, the concrete collar of its retaining wall standing out crisp and clear, every flaw and hollow in the length of it as vivid as if done in an etching.

Then a ripple appeared, faint at first, and rolled outward from the island, all around, just beneath the surface, like a representation of radio waves. With the ripple came a muttering, a grumbling, as though boulders sheathed in wool were being rolled together in some deep cave. And the ripple came outward, outward, not slackening, not losing power, with more ripples emerging behind it.

Planetwatch III lay abeam the island, portside facing it, preparatory to lowering its launch. That first ripple, now visible as a strong surge just below the waves, hit the ship all along its port side and rocked it like a cradle. Crashing sounds came from everywhere aboard as anything on the ship that wasn't tied down was flung away. Half the ship's passengers and crew lost their feet, falling awkwardly, bruising elbows and knees and heads.

Planetwatch III righted itself groggily, a fighter who's been hurt but not yet downed, and Captain Cousseran shouted in French to the steersman. And the next ripple came steadily on, rolling closer.

Jerry Diedrich had been knocked painfully sideways against

the metal wall of the bridge, narrowly missing the sidemost large window pane. Now, his left arm streaked with pain, his chest aching, he cried, "Captain! What are you doing?"

"Moving," the captain told him, short and unapologetic. He was master of his bridge, and of his ship. "We're too close," he said, and *Planetwatch III* started the slow process of its turn, away from the island.

Jerry clung to the rail. "But…what about Kim?"

Captain Cousseran gestured at the sea and the island. "See for yourself."

Jerry saw; he had to admit he saw. Closer to the island, the sea had begun to boil, with whitecaps that leaped like dolphins. The discrete ripples rolled outward like moving rings of Saturn, and the island itself had begun to change, as though it had abruptly gone out of focus. The land seemed to shudder, and the buildings to oscillate wildly, as though an inanimate place could feel agony.

The second ripple hit when *Planetwatch III* was midway through her turn, so that it helped as much as it harmed, pushing the ship along, farther from the island, at the same time that it battered them all once more, with a harder punch at the stern that rattled doors and strained rivets throughout the ship.

Jerry clung to the waist railing along the wall of the bridge, and stared back toward the island and the sea. Buildings were being sucked down into the ground over there, the land itself had turned into brown sluggish waves, everything within the retaining wall was an eruption of mud.

The sea from there to here was empty, rolling with the energy that punched outward from the island. Jerry stared hard at that water, but there was nothing to see. Not Kim, not Kim's body; nothing.

How had he done this? Was he responsible for this? He had wanted to destroy Richard Curtis, but he had only destroyed an eager and trusting child.

And himself?

7

"Six," George Manville said.

So that was the last of the explosions. Manville and the three money people stood in the forward lounge, beneath the bridge, gazing out through the windows at what was becoming of Kanowit. The *Mallory* was nose-to to the island, tethered by the sea anchor, and it withstood the shock waves far better than that lumbering tub of an ex-freighter over there, now waddling desperately away, rocking and bouncing like a bathtub toy.

Manville studied the island through binoculars, and what he saw was good. The land was liquefying, erupting like slow-boiled water. The structures on the island were breaking apart, collapsing into the mud. The ring wall had held.

Another shock wave passed beneath the ship, tinkling glasses on the back bar, causing Madame deCastro once again to clutch at the railing beneath the windows. She said, "How much longer does this go on?"

"Another two or three minutes," Manville told her, and Richard Curtis came in from the ladder—actually a wide flight of wooden stairs down from the bridge—just outside. His heavy face was smiling, his tan seemed ruddier.

Manville offered him a smile and a congratulatory salute. He liked this boss, his most recent boss, liked Curtis's determination and decisiveness, liked the way he described a problem and then got out of the way of the experts. A hefty but solid man of 54, just under average height, Richard Curtis moved through life with a kind of unconscious aggression, as though at all times he were bulling his way through an unresponsive crowd.

Now, he acknowledged Manville's salute with a nod and said, "We've done it."

Curtis looked out toward the island, and the others followed his lead. The turmoil out there continued.

"Yes, sir, we have," Manville said.

8

Jerry Diedrich stood at the fantail, looking back at the distant island. The ripples had ended at last, or the ship had outrun them. The sea was itself again, moderate and unthreatening. The air was the same, soft and warm. Even the sky was just as blue as before, all as though nothing had happened. Only that, on the island, everything had changed.

And somewhere in the water, Kim Baldur drifted, dead.

And the reef, the coral? Had anything happened to that, any structural damage, any death of the living coral to make up for the death of Kim?

He didn't think so. It was a bitter pill, but it seemed to Jerry that Curtis and his engineers had been right, after all. Time would have to pass, experts would have to dive and study the terrain, but Jerry knew this subject, knew it well, and there were none of the telltale signs of environmental damage, no broader upheaval of the ocean, no debris. The retaining wall around the island hadn't collapsed, so the coral footing beneath it must still be sound. The injuries to the fragile barrier reef they'd predicted and feared and had tried to guard against hadn't happened.

It was such a delicate thing they had just done over there. If Curtis and his engineers had been off in their calculations, just a little off, the destruction *would* have occurred, Jerry knew it. And he hated also the knowledge of himself he now had; at this moment, in his heart, he wished the catastrophe *had* come about, that some terrible harm had been done to the reef and the sea creatures and the sea itself, for no reason other than to prove to the world that Jerry Diedrich was right and Richard Curtis wrong.

"Jerry?"

He turned, and it was Tim, a member of the group, a college student from San Diego, with the bleached hair and eyes and flaking skin of a surf bum but the intense look of the devoted volunteer. Except that Tim now looked mostly worried.

Does he blame *me*, Jerry wondered, and wiped at his face. "Spray got me," he said.

There was no spray up here, but Tim ignored that. He said, "The Captain wants to see you, Jerry."

"Be right there."

Tim looked as though he wanted to comfort Jerry somehow, pat his arm or say something encouraging, but couldn't find a way to do it. So Jerry patted Tim's arm instead, and went away forward, and up to the bridge, where Captain Cousseran said, "We have been in further conversation with the *Mallory.*"

Steel yourself, Jerry thought, don't show any weakness.

He couldn't wait to be alone with Luther, when he could release all these tense muscles, let the misery have him. His face as expressionless as he could make it, he said, "Have we? And what does the *Mallory* have to say for itself?"

"They're sending launches to the island, to inspect," the Captain told him, and looked past Jerry to say, "in fact, they've started."

Jerry turned, and saw the two small boats, partly enclosed, bright red and yellow to be visible in an emergency, just moving out from under *Mallory*'s white flank.

Captain Cousseran said, "They've warned us away. If we try to bring our own launch in close, they'll call us trespassers, and repel us. They say, with force, if necessary."

Jerry looked into Captain Cousseran's eyes, hoping to find

sympathy there, or comradeship, but found only a correct dis-passion. He said, "Captain, we can't just— We can't just leave."

"You're thinking about the diver," the captain said. "The captain of the *Mallory* promises his crew will search. If they find...the body...they'll bring it on to Australia."

And use it in the campaign against us, Jerry thought. He said, "Captain, can't we—"

"No." The captain shook his head. "I won't permit my crew to go where they have been threatened with physical harm. We did not order that person into the water, we didn't want him to go—"

"Kim," Jerry said. "It was Kim Baldur."

The captain raised an eyebrow, then nodded. "It would be her, wouldn't it? A pity. A nice girl. Over-eager."

Her epitaph, Jerry thought, and looked out to where the launches slowly moved toward the island. He said, "What do we do now?"

"We go back to Adelaide," Captain Cousseran said. "We report the incident. We hope for the best."

The best. Jerry watched the red-and-yellow launches, out there across the gray water. They were closing with the island. The best seemed farther away than ever.

9

Curtis rode in the lead launch, Manville in the one behind. There were two crew members in each launch as well, and all eyes were supposed to be on the lookout for the body of the diver, but Curtis couldn't stop staring at the island, as they moved out away from the *Mallory*.

Mud. Soup, as he had predicted, in which every mark of man had sunk and crumbled and disappeared. And when he was ready, the same thing, the same sudden stripping away and finality, would happen again, on a much vaster scale. The buildings that fell then, when he was ready, the buildings that would crumble and melt away into the sudden soup, would not be low half-rotted barracks, but skyscrapers, concrete and metal and glass, some of which he himself had built, or helped to build.

I gave them, he thought, I'll take them away. And with just as much pleasure, just as much skill, just as much *efficiency*, the buildings he had helped put up he would knock down again.

Until recently, when he visualized that destruction, the image in Curtis's mind of the toppling skyscrapers was immediately supplanted by the image of the ancient bastards in Beijing, the shock and the fear on those age-lined pig-faces when they heard the news: someone has killed your golden goose. The image of those faces had been enough for him, could bring him a smile every time he thought of it.

But just in the last few days, he'd found himself, not willingly, thinking about the people inside the buildings. There would be no warning, merely a low rumble in the earth and then the buildings would go over like chainsawed trees. No escape.

Those people in the buildings weren't his enemies. But he wasn't going to worry about them. They'd made their choice · when they'd decided to stay, after the bastards from the mainland took over. They could have gone away, almost every one of them could have gone away. They could have gone to Macao, or Malaysia; many could have gone to Singapore (as Curtis had), or Canada, or a dozen other places in the world. But they chose to stay, so what happened was on their own heads.

Still, now that he was thinking about it, it seemed to him, for a number of reasons, he would be better to make it happen at night. He'd always visualized it in daylight, in bright sun, the gleaming glass buildings as they went over, but that wasn't necessary. He certainly wouldn't be there to see it.

At night, it would be easier to make the collections.

It would be easier to get away without question. And, at night, the buildings would be nearly empty, all of the workers, the clerks, the bosses, all off to their bedrooms on the mainland, only a few left to feel the sudden sway as the floors shifted beneath them. It was their choice, it was not on Richard Curtis's head; and yet, it was better to do it at night, when there would be fewer people in the buildings.

The island was very close now. The crewman at the wheel steered the launch forward slowly, cautiously, watching for coral. Curtis opened the leather case and took out the video camera, knowing Manville would be doing the same thing on the other boat.

When he looked back, Manville's boat was already turning away to port. While Curtis circled the island to the right, Manville would circle it to the left, until they met on the far side. All the way, they would tape the island, showing its condition and the condition of the retaining wall.

Seen through the viewfinder of the camera, the island seemed smaller, and the light brown mud looked almost solid enough to walk on, though Curtis knew it was quicksand there now, it would eat anything it was given.

The launches moved slowly around the island, and the steersman next to Curtis gave a shout when he saw the second launch come around into view ahead of them. Curtis kept filming until his and Manville's boats met, and then, in the bobbing water just offshore, they both put their cameras down and grinned across the peaceful water at one another. Manville made the A-OK signal, thumb and first finger in an O, and Curtis nodded.

They were almost alone now, on the sea. From here, the *Mallory* was hidden by the bulk of the island, and the environmentalists' ship was still in full flight toward the horizon, merely a dark blotch on the ocean. Looking over at Manville, Curtis made a sweeping pointing gesture, to say they should go back around the island now and return to the ship. Manville nodded, and Curtis told the steersman, "We'll head back now." Then he turned to stow the camera away, as the launch put about.

It was the second crewman who saw it, part of the way back, a muted thing floating off to port, half-submerged in the slightly deeper water near where the other ship had stood. He called and pointed, and then Curtis and the steersman also saw it, and they veered that way, while Manville and the second launch waited on their original course.

It was the diver, face up, air hose still clamped in mouth, wetsuit zippered shut over body and head, leaving only that blue-gray face exposed.

It was a woman.

The air tanks were still attached to the body, underneath it as it bobbed in the water, making trouble when they tried to grab hold and haul her aboard.

While one crewman held an ankle and the other a wrist, Curtis bent over the launch's side and managed to unhook the straps holding the air tanks in place.

They drifted free, silver, glistening, and Curtis yanked the air hose from the diver's mouth and helped the two crewmen drag her up over the rail and into the bottom of the boat.

The body landed face down. Curtis went to one knee beside it, rolled it over, and unzipped the top part of the wetsuit, wondering if the diver carried ID. It would prove they had the body if they could radio the other ship the diver's name.

The wetsuit's head piece was peeled back, and ash blonde hair spilled out, not long but very curly. The face within that halo of hair was young, unlined.

Curtis leaned closer. Tiny droplets of blood seeped from the nostrils and the ears. Beneath the pale flesh of the throat, on the right side, a small bird fluttered. A pulse. She was alive.

"Damn," Curtis said.

10

When Luther Rickendorf got back to their cabin with the two drinks, held in the big palm of his left hand, he thought at first that Jerry had fallen asleep, and was glad of it.

But then Jerry stirred on his bunk, having heard the door open, and rolled over. His face looked a mess, blotchy and drawn, the eyes still frantic. He blinked a lot, and stared at Luther as though he had no idea who Luther was.

"Here you are," Luther said, and extended toward him the vodka and orange juice, keeping the plain club soda for himself.

Jerry propped himself up on the bunk, back against the bulkhead, and accepted the drink. He gulped some, spilling orange on his chin and T-shirt, then wiped his face with his free hand, looked less manically at Luther, and said, "Thank you."

"The least I could do."

"What's that you've got?"

"White wine spritzer," Luther lied. "To keep you company."

The truth was, Luther had no desire and little liking for alcohol. He could not remember ever having felt the need to have his mood altered. He remained the same no matter what, an optimistic realist, and let the world swirl around him.

It was because of Jerry that he was aboard this ship, not like the others out of any conviction or sense of mission. Tall and blondly Teutonic, Luther had grown up in Munich, his father an industrialist in the new Germany. He had known he was gay from his early teens, and with his strong good looks had never had trouble finding partners. When his father learned about him, shortly after Luther's seventeenth birthday, he had proved to be an enlightened parent, up to a point. He would still consider Luther his son, would support him as necessary and acknowledge him as needed, but only so long as Luther stayed out of Germany.

Luther's exile began auspiciously. His father paid his tuition and expenses through three years to a bachelor of arts degree at Stanford University, in California. After that, with some financial help from home, he had become a ski instructor at Aspen for a few years, then had followed a lover from there who spent his summers as crew on the tourist sailing vessels in the Caribbean. He stayed when the ex-lover returned to the states, quickly became practiced around sail himself, met Jerry Diedrich one night in a bar on Anguilla, and his life as an environmental do-gooder began.

When he thought sometimes of what an instinctive, unrelenting, unrepentant polluter of air and water and land his father was, Luther could only smile. To his father's question, in one letter accompanying a check, "What after all is Planetwatch?" he had replied, "Something much much worse than homosexuality."

Now he sat on the other bunk and watched Jerry slurp his screwdriver. There were no large cabins on *Planetwatch III*, and this one was just big enough for the two bunks bolted into opposite walls, the drawers built in at one end, and the door at the other. If you wanted to make love, you crowded the two mattresses side by side on the floor between the bunks, and were careful to restore everything afterward, not to scandalize the others.

Jerry said, "Did Kim have anybody on the boat? A boyfriend?"

"I don't think so."

"Not sleeping with anybody?"

"I have no idea," Luther said, "but I doubt it."

Jerry took more of his drink; about a third of it was left. He blinked past Luther at the wall. "You don't suppose," he said, his voice mournful, "she died a virgin."

Luther laughed; he couldn't help it. "Nobody's a virgin," he said.

"But she was so young."

"Jerry," Luther said, "she did it to herself. Nobody sent her, nobody wanted her to go. Everybody wanted her *not* to go. Sooner or later, you'll have to accept that. She did it to herself, and there was nothing you could have done about it." He spoke with a faint accent, which usually gave him a pleasant and amusing sound, but when he was trying to comfort someone— though he had no way to know this—he came off mostly like a Viennese psychiatrist, remote and only professionally caring, not emotionally involved at all.

Jerry said, "If anybody's responsible, it's Curtis."

And, as usual, his voice roughened, became harsher, when he spoke Curtis's name.

Luther wanted to tell him, "Forget Curtis. It's over. Think about something else." But he knew he'd be wasting his breath (even if it were possible for him to sound sympathetic), so he said, "What are you going to do?"

"Singapore," Jerry said.

Luther was surprised. "Leave the ship? Why Singapore?"

"Because that's Curtis's base," Jerry said, "now that he's out of Hong Kong. Because I have to know what he's going to do next."

I I

There was no doctor aboard the *Mallory*, but Captain Zhang
had taken a number of accrediting courses, enough to qualify
him as a medical orderly, which was sufficient for the safety
standards required in a ship of this size and purpose. Once he
had the diver safely stashed, Curtis went directly to Zhang, on
the bridge, and said, "I need you to look at the diver."

Curious, Zhang said, "To establish death?" The helmsman
was over on the other side of the bridge. Lowering his voice,
Curtis said, "To establish life." Then, before the man could
make a startled comment, he added, "This is between us. No
one knows. Come down and take a look."

"Of course."

Zhang turned to give orders to the helmsman, who would
command the bridge during the captain's absence, then picked
up his bulky vinyl medical kit and he and Curtis made their way
down through the ship.

When the launch carrying Curtis and the diver had returned
to the *Mallory* and been lifted into position so they could step
through the gate in the railing onto the deck of the larger ship,
Curtis had surprised the crewmen by insisting that he help to
carry the unconscious woman. He lifted her under the arms,
and one of the crewmen took her ankles, and they set off.

The crewmen thought she was dead, and Curtis had said
nothing to correct that idea. While still on the launch, he had
zipped shut the wetsuit around her head again, and her
breathing was so shallow that no one who wasn't carrying her
by the torso, as he was, would notice.

He'd taken her down to stateroom 7, with the crewman holding her ankles to lead the way. This was the smallest cabin on the ship, rarely used, with a single bunk and one small round porthole and not much floor space. Curtis and the crewman had left her on the bunk, still in the wetsuit, and after locking the cabin door and taking the key with him, Curtis had come for the captain.

Now they were back at stateroom 7. Curtis unlocked the door, they stepped in, and he shut the door again behind them. "What I want to know is," he said, "is there much chance she'll go on being alive. She's bleeding out of her nose and ears."

"Concussion," Zhang said. He was a thin man with a round face, about forty, his black hair very thin, so that streaks of amber skull could be seen. He'd worked as mate on commercial ships—cargo, never passenger—and had been with Curtis for nearly three years now, and very much liked his job. If it were possible for him to satisfy Curtis's wishes, he would.

Now he leaned over the figure supine on the bunk, with its blue-gray cold face, and said, "We must get this wetsuit off her, to begin. She needs to be warm."

"Fine."

They worked at it together, and Curtis found it strange to be undressing an attractive young woman with no sexual element involved in it. But there *was* no sexual element involved. His preference for this body was that it be dead, though he would much prefer that she did the dying on her own.

Once the wetsuit was bundled onto the floor, out of the way, the girl remained dressed in the top half of a light green bathing suit, white panties, and white socks.

Zhang removed the socks as well, but left the other garments. He tested her pulse, listened to her chest and her breathing, lifted back the lids to look into her eyes. He took her temperature by ear, felt her armpits, kneaded her rib cage and her legs, and forced open her mouth to study her tongue.

Curtis stood watching, growing impatient. We aren't here to save the girl, he thought, but didn't quite say. We're here to be certain she can't be saved.

Finally Zhang finished his examination. As he put his equipment back in the medical kit, he said, "The bleeding has stopped. That was only temporary, from the concussion. She may have cracked ribs, I can't be certain, but no other bones seem to be broken. She's in shock, and she shows some signs of hypothermia. She needs sustenance. I wish I could give her an intravenous drip, but I'm not equipped for that. When she wakes up, she should be given hot soup. And then I can talk to her about her ribs, how they feel."

Zhang turned away to put a sheet and blanket over the girl, while Curtis stood thinking. He watched Zhang turn the top of the blanket down around her throat. He said, "You think she'll live."

"Oh, yes, of course." Zhang tucked in the blanket along the side of the bunk, and smiled at Curtis. "She's a healthy young girl, she should survive this."

"You're absolutely certain."

"Well," Zhang said, "I don't know *that* much about medicine. Absolute certainty is…more than I can promise."

"So she might not make it?" Curtis said, trying to keep the words from sounding pointed. It wouldn't do to be too obvious. But Zhang was no fool. Surely he could read between the lines.

The captain hesitated, thought about his answer before he spoke the words.

"She *might* not. But I would think she most likely will. It isn't *certain*, but…"

"Likely."

Zhang nodded.

"Well," Curtis said. "That would be wonderful, of course. But we can't count on it."

"No," Zhang said.

"She might die."

"I really don't think she—"

"I'm just saying she might," Curtis said. "And I'm sure you know, no one could possibly find fault with you if she did. That girl was badly injured. You are doing what you can, but in the end... Even the finest doctor can't save every patient. Even the finest doctor, working with the best equipment, in a first-rate hospital, which is not what you have here."

Zhang nodded. He understands, Curtis decided.

Curtis patted the man on the shoulder and headed to the door. "You will do your job, I know," Curtis told him.

12

Curtis and the three money people would copter back to the mainland tomorrow. For tonight there was a celebratory dinner in the *Mallory*'s glass-roofed dining room aft on the top deck. Outside, the black sea breathed in slow respirations, illuminated with gentle brushstrokes from a quarter moon. Above, the thousand thousand stars formed incomprehensible but calming patterns in the black sky. Within, in subdued lighting, Curtis and Manville and the money people sat around the oval table covered with white cloth, and ate off gold-rimmed china with one entwined red RC interrupting the gold ring circling each plate.

Stewards in white served the meal, and nobody talked business. They mostly discussed politics, some economics, and at one point Bill Hardy described at length and with gusto the story of a movie he'd recently seen on tape, about a Concorde in flight threatened by terrorists.

Over the crème brûlée, Madame deCastro said, "I'm told you found that poor diver. He was dead, was he?"

"A girl," Curtis said, "Yes, a surprise to me, too. An attractive thing, a pity."

Bill Hardy said, "So she is dead."

"Oh, yes," Curtis said. "Surprisingly unbattered, but... No one was going to survive out there."

"I take it," Abdullah Wayarabo said, "she's somewhere in cold storage."

"No, not cold storage, we're not really equipped for that," Curtis told him, and smiled around at the table. "We're certainly not going to take all our own food out of our only freezer to put a dead body in it."

Manville said, "Where is she, then?"

Carelessly, Curtis said, "In an unused cabin."

Madame deCastro said, "Isn't that—I don't know how to phrase this delicately, over dinner. Isn't that a little *warm*, for a corpse?"

"We turned the air-conditioning on full," Curtis assured her. "And the ship will make dock at Brisbane some time tomorrow night. It won't be a problem." He raised his Château d'Yquem and smiled around at them all. "In the morning," he told them, effectively ending that conversation, "when we board the helicopter, I'll have the pilot take us over Kanowit, so we can all see how our island's coming along."

13

After dinner, after the others had retired to their cabins, George Manville found himself restless, dissatisfied. And yet, today had been a triumph for him. A comfortable future, even a wealthy future, was now assured for him at RC Structural.

He was an engineer, not a scientist, but he had read the papers the scientists had published, he'd understood the principles, and he'd gone them one better. They had created the soliton in their laboratories; he had created the soliton in the real world, in an island in the ocean. He had seen it work, and he knew it was all his.

And he knew Richard Curtis appreciated him. Curtis had stayed with him every step of the way, showing a genuine interest, asking questions, even taking notes, following what Manville did, until by now Curtis could probably create the same effect himself. They'd been that closely tied together, the last few months.

George Manville was a stolid engineer, 34 years old, more comfortable in a construction trailer on a building site than anywhere else in the world. He'd been married once, just out of college. Jeanne was artistic, without being arty or phony; she acted in amateur theater groups, without convincing herself that Broadway had lost a great star when she'd married young; she was interested in classical music concerts and in opera, and would never find a blueprint fascinating, or want to hear the details of how a problem in stress-weight materials had been elegantly resolved.

Since the fairly amicable divorce, nine years ago, Manville had been lonely but content, and sometimes even happy. And tonight he should be the happiest of all. He had today's success. He had the confidence and respect of one of the major builders in the world. And yet, after midnight, the stars still fixed across the black sky, the sleeping *Mallory* running with the minimum of lights, Manville still paced, discontented, troubled. He wasn't an introspective man, but now he had to be: What's wrong tonight? Why can't I just go to sleep, like everybody else?

It was the diver. He knew it was the diver, he'd known it all along, but there was nothing he could do about the diver, not anymore, so he'd been avoiding the thought. But it was the diver, and there was no getting away from it.

From the instant, this afternoon, when that orange-suited figure had gone over the rail of the other ship, disappearing into the sea, Manville had been tense, frightened, hoping against hope. Because if the diver died, he was the one who had done it. He was responsible.

There should have been a fail-safe mechanism, a way to abort the experiment if something unexpected happened. Of course there should have been some way out, as the people on the other ship had insisted, but it had never occurred to him that such a thing might be needed. The experiment seemed so simple, so clear-cut; why would there be a need to abort?

He should have thought about it. His job was not to foresee the unforeseeable, but it was to guard against the unforeseeable, and he hadn't done so. He hadn't done his job. And now a human being was dead.

Somehow, it being a girl made it worse. It shouldn't have, he knew that, a human being is a human being, but nevertheless it did. She's young, and now she's dead, through George Manville's failure. Her life won't happen, because of him.

And nothing to be done, not anymore. Nothing except roam the empty rooms and decks, waiting to be tired enough to sleep.

He wanted to see her. Was that morbid? He didn't know why, maybe just to say the words *I'm sorry* in her presence, but he wanted to see her.

Curtis had said the body was in an unused cabin. The five on the upper level were all occupied, so it had to be one of the two below. So Manville at last decided he would go see her, he would tell her he was sorry, and then he would, no arguments, go to bed.

The interior corridors were dimly lit at night. Manville made his way to the lower deck, along the corridor, and opened the door to cabin 6. The light switch was just inside the door; flicking it on, he saw an empty room, an unmade bed. He clicked the light off again and turned to cabin 7, across the way.

The door was locked. Curtis must have locked it, to keep anybody from stumbling in there unawares. But it only stymied Manville for a second, until he thought, This door isn't locked against me. I already know what's in there.

I'm not violating anything if I ignore the lock.

In one pocket, Manville kept a card that gave, in black letters and numbers on white, equivalences: pounds to kilos, quarts to liters, that sort of thing. It was about the size of a credit card, but thinner, more supple. Manville took it from his pocket, slipped it into the crack between door and jamb, and slid back the striker on the lock.

The door eased open, darkness within. Manville stepped inside, switching on the light, leaving the door open. And there she was, in the bed, on her back, covered to her chin.

That was the first oddity that struck him, that her face wasn't covered. Then he realized the room wasn't at all cool, it was warm; the air conditioner hadn't been turned higher at all.

Somebody's mistake, obviously. Somebody on the crew had misunderstood Curtis's orders. So it was a good thing Manville had come down here, or things might have got very unpleasant.

He was going to turn the air-conditioning up, but before that, he thought he should cover her face. And look at her, and offer his belated and useless apology.

He stepped closer to the bunk, and looked at her, and she was really very good-looking. And young. Twenty?

There was even, somehow, faint color in her cheeks.

No. That made no sense at all. Manville, not wanting to, reached out to touch that cold stiff cheek and it was warm and yielding.

He pulled his hand back as though he'd been burned. She was alive, not dead.

How could Curtis have made such a mistake? Or Captain Zhang, he was the one who handled medical duties aboard the ship. Couldn't they tell the difference between her being alive and her being dead? It made no sense, no sense at all.

Unwillingly, Manville found his methodical mind giving him the answer. Richard Curtis had several times in the last months told Manville that he had a nemesis in the ranks of the environmentalists, a fellow named Jerry Diedrich. Why Diedrich had that special hatred or rage toward him, Curtis professed not to know; he only knew, with certainty, that it was there. He'd told Manville a week ago that he half-expected Diedrich would try to make trouble at today's experiment, and in fact Diedrich had.

And then the diver had happened, and Diedrich was on the defensive. The diver had happened, and Curtis had immediately made it clear he would use the incident to defuse the problem of Diedrich. He'd left no doubt that he had no sympathy to waste for the diver, that the diver's dead body would be the

centerpiece of a legal action to get Diedrich out of his way forever. Because...

Because there was something else coming, something larger.
"We'll be using this soliton thing again," Curtis had told him,
"and in a much more significant way, you wait and see." And
that was the project Curtis wanted to keep Diedrich away from,
for some reason desperately needed to keep Diedrich away
from.

Desperate enough for him to make certain he had a dead
body to deliver to the authorities in Australia? Manville knew
Curtis was a hard man, in business he was famously ruthless
and cold, famously hard. But was he that hard?

Could he be?

Manville looked at the girl. Her breaths were shallow, but
regular. She was not dying, but mending.

He didn't know what to believe, or he was afraid to know
what to believe. It was better now, at least for now, that nothing
made sense.

He turned away at last, switched off the light, and left the
cabin, letting the door snick locked again behind him. As he'd
promised himself, he went straight from there to bed, but it
was hours before he got to sleep.

14

Snick.

That was the first sound since the shock wave had taken her that penetrated into Kim's stunned brain, to bring her up from the cocoon she'd been pending in. Her brain heard the sound, tried to process it, failed to give the sound a meaning, and the resulting unsatisfied curiosity, unanswered question, drove her up closer to consciousness, and more bewildering sense impressions. Her body felt a thrumming vibration, like a ship, but very unlike *Planetwatch III*. The sheets above and below her were a texture different from what she was used to. The faint odor in her nostrils was like polished wood (the odor on *Planetwatch III*, not that faint, was of diesel oil). Confused, troubled by the incomprehensibility of where she was, she came closer again to consciousness.

And memory. That great underwater blur roared toward her again, and her eyes popped open, and she was terrified.

Now it came in a rush, just as the shock wave had done. She'd been on deck, on *Planetwatch III*, and she'd listened with the others to the ship's PA system relaying the debate between Jerry and the people on the yacht. She'd realized they weren't getting anywhere, she'd believed Jerry's insistence that there had to be a way for Curtis's people to halt the experiment, and she'd finally decided the only way to force the issue was to throw herself in harm's way. Like the student who'd stood in front of the tank in Tiananmen Square.

In the water, just beneath the surface, she had at first swum strongly toward the island, seeing the jagged landscape of coral below her. But then she'd decided she shouldn't get too far from the ship, she should stay close enough so they could signal her when the experiment was called off, so she turned about and headed back, arms at her sides, flippered legs scissoring in strong rhythm as she looked down through the facemask at the coral seabed, receding in bumps and jags as she moved into deeper water.

Some trembling in the sea around her made her look over her shoulder, and at first she couldn't understand what she seemed to see back there. It was like trying to watch a movie with the projector out of focus. It was a blur, a thick gray-blue-silver-black blur, fifteen or twenty feet from top to bottom, as wide as the whole ocean, and it was rolling at her like an avalanche, like a bulldozer burying an anthill.

In panic, seeing that thing hurtle on, she yearned upward, and her flippers gave one strong kick to propel her toward the surface before the blur caught her and shook her like a puppy shaking a rag doll, and her last thought was, Stupid me, now I've killed myself.

She stared upward in darkness in this strange cabin, reliving the moment, clutched by the panic, unable to think, barely able to breathe, living that panic and that surge of impossible power all over again, her entire body clenching until the pain in her chest forced her to let go, to ease back, to take a long slow (painful) breath and get that terrified butterfly brain inside her head to slow down, slow down, settle, settle.

I'm in a bed, she thought. I'm in a cabin on a ship, but not my own ship. The yacht? Why didn't my own people rescue me?

She turned her head, and her neck and back gave her twinges of pain. In the thin light that seeped into the cabin under its door, she looked at where she was, simple and plain, but also elegant. She thought to roll onto her side, so she could get up and go over there to open that door, but when she made her first move *everything* gave her a jolt. The fiercest pains were in her chest, as though she might have broken some ribs, but everything else hurt as well. It was like the soreness after too much exercise, but magnified a hundred times.

She couldn't move. The effort made her dizzy with the pain. She very slowly turned her head back to where it had been. She felt weak, groggy. She was afraid she might lose consciousness again. She breathed slowly, carefully, trying to avoid the whip-stroke of pain that came sometimes to her chest, and again she remembered the blur, how fast it came, how immensely powerful it was, unimaginably powerful.

And once more she remembered her own final thought: Stupid me, now I've killed myself. But now she remembered more; she remembered what was inside that thought. Inside the panic and the desperate useless lunge toward the surface, and much more real, had been acceptance.

Resignation, and calm acceptance. She had known, for that second or two seconds, that she was going to die, and she'd accepted the fact, without challenge. She hadn't even been unhappy.

How easy it is to die, she thought, and realized she'd always assumed it was hard to die, that life pulsed on as determinedly as it could until the end. It was a grim knowledge, that life didn't mind its own finish, and she felt she had been given that knowledge too soon. I shouldn't know that yet, she thought, and began to cry. She struggled to keep her breathing regular, to avoid the pain, and tears dribbled from her eyes, and then she opened her mouth and sighed and gave up the struggle and faded from consciousness.

15

Richard Curtis woke early, feeling doubt. He didn't like the feeling, had no use for doubt. In his mind, indecision was a sign of weakness, second thoughts the practice of losers. He himself was swift and decisive, and known for it, and relished the reputation. Doubt, on those rare moments when it came to him, irritated him, and he did his best to thrust it immediately away.

Hard to do, now. It was far too early to get out of bed, with the fresh sunrise a soft pink on the curtains, giving his cabin a soft rose glow, as though he slept inside a ruby. Too early to get up, but could he fall back to sleep?

He was afraid—this was the doubt, not going away—afraid he'd made a mistake last night. When asked if the diver was dead, he hadn't hesitated for a second. *Yes.* Of course she was dead. It was necessary to his future plans that she be dead, so obviously she was dead.

But was it true? Would it be as true as he needed it to be? Could he rely on Zhang?

These were murky waters for Richard Curtis. He'd asked men to commit crimes for him before, mostly of a financial nature, or a lie to get around a regulation, and he'd committed such crimes himself without regret. But this was the death of a person, this was something larger, more severe, something of a different kind. Would Zhang do what he knew he was supposed to do?

In his mind, Curtis didn't use the word 'murder' or even 'killing.' She was a severely damaged woman dragged mostly dead from the sea. Zhang was a skilled medic, but hardly a doctor, and this was, as he had taken pains to point out, hardly a hospital —not even a hospital ship. By their deficiencies of equipment and knowledge, enhanced by their neglect, couldn't they assure she would not survive? And if the flame of life insisted on sputtering inside her, might not Zhang assist its snuffing in some way?

(Curtis was vague on that part. Some medicine? The wrong one, or given in the wrong dose? Or a pillow pressed for just a moment or two on the face? Something barely intrusive in any event, more an encouragement to nature than anything else.)

But here was the source of the doubt. Would Zhang do this thing he knew Curtis wanted? Would he too see it as merely assisting nature, encouraging the proper outcome? Or would he think it was something more significant than that, and falter?

If Curtis hadn't said *yes* last night, he would have more room to maneuver now. If the girl's condition had been left unstated, and if Zhang were to turn out not to be up to the task, then once they reached port Curtis had other people he could turn to. But what he'd done, when he'd told his guests firmly that the girl was dead, he'd made it necessary that the girl be dead, now, while they were still at sea.

And if Zhang wouldn't do it?

Curtis closed his eyes against the pink morning light. If Zhang wouldn't do it, and if it had to be done before Curtis left the ship, early this afternoon, then there was only one person left to turn to, and *that* person had never done such a thing, either. He had planned deaths, he was willing that people should die, he could order death, he could be responsible for death at a distance (and planned to be, in a large way, very soon), but could he do this other thing? Could these hands press the pillow down? Could he be *present* in the room when it was actually happening?

And so the doubt. And he wouldn't be sleeping any longer this morning.

16

Captain Zhang was on duty on the bridge from eight every morning, but today he arrived fifteen minutes early, relieving the mate, who had stood the night watch. This morning was windier than yesterday, the *Mallory* rocking more noticeably in the increased swell. To the east, the pale sky was clear, a great pastel wash around the hot yellow furnace of the sun, but to the west, toward Australia, darkish clouds were piled like low foggy hills on the horizon, and would soon be coming this way. Zhang listened to the satellite weather service, listened to radio traffic generally, watched the sky and the sea, and tried not to think about what Richard Curtis wanted.

Zhang was 43, a coastal Chinese from Qinhuangdao on Liaodong Wan Bay, just across the Yellow Sea from Korea. He'd grown up loving the sea and hating politics, hating having to *care* about politics, and was 15 when he first shipped out, on a cargo ship from Tientsin. He retained his Chinese passport, but had not lived on the mainland for many years, and now had a wife and three daughters living in Kaohsiung, on Taiwan.

His wife, Yanling, was Taiwanese, and they had lived in Hong Kong until the changeover, when it had seemed safest for her to relocate back home. Taiwan was still, in all the ways that mattered to them, China.

The life Zhang Yung-tsien and his wife and children enjoyed was a good one, an enviable one, and it was made possible almost exclusively by Richard Curtis. Without this job, a semi-stateless Chinese with first-mate papers only—he had not yet qualified for master's papers, and it hadn't seemed urgent to do so—he could surely find more work, but not at these wages. He would

live on a third of his present income, at best. They would lose
the house in Kaohsiung, that was certain. The private school
his daughters went to would be beyond his means.

Until now, there had never been any reason to worry about
his position. He knew Richard Curtis appreciated his skills and
discretion and had no fault to find with him. He did his job
well, he was not fearful, and there had been no reason to suspect that anything would change.

But now. Now.

If only they hadn't found the damn woman, out there in the
sea! Or, finding her, if they'd only left her there.

Who wanted her? Why keep her?

What kind of thing was this to ask of a man? He wasn't that
sort, he never could be. If anything, Richard Curtis was more
the cold and emotionless type that was needed for a thing like
this. So why did it have to come down on the shoulders of poor
Zhang Yung-tsien?

What am I going to do, he asked himself, and watched the
sea, and the slowly approaching storm front from the west. I
know *what* to do, of course, he thought, that's simplicity itself.
I inject a bubble of air into her veins, as plain as that. No one
will find it because no one will suspect it, and therefore no one
will look for it. She should be dead, anyway, so what difference
does it make?

But Zhang knew the difference. From today on, he would be
the man who had murdered a human being. That would be
him, that and nothing else; could he live with that self?

But what else was there? What real choice did he have?

He didn't know this troublesome woman; he knew Yanling
and his daughters.

But *could* he do it? When the instant came, would he be able
to do it?

"Morning, Zhang."

Zhang started, yanked from his concentration, and turned to see Curtis standing there. Just inside the doorway, smiling a greeting at him, easy and confident. "Good morning, Mr. Curtis," Zhang said, and blinked at the man.

Curtis looked out at the sea. "What news of our patient?"

"I...haven't looked at her yet this morning."

Curtis seemed mildly surprised. "You haven't? I should think you'd want to keep tabs on her. For all you know, she took a turn for the worse during the night."

"That's possible, of course," Zhang said.

"You will see her for me, won't you?" Curtis asked him. "You will take care of things."

Zhang found it impossible to meet those cold eyes. Looking fitfully here and there, as though some instrument, some gauge, demanded his attention, he said, "Mr. Curtis, I, of course, I have some skills, but I'm not sure I can, I'm not a doctor, of course, I think...."

Bleak, he now did face Curtis's bleak eyes, and said, "You might have someone else, someone in all your great organization who's better qualified than I am."

"But no one else is here," Curtis said. He was almost kindly, explaining the situation. "Only you, master of this fine vessel, which I know you enjoy. Don't you?"

"Yes, I do," Zhang agreed. "Very much."

"So here we are, out at sea," Curtis said, "and you're the only one I can count on. I can count on you, can't I?"

Zhang was silent. He wanted to speak, but he couldn't.

"I need to count on you," Curtis said, his voice a little raspier, a little harsher. "I need word about our patient, Captain Zhang. I'll be leaving after lunch, if that storm out there holds off. I'll need word about our patient before I go. Do you see what I mean?"

Miserable, "Yes," Zhang said.

17

Manville, having slept little, got up early and went looking for Curtis. He saw him, up on the bridge, in tense conversation with Captain Zhang, and thought he might know what the subject was. So he waited in the forward lounge, below the bridge, where he would be sure to intercept Curtis when he came down.

Standing by the big windows, seeing the flattened island off to starboard and the beginnings of storm clouds to port, far off at the horizon, he thought about what he would do and how he would go about it. There was very little question in his mind that Curtis knew the girl was alive, but he felt, at least at the beginning, he had to give the man the benefit of the doubt. Because if Curtis knew she was alive, but had announced last night that she was dead, it could only mean he was determined to *make* her dead, and his motive would be the hobbling of Jerry Diedrich.

Could that be reason enough for murder? Or was Manville about to make a serious mistake, at the very moment his career was assured?

I'll have to say it to him straight out, he thought, and see how he reacts. I'm no good at subtlety, anyway, I'll just have to be myself, and I'll know, I'm sure I will, the instant I see his reaction. And here he comes now.

Manville turned at the sound of footsteps coming down the outside stairs. Curtis came through the swing door into the lounge, his expression grim, deep in thought, and he abruptly switched to an enthusiastic smile when he saw Manville: "Good morning!"

"Morning, Mr. Curtis."

"Going in to breakfast?"

"In a minute," Manville said.

Curtis looked at him more closely. "Something wrong, George?"

"I looked in on the girl last night," Manville said.

Well, he'd been right: He would know instantly from Curtis's reaction. Curtis stared at him for a second, then looked very angry and seemed about to yell something, and then just as quickly gave up anger, shook his head in exasperated defeat, and said, almost pleadingly, "Now why did you do that?"

"I felt responsible," Manville said. "I thought she was dead, and I'd done it, and I—"

"*You?* For God's sake, why you?"

This isn't the right subject, Manville thought, but he found himself saying, "The fail-safe device, I should have thought to—"

"All right, all right." Curtis, always a fast study, understood immediately what had gone through Manville's mind. "You felt responsible. So you went down there to apologize to a corpse…"

"And she's alive."

"She's very badly hurt, you know," Curtis said. "She's still alive, but Captain Zhang isn't at all confident she'll—"

"She's improving," Manville said. "I'm not claiming any great medical knowledge, but anybody can see she's improving."

"If she were bleeding internally, we wouldn't—"

"She'd be feverish by now," Manville said. "Her skin would be clammy. She'd show the signs."

Curtis looked increasingly annoyed. He said, "George, this isn't our expertise, neither of us. You do what you're good at, and I'll do what I'm good at, and that girl will live or die, and neither of us can say which it will be."

Manville said, "If she's dead when we reach Brisbane, I'll have to tell the authorities that she didn't die as a result of what happened to her in the water."

Curtis frowned at him. "What could you prove?"

"I don't have to prove anything, Mr. Curtis," Manville told him. "I only have to tell them there's a problem. They'll do their own proving."

Curtis stood thinking, clearly trying to figure out how to handle this situation. Then he said, "Are you particularly hungry, George?"

"For breakfast?" Manville asked, surprised. "Not very much, this morning."

"Neither am I," Curtis said, and touched Manville's arm, and gestured at the cluster of soft maroon swivel chairs over by the windows. "Sit with me a minute, listen to what I have to say."

"All right."

They sat in adjacent chairs, turned slightly away from one another, and Curtis leaned forward, hands on knees, to say, "I've already told you, I have another use for this soliton of yours."

"Yes."

"Something far better than just clearing land to build a resort. Something much more ambitious. And lucrative."

"All right."

"I told you it had to be a secret, and it still does," Curtis said, "but I didn't tell you why. The fact is, I'm not as rich as people think I am. Not anymore."

"You aren't poor," Manville said.

Curtis smiled. "No, not poor. But I've borrowed a lot, from a lot of banks. No one has seen an accurate financial statement from me in three years, not since before they threw me out of Hong Kong, because an accurate financial statement would show I owe probably four times as much as I'm worth."

Manville, surprised, gestured to include the *Mallory*, Kanowit Island, everything. "But, how can you…then how can you do all *this*?"

"Front," Curtis told him. "I'm spending to create the perception that I'm rich because only the perception that I'm rich will permit me to borrow the money to go on spending."

"That's a—" Manville started, and across the way Captain Zhang entered from the outside staircase, his medical kit hanging from his left hand. He turned aft, and Manville looked at him.

Curtis looked from Manville to Zhang, then called, "Captain!"

Zhang turned around. His face was gray and unhealthy and deeply worried. "Yes, sir?"

"Why not see your patient a little later?" Curtis suggested. "After George and I have had our talk, I'll come up and we'll have a word."

Zhang looked confused, as though he wasn't sure whether this was a reprieve or not. "Yes, sir," he said, but seemed for a few seconds unable to reverse his motion. What he'd been going to do was so deeply fixed in his mind—because it was so difficult?—that he found it hard to give it up. Then, with a kind of lurch, he did turn around, and go back out through the swing door, and Curtis turned to Manville to say, "You were going to tell me, I think, that what I'm doing can't last, that eventually I'll be so deeply in debt there'll be no way to hide the fact, and that already I'm probably so deeply in debt I'll never get clear."

Manville said, "Are you?"

"Yes," Curtis said.

Manville leaned back. He didn't know what to think, couldn't even imagine why Curtis was telling him all this. Bewildered by what Curtis was saying, he found he was thinking mostly about himself. Had he hitched his wagon to a falling star?

Curtis said, "At first, I thought it was only a temporary expedient, I could dance on the edge of the cliff until I got everything back the way it used to be." Pointing off to starboard, he said,

"Fifteen years from now, Kanowit will be a money machine, but I don't have the time to wait for it. I have other money machines, but they all require too much priming of the pump, too much money going in before any comes out. And even with all of my efforts, I'm doing most of this for other people. Do you know how much of Kanowit is mine? Ten percent. My three partners here, each of them thinks *he's* the only one with thirty, that the other two have ten each and I have fifty. And each of them thinks the other two have been lied to, have been told that he has only ten percent instead of thirty, so none of them will ever compare notes." With a bitter smile, he added, "None of them will go to apologize to a corpse."

"What risks you're taking," Manville said.

"At first, it was because I was angry," Curtis explained. "That last year in Hong Kong, the bastards were squeezing and squeezing, they wanted me out, but they wanted everything I owned to stay behind. I fought the best way I could, I moved the operation to Singapore, I kept the business going with borrowed money while trying to salvage what I could from Hong Kong, and my anger at those fucking *thieves* got in the way of my caution. I overextended myself, and the only cure was to overextend myself even more."

Manville shook his head. "Mr. Curtis, why tell me this? I'm sorry for the fix you're in, I had no idea—"

"No one has any idea," Curtis said, his face grim. "I'm risking a lot, telling you this."

"You could deny it, if I tried to say anything," Manville said. "But you know I won't. I can sympathize with you. I know the Chinese broke a lot of promises when they took over Hong Kong—"

"As everybody in the world except for a few brainless British politicians knew they would."

"But what does that have to do with that girl, down in cabin seven?"

Curtis thought about his answer, then said, "All right. The fact is, I have a way out of this mess. I am going to be rich again, very rich, a lot richer than I ever was before. But I have to be extremely careful, George. What I'm going to do is dangerous, and it's illegal, and I have to admit it's going to be destructive."

"With the soliton," Manville said.

"I was going to do it without you," Curtis told him, "and I still can. I'm not asking you to be at risk, not for a second. But you could share in the profit."

"Because of the work I did over on Kanowit? Or because of the girl?"

Curtis shook his head. "To do what I'm going to do I have to be able to move without being observed, without being tracked and trailed every goddam place I go. You saw how Jerry Diedrich showed up out there yesterday, as I *knew* he would, even though this was far from being a publicly known event. It didn't have to be, it wasn't illegal, and despite Diedrich and his simple-minded friends, it wasn't harmful to the reef. But the point is, he was *here*. He has friends in my own company, clerks, who knows who they are, they keep him informed, let him know what I'm doing, where I am."

Manville asked, "What does Diedrich have against you?"

"I have no idea!" Curtis was so obviously exasperated that Manville had to believe him. Curtis said, "He's been after me since just around the time I left Hong Kong, and it's me he wants, not polluters or environmental criminals or any of that, it's me. Most of that Planetwatch crowd is off doing something about the ozone layer or some fucking thing, but he's got this one bunch to fixate on me, he's got them convinced it's a crusade and I'm the evil tycoon that has to be brought down."

"And you need to get away from him," Manville said, "to do what you want to do next."

"It's ridiculous," Curtis said. "I should be able to bury him under lawyers, clog him with money, but every move I make to protect myself just inflames them all the worse and brings another dozen volunteers out of the colleges and onto my tail. I need him *off* my tail, George."

"Then why not have Diedrich killed?"

"Because I don't know how." Curtis grinned, with not much humor. "I've thought of it," he said, "of course I have, but that's not the business I'm in, George. I wouldn't know how to go about it. I don't have people killed."

"What about here? What about now?"

"Death through neglect, death through...ignorance."

"It'll take more than that," Manville said.

"I hope not," Curtis said. "But in any case, it will give me the leverage I need to get Diedrich and his little friends off my back just until I get this done. A few months, maybe less." Curtis leaned forward again. "George," he said, "you're a good man. You're also a brilliant engineer. You could have your own business, accomplish... I'm not going to tell you what I have planned, but I will include you in the profit." Then he leaned back and considered Manville, and didn't quite smile. "I've mentioned your profit twice now," he said, "and you still haven't asked me how much."

"It didn't occur to me."

"Ten million dollars," Curtis told him. "That's your share. You can have it right away, in gold, if you like, right after it's done. Or you can wait a week or two and it will become nothing but a number in a bank account."

"Gold?" Manville said.

"I've told you enough," Curtis decided, but smiled to show they were partners now. "George," he said, "I have to go up and talk to Captain Zhang. What do you think I should say to him?"

Manville thought. He knew that Curtis was telling the truth about it all; his current financial mess, the existence of a risky and illegal scheme to get himself out of the mess, and the ten million dollars that would be his own if he merely went away and didn't say anything and didn't make trouble.

The money didn't tempt him, which surprised him a bit. His hesitation was caused instead by his fellow feeling for Curtis. The man had truly been mistreated and was truly in a bind. But a poor dumb well-meaning girl shouldn't be *murdered* to help Curtis get out of his troubles, and that's what they were talking about, after all. It was an escalation too far.

Manville sighed. "I'm sorry, Mr. Curtis," he said, "but I think you have to tell the captain to take very good care of that girl, because if she doesn't survive the trip to Brisbane there will be too many questions."

Curtis said, "You're sure about this."

"I'm sorry."

Curtis looked out the window toward the sea. "Well," he said, "if she has to be kept alive, it might be better to get her to the mainland right away. We could strap her to a mattress, carry her along in the helicopter this afternoon."

"Then I'd come along, too."

Curtis frowned at him, showing some of his anger, and stayed silent for a long moment. Then he said, "You're making an enemy, George. Not a good enemy to have."

"I know. I'm sorry." Manville spread his hands. "It just isn't something I can do."

Another long thoughtful pause. He's trying to figure out, Manville thought, how to kill me, too. Then Curtis nodded, briskly, in agreement or farewell, and got to his feet, and went off without another word for his talk with Zhang.

Manville sat on, looking out the window, seeing nothing. What a rotten position to be in. Well; what a rotten position they were all in.

He never did eat breakfast that morning.

18

A mistake had been made. Curtis understood that, now; he'd made a second mistake, while trying to adjust for the first. And both mistakes came down to the same error of judgment. He had gauged George Manville too poorly, dismissing him as just an engineer, which was certainly true, but without stopping to think what that meant.

Yes, Manville was just an engineer, and what that meant was, he had too much integrity and too little imagination. Dangle ten million in front of him—in gold, George, in gold!—and he hasn't the wit to be seduced by it. First he has to take responsibility for the accident to the diver, a responsibility that was never for a second his, but which he assumed for himself simply because he was the project's engineer. That unbidden, unasked-for scrupulousness leads him to learn the truth about the diver, which makes him a threat to Richard Curtis, to which Curtis responds by making mistake number two. Not taking time to judge his man, he tries to enlist Manville on his side, and tells him too much.

Before this, Curtis had once or twice wondered, if there were unexpected complications down the line, whether or not he'd be able to recruit Manville, and had guessed that a combination of cupidity and the engineering challenge would turn the trick, but now he knew he'd been wrong. Manville was too blunt-minded to be affected by cupidity, and his engineer's honor would keep him from being caught up by the engineer's challenge. If he could balk at finishing off one half-dead idiotic girl, how would he react to what was going to happen to all those people in the buildings?

No, Manville could never have been an ally, and now he's become a danger, a bigger danger than the girl, who was merely a club to beat Jerry Diedrich with. And Manville was now an even bigger danger than Diedrich, because Curtis had told him far too much.

The both of them, Curtis thought, and considered the personnel available to him in Australia, and saw how it could be done. The both of them, when they landed at Brisbane.

Curtis spent the late morning in his cabin, on the telephone to Brisbane and Townsville, looking for the people he needed, assuring himself they would be in the right places at the right time. He couldn't say very much over the phone—there was no security on these things, particularly the ones that bounced off satellites—but he could at least get them in position, so he could tell them in person, and very quietly, what was needed.

Content with the moves he'd made, pleased that at last the mistakes had come to an end, Curtis went aft to the dining room for the farewell lunch with his three money people. Manville was there, looking worried and uncertain, and Curtis went out of his way to be friendly, to reassure the man. Patting Manville on the arm, being his heartiest, he said, "Forgotten, George. Don't worry about it. I don't know what I was thinking before. Desperation, I suppose. I'll find some other way to deal with my problems, and you're still my man. All right?"

Manville was obviously surprised, then grateful. Of course, the man without imagination *wanted* to believe that everything could be all right, that simply, that easily. "Thank you, Mr. Curtis," he said, answering Curtis's smile with his own tentative grin. "I am sorry, the situation you're in, and you can count on me to keep my mouth shut."

"I know I can, George. I don't have the slightest doubt." And, with another pat on the dead man's arm, Curtis turned to the other three, saying, "Good news. It turns out, I was told wrong. The diver *isn't* dead, she's still alive."

Beaming at everyone as they expressed their own surprise and pleasure, Curtis said, "We only hope we can keep her that way. Don't we, George?"

19

Captain Zhang stayed on the bridge to watch the helicopter take off, not wanting one last encounter with Richard Curtis. He was still frightened, still depressed, and still very confused.

Would he have killed the girl? Even when he checked his medical kit to be sure he had a fresh syringe, even when he carried the kit with him down from the bridge, he hadn't known for absolute certain what he would do when he reached cabin 7. He knew what he felt and believed he should do, which was protect his family, save his job, not permit some stupidly intrusive unknown stranger to destroy his life. But could he have done it?

He didn't know. All he was certain of was, when Mr. Curtis called to him, in the lounge, and told him not to go down to the patient yet, not until Curtis and the engineer had finished their conversation, Zhang had not immediately felt relief, or pleasure, or anything like that. He'd felt confusion, of course, but also he'd surprised himself with a strange welling up of frustration, as though he'd just been thwarted in the accomplishment of something that had been his goal all along.

But what accomplishment? Killing her? Not killing her, and nobly suffering the consequences? Now he would never know what his decision would have been, and in some terrible way that was even worse than having the decision still out in front of him.

When Mr. Curtis had come up to the bridge, after he and the engineer had finished, he was very angry, red-faced, banging his fist against tabletops, and Zhang knew it was Manville who had made him so angry. "We are going to *take care* of that girl, Zhang," he announced, showing his teeth in a snarl. "We are going to keep her alive. Do you understand me?"

"No, sir." Zhang watched his employer warily, not wanting all that rage to turn in his direction.

"We're not going to do what we were going to do," Curtis snapped, and grimaced with his fury. "Mr. Manville won't let us, you see? Zhang, that girl stays alive until you dock at Brisbane, no matter what. From then on, we'll see, won't we?"

"If you say so, sir."

"I say so," Curtis repeated, mocking him, then showed him a hard false aggressive smile and said, "Well, at least it's a happy ending for *you*, isn't it? I know you didn't like the idea."

"I want to do what I can to help you, Mr. Curtis."

Curtis could be seen to force himself under control, and when next he spoke he was calmer, more controlled, more himself. "I appreciate that, Zhang. These have been...difficult times for me. Well, it'll all work out, and I know you're a willing man, Zhang, and I won't forget it."

"Thank you, sir."

"And I'm glad, for your sake," Curtis said, with a shrug, "you don't have to do it after all."

"If there's anything—"

"No, no, that's it, that's all of it," Curtis said, and shook his head, and left the bridge, and Zhang, alone, dropped heavily into his chair at the chart-table and wiped the perspiration streaming down his face.

But of course, that wasn't all of it. Curtis spent much of the morning on the telephone in his cabin, and Zhang suspected he was making other plans, dealing with people far better at this sort of thing than Zhang could ever be, and that was confirmed just after lunch, while the other guests were in their cabins, packing for the helicopter trip back to Australia. That was when Curtis came up again to talk with Zhang on the bridge. Zhang saw him coming, and waited, polite on the outside, trembling within.

As usual, Curtis wasted no time on pleasantries. Coming onto the bridge, he said, "Captain Zhang, you intend to dock tomorrow night around seven, early evening, am I right?"

"Yes, sir."

"We're going to change that," Curtis told him. "Without being obvious about it, don't make your best pace. I don't want you to round Moreton before one in the morning."

Moreton was the island that ran along the seaward side of Moreton Bay, with Brisbane at the inner end of the bay. Zhang could make that adjustment, of course, he could travel just a bit more slowly, take a slightly more curved route. A few of the more experienced crewmen might be aware of the difference, but no one else. Certainly not the engineer, Manville, and Zhang was sure the engineer was the reason for this change.

Which Curtis confirmed by what he said next: "I'll want you to take the bridge tomorrow night, by yourself. No one else has to be up and around at that hour."

"No, sir."

"And if it happens," Curtis said, "that a boat comes alongside, even grapples on, you don't have to pay attention."

"No, sir."

"Understood?"

"Yes, sir," Zhang said.

Curtis looked keenly at him, and Zhang felt he had to meet the man's eyes. Curtis's mouth was smiling, but his eyes were icy cold, very hard. Zhang thought, I don't know if he's crazy or just brutal, but it doesn't matter. Either way, I don't want him to think *I'm* one of his enemies.

It was very difficult to meet that inhuman gaze, not to flinch or turn away, but Zhang held himself in, waited it out, didn't even show a tremble, and at last Curtis nodded and said, "I know I can count on you."

"Yes, sir." Zhang's mouth and throat were dry, the words came out crumpled.

Curtis patted Zhang's arm—Zhang didn't flinch—and twenty minutes later, as he watched the helicopter with Curtis and his guests aboard lift off from *Mallory* and swing over to look at the muddy blank they'd made of Kanowit Island, that spot on Zhang's arm still burned.

What am I going to do? Zhang wondered. I am on Kanowit Island, and I'm slowly being sucked under. To do nothing doesn't save you, you'll still be sucked under. But what can I do?

20

Manville was very aware that he was alone on the ship. Once Curtis and his financial people flew off, there was no one on the *Mallory* that he had ever even had a conversation with, except Captain Zhang, and he expected little comfort from that quarter. The people who'd worked with him on the island, setting the charges and flooding the tunnels and sealing the areas where the explosives would go off, had all flown in from Australia, construction crews of Curtis's, in two planes that came down on the old Japanese landing strip on the island and then took the crews back home the day before the test.

Usually, Manville didn't mind being alone. There were always projects he was working on, problems to be solved. But now, for the first time in his life, he was aware of being in personal physical danger, of being threatened by another human being, and he didn't know what to do about it. He didn't even know how to think about it. He wasn't a soldier of fortune, a man of action, a man of violence. He was an engineer, he had tools, not weapons, and his primary tool was his brain.

It would help if there were a friendly face on the ship, an ally, someone to discuss the situation with. Because he wasn't at all sure he was up to this kind of thing. The main point now, he supposed, was to try to protect the girl. Whatever came at him, Zhang or members of the crew, or somebody else entirely when they reached Brisbane, at least he should be with the girl, not leave her exposed and helpless.

He wished he could move her, possibly to his own cabin, but he was afraid to, not knowing exactly what her condition was.

She'd been battered by the sea, and though she was surely going to live—if nobody interfered—she might have broken bones or other injuries. So the best thing to do, if he couldn't move her, was to move himself.

After the helicopter lifted away from the *Mallory* with an excited flutter of rotor blades, and swung over to take a last look at Kanowit, Manville went on back down to cabin 7 and let himself in again with his equivalence card. Then he propped the door open while he went across to cabin 6 and picked up a pillow and blanket there. Returning to 7, he let the door snick shut and locked, then put the blanket on the floor at the opposite end of the room from the entry, under the porthole. He propped the pillow against the wall there, took his paperback book from his hip pocket, and sat down, back against the pillow against the wall, face toward the door.

The porthole above his head gave plenty of light for reading. His book was a collection of Maugham short stories of the South Seas; a very different place, then, but he supposed the people were much the same. The stories were comforting, because no matter how serious the problem, there was always some sort of acceptable resolution by the end. Reading, he could hope for the same sort of resolution for himself.

Her head on the bunk was just to his right, and after a while he became aware of her breathing. It was less shallow than before, and less rapid, long slow breaths now, regular, without strain. It seemed to Manville that she had undergone a transition, from being unconscious to being asleep. Which meant she might soon wake, and then he'd have somebody to talk it over with. In the meantime, he read.

21

Kim looked at the ceiling. Daytime. The ship was in motion, and grayish light reflected from the passing ocean came in through the porthole to fidget on the pale ceiling.

She realized she was awake again, and had been awake for... for a while.

She remembered everything this time, and remembered most sharply that her body contained many pockets of pain that would activate if she made any move at all. So she lay still, on her back, and looked at the ceiling, and wondered where she was and what would happen.

A page turned; a faint sound, but clear. Close by, to her left. Cautiously, she turned her head just slightly, waking soreness in her neck and back and shoulders. She looked sidelong, and a man was there, next to her, in profile. He was seated on the floor, head tilted down, legs bent up, reading a paperback book propped against his knees. She had never seen him before in her life.

Slowly she moved her head back to position one, and closed her eyes. He must be a guard of some kind; so she was a prisoner. On Richard Curtis's yacht? Why a prisoner?

Are they going to arrest me? Is Richard Curtis going to make an example of me, and have me charged with trespassing and endangerment and all sorts of things, and have me thrown in jail? And where? In Australia, or in Singapore?

She found herself afraid of Singapore. It was known to be very stern with lawbreakers, and very accommodating to its businessmen, and Richard Curtis had become one of Singapore's most significant businessmen since he'd left Hong Kong.

How could she escape? She could feel she was nearly naked, and the wetsuit wasn't to be seen anywhere in the cabin. Even if her body weren't so battered, she couldn't possibly leap from a moving ship in the middle of the ocean.

Jerry will help, she thought. Planetwatch will help, they have lawyers, they can do a lot. Once they find out where I am, and what's happening to me.

The scratch of a key in a lock made her eyes automatically snap open, and she saw the door start its inward sweep, felt movement to her left as the guard started to get to his feet. They should think I'm still unconscious, she thought, trying to find some advantage for herself somewhere in all this, and shut her eyes.

The newcomer spoke first, sounding surprised: "Mr. Manville!"

"Hello, captain," her guard said. "Come to see your patient?" He sounded sarcastic, which surprised her.

"Mr. Manville, please," the captain said, as though he'd been insulted or demeaned in some way. "I'm not going to hurt her."

"You would have," the guard said.

"I don't know." Now the captain only sounded unhappy, and she recognized his as the voice she'd heard on the *Planetwatch III*'s sound system, arguing with Jerry. *I am asked to inform you...* Now he said, "I'm not sure what I was going to do, and that's the truth. Mr. Manville, I'm not a bad man."

"Richard Curtis is," the guard said, which surprised Kim a lot. Wasn't she on Curtis's ship? Wouldn't the guard be one of his men? She listened, wondering, and the guard went on, "Captain, don't do his dirty work."

"I will not harm her," the captain said. "I promise you, Mr. Manville. May I look at her now?"

"I'll stay here."

"Of course."

"I'm awake," Kim said, because they would soon discover that anyway, and opened her eyes, and studied the two men standing there. The captain was Asian, middle-aged and worried-looking, wearing his dark blue uniform and braided cap without pride or distinction. The other man didn't seem like a guard at all. He was rugged enough, she supposed, but something in his face seemed at once more intelligent and less brutish. And the man had been sitting and reading, after all.

They both looked at her, and both seemed pleased that she was awake. The guard or whatever he was even smiled at her, as though to offer encouragement, as the captain went to one knee beside the bunk, gazed seriously at her, and said, "I am Captain Zhang of the motor ship *Mallory*. You were found in the water near Kanowit Island. That was yesterday. At first, it was thought you would die."

"I'm very stiff," she said, and the effort of speaking made her cough, which hurt her torso. "And dry," she whispered. "Very dry."

"In a moment," the captain said, "we'll help you to sit up. But first, if I may? We have not been able to be certain of the extent of your injuries."

Gently he moved the blanket and sheet down away from her upper body, exposing her down to the bellybutton. She became very conscious of her nakedness, and in a small voice said, "I'd like to have some clothing."

The guard said, "We'll find you some. It'll have to be men's things."

"That's all right."

"But I'm sure we can find something that fits. Right, captain?"

"Oh, yes," the captain said, but he was absorbed with other

questions. He said, "Miss, you may have cracked or broken ribs. Excuse me, I must test. Tell me if this hurts."

"Yes!"

"Ah, yes, there and…here?"

"Ahh!"

"And then the stomach, the internal organs. Forgive this." His hands were blunt-feeling but somehow comforting. He pressed down in several places around her stomach and lower sides, asking each time if she felt pain, and she never did. "Very good," he said at last, and moved the covers back up over her, then used the edge of the bunk to help him get back to his feet. "You have three cracked ribs," he told her. "I am going to wrap your torso, just beneath the breasts, with an expanding bandage."

"Ace bandage?" she asked.

"Yes, exactly," he agreed. "We want the ribs to rest and remain still, so they can heal, but every time you breathe you strain them again. This is to keep them from moving too much. You'll feel the constriction, it won't be very comfortable, I'm sorry to say, but the sharp pains should be less, and in a few days, if you don't move around too much, exercise yourself too much, it can come off."

"I ache all over," she told him. She found she automatically trusted this man.

"Yes, of course you do, you were very strongly battered. But I believe there's nothing else broken, and the stiffness will ease." Then, with a small sad smile, he said, "If you are my patient, I should know your name."

"Oh, sure," she said. "I'm Kimberly Baldur. Everybody calls me Kim."

"And how do you spell your last name, please? I must put it in the log."

She told him, and he asked her age, and she said, "Twenty-three. And I have to go to the bathroom."

"Well, yes, of course," the captain said. "You've been unconscious quite a long time. Mr. Manville? Would you help Ms. Baldur to sit up?"

The captain offered her his hands to grasp, so she could pull herself up, while Manville crouched against the head of the bunk to put his hands behind her shoulders and lift.

Pains shot through her, especially around the chest, and she gasped and clenched her teeth, and sat slumped and miserable while the captain reached under the blanket to pull her legs sideways, and Manville helped to turn her, until she was seated on the edge of the bed with her bare feet on the floor, blanket still covering her from waist to knee.

"Mr. Manville," the captain said, "would you help her to stay there, please, while I get the bandage? I'm sorry, Ms. Baldur, we'll have to do the bandage first, before you leave the bed."

The pain was so intense she felt she might faint. "That's all right," she whispered, and Manville sat on the bed beside her, one hand on each shoulder to keep her upright.

The captain had a medical bag with him, on the floor, and while he rooted through it the other man said, "I'm George Manville, I was the chief engineer on that test on the island. I'm the one who didn't think to put in a fail-safe. So I'm to blame for what happened to you."

She tried to look at him, surprised, and saw his earnestness, and said, "Oh, no, I don't have anybody to blame but me. All of my grand gestures end in pratfalls, Mr. Manville, don't blame yourself for it."

"Here we are," said the captain, and he wound the tan elastic bandage around her torso three times, not too tight, fixing the end with two small metal clips. "That should make things a little easier," he said.

It did. Breathing was somewhat harder, but when she moved there was much less pain. "Thank you."

"Let us help you to your feet."

God, she was shaky! Her legs felt like Play-Doh. When she was standing and they let go of her, she swayed back and forth like a sapling in a wind. "I don't know," she said, but somehow kept her balance.

They helped her across the narrow room to the lavatory door. "We'll wait in the corridor," the captain told her, and Manville gave her another encouraging smile, and they went outside, shutting the door.

She heard them talking together in the corridor as she weakly pulled open the lavatory door and hobbled inside. In the mirror there, she saw what a haggard wreck she was, how her hair looked like last year's bird nest and there were great dark crescents under her eyes. And all over her body were large irregular bluish-gray bruises. That would be blood, wouldn't it, under the skin. God, I really did hurt myself, she thought, and felt grateful wonder that she'd survived.

Getting up from the toilet was the hardest part. But then she made it successfully all the way back to the bed by leaning on the wall the entire way. They were still talking outside, a murmur in which she could make out no words, and she wondered at their relationship. They'd seemed like antagonists at first, with Manville so clearly distrusting the captain, but now they were more like partners, at least in the matter of taking care of her.

She arranged herself in the bed, sitting up, back against the wall, covered again with the blanket, and called out, "All right."

They came in, Manville first, and the captain said how pleased he was that she'd done the whole thing by herself. "You're a young and healthy person, you'll recover very quickly."

Manville said, "By tomorrow, when we reach Brisbane, you'll be ready to walk off the ship under your own steam." To the captain, he said, "We'll be docking around seven tomorrow night, won't we?"

"Well…" All at once, the captain was evasive, Kim could sense it, but couldn't imagine why. "It may be later," he said. "I think probably we won't arrive until two or three the next morning."

Manville must have sensed the change in the captain, too, because he frowned at him, but all he said was, "That late, I'm surprised."

The captain looked away from him, and at Kim, telling her, "I will have some soup brought to you, and some clothing. You should eat the soup, and then you should sleep some more."

"I am…tired," she agreed. "But soup, yes. I'm hungry first. Thank you."

"I'll be handy," Manville told her, and it seemed to Kim he was saying it as much to the captain as to her. "If you need me."

22

Manville had gradually reached the conclusion that the threat would now come from elsewhere. Originally, Curtis had ordered Zhang to make sure Kim Baldur didn't live to see Brisbane, but after his confrontation with Manville he'd obviously changed that order. It could be seen in the attitude of Zhang himself; the man was weak and frightened, and would have done whatever Curtis asked of him, but would have been miserable while doing it. Now Zhang was a man from whom a heavy weight had been lifted.

But not entirely. Curtis would not give up, he wasn't the kind of man to accept defeat gracefully; or at all. He had two enemies now between himself and whatever this money-making scheme was, and one of them was Jerry Diedrich and the other was George Manville. He could get at Diedrich through Kim Baldur, but he would get at Manville much more directly.

Why would they be arriving in Brisbane so much later than originally planned? It seemed to Manville that Zhang had been hiding something when he'd told them that, and what could it be but an attack from Curtis? But where, and when? Sometime before they reached Brisbane, and apparently Curtis needed the extra time to get it ready.

In the meanwhile, though Manville felt he and Kim Baldur were both for the moment safe, he still took precautions. He moved himself into cabin 6, across the hall from her, and, while he was there, bolted shut the bulkhead doors at both ends of the passage.

The girl mostly slept, and whenever she awoke she was

starving. She moved on from soup to stew and bread, then some red wine, and improved by the hour.

Manville ate his own meals with Zhang, in the crew's mess, on the same level as cabins 6 and 7 but farther aft. Zhang was still hangdog, but pleasant, and they talked about neutral things: engineering, coastal shipping, the *Mallory*.

With Kim Baldur, he had only one real conversation, and that was about Jerry Diedrich. He stood in the doorway and watched her eat a bowl of stew, and said, "Do you know why Diedrich has it in so much for Richard Curtis?"

She looked at him in surprise, and said, "He's a major polluter. Planetwatch is after *all* those people."

"I'm sorry, Kim," he said, "but that isn't exactly true. Curtis is in construction, he's no saint when it comes to environmental laws, but he's no worse than any of the others, and better than a lot of them. It's Jerry Diedrich who has a personal vendetta against Curtis."

"Well, he despises Curtis," she said, "because he's a threat to the environment. But it isn't *personal*."

"You all showed up at Kanowit because of Diedrich," Manville pointed out. "That day, I'm sure there were a lot of threats to the environment, here and there around the globe, but what we were doing at Kanowit wasn't one of them."

"The risk to the coral—"

He shook his head. "There was none. We didn't even want to endanger the seawall, much less the coral, because Curtis and his partners have a use for that island. They don't want to destroy it."

"The chance you took—"

"I'm an engineer, Kim. Forgive me, but I know the risks better than Jerry Diedrich, and when he showed up at that island it wasn't because the reef was going to be destroyed,

because it wasn't. It was because Jerry Diedrich has a personal
vendetta against Richard Curtis and wanted to harass him."

"That isn't true," she said, and he could see from her face
that she was angry, closing down against him.

"Okay," he said, because it was obvious she had no idea why
Diedrich had it in for Richard Curtis. "How's the stew?"

She took a second to decide if she wanted to hold onto her
anger, then abruptly smiled and said, "It's great."

"Good."

"And I do want to thank you."

He laughed, and said, "Don't thank me yet, wait'll I do something."

That conversation was in late morning of the day after she'd
regained consciousness. That evening, Manville had dinner with
Zhang, and said, "Captain, originally, we'd have been coming
into Brisbane just about now."

Zhang looked worried and defensive. "Yes. That's true."

"Curtis told you to slow down, to give him time to set something up to deal with Ms. Baldur and me."

Zhang looked down at the food on his plate, and didn't
respond.

"Captain, I know you felt relieved when Curtis told you not to
try to...hurt Ms. Baldur. But if you do nothing and say nothing,
you'll be hurting her. At least let us know what's supposed to
happen."

Zhang looked very deeply troubled. He chewed a mouthful
of food, slowly, and at last swallowed it, and drank water, and
said, "Mr. Manville, I don't want to hurt anyone. But I don't
want my family to suffer either."

"I can understand that."

Zhang sighed. He couldn't meet Manville's eye. He said,
"Someone, some people, will board us tonight, around one,

when we go past the end of Moreton Island. I was told I should be alone on the bridge, everyone else should be asleep, I should pay no attention to whatever happens."

"Some sort of ship will come alongside? Grapple on?"

"That's what I understand."

Manville leaned back. "So when you dock at Brisbane, I won't be on the ship anymore, and Ms. Baldur will have died of her experience in the sea off Kanowit."

"I don't know," Zhang said miserably. "I'm not supposed to know anything, and I don't know anything."

"Captain," Manville said, "what are we going to do? To protect you, and your family, and to protect Ms. Baldur, and to protect me. What are we going to do?"

Slowly, Zhang shook his head. "I can't think," he said. "If there was something— As you say, to protect us all. But I can't think what."

"Let's put our heads together," Manville said.

23

A hand touched her shoulder, and a voice softly said her name. Kim frowned, not wanting to be awake, because to be awake was to be in pain, but in thinking that thought she knew it was too late, she was already awake, and not going back.

She opened her eyes and saw the dim room, the door propped open and the corridor light giving shape to George Manville, on one knee beside the bunk, still holding her shoulder, leaning toward her, something hushed but urgent in his manner. She felt afraid, and didn't know why, and said, "What?"

"Kim, listen," he said, his voice still low, but with that tremor of urgency in it. "Some people are coming to the ship later tonight, to do us harm. We have to keep away from them."

"Curtis?" she asked, and wondered why he'd want to do her harm. Or do George Manville harm.

"People of his," Manville said. "Kim, if you're dead, he can use that as a lever to pry Jerry Diedrich off his back. It's that important to him, I don't know exactly why, and he was hoping you'd die all by yourself, here on the ship. Since you won't, he's sending people."

She stared at him, not wanting to believe, but believing. "To *kill* me?"

"Captain Zhang and I talked over what to do," Manville told her. "We're releasing one of the launches, to try to convince them we already got away."

"Well, why don't we?" Feeling the urgency, she moved to sit up, and the stiff pain jolted through her, and she caught her breath with a sudden gasp.

"That's why," he told her. "You're mending, but you're still very battered. Eight hours in a small launch, on the open sea, would be too much for you."

"*You* could get away. Then he wouldn't dare do anything to me, because you could tell."

He shook his head. "Who would I tell? Who would I tell, and be believed against Richard Curtis?"

They've thought this through, she realized, Manville and Captain Zhang. Stop struggling, stop arguing, just do it, whatever it is they want. You're not going to have better ideas than theirs. "All right," she said.

"We'll scuttle the launch," he said, "so these other people won't come upon it accidentally in the water. Then we'll put you in one of the other launches, cover you with blankets, and hope they believe we already left the ship."

She could tell immediately that this was a very flimsy plan. "Where will you be?"

"Keeping out of their way, or trying to."

Very flimsy. But maybe it was the best they could do. "All right," she said.

"I have jeans and a sweater here for you," he said, holding them up for her to see. The jeans were faded, with bumpy knees, and the sweater was a dark green acrylic. "They're clean," he promised her, "and they should fit you."

"Thank you."

"I'm afraid these are the only shoes we could find," he said, and held them up.

She couldn't help it; she smiled at the shoes. She'd seen people wear shoes like this, when *Planetwatch III* docked sometimes, but had never guessed she'd one day wear them herself. The bottoms were roughly sawed out of the sidewall of an old tire, with a loose piece of canvas stapled across the top, and no heel. One size fits none.

"Can I help you sit up?"

"Yes," she said, lifting an arm for him. "Thank you. I'll be all right after that."

But she wasn't, not really. He had to help her put the sweater on, pulling it down over the elastic bandage that held her together. Then he put her feet into the legs of the jeans, helped her to stand, and pulled the jeans up to her waist.

"I've never been dressed by a man before," she said, feeling awkward as she zipped the fly shut and fastened the canvas belt.

Manville didn't say anything to that. His concentration was on the shoes, as he held her elbow and said, "Just step into them. There you go."

Actually, they were better than she'd expected, the rubber firm but not too hard, the canvas stretching to hold her foot. "I'm ready," she said.

When she started to walk, she realized how weak and dizzy she still was, and she was grateful for his hand holding tight to her upper arm. They left the cabin and started down the corridor, and he said, "Only the captain knows about this, so we have to be quiet."

She was looking at her surroundings. How plush it all was, in comparison with *Planetwatch III*. Real wood floor, cream-painted walls, and actual carpeting on those stairs out ahead of her.

Why couldn't Richard Curtis be content with all he had? Why did he have to ruin the planet to get just a little more?

Manville said, "I'll carry you up the stairs. It's just up one deck."

"Can't I walk?"

He shook his head. "I don't think so, Kim."

It was stupid to be so weak, to have to be carried around like an invalid. But she knew he was right; those stairs looked a mile high, and already she could feel what little strength she had draining away. "All right," she said, and stood obediently still, and he picked her up, one arm under her back, the other under her knees, and she put an arm over his shoulders, for balance.

He carried her slowly up the stairs. At the head of the stairs, he let her stand again, but kept that supporting hand on her arm as they went down a corridor past open doors showing much larger and more elaborate cabins, with large windows rather than portholes to show the black night outside.

At the end of the corridor he guided her through a wide teak door with two diamond-shaped windows in it, and then they were on deck, and immediately she could feel the movement of the ship more distinctly than when she'd been inside. Or was that just from seeing the dim whitecaps passing below?

The captain stood in darkness off to the right, forward, where one of the launches hung in its divots, just beyond the rail. When they walked toward him, Kim saw that a part of the rail was hinged to open inward as a gate, next to the entry steps to the launch.

"Good evening, Miss Baldur," he whispered, and nodded a greeting. He looked and sounded very worried.

"Good evening. Thank you for helping me."

"I wish it were not needed," he whispered. "But since it is, I am happy that this is what I can do."

To oppose Richard Curtis, she understood him to mean, instead of to give him what he wants, even though the captain worked for him.

Manville stepped onto the launch first, then took her arm to guide her aboard, the captain holding her other arm to steady her. "You'll stay in the cabin," Manville told her.

Most of the launch was open, with plank seating along both sides, but the front quarter was roofed in gleaming wood, with a low door next to the steering wheel. Manville opened the door, then steadied Kim as she bent down to step in, finding it so low in here she couldn't even kneel upright. There were two bunks side by side using most of the space, both neatly made with drum-tight woolen blankets, plus many storage bins and cabinets.

"What you should do," Manville said, leaning into the small space, "is lie on one of the bunks and cover yourself with the blanket from the other one. Cover yourself completely, if you hear anybody moving outside."

"I will."

He gave her leg an encouraging pat, and backed out of the doorway, then closed the door, leaving her alone in the dark.

Not total darkness; it wasn't completely black inside the cabin. Two narrow slit windows were in the forward end of the prow on both sides, just under the roof; some light from the ship leaked in through the window on the right. In its illumination, Kim pulled the blanket off the right-hand bunk, lay back on the other, and pulled the blanket over herself. And by then she was exhausted.

But not sleepy, not the way she'd been before. Now she was too tense to be sleepy, too worried, too frightened. People coming here to this ship to kill her? It was unbelievable, and yet she had to believe it.

Would she hear them arrive? Would they find her?

Would Manville and the captain be able to help?

She couldn't sleep, not at all. She lay there in the darkness, eyes open, looking at nothing, and nearly two hours later she heard the distant thump.

24

Morgan Pallifer once had his own ship, but that was years ago, in a completely different ocean. He had the ship because he and the Colombians were useful to one another, and then he lost the ship because the situation changed.

Oh, he was still useful to the Colombians; it's just that he was useful in a different way. He became useful to the Colombians as a bargaining chip in their sub rosa dealings with the American authorities. They would permit Pallifer and his lovely sloop, the *Pally*, to be caught by agents of the Drug Enforcement Administration when he made landfall at South Carolina with the cabin of the sloop full of duffel bags full of white plastic bags full of cocaine. The *Pally* was impounded, having been used in the drug trade, and Morgan Pallifer spent seven hard years in a Federal maximum-security prison, and now, gracious me, Morgan Pallifer can't vote in American elections anymore. Hah!

Oh, he understood how it worked, he wasn't bitter. The *Pally* had been in his name, but the Colombians had actually bought it for him, so it was really theirs, so they could take it away from him and give it to the DEA if it suited their needs. And he'd had four terrific years sailing the Colombians' ship and spending the Colombians' money, so it wasn't a bad deal to pay for it with seven years cowering like a cur in that Federal kennel. The American authorities were enabled to rack up yet another wonderful public success in their war on drugs—success after success, and yet nothing changes—and they got to do it by putting away some scruffy unimportant American citizen without harming their vitally important geopolitical interests with the Colombians.

Morgan Pallifer wasn't bitter, but he wasn't stupid, either. He did his seven years hard, he worked in a marina in Newport Beach, California for the three years of his parole, and the instant he was a completely free man he applied for and got a new passport and got the fuck *out* of that country. He'd been a citizen of the Pacific Rim ever since, nearly thirty years now, working when he had to, stealing when he could, living on the sea as much as possible, working other men's boats but never his own.

Sometimes the boats belonged to Richard Curtis, a good man in Morgan Pallifer's estimation, who occasionally needed to get around various regulations by bypassing the normal import-export routes, and when that happened, Curtis knew Morgan Pallifer was someone he could depend on, and Pallifer knew Richard Curtis had good money and good boats.

Today, Morgan Pallifer was 62, lean and leathery and mean as a snake. His faded blue eyes could almost look kindly at a distance, but they were not.

Tonight's work was straightforward, and lucrative. Pallifer had a good power launch of Curtis's, and a three-man crew of his own, people he could rely on. He'd done this kind of thing before, though not for Curtis, so this was a new level of their business relationship, and one that Pallifer was happy with. He would do his customary efficient job tonight, and Curtis would be pleased, and who knows what other interesting work might lie ahead? He might even have his own ship again one of these days, in waters not polluted by the Americans' high piousness and low dealings.

They came out from Brisbane Bay after dark, and made their approach to the *Mallory* keeping the bigger ship to port, so the bulk of Moreton Island lay behind them, to make them just that much harder to be seen. They swung around behind the white yacht, as it sluggishly moved shoreward like some fat nun waiting for the bandits, and Pallifer, at the helm, saw the space along the starboard side of the yacht where a launch was missing.

Did the birdies fly away? Or do they want poor old Morgan Pallifer to *think* they flew away?

Pallifer was good with boats. He brought this launch in tight to the *Mallory*'s flank without quite touching her, and behind him Arn swung the grappling hook forward and back, and in the darkness it looked like an unlit chandelier. Arn flung it high, and the curved arms of it cleared the rail up there, and at once Pallifer turned the wheel, so that the launch eased away from the white side of the yacht, making the rope more taut, out at an angle from the ship, so skinny little rope-muscled Arn could shinny up it without trouble.

Pallifer had not brought with him the ship's plan of the *Mallory* that Curtis had loaned him, but he remembered the layout, and had planned accordingly. Just ahead of him on this side was the door to the storage area, for loading supplies, a plain white metal door in the ship's white skin that was barely visible and that would be at deck level when *Mallory* was in port. Now, once Arn was aboard and had tossed the grappling hook back down into the sea between them for Frank to reel in, Pallifer eased the launch forward to that door. Above, Arn would be scurrying inside the ship into the main corridor, racing down the interior stairs, and then hurrying forward to the storage area. In just a minute, this door would open, and there it was, and there was Arn.

Frank and Bardo were the muscle. While Pallifer held the launch steady beside the open door, those two leaped across the moving space, holding onto the ends of ropes. Aboard, they looped the ropes around small stanchions just inside the doorway, to make the launch fast to the yacht, causing only one thump to sound when the two vessels came together. Once they were secure, Pallifer switched off the launch's two engines and stepped aboard the *Mallory*.

This wasn't his kind of ship. It was more like a country house than something seaworthy, with its carpeted stairways and expanses of glass. This wasn't the sort of vessel Pallifer loved to sail on and craved to own.

But he wasn't here to put an option on the *Mallory*, was he? No, it was a simple killing he was here for, that's all. Two killings, to be turned into one natural death and one disappearance.

Except that the subjects weren't where they were supposed to be. Pallifer and Arn and Frank and Bardo padded through the ship, undisturbed, knowing the crew would all be asleep and the captain obediently blind and deaf on the bridge, and when they got to cabin 4, where the disappearee was supposed to be bunked, the place was empty. No clothing, no personal possessions left behind. He'd moved out.

They went down one deck to cabin 7, where the natural death was to be waiting, and it, too was empty, but here at least the bed had been used and left mussed. And so had the bed in the cabin across the way, number 6. So the man had come down here to guard the woman, but then they'd both gone somewhere else.

Where? Off the ship? Pallifer didn't believe it, not from Curtis's description of the girl's condition. No, more likely, the two of them had set loose that launch and then hidden themselves somewhere aboard the *Mallory*, because they'd be thinking all they were up against was some simple stupid riff-raff. They wouldn't be expecting Morgan Pallifer.

The four men stood in the corridor between cabins 6 and 7, and Pallifer said, "All right, we'll find them aboard somewhere, but I'd best check in first with Curtis. He wanted me to ring if there was a complication."

They all went back up to cabin 1, which was Curtis's when he was aboard, and where the telephone was located. Pallifer dialed the number Curtis had given him, and the man answered on the second ring; so he'd been waiting right there for the call, it was that important to him. "Yes?"

"Not in their cabins," Pallifer said, being terse because there was no real privacy on a phone like this. "One launch is gone."

"No," Curtis said.

"I agree. We'll look around."

"Crew last."

Of course; only disturb the crew if it was absolutely necessary. Pallifer said, "Do you suppose the captain's been talking to them?"

There was a silence on the line, filled with electronic rustle, and then Curtis said, "I don't think so. I think he noticed it slowed down."

"That's possible," Pallifer said. "Means he's pretty smart, though."

"He is."

"Should I discuss it with the captain?"

"If you think you should," Curtis said. "But discuss it gently."

Palliser shrugged, a little irritated. Gentle discussion never accomplished anything, "I'll call you before we leave," he said.

25

Manville moved back from the doorway to cabin 1 while the leader was still telling his men what he wanted done. The leader hadn't believed for a second that he and Kim had fled on that launch, had he? No. A waste of time.

Manville had heard the thump of the two ships meeting, and had looked over the rail to see the last of them, the leader, as he moved from their launch into the *Mallory*. He'd trailed them ever since, as they went first to his cabin and then to Kim's— Curtis had prepared them thoroughly, all right—and then back to cabin 1 for the leader to make that call.

What now? If he were alone, Manville would try to circle around them, get into an area they'd already searched, and then possibly get to their own launch and take off in it. But he also had Kim to consider, who couldn't run, who could barely walk, and would not be able to defend herself.

What he needed was a weapon, some sort of weapon. Those four all had pistols stuck down into their belts, and at this point he had nothing. But if he could find *something*, and then get his hands on one of those pistols…

He'd always been a pretty good shot, against targets, never against anything alive. He'd belonged to a gun club for a few years, people who liked to plink at targets, try to compete against their own previous scores, but then the club was taken over by a group of hunters, "sportsmen" who wanted to politicize the organization and make it a mouthpiece for their own ideas, and Manville was one of those who'd dropped out. But he thought he was probably still pretty good, against something that didn't move, and didn't shoot back.

But the first thing was to find a weapon, some way to defend himself, and the second thing was to stay ahead of the search until he could circle around behind it. They were starting to look at the top deck, ignoring for the moment the bridge, moving from forward to aft, two of them on each side of the ship, taking their time. So Manville moved on ahead, and entered the large glass-domed dining room, and from there he went into the small service kitchen.

There were a lot of knives in here, some big cleavers, too, but Manville hoped for something better. Something like a club, to knock somebody out. He didn't want to go around cutting people, wouldn't know how to do it, probably didn't have the stomach for it. The idea of stabbing another person made him queasy.

He looked past the peppermill two or three times before he finally focused on it. It was a large thing, darkly lustrous, like a rook in a giant's chess set; probably a foot and a half long, it was made of rosewood, and when Manville picked it up it was as heavy as a baseball bat, with most of the weight near the base, where the metal grinding mechanism was fixed.

The peppercorns inside rustled when Manville hefted the thing, and he felt at first that it was too ridiculous to think of defending himself with a peppermill. But it was *heavy*, and it had the right shape for a club, and there was nothing else in here.

Carrying the peppermill next to his leg, Manville left the serving kitchen and went back through the dining room.

The four men were slowly moving this way, two through the central corridor, checking every door along their route, and one on each side, along the outer decks. Manville would have preferred to tackle the leader, who was older and scrawnier than the other three, but he needed to go after somebody who was alone, and that meant one of the bruisers searching along the deck.

At the aft end of the dining room, glass-windowed doors on both sides led out to the decks. On the starboard side, another door, solid wood, just aft of this one, led to a stairwell going down. The searchers were entering through every doorway they reached, looking inside, then backing out again. Manville stationed himself just inside the dining room door, gripped the peppermill hard, looked through the window, and waited.

Here he came. A big man, he walked with hunched shoulders and with head thrust forward, as though sniffing out his prey. His pistol was in his right hand, and he stepped cautiously, looking over his shoulder often, pausing before entering a doorway, then backing swiftly out again.

The man reached that stairwell door. Manville hung back, looking through the window in the door, seeing only the right side of him, the dark pants and black sweater, the right arm bent, pistol beyond Manville's range of vision. The man stepped forward, disappearing, and Manville took a deep breath. He'd never done anything like this before, never *anything* like this. But there was no choice, and the time was now.

He pushed open the door, eased outside, stood with his back to the wall beside the open stairwell door, right arm cocked up across his upper chest, peppermill held up beyond his left ear, and waited for the man to back out to the deck, and from the other side of the ship he heard the scream.

It threw him off. All he could think was: They found her! And it immobilized him for just a second, while the searcher, as startled as he was by the sound of that scream, came lunging out of the doorway, forward rather than backward, pistol right *there*, and he actually saw Manville before Manville thought to swing the peppermill as hard as he could. It hit the man in the face, at the top of the nose, between the eyes. It knocked him back a step, but it didn't knock him out. It wasn't heavy enough, the damn thing wasn't heavy enough.

And the man still had that pistol. Desperate, Manville swung again, and the heavy base of the peppermill thudded down on the man's right wrist, and the pistol fell to the deck and went sliding away,

I *need* that pistol! Manville swung the peppermill with all his might, like a carpenter driving a masonry nail into a brick wall, three hard pounding frantic punches at that face, and then the peppermill cracked diagonally in two, the base and a long triangle of the handle bouncing off the man's chest to fall at his feet, leaving in Manville's hand a kind of long jagged wooden dagger.

The man was still on his feet, though goggle-eyed and reeling, hands groping as though for an opponent he couldn't see. Manville lunged at his face with this new dagger, and the man staggered back, lost his footing, and toppled backward down the steep flight of stairs.

Pistol first. Manville ran to where it still moved on the deck, the polished metal sliding over the polished wood surface with every tremor of the ship. Hurling away the remnant of the peppermill, he snatched up the pistol, then ran back to point it down the stairwell. Only then did he look past the barrel of the gun, to see the man in a twisted heap down there, unconscious or dead.

Kim. Manville hurried back into the dining room and across it and out the door on the other side, and down there to his left, dimly illuminated by the night lights within the ship, he saw the group of them, the three men just now dragging Kim from the launch to the deck while she weakly and uselessly struggled.

Manville was about to run down there, to stop them and save her, when he suddenly realized he didn't know this pistol he now clenched so hard in his right hand. It was a tool, after all, and you're supposed to know your tools, and he didn't know this tool. It would have a safety, he knew that, but was the safety at this moment on or off? He didn't know.

He stood just out of sight of the people on deck, and studied the thing, a revolver with a bit of bullet showing at the back of each chamber. This small lever here on the side, handy to the right thumb; wouldn't that be the safety?

The lever moved up and down, and when he first tried the thing it was in the down position. Would the man have done his searching with the safety on or off? There was nothing written on the pistol, no icons, no hint.

I'm an engineer, Manville thought, if I were the one who'd designed this, which way would turn the safety off, which way would turn it on? I would want the more speed when turning it off, would have less reason for speed when switching it on. The quickest simplest motion here is for the thumb to push this lever down, so if I were the engineer on this project I'd design it so the safety was off when the lever was down. The lever's down.

If I'm wrong, I'll know it when and if I have to pull the trigger. With luck, I'll still have time to put my thumb under the lever and push it up. Without luck, I'm dead anyway, because this is nothing I know anything about.

Manville stepped forward onto the deck, the pistol held out in front of him, and moved toward the group, all of them now on deck, clustered around Kim, half-supporting her. The leader was saying, "—down to her cabin," and of course that's what they'd want, for Kim to be dead in her cabin, smothered with a pillow.

"Stop!" Manville shouted. "Put your hands up!" They looked

at him with astonishment, but without fear. Because they were dragging Kim, none of them had a pistol in his hand, and yet they looked at Manville and he could see they were unafraid of him, unimpressed by him. They know, he thought, they know this is their world, not mine.

It was like meeting a dangerous dog: Don't show your fear. "Everybody hands up!" he yelled. "Kim, get out of the way! Lean against the rail!"

The tableau they presented to him was this: The leader stood in the middle, one arm around Kim's waist, holding her up, with the other big man to the right and the smaller man to the left. None of them obeyed him, none put their hands up. The leader didn't release Kim, but held her even tighter. None of them even seemed worried.

Manville was about fifteen feet from them now, and reluctant to get any closer. He held the pistol out at arm's length, aimed at the leader's head, just next to Kim's, and he called, "I'll shoot! Let her go!"

"Oh, I don't think so," the leader said. He had a raspy scaly voice, like the whispery sound of a lizard moving on a stone wall. "You ever shoot a gun, mister?"

"Yes," Manville said, and felt immediately calmer, because it was true. "I'm a good shot, as a matter of fact," he said.

The leader grinned at him. "Ever shoot a man? Not everybody can, you know,"

"I can," Manville said, but the calm had fled him, because he wasn't at all sure now that he was telling the truth. He had captured this pistol, they were supposed to obey him, but they didn't believe he was a threat. They believed he was an amateur, a baby in their hard world. He might interrupt them for a few seconds, but then they'd contemptuously brush him aside and get on with their bloody work.

Yes. The leader turned to the big man, to his left, and said, "Bardo, kill this cocksucker and let's get on with it."

It was because Manville was thinking mostly about the safety that he could do it. He wasn't thinking about the shooting of a human being, he was thinking about time. If I'm wrong about the safety, he thought, I won't have time for a second chance. That's why, before Bardo could finish drawing his own pistol out from under his belt, Manville shot him in the chest.

Well. He'd been right about the safety. Good engineering.

They were all amazed, he could see that, and it gave him strength. Pointing the pistol at the leader again, he said, "Let her go."

This time the leader did, releasing Kim and stepping one pace back, looking now mostly irritated and frustrated, but still not at all afraid. The other man, arms held out from his sides to show he didn't mean to start any trouble, stood watchful, wary, but also not frightened.

These people are very dangerous, Manville thought. I've never dealt with such dangerous people. They're waiting for me to make one tiny mistake, any tiny mistake, and God knows I'm likely to make a dozen mistakes. Except, no; one mistake is all they'll give me.

He said, "Kim, get to the side, get out of the way."

She did, stepping around behind the one he'd shot, who lay now on his back on the deck like a drowning victim who's just been dragged aboard. She was tottery, but she could walk, she could take care of herself. Looking at Manville past the one he'd shot, she said, her voice shaky and weak, "George? Is he dead?"

"I really don't care," he told her, truthfully, and the leader surprised him with a snort of amusement, and Manville knew he didn't have much time to press this advantage. "Kim," he said, "get around behind them, get those pistols, hold onto them. Don't let anybody grab you."

"Don't worry," she said, with a weak smile. "I don't want to be a shield. I think you'd shoot them right through me."

That made the leader turn his head to give her an inquisitive look, and to say, "Is that right?"

Manville said, *"Now,* Kim."

Kim moved, around behind the leader, who was now studying Manville as though to memorize him, or read him. As Kim put one cautious arm around him to pluck the pistol out from his belt, the leader said to Manville, "You're some kind of ringer, I think. You're not what I was told I was gonna find here."

Oh, yes, I am, Manville thought, but I'm happy if you don't believe it. And he knew it would be best if he didn't say anything at all to that. The strong silent type, that's me.

Kim got both pistols, and went back to lean against the rail. She looked very weak, and not as though she could possibly use those guns now dangling from her hands at her sides, not to save her life.

Manville said to the two men, gesturing at the one he'd shot, "Pick him up." Not because he needed the man moved anywhere, but because he wanted to keep these last two occupied.

The leader and the other man obediently stepped over to crouch above the one he'd shot, and the leader said, "I think he's still alive."

"Pick him up."

"We oughta get the captain down here," the leader said, "get my man Bardo some medical attention."

"Pick him up or I'll shoot you," Manville said.

The leader shrugged. "Not the way it was supposed to be," he commented, and he and the other one picked up the wounded man, the leader at his ankles, the other man at his head.

Following Manville's orders, they went back down through the ship, the killers first, muttering privately together over their unconscious mate, then Manville, and Kim last.

They made slow progress, because of the weight the two in front were carrying and because of Kim's weakness and Manville's fear that if he put any concentration on her, to help her, they'd find some way to take advantage.

He directed them through the ship down to the storage room, where they'd boarded. The outer door stood open there, the moving night sea hissing outside, the two ropes snaking in to the stanchions, their powerful launch nestled snug against *Mallory's* side. There, Manville ordered them to put the wounded man down on the metal floor and then to sit next to him. "Take off your shoes," he told them, and said to Kim, "Throw those pistols into the launch."

The leader said, "You're gonna take our boat?"

Manville ignored him. "Kim, get their shoes. Don't get between me and them. Take the laces out. You two. Face down on the floor."

The leader said, "I don't think I can let you do this."

He's dangerous, Manville reminded himself, and he meant to kill me, so this is what I'd better do. He pointed the pistol at the leader's head, just as the leader was putting a hand behind himself to lever up, to stand.

But then the leader looked at Manville's face, and as Manville was about to squeeze the trigger the leader abruptly dropped back, hands up in front of his face, saying, "All right. All right." And now, for the first time, a small flicker of fear did show in the man's eyes.

I would have killed him, Manville thought, astonished at himself, a little disapproving of himself. I was *going* to kill him, and he saw that.

The two men lay face down on the metal floor, as he'd ordered. He said, "Hands behind your backs. Kim, use the shoelaces, tie each one's thumbs together. Tie them tight. Use a lot of knots."

"Not their wrists?"

"No. If you tie their wrists, their hands are still free, and they can untie one another. If you tie their thumbs, they can't use their hands anymore." He had no idea how he knew this, or how it had occurred to him, but he knew he was right.

Once Kim was finished, Manville used the other two laces to tie their ankles, then helped Kim into the launch, saying, "I'm sorry, we're going to have to do the bumpy trip, after all."

"That's all right," she said, "I'm a lot better."

Manville climbed into the launch and started the engines. Then he went back to the open door to deal with the ropes, and the leader had twisted around, was propped on one elbow, staring at him. Their eyes met. The leader said, "I'd like to run into you again some time."

"I wouldn't," Manville said, and freed the ropes.

TWO

I

Kim had never felt so alone, or so vulnerable. The late morning sun was hot, the day was beautiful, Brisbane reared up all around her like a glass version of the city of Oz, but alone here on this launch on the Brisbane River, tied up to a support at the southern end of the William Jolly Bridge, still she felt cold, with an interior cold the warm sun and the inviting city couldn't reach.

She was alone in the world. Would George Manville come back? He had saved her life, out there on that ship, he had carried her here, and he had promised he would come back, but would he? Wasn't it time for him to start taking care of his own life? Hadn't he made it clear that from here on she was only a burden, an added difficulty when he had his own safety and his own future to worry about?

There had been no conversation at all at first. The night-time journey in from the *Mallory* had been slow and bumpy, and had taken all of Manville's concentration. Not that it had been hard to find the way; Brisbane was a bright pink dome of light against the blackness, just ahead of them to the west. But they were running without lights, in case Curtis's killers decided to pursue them in one of the *Mallory*'s launches, and there was no telling what might be anchored or floating in the darkness out ahead. They didn't want to foul their propellers with some fisherman's cast-off net or somebody's lost rope.

This launch was larger and more elaborate than the ones belonging to the ship. It had a proper cabin, with a galley and two proper bunks, one above the other, and Kim spent most of the night on the lower bunk, to ease the soreness as they jolted their way across the bay. Manville had to stay up at the wheel, so there was no conversation between them until, in early morning, she at last climbed out to look at the nearby city sparkling in the fresh sunlight and say, "What do we do first?"

"Hide," he said, "while I try to find somebody who can help."

Surprised, she said, "Hide? Aren't we going to the police?"

"To say what?"

"But— They tried to kill us!"

"Who did? Kim, Captain Zhang isn't going to back up anything we say, and why should he? And without him, who are we? A disgruntled ex-employee and an environment nut. You don't even have ID, or a passport, or a visa for this country. What are you going to tell the police, and how are you going to prove it? You can't even prove who you are."

"But— They can't, they can't just do things like that, and get away with it!"

"Of course they can."

Morning water traffic was coming out of the wide river mouth now, past the harbor cranes and warehouses and fuel storage tanks; commercial fishermen, barges, private sailboats, excursion boats to take the tourists to see the birdlife on St. Helena Island in the bay. Heading inbound against most of that traffic, Manville had to keep his attention on his steering, while Kim sat on the white vinyl-covered bench behind him and watched the city come closer and the day begin, and she wondered, once they got ashore, what they could possibly do.

The Brisbane River, as twisty as a discarded piece of string, meandered through nine miles of switchbacks through the city, flanked by new glass skyscrapers stacked next to colonial-era buildings of stone and brick. Kim felt she must look very strange, with her matted hair and her borrowed grubby sweater and jeans, and these rubber-tire-soled shoes, but there was so much river traffic, and so much going on ashore as well, that she soon decided nobody was paying any attention to them, and she relaxed a bit.

Several high bridges crossed the river, connecting the two halves of the city. Manville passed a number of them, then said, "Isn't that a railroad station?"

It was, over there to the left. Just visible beyond some sort of park or fairgrounds. She said, "You want to take a train somewhere?"

"No. But they'll have phones and phone books, and an ATM, and probably whatever else I need. Curtis knows by now that we got away, and I don't know exactly what he'll do, but he'll certainly try to find us and at the same time he's sure to try to make us look like criminals or crazies or something, just to protect himself. *You* might be able to get out from under, with that Planetwatch group to help you, but he could pretty well put a stop to my making a living anywhere in the world."

"Oh, my God! I hadn't even thought."

"I can't waste a lot of time," he said. "I've got to get hold of some friends, start fighting back. There; we'll stop there."

It was a bridge. Just beyond the next curve in the river, the William Jolly, at a quieter place than that fairground back there. Manville cautiously steered them in toward the shallower water, tied the launch to a stanchion where he could get ashore and up to the roadway, and said, "You'll be all right here for a while. I'll get back as soon as I can."

"Okay."

"If the river police come by, tell them your boyfriend went for beer."

She smiled at that, and shook her head. "I'll tell them you went for sunblock. Because that I could use."

"I'll bring some," he promised, and said, "See you soon," and left her there.

For how long? It seemed like hours. The sun was much higher in the clear sky, the humidity was moving from soft toward oppressive, and the constant river traffic kept the little launch bobbing at its tether. George Manville must have realized by now that he was much better off from here on doing things on his own. He'd even said that she'd be all right, better off than him, because she had Planetwatch to look out for her, and that he didn't have any time to waste. So this would be the easiest way to get rid of her, wouldn't it? He'd done the right thing up till now, he'd done wonderful things, rescuing her, saving her from being murdered, facing down those thugs. He even *shot* one of them, as startling to Kim as it was to the men who'd grabbed her. But now he was finished, she was safe, and he had his own life to worry about. So why would he come back?

So he isn't coming back, she decided at last, and was depressed but not surprised at the idea. And now the question was, what should she do on her own? She had no money, no identification, knew nobody in Australia, and had probably been declared dead by the people of Planetwatch. She had a story no one would believe, and no other story to put in its place because it was true.

Should she try running the boat somewhere, farther inland? Should she leave the boat and walk to that railroad station and try to find a policeman to surrender to? That was probably best, though she couldn't help a strong reluctance to leave the known world of this launch for the unknown world ashore.

Still, it was the thing to do, and she knew it, and she actually had one leg over the side of the boat when she looked up and saw him, coming down toward her from the bridge approach.

Manville, solid and serious, arms loaded down with supplies, concentrating on his movements.

She felt such relief at the sight of him that she made a surprised cry, a "Hah!" that made him look up and call, "Wait. I'll be right there."

She stepped back aboard, and watched him come down. When she'd believed he wasn't coming back, she'd done her best to hide from herself how deep was the disappointment she felt, but now she let it all come to the surface, how much she needed him right now, how frightened she was of being alone, in this place, at this time.

He clambered onto the boat, put down the bags he was carrying, and took a tube from his pocket. "Sunblock. Better put it on while we talk."

"Oh, yes, thank you." She took the tube and started spreading the white lotion on her forehead and nose and the back of her neck.

He said, "I've tried calling friends in San Francisco and in Houston, left messages for them both, I want to find out what's going on with Curtis. But for now, what we should do is leave this boat right here, and take off."

"Where?"

"The Gold Coast," he told her. "Just south of the city, it's the Australian version of Miami Beach, full of tourists. Very crowded. Nobody will find us there." He lifted a shopping bag, held it out in her direction. "And you'd probably like a change of clothes," he said.

2

Richard Curtis was supposed to be in Singapore right now. He was not supposed to be in this suite atop the Heritage, with its views out over the gaudy Botanic Gardens and Town Reach of the river, a fine hotel, a fine view, everything perfectly fine, except that Richard Curtis was not supposed to be here now, and the fact that it had become necessary was making him furious.

Morgan Pallifer was as furious as Curtis, and embarrassed and ashamed as well, which made him pace the sitting room like a wolf, punching his knuckles together, staring out past the terrace at the river as though magically he would see George Manville and the girl out there. He'd gone out last night with three men to do what should have been a simple task, getting rid of an already-injured girl and an engineer, and he'd come back with two men dead and the job not done. "He isn't what you said he is," he insisted, so angry and discomfited he was even daring to take out his feelings on Curtis.

All right. Curtis would permit that, just this once, for a little while. He understood and sympathized, up to a point. Pallifer had always been reliable and discreet, a good man for bad work, and Curtis could cut him a little slack. "Manville always used to be who I said he was," he answered. "I don't know what happened. Maybe he has some kind of Green Beret background I don't know anything about."

"I think your Chink captain told him we were coming," Pallifer said.

"I don't much care, one way or another," Curtis said, and shrugged. "It's over, and the only question is, what next."

He had still been up north in Townsville when Pallifer made that second call last night, being so damn circumspect over the telephone that Curtis finally realized he was going to have to fly down to Brisbane and meet the man face to face this morning just to find out what in hell had gone wrong, even though he was *supposed* to fly to Singapore today, the three thousand miles over the land mass of Australia and the thousand islands of Indonesia to his new home at the tip of Malaysia. He had business there, other details of his construction deals around the world, but clearly it would have to wait.

Coming down here, he hadn't believed it possible that both Manville and the girl could have escaped from Pallifer, both still be alive. He'd thought something had screwed up involving the crew of the *Mallory*, or maybe one of Pallifer's team had turned out to be untrustworthy.

But, no. It was Manville, and he'd got clean away, and killed two of Pallifer's people en passant.

Would Manville and the girl have come on to Brisbane? Yes. Manville wouldn't want to keep her jouncing around on the water any longer than necessary, so they would certainly have come here, probably arriving an hour or two ago.

And then what? Do they go straight to the authorities? What do they say, and how much can they prove? And is there a way to head them off?

Possibly. Pallifer had been waiting here in the suite, pacing and raging, when Curtis had arrived. He'd told his story, in gruff monosyllables, and even before he was finished Curtis was making his first phone call, to Geneva. Nine hours earlier there, or fifteen hours later; in any case, around midnight. Bendix was not an early riser, Curtis knew. He left a message with Bendix's secretary at the estate, then listened to the rest of Pallifer's story, and now he was simply waiting.

Robert Bendix was a competitor of Curtis's, in construction and finance. At their level, being competitors meant they were mostly partners, rarely fighting for an entire pie, usually content to share slices of the very large pies that came their way. Bendix was not one of the people he'd approached about the Kanowit Island deal, because Bendix was far too shrewd, far too skeptical; he'd have seen through Curtis's Ponzi scheme in a minute. But there were other ways in which Robert Bendix could be of use to Curtis, just as, once or twice, Curtis had been of use to Bendix.

Now there was nothing to do but wait for Bendix to return the call, and in the meantime see if there was any way that Pallifer could still be useful, could make up for last night's failure, God knows the man was willing. Glaring out the glass doors of the terrace, showing his teeth, Pallifer said, "They're around here somewhere. The girl's as weak as a kitten, they won't travel a lot."

"How would you find them?"

Pallifer said, "If they go to the law, the law's gonna come to you, and that puts me on their tail. In a big city like this, automobile accidents happen all the time."

"What if Manville doesn't go to the law? He doesn't have a very good hand to play with them right now, no proof, no witnesses. What if he's smart enough to hide out for a while, until he and the girl can go somewhere else?"

Pallifer nodded, considering that. "You say the girl came off another ship. No documents on her?"

"Identification? None. No passport, no driver's license, nothing."

"If I was them," Pallifer said, "and I didn't want to bother with the law just yet, I'd hole up in one of the tourist sections around here, up or down the coast."

"And how would you find them?" Curtis asked. "Drive up and down the beach?"

"Well, he has to pay his way, doesn't he?" Pallifer said. "He'll use credit cards, won't he?" Pallifer turned his head to look at Curtis, and he was almost smiling. He said, "How hard is it to get a look at a man's credit card history?"

"Not hard," Curtis said, "if you want to wait two weeks or a month, to find out where they used to be."

"He's an American," Pallifer pointed out. "Lots of tourists around here, but damn few of them American. He's got to use his own name, because that's what's on the card. The transactions go through one of the banks here in Brisbane, don't they?"

"I'm not sure how that works," Curtis said, "but I have people who know. We're looking for an American credit card being used somewhere around here today."

"When I find 'em," Pallifer said, "is it the same as before?"

"The girl should disappear," Curtis told him. "No body, no questions, she doesn't get to tell anything to Diedrich. If you can hold onto Manville, do, and let me know. He's the engineer, he could still be valuable."

"He could be trouble," Pallifer said, and the phone rang.

"If he's trouble, of course, you kill him." Curtis picked up the phone: "Curtis."

"Richard. It's Robert here." Bendix, though American, had been living in Switzerland for so long, avoiding U.S. Federal tax indictments, that he was beginning to develop a faint German accent.

Curtis said, "Robert, I have to admit I'm a little disappointed in you."

Surprised, Bendix said, "What? Have I done something?"

"I have an engineer that works for me," Curtis told him, "a brilliant man, George Manville."

"I've heard the name."

"Of course you have. I just now learned that he's been betraying me."

"I'm shocked to hear that," Bendix said, sounding calm.

"He offered several of my business secrets for sale," Curtis said. "Bids on projects, sourcings of materiel, things like that."

"These grubby little people," Bendix said. "Tsk, tsk." He said it that way: *tsk, tsk*.

"He offered this information to you," Curtis said.

"Why, the swine," Bendix said. "I hope I threw him out on his ear."

"I'm afraid," Curtis said, "you gave him a hearing. I believe you even looked at some of the documents he'd stolen from me."

"Perhaps I was drunk."

"I'm here in Brisbane now," Curtis went on, "where I just discovered this thievery, and I'm sorry, Robert, but I have no choice but to go to the police."

"Perfectly understandable," Bendix assured him. "Unfortunate, of course, but I quite see where you have no alternative."

"None. It will probably mean, as well, that I'll be forced to say some unpleasant things about you in the press."

"Speaking of swine," Bendix said. "Well, I've been spoken of unkindly before."

"I'm sure you have."

"Now, you know, Richard," Bendix said, "I'm certainly not going to admit to having encouraged this fellow."

"No, of course not."

"However," Bendix said, "I suppose I could manage not to deny it very forcefully either. I'm rather good, in fact, at being coy."

Curtis laughed. "I'm sure you are. I'd like to watch some time."

"Never. How's Brisbane?"

"Warm. How's Geneva?"

"Cold. Nice talking to you."

"And you, Robert." Curtis broke the connection, then dialed the hotel operator: "Police headquarters, please."

3

Luther walked into their cabin and Jerry was still seated there, crosslegged on his bunk, gazing moodily at nothing at all. "We're there, Jerry," he said. "Come outside and watch."

Jerry came back from far away, and gave Luther a bleak look. Sighing, he said, "I'm dreading this, Luther."

"The parents, you mean."

"Of course the parents."

"Well," Luther said, "brooding in here isn't going to get it over with any faster. Come out on deck, look at the world."

"The world," Jerry said, as though repelled by the idea, but he did obediently get up from his bunk and follow Luther out of the cabin. The two went single file down the narrow corridor and up the ladder to the foredeck.

Planetwatch III had already rounded South Head and was well into the harbor waters called Port Jackson, surrounded by the hugely sprawling city of Sydney. Ahead soared the perfect arch of Sydney Harbour Bridge, uniting the two halves of the city, while just this side of it and to its left sat poised the Opera House, that great gleaming white bird with folded wings.

Usually Jerry both enjoyed this view and was appalled by it, the great spread of massive buildings up the hillslopes from gleaming beaches both beautiful in themselves and horrible in their implications of massive environmental damage. He could dwell endlessly on the contradictions as their little ship steamed slowly westward into the harbor.

But not today. Today, Jerry saw nothing, because out there in front of him, somewhere in all that muscular teeming space, were Kim Baldur's mother and father.

Of course they'd been told, as soon as possible. Two days ago Kim had gone over the side and disappeared, most certainly dead. As soon as *Planetwatch III* had gotten out of range of those deadly waves, Jerry had radioed to the Planetwatch office here in Sydney to report what had happened, and they in turn had notified the main Planetwatch headquarters in Seattle, who had informed Mr. and Mrs. Baldur in Chicago. Who had immediately flown here, and had been waiting for the slow-moving *Planetwatch III* since last night.

It was Jerry's responsibility. It was his responsibility that Kim had done that rash thing, that foolish thing, thinking he would want her to do it, and so it was his responsibility to face the parents, answer their questions, accept whatever blame they wanted to put on him.

Today. Now. In that city, closing around him as the ship turned to port to enter Woolloomooloo Bay, closing around him like the gleaming white teeth in the jaws of the world's most massive shark.

Planetwatch maintained a storefront office on George Street in The Rocks, a lesser tourist and shopping area overlooking Sydney Cove. Amid the restraint of the restored 19th-century buildings of the neighborhood, Planetwatch's shop window of color photographs of ecological horrors blown up to gargantuan scale struck a strident note that only Planetwatch's supporters couldn't see.

It was in the conference room behind the store area that Jerry and Captain Cousseran, along with three local Planetwatch volunteers, met the parents, all of them seated on the uncomfortable green vinyl chairs around the free-form cream-colored

Formica coffee table under the fluorescent ceiling lights, in the conversation area away from the main long rectangular conference table. Michael Baldur was a large man in his mid-fifties, with large jowls and black-framed eyeglasses and thinning gray hair; he was dressed in the same discreetly expensive dark blue pinstripe suit and white shirt and dark figured tie he would wear to his executive's office in a large merchant bank in Chicago's Loop. Kristin Baldur was a tiny woman who tried not to look as though she were in her late forties. Her medium-length ash blonde hair was carefully informal, her makeup insistently discreet, her Hermès scarf casually but perfectly draped over her padded shoulders. She had clearly been a beauty in her youth, of a delicate and more powerful sort than her healthily attractive daughter.

After awkward introductions, after a general refusal of an offer of coffee from one of the volunteers, after an uncomfortable pause, Jerry blurted out, "I want you to know, I feel horrible."

They looked at him mildly, as though they didn't know it was his fault, as though they thought he were just being conventionally sympathetic. Kristin Baldur even managed a polite smile as she said, "It must have been a terrible shock for you. All of you, on the ship."

"It was," Captain Cousseran said.

"We've been told," Michael Baldur said, "she was volunteering in some way. I don't entirely understand it."

Jerry closed his eyes, and took a deep breath. This was the moment. Opening his eyes, he said, "She did it because she thought I wanted her to."

Now they looked at him more closely. The father said. "Did you want her to?"

"No!"

Captain Cousseran, in the chair to Jerry's right, said, "There was no warning. She told no one, asked no questions, merely leaped into the sea."

Jerry wasn't about to let himself be let off the hook that easily. Turning to the captain, he said, "But she heard me say there had to be a fail-safe. You know she did. She heard me say it was going to be safe, that's why she went ahead."

Captain Cousseran could be stubborn when he wanted. Shaking his head, setting his jaw, he said, "She went without warning, without discussion."

Michael Baldur said, "My daughter was an impulsive girl, I know that."

"But she wouldn't have gone," Jerry insisted, "if she hadn't listened to me."

Kristin Baldur smiled sadly at Jerry, and said, "Kim didn't really listen to you, Mr. Diedrich. She would always jump first, and think about it afterwards. I don't think she ever really understood the idea of personal danger. I was always afraid that, some time…"

Michael Baldur reached over to grip his wife's forearm. Her smile had become fixed, her large eyes brighter.

Captain Cousseran broke through the moment, saying, "My regret is that we were unable to look for her ourselves. There was no question, of course. Still, it should have been our job to look for her and, if possible, find her."

Michael Baldur said, "That's something else I don't entirely understand. Why *didn't* you stay to help search?"

"We were trespassing," Captain Cousseran told him. "We had been ordered away, and we had no choice but to obey. The other ship lowered two launches to study the island after the explosions, and to look for the—for your daughter. Captain Zhang assured me they would search for her, and I'm sure he did."

"He wasn't much help, I must say that," Kristin Baldur commented.

Captain Cousseran, with obvious professional courtesy toward another mariner, said, "I'm sure he and his crew did everything they could."

"No," she said, "I mean when we talked to him."

Jerry said, "When *you* talked to him?"

Michael Baldur explained, "The *Mallory* came into Brisbane early this morning. We flew up there to speak with the captain."

"As much as we could," his wife said. "He has practically no English at all. We could barely understand a word he said, and I'm not sure he ever grasped what we were trying to say."

Jerry said, "But—" then left the thought unexpressed, bewildered by it. His memory of Captain Zhang's voice on the loudhailer was still all too clear: "*I am asked to inform you…*"

Why had Captain Zhang pretended not to understand or speak English? Had he been embarrassed in the presence of Kim's parents, made uncomfortable by their grief? (Though in fact they were being very restrained, all in all.) Had it actually *not* been Captain Zhang who'd talked to them by radio from the *Mallory*, but some other crewman, or somebody connected to Richard Curtis? Or did Captain Zhang have something to hide, and that's why he'd evaded the Baldurs? But what could he have to hide?

Before Jerry could respond, Captain Cousseran did, saying, "I never had trouble with Captain Zhang's English, on the radio."

"Well," Kristin Baldur said, "if you can communicate with him, that's wonderful. There are questions…well, we just wanted to *know*, know what happened, what it was like, and… even what the search was like. Captain Cousseran, if you and

Captain Zhang can speak together, and understand each other, would you ask him that? How much did they look for Kim? How long did they spend on it? What made them give up when they did?"

Maybe Captain Cousseran had belatedly realized, like Jerry, that there must be something odd going on here, with Captain Zhang suddenly bereft of English. He looked uncomfortable as he said, "I'm not sure how to get in touch with him, I have no idea where *Mallory* is by now, or where it's going."

"It's in Brisbane," Michael Baldur said. "It will stay there at least two weeks."

Captain Cousseran didn't look happy at that news. He said, "Are you certain? The owner can call for the ship at any—"

"Not now," Michael Baldur told him. "It lost one of its launches on the way back. Apparently, some crewman did a very poor job when it was hauled back aboard after the search, and in the night it dropped off and was lost."

Captain Cousseran frowned. "That's very unlikely," he said.

"But that's what happened," Michael Baldur said. "That's what we were told in Brisbane. What with one thing and another. Captain, I must say I got the impression that's a very sloppily run ship. In any event, the harbormaster in Brisbane won't give the *Mallory* permission to sail until it has all its lifeboats, and it will be two weeks before they can replace that one and adapt it to the ship."

Jerry said, "I'll talk to him."

They all looked at him in surprise. Michael Baldur said, "Talk to who? Captain Zhang?"

There's something wrong here, Jerry thought. I have no idea what it is, and I don't dare even to think it might mean that somehow Kim is still alive, it almost certainly doesn't mean that at all, but something is definitely wrong. Captain Zhang loses his command of English. The *Mallory* loses one of its launches. There's something wrong.

"Yes," he said. "I'll leave in the morning, go up to Brisbane, talk with Captain Zhang."

"I wish you the best of luck," Kristin Baldur told him, as though to say she thought he'd need it.

4

On the drive south out of Brisbane on Pacific Highway, Manville and Kim discussed what they should do. He hadn't managed yet to get in touch with either of his friends, the one in San Francisco or the one in Houston. The test at Kanowit Island had been on Tuesday, this was Thursday, and he needed to reach one or both of those guys before the weekend, which meant by noon, their times, tomorrow.

The question was, what would he say to them? What position was he in now, and what position was Kim in? Richard Curtis had clearly found himself in an escalating situation beyond what he'd originally intended, but where was he now? He'd gone from the simple hope that the Planetwatch diver wouldn't survive, so as to free himself from Planetwatch's— Jerry Diedrich's—intense surveyal, on to acquiescence in a kind of passive killing of the diver, on to an active scheme to murder her, on to a feeling that Manville had to be murdered as well, because of Curtis's own indiscretion. But what was his situation now? Had the threat from Curtis receded, or was it still as strong?

The original idea, that Kim should die in order to render Diedrich harmless, was no longer workable. She was off the boat, she was known by at least a few neutral observers to be alive, the scheme could not play out. On the other hand, though Manville and Kim could report they'd been attacked by Curtis's people, they had no way to prove it. And although they knew Curtis was up to something illegal and dangerous, they didn't know what it was—just something involving a soliton wave, and good luck explaining that to some policeman in a Brisbane precinct house. So, at this point, did Curtis consider them a peril, or merely a nuisance, or nothing at all?

Before they showed themselves to anyone, official or otherwise, they had to know how much danger they were in. They'd been lucky to escape from that first batch of men Curtis sent after them, but they weren't apt to be that lucky again, and Curtis could hire all the men he needed.

So once they found a safe hiding place, they both had some telephoning to do, discreetly. Manville would try again to reach either Tom in San Francisco or Gary in Houston, while Kim wanted to talk to Jerry Diedrich, to let him know what had happened and to find out if he had any idea what Curtis's scheme might be. First, though, to hide out, in a crowd.

The little red car Manville had rented was an Australian-made British-designed Ford, with the steering wheel on the right, because Australia follows the British system of driving on the left. "I feel as though I'm driving," Kim said at one point, in the passenger seat beside him. "I keep pressing down on the brake, and there isn't one."

Barely half an hour south of Brisbane, the pastel world of vacationland began. Men and women and children dressed in pink and topaz and aquamarine strolled in couples or ricocheting family groups past buildings painted in pink and topaz and aquamarine. Sunburned overweight undressed bodies were everywhere. A glittery sheen of grease and excitement vibrated in the warm humid air. Then at Coomera, the northern rim of the Gold Coast, less than forty miles south of Brisbane, the crowds grew even denser, tourist hordes packed hip to hip and camera bag to camera bag. "One thing for sure," Manville said, "nobody will find us here."

Expensive high-rise hotels fronted the beach along Cavill

Avenue, the main drag, but a block or two back from the sea were the economy motels. While Kim waited in the car, Manville checked into one of these. The room was clean and anonymous, with one bed along each side wall, and except for the cute paintings of koala bears over the beds could have been anywhere in the world.

Kim went straight to the smaller bed, a single along the right wall. "I'm starving," she announced, and lay on her back atop the bedspread. "I'll just rest for a minute, and then we'll go get something to eat." And fell sound asleep.

"What time is it?"

Manville looked up from his paperback, to see Kim half-risen, blinking at him in the dim illumination from the bedside lamp. "Hi," he said, and looked at his watch. "Quarter to nine."

"Day or night?"

He had shut the blinds over the only window. "Night."

Slowly she blinked again, absorbing that information, then looked startled and said, "My God. I've been asleep..."

"Almost ten hours."

"Why didn't you wake me?"

"I thought you needed it."

"I thought I needed lunch." She sat up the rest of the way, wincing and clutching briefly at her rib cage, then said, "Now I'm *really* starving. Now I need lunch and dinner both."

"Fine."

She rubbed her eyes. "What's that you're reading?"

He showed her the cover. "It's a caper story, called *Payback*, by an Australian writer named Gary Driver. He's imitating the Americans, but he's pretty good. He's teaching me how to behave in dangerous situations."

Grinning at him, she said, "You behave fine."

"Thank you." With a nod of the head toward the packages on the bed next to him, he said, "I got you some stuff. Toothbrush, toothpaste. Some more clothes. Don't know if they'll fit."

"Oh, that's wonderful." She put her legs over the side to sit on the edge of the bed.

"Maybe you want to shower and change before we go out."

"I would. Is that okay?"

Getting to his feet, dropping the paperback on the empty bed, he said, "I'll just try my friend in Houston again while you shower."

She blinked around at the room. "Oh. There's no phone."

"There's one by the office."

"You're going to call someone at this hour?"

"Thirteen-hour time difference. It's quarter to ten tomorrow morning in Houston, Gary should be just coming into the office this minute."

Rising, tottering a little, she said, "When you come back, I'll be transformed. And hungrier than ever."

"I'll be quick," he promised, and left the room, and walked around to the front of the building.

The pay phone was in an alcove just inside the office door, separated from the main part of the office by a plywood partition; not a lot of privacy, but some. Manville used his phone card to make the call, and after one false try got the receptionist at Gary's offices. "Millbrook and Tennyson."

There was no way to tell from that what sort of firm they were, but Gary Millbrook and his partner were architectural consultants, not the designers of structures for the most part but the people brought in by large corporate clients to vet the designs of others and make corrections and improvements where needed. George had worked with the company several times over the years, and he and Gary had gradually moved from a business relationship to an easygoing friendship.

"George Manville for Mr. Millbrook."

"One moment."

It was about three moments, in fact, and then Gary's familiar voice came on, saying, "If you want to know do I believe it, of course I don't. Is there something I can do to help?"

"What?" It seemed to Manville that Gary was starting well into the conversation, reacting to Manville before Manville had told him anything.

"I don't know how you got Richard Curtis mad," Gary went on, "but I assume he's playing dirty pool here."

"Gary, Gary, back up a little. What are you talking about?"

"*The Wall Street Journal*, of course."

"What about it?"

"George? Aren't you calling about the piece in today's *Journal*, that I just read maybe three minutes ago?"

"I'm in Australia," Manville explained. "I haven't seen the *Journal*."

There was a startled pause, and when Gary spoke again his manner was subtly different: "You mean you *are* in Australia?"

"Yes. Why? What does the *Journal* say?"

"It's a short piece deep in the paper, they don't make a big deal out of it."

"What does it say, Gary?"

"It says that yesterday Richard Curtis swore out a warrant against you in Brisbane, Australia—"

"A warrant!"

"—for industrial espionage. You're described in the piece— It's short, I could read it to you, if you want."

"Just tell me what it says."

"It says you've been working for Richard Curtis."

"That's true."

"And it says you were doing things for him having to do with a new destination resort he's building out on the Great Barrier Reef."

"Still true."

"And that Curtis just now found out that you tried to sell trade and business secrets to a Swiss company called Intertekno, whose principal owner is a financier named Robert Bendix."

"I've never heard of Robert Bendix, or Inter whatever."

"He claims you went to Bendix personally and showed him some documents," Gary said. "According to the *Journal* piece, Bendix neither confirms nor denies, and Curtis has a warrant for your arrest on various felony charges, including theft of privileged documents belonging to him, and you have disappeared. You were last seen in Brisbane."

"I'm still in Brisbane," George said. "Or near it."

"Well, that's probably not a good career move, George. On the other hand, you really shouldn't try to come home, or leave that country for anywhere else, because they'll surely grab you at the airport and then you will look guilty."

"Oh, he's done it to me, hasn't he?"

"Give me your number," Gary offered, "I'll ask around, get the name of a good lawyer for you over there."

"I'll have to call you back," Manville said. "What if I call you at noon your time, would that be too soon?"

"No, fine. I should have something by then."

"Thanks, Gary."

"You're in a mess, huh?"

"A rotten one."

"Tell me about it when it's all over."

"I'm looking forward to the day."

"I'm afraid you broke the old rule, George," Gary told him. "Never fight with somebody whose pockets are deeper than yours."

"Now you tell me," Manville said, but he didn't feel much like joking. "I'll call you in two hours."

"I'll be here."

Walking back to the room, wondering what he would tell Kim, Manville thought, Curtis doesn't have to have me killed, not anymore. He doesn't have to kill me, because he just did.

5

The pleasant pale green skirt was a wraparound, which meant it had to fit her. The blouse was loose, creamy white, scoop-necked. The panties were stretchy, and would do for now. He had wisely not tried to buy her a bra.

All in all, Kim was satisfied not only with the clothing, but with Manville himself. From time to time, when she remembered the suddenness with which he'd shot that man on the ship, she felt astonishment all over again, because he just didn't seem like that kind at all. He was so reserved and low-key most of the time that you didn't ever expect anything sudden from him, and certainly never anything violent.

She had gotten over both her panic and her deep exhaustion by now, and was beginning to return to her normal optimistic self. She'd removed the Ace bandage in order to shower, and though her torso felt stiff and achy without it, and there were still twinges in her rib cage if she breathed too suddenly, she felt she'd rather try to live without that wrapping from now on. The long sleep had helped, the shower had helped, the fresh clothing had helped, and the knowledge that George Manville was reliably at her side helped a lot.

She heard him come back into the room after his phone call, and shouted, "Be right out!"

"Take your time."

"Oh, no," she said, but not to him, to her reflection in the mirror. "I'm too hungry to take my time."

She finished with her hair—not much she could do about it, really—then washed the underwear she'd had on for the drive and hung it on the towel rack, and went out to find him seated cross-legged on his bed, reading his paperback novel again. He put it aside, stood, looked her over, smiled tentatively, and said, "Not so bad, I guess."

"I've had better compliments," she said.

He looked flustered: "No, I meant my part. The clothes."

"They're great," she assured him, and turned in a circle, arms out. "But now," she said, "I really have to put some food in here, before there's nothing under these clothes but skin and bone."

"There's some kind of diner or cafe just down the street, doesn't look too bad. We just have to be back here in two hours, so I can make another phone call."

"You talked to your friend?"

"I'll tell you all about it," he promised, "while we eat."

The best thing you could say for the place where they had their late dinner was that it wasn't as garishly overlit as the similar place across the street. The food was acceptable, and there was beer; Fosters, in cans. Ladies could have a styrofoam cup with their beer, on request. Kim decided not to request.

Over the various fried foods, George told her about his phone call and what Richard Curtis had done. She stared at him, appalled: "But why?"

"Destroy my credibility," he said. "No matter what I do now, it isn't a case of me charging Richard Curtis with something, it's just me reacting to the charge he's made against me."

"What an awful man he is," Kim said, "Jerry Diedrich was absolutely right."

George shook his head at her. "Not absolutely right," he said. "He was sure I was going to destroy the reef."

That made her stop eating to consider him thoughtfully and then say, "Two days ago, you were my enemy."

"And now?"

Suddenly, she felt awkward. "Well, you're not my enemy," she said. "We know that much."

When he came back to the room from his second phone call, she was feeling very sleepy again, probably because of all the food and the two beers, but she needed to stay awake to know what was going on. And also, her ribs were hurting again.

He came in and looked a little less grim than when he'd told her about Curtis's mad accusations back at the cafe. "There's somebody for me to call in the morning," he said. "A business friend of my friend's, here in Australia."

"What can he do?"

"No idea. Maybe nothing. I'll find out tomorrow morning." He stretched, like a man who's been too stiff and cramped in a too-confined space for far too long. "Right now," he said, "I think we both need sleep."

She said, "I shouldn't have left that bandage off, I'm getting very sore again. Could you help me put it on?"

She picked the soft roll of it up from her bed, and handed it to him.

"Sure."

As he took the two snaps off the bandage, she said, "Wait, I have to—" and pulled the blouse off over her head. "Okay."

He looked at her, and became awkward again. "I didn't know how to buy a, I don't know how the—"

"That's all right." She held her arms out from her sides, so he could wrap the bandage around her torso. When he stepped close, it was only natural to rest her hands on his shoulders. He put his arms around her to start the bandage and she lifted her face up to him, and they kissed, and that was natural, too.

When they kissed again, he'd dropped the bandage onto the

floor, so he could stroke the skin of her back with both palms. She murmured, and their teeth bumped, and she held him tighter, but then he pressed her close and the sudden pain in her ribs made her gasp and pull away.

"I'm sorry," he said, "I forgot."

"No. *I'm* sorry," she told him, still holding to him, not wanting to let go. "Damn these ribs! George, what can we do?"

Slowly he smiled. "Well, it's an engineering problem, isn't it?" he said. "And I'm an engineer."

6

Andre Brevizin entered the offices of Coolis, Maguire, Brevizin & Chin at exactly ten-thirty Friday morning, as was his wont. He exchanged the usual greetings with Angela Brother, the firm's excellent receptionist, strolled down the hall to his own office, paused to look out at the usual morning bustle at the corners of George and Margaret Streets one flight below, sat at his vast desk, reached for the stack of newspapers placed there as usual by Angela, and the phone rang.

He blinked. He didn't much like such suddenness. A lawyer in a highly respectable corporate firm with offices in one of the most prestigious and attractive locations in Brisbane, Andre Brevizin preferred a certain stateliness in his life, a certain moderation and order.

He lowered a severe brow at the telephone—an internal call it was, not external—permitted it to ring a second time, and only then did he pick it up: "Angela?"

"Jimmy Coggins on the line for you."

Ah. Jimmy Coggins was an important corporate client, a construction company man and developer partly responsible for the ever-widening suburban sprawl around the center of the city. As such, he was both to be deplored and catered to. And of course, he was calling at this exact moment because he was well aware of the comfortably precise routines of Brevizin's days.

"I'll take it," he decided, and pressed the button on the phone, and said, "Well, Jimmy, you know all my habits."

"Only the least disgusting ones," Jimmy assured him. "I take it you haven't read the papers yet."

"I was just reaching for them."

"Take a look at the business section of the *Herald*," Jimmy suggested. "Page forty-two."

The *Sydney Morning Herald* lay beneath the Brisbane paper on Brevizin's desk; the usual order. He brought it out, opened it flat on his desk to the appropriate page, and said, "What am I looking for? I don't see your name here."

"No, thank God. We'll save those revelations for another day. The Richard Curtis piece."

"Where— Oh, down here."

It was a brief piece, tawdry, under the slightly misleading headline AMERICAN SOUGHT IN BRISBANE IN SPY CHARGE. Industrial spying, it was, the usual disgruntled ex-employee. All of them Americans, though it had happened right here in town. Or been reported here. "And?"

"Manville says he didn't do it."

"Jimmy, they all say they didn't do it. When your turn comes, *you'll* say you didn't do it."

"Somebody has to be innocent, Andre."

"You think so?"

"Manville's a friend of a very good friend of mine," Jimmy said. "Also an American. My friend vouches for Manville, and that's good enough for me."

"But not good enough for a judge, I shouldn't think. Jimmy, are you sending me this fellow?"

"I'd like to. On the QT."

"On the dole, as well?"

"Oh, I think he could probably pay a modest fee. He doesn't have Richard Curtis's money, however."

Brevizin had heard of Richard Curtis, here and there, but

had never had direct dealings with the man. He had a vague impression of ruthlessness. He said, "Jimmy, I'm not a criminal lawyer, I couldn't very well go to court with this fellow."

"He needs advice, Andre, he needs to know what his options are. Apparently, there's quite a bit more to the story."

"There always is." Brevizin sighed. "All right, have him give me a call."

"He will," Jimmy said. "At eleven-thirty, after your tea."

Brevizin laughed. "You already told him to call, and when? Jimmy, you do know me too well."

"And later," Jimmy said, "you'll tell me all about it."

Brevizin's first impression of George Manville, when the man arrived for his two-thirty appointment that afternoon, was not encouraging. He had a scuffed and ragged look about him, the hangdog manner of the already defeated. Well; adversity can take it out of a man.

Later, he would wonder if that first impression had simply been his expectation of what the man in today's newspaper would be, or if in fact Manville had been that close to despair. Impossible to tell.

So here he was, recommended by the far-off friend of a business acquaintance. The things we get into, Brevizin thought, and came smiling around the vast desk as Angela let the fellow in. "Mr. Manville, how are you? Did Angela offer you coffee, whatever?"

"Nothing, thanks," Manville said, and turned to smile a bit wanly at Angela. "Thanks."

"It was easy," she assured him, and backed out, smiling, and shut the door.

So Angela's taken with him, Brevizin thought. Her instincts were usually good. "Come sit over here, it's more casual," he said, gesturing to the conversation area, an L of soft gray sofas and a large distressed-wood coffee table.

They sat catty-corner, and Brevizin leaned forward to touch the long pencil resting on the yellow legal pad he had waiting there. "All I know about you, Mr. Manville," he said, "is what I read in the *Sydney Morning Herald*."

"I've made the *Wall Street Journal*, too," Manville said.

"Not in the way you'd have preferred."

"No."

"Jimmy Coggins says you deny the charge."

"I don't know Mr. Coggins," Manville said, and met Brevizin's eye. "Talked with him once on the phone, that's all. I appreciate what he's done, I'm grateful. But I don't really mean anything to Mr. Coggins, so if you decide, at some point, you don't want any more to do with all this, it's okay."

Brevizin found himself surprised and somewhat interested. Normally, a fellow in George Manville's situation would cling to whatever help or encouragement he could find. To begin the conversation by assuring Brevizin that Jimmy Coggins wouldn't go to the wall for him was unexpected. He said, "Thank you. But let's not part company just yet. I really should hear your story."

"I'd appreciate it. The first thing," Manville said, "is that the published story is one hundred percent false. Curtis made it up. I've never met this man Bendix, never heard of him before last night. The documents Curtis is talking about are pretty vague, I couldn't tell from the newspaper exactly what they were, but they don't sound like things I ever had access to."

"You're saying Richard Curtis has gone out of his way to tell whole-cloth lies about you."

"Yes."

"And that he swore false statements in having that warrant made out."

"Yes."

"Not a thing we'd expect from a man in his position," Brevizin pointed out.

Manville's smile was bleak. "Part of the problem," he said, "is that Curtis's position is not what everybody thinks it is. I know the truth, and I know more than that. I suppose he thought I might talk, go to the police myself, so he did this... what do they call it? Pre-emptive strike."

"What is the truth, Mr. Manville?"

"Curtis is broke," Manville said, "or worse than broke. Conning his business partners, going deeper into debt every minute. He over-extended when he was trying to protect his Hong Kong businesses from the Chinese, and he hasn't been able to get back."

Brevizin dropped the pencil onto the pad and leaned back. He would have a story for Jimmy Coggins after all. Smiling at Manville, he said, "The reason I'm beginning to believe you, Mr. Manville, I myself have heard some very vague rumors that Richard Curtis might be in some sort of financial trouble. This firm's corporate clients include a number of builders, some private bankers, venture capital investors, people who have had or might have dealings with Curtis's companies. People are beginning to tell one another to be careful of doing business with Richard Curtis, though nobody knows exactly what the problem is."

"He's his own Ponzi scheme," Manville said. "He's losing money every day, and he has to keep bringing more in to keep the facade going. And he knows it can't last much longer. I didn't know there were already rumors starting about him, but he may know."

Brevizin said, "He *told* you how much trouble he was in?"

"Yes. He was trying to enlist me on his side."

"In what?"

"I'm not sure," Manville said, and spread his large hands, workman's hands. "He told me he had a way out, it was illegal and dangerous, but it was going to make him a whole lot of money, and if I kept quiet my share would be ten million U.S. dollars, in gold."

Brevizin squinted. "He said what?"

"Now you're beginning to not believe me again," Manville said. "Mr. Curtis told me my share could either be ten million dollars in gold or, if I'd wait a little while, the same amount in a Swiss bank account. I think I was supposed to be impressed."

"Why were you having this conversation?"

Now Manville too sat back in the sofa, though he didn't seem very relaxed. He said, "I've been working for Mr. Curtis for over a year, on a project out by the barrier reef. I've been developing a new technical way to deal with landfill, a cheaper way to convert land to new uses, and we just tried it, Tuesday of this week."

"Tried it."

"We set off measured explosions in tunnels in an island out by the reef," Manville explained.

"That sounds risky."

"It isn't, really," Manville said, "but we did have some environmental protesters, from a group called Planetwatch."

"Oh, you touch another button," Brevizin told him. "Planetwatch has been an irritation to more than one of my clients. Including Jimmy Coggins, come to think of it. All right, what happened?"

"A diver from their ship," Manville told him, "a woman, went into the water just before the explosions, even though they'd all been told there was no fail-safe, no way to stop the countdown. Which was my fault, I should have taken every contingency into— Well. That doesn't matter here."

"She was in the water, near the island, when your explosions went off?"

"Yes."

"And she was killed."

"Well, no." Manville did that bleak smile again. "Though Mr. Curtis would have preferred it. For a while, we all thought she was dead, but she survived. And then Curtis wanted to kill her, as though the explosion—or the shock wave, really—had done it, in order to get Planetwatch off his back."

Brevizin said, "Mr. Manville? Are you sure?"

"Absolutely. It was because I didn't want him to do it that he told me what his situation was, and offered me the ten million dollars."

"If you'd kill the girl?"

"No, simply if I'd step aside."

Brevizin looked over at the window, then back at Manville. "You're saying he's that desperate."

"I think anybody would be," Manville said, "in his situation. There's a fellow with Planetwatch named Jerry Diedrich..." He paused and looked at Brevizin.

Who shook his head. "Don't know the name."

"Well, for some reason, he has a personal vendetta against Richard Curtis, and shows up wherever Curtis is doing anything at all that involves the environment. Curtis definitely doesn't want Diedrich around when he makes that move of his to get all the money, and he thought a dead diver could tie up Diedrich and Planetwatch in the Australian courts long enough for Curtis to finish whatever he's doing."

Nodding, Brevizin said, "It might. But we're a long way from you and Robert Bendix and industrial espionage."

"Well, I wouldn't go along with him," Manville said. "I told him I didn't want Kim to die."

"Kim. You knew this woman?"

"We met this week, after the event. What happened was, Mr. Curtis and the people investing with him in Kanowit Island —that's where we were—they helicoptered off on Wednesday. Wednesday night, I found out from the ship's captain that he'd been ordered to slow us down so we could go past Moreton Island late at night, so some people could come aboard to kill the two of us. We managed to get away, and now Mr. Curtis is afraid we'll go to the authorities, so he made that charge of his own first. Ruin my credibility before I say anything."

"It should work," Brevizin said. "I don't suppose you have any evidence, any proof, any signed confessions?"

"No, I'm sorry," Manville said, and sounded as though he really was. Too worried, in other words, to have much sense of humor.

Brevizin said, "Well, do you have *anything* that would serve to substantiate your story?"

"I've been thinking about that," Manville said. "I don't have much. I have my own reputation, over the years. Kim and I both tell the same story, and we never knew one another before this week. And the *Mallory*, the ship we were on, might still be in harbor here. It lost a launch as a result of the business with us, they won't be able to sail until they replace it."

"The *Mallory*," Brevizin said, and made his first note of the meeting.

"Since I don't know this man Bendix," Manville said, "I can't think why he'd say I tried to sell him anything."

"He and Curtis could be friends," Brevizin said, dismissing it. "That aspect doesn't bother me."

"Tell me what bothers you," Manville said. "If it's something I know anything about, I'll tell you."

"I believe you're probably accurate about Curtis's finances,"

Brevizin said, "and I can make a few calls after this meeting to confirm. I find it hard to believe that any businessman, legitimate businessman, would send out killers to murder two people. Hard, but not impossible. I believe, if I check into it, a ship called *Mallory* will be in harbor here, missing a launch. I believe it is possible you were framed, for the purpose of shutting you up. I believe it is also possible that everything you've said is the invention of a desperate man who's been caught with his hand in the cookie jar."

"It could look that way," Manville agreed, "I know that."

"Unfortunately," Brevizin said, "if I choose to believe your story, then I must also believe you don't have the answer to what's still most troubling me. Which is, what does Curtis plan to do that's illegal and dangerous, and when does he plan to do it? And, come to think of it, where? Here?"

"You're right, that's the part I don't know," Manville said. "I'm sorry. I get the impression it might have something to do with Hong Kong, but only because those are the people he blames for his troubles. And even if that's right, I don't know what the plan is."

"And it must be intended to happen fairly soon," Brevizin pointed out, "if it would be before Planetwatch got over the legal embarrassment of negligently causing the death of one of their own divers."

"Oh, yes," Manville said, "I'm sure it's soon. I don't think that house of cards of his can last very much longer."

"All right," Brevizin said, "conditionally I believe you. I should probably advise you to turn yourself in to the authorities, to let me begin the legal process, but that would leave your friend Kim alone, and if someone has tried to kill her before they might try again."

"I think so, too," Manville said.

"Do you want to tell me where you're keeping yourselves?"

"Down on the Gold Coast."

"Good God. Can you stand it?"

"For a while," Manville said.

"Then you'll have to stand it for the weekend," Brevizin told him. "There's nothing more to be done today. I'll talk to some people, look into the situation. Assuming I don't run across anything that suggests you're a really accomplished liar and fantasist, you should ring me Monday morning at…eleven o'clock."

"I will. Do you want to meet Kim? She's three blocks from here, in one of the street cafes on the Mall."

"Monday will do," Brevizin told him. "I'll probably want you to bring her with you then."

"She wanted to make a phone call of her own," Manville said. "To this guy Jerry Diedrich, from Planetwatch. They have an office down in Sydney, she thinks she can find him through there. I said I'd ask you, and she'll call him if you say okay."

"I don't see why not," Brevizin said, "if only on the concept that the enemy of my enemy is my friend. Diedrich is unlikely to betray either of you to Richard Curtis."

"Very unlikely," Manville agreed.

"And Planetwatch," Brevizin went on, "no matter how much they might irritate my clients and me in other contexts, they do have an organization and they might be of help to you." Brevizin rose, and reached across the coffee table to shake Manville's hand. "Keep out of sight over the weekend," he advised, "and ring me Monday."

"I will. And thank you, Mr. Brevizin, you've given me hope."

"Not too much hope, please," Brevizin cautioned. "Not yet."

7

Kim sat over her second cappuccino, now long cold, and watched the pedestrians surge endlessly by. It was as though two giant machines, just out of sight, one at each end of the Mall, kept spewing these people out, in their amazing diversity, and sent them striding or strolling forward along the Mall, finally to be gobbled up again by the machine at the other end, altered into new sizes and shapes, and pushed back out to do the same thing the other way.

The Mall was two long blocks of Queen Street, here in the heart of Brisbane, where motor traffic was not permitted. Stores and restaurants filled the buildings along the way, upstairs as well as down, and spilled out into open-air cafes like the one where Kim sat and waited for George to finish with the lawyer. Shoppers and tourists and simple strollers filled the Mall from end to end, as crowded and noisy and lively as the streets of the Gold Coast, but more upscale.

Kim wondered how much longer George would be. He'd left her forty Australian dollars, so she could go on ordering cappuccino forever, but that lost its charm eventually. Also, the Ace bandage, around her torso again, was beginning to feel too tight, and starting to itch; she'd love to be back in the little room in Surfers Paradise, comfortably naked. With George. She sighed, looked around at the people at the other tables here in the cafe—couples or families, she the only single—then looked out again at the schools of passersby, and saw the killer.

It was him. He walked with two other men she'd never seen before, he in the middle, talking intently, they listening intently, and she recognized him at once. She'd never forget that man, or how he'd looked when he'd taunted George, asking if he could shoot a human being, saying George couldn't do it, and then George did it.

Of course he's here. Brisbane is where the *Mallory* was coming, and the Mall is where everybody in Brisbane walks sooner or later. But why *now*? Why not half an hour from now, when I'm gone from here?

Kim looked down at her trembling hands in her lap, hoping to seem like someone searching in a handbag for a tissue or change or whatever, hoping the man would just keep moving by, keep on with his intense conversation, pay no attention to the world around him, and when she looked up she stared directly into his eyes. The three of them had stopped out there, like a rocky island in the sea of pedestrians, and they were all staring at her.

Everybody moved at once. The killer shouted something to the other two, pointed at Kim, and the three leaped forward, at the same instant that Kim jumped to her feet, knocked over her chair behind her, turned to her right, and ran.

Through the tables, through the tables, breathlessly apologizing to the people seated there, afraid to look back. Hedged planters marked the boundary of the cafe, with a narrow space between two. Too narrow; something plucked at the wraparound skirt, tried to pull it off her. She clutched at bunches of skirt at both hips and kept running.

Now she looked back and they were farther away, but still chasing her. They'd had to go around the planters, but they were moving fast, and they were big enough to simply knock people out of their way, while Kim had to duck and dodge around the strollers.

The Myer Centre. She ran in, snaking around shoppers laden

with bags, nearly bowling over a girl trying to offer a perfume sample, dodging to the left only because the aisle ahead was too clogged.

She wanted to call for help, but who would understand? What would she say? She didn't have time to think, only to run.

They were back there, behind her, two in the same aisle as her, one coming faster along a more open aisle to the right. One of them was shouting; the killer, straight behind her, he was waving his fist and shouting.

"Stop! Stop! Stop, thief! She stole my wallet! Stop her!"

No, no, that's ridiculous, that isn't real. But it is real. And if somebody were to stop her, hold her for them, they'd finish her off before she could explain. And already people were reaching for her, wide-eyed and astonished but with clutching hands to stop the running girl.

An exit. She had to get out of here, outside, away from confinement, narrow aisles, too many bodies. Brushing aside the hands that tried to hold her, she hurtled out the exit onto some different street, not the Mall at all, but a regular street with traffic through which she ran heedless, while astonished drivers slammed on their brakes and blared their horns.

An alley. It was Elizabeth Arcade, running between Elizabeth and Charlotte Streets, though she didn't know that. She ran into it, past a hamburger restaurant called Parrot's on her right and a sign for an upstairs vegetarian restaurant called Govinda's on her left, and straight down the arcade.

Another look over her shoulder. They were still back there, still running hard, the killer still shouting his horrible absurd demand.

The end of the arcade. She veered left, because that way there were fewer people in her path. She ran, leaving a sea of startled faces in her wake, and at the next corner there was a crowded bus just taking on passengers, the last man pressing in, pushing himself on, the door about to close.

Kim ran full tilt into the bus, slamming into the last man's back, shoving a whole phalanx of people deeper into the bus ahead of her, as the door snicked shut behind her, and the bus moved away from the curb. She ignored the comments and the dirty looks, ignored the crush, and managed to twist around just enough to look over her shoulder, out the window. They had stopped back there, panting, holding their sides, moving together to confer.

The bus was so crowded she had no opportunity to pay before it stopped again, not far enough along this street.

She jumped backward to the curb the instant the door opened, spun around, looked only straight ahead, and ran.

Two blocks later, out of breath, she slowed to a walk, and looked back, and they were gone. She stopped. She'd lost them.

And herself. Slowly catching her breath, she looked around at this new street. She hadn't the slightest idea where she was.

8

She wasn't there.

Manville double-checked, walked both ways along the Mall, frowning at the people at the tables in other open-air cafes, and she was at none of them. He'd been right the first time; *there* was where he'd left her, at that table in the middle of that particular cafe, where the young couple now giggled together like the newlyweds they no doubt were.

Where was she? She wouldn't just leave. That didn't seem right. Did something spook her?

Whatever had happened, there was nothing for Manville to do but wait here. Wherever Kim had gone, she would certainly come back to this spot to find him.

There was an empty table in the second row. He took it, waited a couple of minutes for the waiter to arrive, ordered a cappuccino, then looked off to the right, the long way down the Mall. All those bobbing heads, all those people, in random movement, no rhythm, no pattern. Would Kim suddenly appear among them?

Movement made him turn his head, and there was now somebody seated next to him. He was in his forties, heavyset, a bruiser with a large round head, thick bone above his eyebrows, a broken nose. Manville had never seen him before, but he knew at once that this man was connected to the killers on the ship. And that something bad had happened to Kim.

The man leaned forward, as though he wanted to deliver a secret. "George Manville," he said.

Manville looked carefully at him. The man's large bony hands rested on the table, empty. He didn't act threatening, he was just there. "Yes," Manville said.

The man nodded. "If you look out there," he said, his voice raspy but soft, his accent showing him to be a local, "you'll see a fella that isn't walking. He's looking at you. He's got his hands in the pockets of kind of a big raincoat."

Manville looked. "I see him." It was another stranger, cut from the same cloth as this one.

The man said, "If I stand up and walk away from this table, and you don't stand up and follow me, that bloke's gonna take a machine pistol out of his pocket and blow your head off. And probably a few other heads around here, too. He's got rotten aim."

Manville said, "Where's Kim?"

The man smiled. "You wanna talk to her? Come along."

"She's all right?"

"Sure," the man said. "Just a little out of breath, that's all."

Manville had no idea what he meant by that, except that Kim must still alive. "I'll go with you," he said.

"I thought that's what you were gonna decide," the man said, and patted the table. "Leave some loot for the waiter, there's a good chap."

Manville did as he was told, and the man stood and walked away, without a backward glance. Manville got to his feet and followed, aware of the other man trailing along behind.

Down at the end of the Mall, on the corner with George Street, stopped illegally at the curb was a large black Daimler limousine. The man ahead of Manville walked directly to it and opened the curbside rear door. "Get in," he said.

Manville did, and the man followed him, as Manville saw, seated in the rear of the limo, the leader of the killers from the ship. From the corner of his eye, he saw the man with the machine pistol get in the front, next to a liveried chauffeur.

Manville was in the middle of the rear seat, the leader to his left, the other man to his right. Kim wasn't here.

The chauffeur started the Daimler purring away from the curb, and the leader smiled at Manville's profile, not in a friendly way. "And now," he said, "the rematch."

9

Morgan Pallifer liked the way things were going. He was closer to Richard Curtis, more important to Curtis, than he had ever been. He had the use of this nice Daimler belonging to Curtis, that even came with a chauffeur hired by Curtis, who knew to do what he was told and keep his mouth shut. He had a nice wad of cash from Curtis, enough to keep him going for months, with more to come, a lot more. And now, three or four days ahead of schedule, he had his hands on George Manville.

Oh, he would have gotten Manville anyway, that wasn't a problem. Curtis's people were watching the banks, and no later than Monday he'd have known where Manville and the girl were hiding out. He'd still know, come Monday, and the way things were, he'd probably find the girl there. She'd lost Pallifer and his new pals, that was true, but she'd also lost Manville, and what else would she do but go back to whatever mouse hole they'd been hiding in, to wait for her protector to return? Where else could she go? Nowhere. So she'd most likely still be there, wherever it was, hoping for the best, when Pallifer and his friends dropped by to scoop her up on Monday.

But for now, he had the more important one, he had Manville. Curtis had wanted Manville alive, at least temporarily, at least if it wouldn't be too much trouble; the girl he simply wanted gotten rid of, so that could happen at any time. Curtis would be very pleased to know that Manville was already in their hands.

Pallifer was pleased, too. The events on the *Mallory* still rankled. He and Arn had had to finish off Bardo and Frank, both wounded by Manville. He'd told Curtis that it was Manville who'd killed them, because you never tell anybody *you* did some killing, but in fact Manville had left the two of them alive but useless. Pallifer couldn't carry them, couldn't nurse them, couldn't fix Frank's broken bones or dig that bullet out of Bardo. He had no more use for them, so what could he do but drop them into the sea, once that miserable Chink captain came slinking down to see what was what and finally agreed to untie him and Arn?

Which was why he'd had to go around among people he knew, people he'd been connected with in the past, to find new partners. Arn had got spooked out there on the *Mallory*, and didn't want any more of this job, so he was out, and these new fellas were in. Steve on the other side of Manville, and Raf up front. Pallifer had already worked with both of them more than once, and knew he could count on them.

And now, after he brought them aboard, the job was turning out so simple and easy, he barely needed them at all. Already he had Manville, and the girl was such a piece of cake he could almost send a cabdriver to pick her up. In fact, maybe that was the thing to do. Make Manville write a note, send it with a cabby, pop the girl in privacy and comfort, at Pallifer's leisure.

Well, that was the pleasure for next week. For now, as the chauffeur purred them out of downtown, skirting Albert Park, heading out Musgrave Road to leave Brisbane toward the west, Pallifer reached forward to the black leather pouch mounted on the side panel behind the door, took out the cellphone, and called Richard Curtis at the hotel. He got a secretary, who said Curtis was out. "Tell him it's Morgan," Pallifer said. "Tell him I took early delivery on that package he wanted. I'm bringing it out to the ranch."

"He'll know what this is about?"

"Oh, yes," Pallifer said, and winked at the stolid-faced Manville next to him on the wide seat. "He'll be happy at the news," he assured the secretary, and broke the connection, and twisted around a bit more to look at Manville head on. "Give me your ear, you," he said.

Manville didn't react at all, so Pallifer poked him in the chest with a hard finger. "And give me your eye, too, while you're at it," he said.

Now Manville did look at him, and once again Pallifer was startled for just a second by how cold and deadly those eyes could look. But then he caught himself, he reminded himself who was in charge here now, and he grinned into those eyes as he said, "I'm about to tell you what's happening here."

Manville said, "Where's Kim?"

"Oh, Kim is it? The hero's been getting his reward, has he? Hear that, Steve? The hero's been getting his reward."

Steve was looking out his side window at the passing bustle of Brisbane, not interested in the conversation. So Pallifer quit his grinning, and said to Manville, "She run away from us. Would you believe that? She run away clean, but that's why we knew you'd show up at the same place."

"Oh," Manville said, and turned to look at the back of Steve's head. "That's why you said she was out of breath."

Steve turned to give Manville his own cold look. "I'm done with talk for today," he said, and turned aside, and looked out the window some more.

Pallifer said, "Steve isn't your social type. Steve is more your killer type. And the situation is, Mr. Curtis asked Steve and Raf and me to collect you and Kim—Kim? is that it?—yeah, Kim. To collect you and Kim, because he misses you. He said to me, he said, 'Morgan, that George Manville is a right smart engineer, I could use his brains some more, so would you just collect

him and bring him to me, so we can let bygones be bygones?'
And I said, 'Mr. Curtis, I will. But what if it turns out this
Manville makes trouble?' And you know how he is, Mr. Curtis,
you know how he talks. He just shrugged, you know how he
does, and he said, 'Oh, if he makes trouble, kill him.' Now, you
know I'm not lying to you, don't you?"

"Yes," Manville said.

"And this isn't a lie, either," Pallifer told him. "You pestered
me out on that ship, you truly did. I didn't like it, and I must say
I don't like you. Now I know Mr. Curtis would like it better if
you didn't make any trouble, but *I'd* like it better if you did.
You follow me?"

"I won't make trouble," Manville said.

"Well, that's a shame," Pallifer told him, "although it will
make Mr. Curtis's day. Now, we got about four hundred miles
to travel, so just you take it easy, don't do any scheming with
that bright brain of yours, and everything will be okay."

Apparently, Manville believed him. To Pallifer's astonishment,
the son of a bitch folded his arms, put his head back, shifted his
body around into a more comfortable position on the seat, and
closed his eyes.

It was more than four hundred miles, though not many more,
all of it almost perfectly due west. Out of the city of Brisbane,
they stayed on route 54 past Ipswich and Toowoomba, on the
rim of the Great Dividing Range, and on to Dalby, where they
left the main road for the almost as big Route 49, dipping
slightly south to run across the Darling Downs, the great fertile
flatlands, boring but fecund, with mile after mile of cotton and
wheat, sprawling ranches, tiny towns, huge sky.

Twice they stopped for everyone to walk off into the fields to
relieve themselves, both times with Manville where the others
could keep a close eye on him. At St. George, with darkness

just creeping up behind them, the sun out in front of them floating downward toward the broken line of hills to the west, they stopped to refuel, again giving Manville no opportunity to make a move unseen.

Beyond St. George, with a great bruised sunset burning its way down the sky, the chauffeur squinting and ducking his head behind his dark glasses, the farms of the Darling Downs petered out, giving way to herds of grazing sheep and cattle, none of whom paid any attention in the gathering darkness to the occasional passage of headlights out on the road. The land looked dryer here, reaching away in brown folds, like a tumbled blanket.

At the small settlement of Bollen, they turned left again, onto a much smaller and more twisty road, climbing into dry hills. They passed Murra Murra, barely a dozen lights in the blackness, and then turned off onto an unmarked dirt road that twisted up into the dark, posting back and forth, detouring around the hillocks. They drove past groups of shaggy-coated cattle that blinked in their headlights and shuffled slowly out of their way, bumping their shoulders together as they went. They drove on for three or four miles, over rolling open country, the Daimler taking the terrain like a good powerboat on a moderate sea, and then all at once they crested a rise and a bowl of lights appeared before them, down a farther hill, like a wide low glass jar full of fireflies.

It was a house, a ranch, what the Australians call a station, a sprawling adobe structure, two stories high, ablaze with light. Spotlights mounted high on the exterior walls flared on the road, showed a helicopter squatted with drooping rotors near the entrance, made tiny sharp black shadows among the tough grasses that covered these hills.

"Look at that," Pallifer said, nudging Manville, who didn't respond, and pointing at the helicopter, as they drove on by it.

"Your friend Mr. Curtis, he's so excited to see you again, he flew
out here already."

The Daimler drove past the front of the house, with its deep
wooden-posted porch dotted with rough wooden benches and
small tables, and followed the faint track of the road around to
the side, where a tan overhead garage door in the flank of the
building, near the rear, one of three such doors in a row, all the
same color as the adobe of the building, was already lifting up
out of the way, welcoming them.

The Daimler drove inside, into a space already flanked by
two other vehicles, under strong overhead lights. The garage
door, one solid piece of metal in an electrically operated track,
angled back down again and snicked shut. A minute later, all
the exterior lights went out.

10

"Let me do the talking," Jerry said.

"I always do," Luther told him.

They'd flown up from Sydney this morning, as Jerry had promised Kim's parents he would, but then had wasted precious time on the wrong assumption that Captain Zhang would be living on his ship. The crew members they'd approached had been no help at all, either not speaking English or pretending not to, but then a smooth young Japanese gentleman in a suit had come by, at the gangplank where Jerry and Luther were frustratingly being held, not permitted even to board the *Mallory*, and the gentleman had turned out to be with the company that was replacing the ship's missing lifeboat. He it was who told them that Captain Zhang was staying at a hotel in town, the Tasman Crest—"As am I myself"—during the time the ship was forced to remain in harbor.

The Tasman Crest was a mid-range smallish hotel near City Hall that seemed to cater to Asian businessmen almost exclusively, which was probably why their cabdriver had seemed surprised when they gave it as their destination. The young woman at the desk rang the captain's room for them without result.

"You could wait for him," she offered, with a gesture toward a seating area nearby.

"Thank you," Jerry said, and they went over to sit on broad low chairs with thick pale green cushions and bamboo arms. A fountain was nearby, a gentle plash of water onto polished stones, an unobtrusive white noise which would make any conversation in this place something close to confidential.

Jerry was feeling more and more frustrated. "We don't know what he looks like, only the sound of his voice. What if he isn't in his uniform? He could go in and out a dozen times, and we wouldn't know."

"She said she called room 423," Luther said. "And the key is in that slot, along with a message. Possibly two messages. Jerry, don't turn around, I can see it fine from here. We just have to wait." And when Jerry didn't respond to that: "What are we going to do tonight?"

They'd decided to spend tonight in Brisbane, staying at a Sheraton because Planetwatch got a group discount, so now Jerry permitted Luther to distract him with a discussion of how they'd spend their evening. There were good seafood restaurants here, and good jazz clubs, and other clubs that might be of interest. They wouldn't be bored.

"Ah," Luther said, and got to his feet.

As did Jerry. Turning, he saw the girl at the counter just handing the key and the message or messages to a man who was indeed not in uniform but in a rather shabby brown suit. The man had a gloomy and defeated air about him.

It was as they crossed the lobby toward the man, who must be Captain Zhang, that Jerry said, "Let me do the talking," and Luther gave his agreement. Meanwhile, the man had turned away from the desk, moving toward the elevators on the farther side of the lobby, and Jerry had to trot to try to catch up.

Though the girl at the desk solved that problem, calling, "Captain Zhang. You have visitors."

The captain turned around, still holding his key and messages, looking more frightened than curious, and very wary when he saw two men he didn't know approaching him.

Jerry stopped in front of him. "Captain Zhang?"

"Yes?"

"I'm Jerry Diedrich from Planetwatch. We talked the other day, by radio."

Now the captain looked like a frightened rabbit, backing away, eyes slipping to the sides, looking for a hole to hide in. "No no," he said. "You must talk to the company, Mr. Curtis—"

Jerry pursued him, saying, "When Kim Baldur's parents came to see you, you didn't speak English."

"I could not talk to them," the captain said. He was almost running backward, unwilling to turn away from them but wanting desperately to escape. "I cannot talk to you. Mr. Curtis has lawyers, you must see them. Please, not me." He was at the elevators now, and one was just opening, releasing three businessmen with briefcases, deep in discussion. The captain ducked around them into the elevator, and Jerry and Luther went in after him.

The captain stared at them in horror. "You can't follow me!"

Luther said, "Of course we can," and leaned forward to press button number 4. "You're in 423," he said.

The door closed; they started to rise. The captain tried to be stern, not very effectively. "I have nothing to say to you," he insisted. "I wrote a report for the authorities, that's all—"

"You *signed* a report," Luther corrected. "Some of Curtis's lawyers wrote it."

The elevator door opened, and the captain could be seen to be torn between horrible choices. He didn't want to stay in here with these two people, but he didn't want to let them approach any nearer to his room either.

Luther held the door, and spoke in an almost kindly way. "Your floor, sir."

The captain stepped out, jittering, and they went out with him. But then he refused to go any farther. He stood where he was in the hall, in front of the elevators, sullen but unmovable.

"I have nothing to tell you," he said. He wouldn't look at them either, but kept frowning at some invisible spot at waist height between them. "I did my report. I was very upset by what happened. I thought I would lose my job. I *need* my job, I have a family, I have daughters, I thought we were all destroyed. I felt…I felt very bad for that girl, so young and pretty and…it was not my fault. I would never hurt another person, you must believe me. I would never hurt anyone. It's not my fault."

Jerry said, "What about her parents? You pretended you couldn't speak English. What about them?"

"I felt so— I couldn't talk with those people, such sad people, I have daughters, I have daughters, what could I say to those people? How everybody looked for her and nobody found her, and if they found her she'd only be dead. They know that, I can't say that. How could I talk to those people? I pretended, because I felt such badness for them." He shook his head. "And I cannot talk to you. If you follow me to my room, I will call the desk and have them send people to take you away, arrest you. You must leave me alone."

He turned away, scurrying off down the wide pale corridor. Jerry would have followed, but Luther grabbed his arm, holding him back. Jerry looked at him, surprised, and Luther shook his head, then turned to push the down button for the elevator.

Jerry watched the captain pause at a door some way down the hall. He never looked back. He fumbled with the key in the door, dropped his messages, scooped them up, hurried inside. The door slammed, as the elevator arrived.

As they rode down, Jerry said, "Why did you stop me? If we just kept at him—"

"No," Luther said. "He's covering up, he's hiding something, and it scares him so much he won't talk. He really won't talk, Jerry, he's too scared. So all we know is, there's something hidden. We'll have to find out what it is some other way."

The elevator door opened at lobby level, and as they stepped outside Luther said, "The first question, of course, is how did he know she was pretty?"

Jerry thudded to a stop, as though he'd walked into an invisible wall. He spun around for the elevators, crying, "We have to—"

"No, Jerry," Luther said, holding him by the arm again. "We'll find out, but we'll find out someplace else. And it is possible, of course, that Kim's parents showed him a photo of her, though unlikely."

"Why would they do that?"

"Exactly. But we know he pretended not to speak English with them because he was afraid of making exactly that kind of slip. So what we now know for sure, there's more to the story. Come on, we'll go back to the hotel and decide what to do next."

Jerry was dissatisfied, but he let Luther lead him. They took a cab across to their own hotel, with its larger and more impersonal lobby, and as they were crossing it a voice called, "Jerry! Jerry!"

Jerry turned, and saw coming toward him, hurrying toward him, face grimacing with strain, the ghost of Kim Baldur. His eyes rolled back in his head, and he fainted.

11

Trembling, Zhang Yung-tsien dropped his two messages onto the floor, while trying to unlock the door to his room.

He was so nervous, so afraid those two strange men would rush up behind him and push him into the room, trap him there, force him somehow to tell them what they wanted to know, that he fumbled with the two flimsy slips of paper on the floor, and lost his balance, and would have toppled forward into his room if his shoulder hadn't hit the doorjamb.

His fingers felt like fat sausages, but he clutched at the crinkled slips of paper, and straightened, and lunged into the room, the door automatically closing behind him. He fell back against the door, eyes closed, the key and messages held tight in the hands crossed over his chest. His breath was loud in his ears.

They did not pursue. No knock on the door, no shouts in the hall. They've given up.

Zhang opened his eyes, and there was the room, his home ashore until *Mallory* should be ready to leave port. It was a small room, but very neat, the colors pale without sentimentality, not like the pastel palette of the Americans. The room's creators were Japanese, not Chinese, but still he had felt more at home here than in the American-made world he had so much to inhabit.

One of his messages, from his wife, Yanling, was in Chinese, the ideograms neatly penned. The other, yet another question from the insurance company adjuster, was written in English, the letters just as neat. He had trouble focusing on either, and held one in each hand, looking back and forth from one to the other, then finally giving up and placing them side by side on the dresser.

He was having trouble with his breath, he couldn't seem to inhale. The air in the room felt cold and lifeless, and it was hard to gain nourishment from it. He crossed to the window to open it wide, and immediately the warm moist air from outside flowed in to conquer the air-conditioning. He could feel it as a soft caress against his skin.

What was he going to do? What *could* he do? The people kept coming to ask questions, and he was so afraid, so confused, that he never knew how to answer, what to tell them, what to try to conceal.

The girl was alive. Could he have told her parents that? But then so many more questions would have come from them, questions he was terrified to answer. What had happened on the ship? What had been *intended*, and by whom? And what was Captain Zhang's role in it all?

The girl was alive, or she'd been alive when she'd left the ship with that engineer. But was she still alive, were either of them still alive, or had some other of Curtis's men caught up with them? Should he say the girl was alive, if he didn't know?

But what if she *were* still alive, and finally came forward, and told everything that had happened on the ship? Then people would know he had lied, and they would demand to know why.

He had never wanted to be involved in this. He was good at his work, and that was all he'd wanted. He wasn't supposed to have these burdens.

He sat on the side of the bed. Next to the telephone were a ballpoint pen and a notepad, the name of the hotel at its top in Japanese and English. Zhang picked up pen and pad and wrote, under the letterhead, "Yanling."

What would he say next? What would he tell his wife? There

was insurance; they would be taken care of. This way, there would be no shame and no disaster. But how could he tell her all that, on a scrap of paper in a hotel room, under a name in Japanese and English?

"I love you," he wrote, and put the pad and pen back next to the telephone, and got to his feet.

It all started because of the girl, the diver. If she had not launched herself into the sea, nothing bad would have happened.

Zhang reached the window, and bent forward. Without pausing, he put both hands on the windowsill and launched himself head-first into the air.

12

"I'm *really* sorry, Jerry," Kim said yet again, and yet again he gave her his rattled martyr look and said, "It's all right, Kim, it really is."

When she'd first seen him collapse like that, downstairs in the lobby, she'd thought he'd been shot, that one of Richard Curtis's killers had found her and fired at her and missed and killed Jerry. But then Luther dropped to his knees beside him, and called, "Jerry! Jerry!" and Jerry's eyes fluttered, and Kim realized he'd only fainted.

Not only; she wouldn't dare say he'd *only* fainted. Jerry was taking it all very seriously. And it's true he'd hit the floor hard, falling sideways, bruising his left hip and raising a shiny bump on his head, above his left ear, just in front of the hairline. Luther kept putting fresh wet, cold washcloths on it, from the bathroom sink, so it wasn't getting any worse, but it wasn't getting any better either.

As Luther and Kim together had helped the quivering Jerry back to his feet, he'd looked at her with still-frightened eyes and said, "You aren't a ghost. You're real."

"I'm real, Jerry," she promised him, and for the first of many times she said, "I'm *really* sorry," and he assured her it was all right, and she and Luther helped him to rise and walk to the elevator. They went up in it together and into their room, which was a surprising mess, clothing and luggage and personal effects strewn just everywhere, the bed rumpled and unmade.

Kim helped Luther straighten the top cover so Jerry could lie down. Luther went away for the first of the wet washcloths, and Kim told her story.

Parts of it she had to tell more than once, particularly the suggestion that George Manville, Richard Curtis's chief engineer on the Kanowit Island project, creator of the shock wave that had reconfigured the island and threatened the delicate coral of the barrier reef and almost killed Kim herself, wasn't a villain after all. Not a bad man, but a good one.

"He saved my *life*," she told them more than once, and described how astonishingly Manville had shot the killer, and how brilliantly he'd arranged their escape from the ship, and how, through some friend of his in Houston, he'd even made contact with a lawyer here in Brisbane who was going to help them all, but how now it was all messed up.

"I don't know where he is," she said. "I don't know what happened to him."

"Got on with his life, I suppose," Jerry said. He still didn't get it.

But Luther did, by now. He said, "You're sure it was just coincidence, them seeing you there. The people who chased you."

"Yes, of course, it had to be," she said. "Only George knew where I was, and if he was going to turn me over to those people he could have done it a long time ago. In fact, he never had to save me in the first place."

Luther said, "Would they have known you were waiting for Manville?"

"Probably. They knew I'd got off the ship with him, they probably figured we were hiding out together."

"So," Luther said, "they might have gone back to where they saw you, deciding that you had been waiting to meet up with Manville again."

"That's what I'm worried about," she agreed. "I got so lost, running away from them, it took me *forever* to find the Mall again, and of course by then he wasn't there."

Luther said, "So either he was captured by them or he escaped the way you did."

"I went to the parking lot where we left the car," she said. "George rented this little red car, and it was still there. I called the lawyer's office, but it was almost five o'clock by then, and everybody was gone. He wasn't at the Mall, and he didn't pick up his car. So that's when I tried to call you two, at the Planetwatch office down in Sydney, and the people there said you were up here, and which hotel, so I just waited in the lobby. And I'm *really* sorry, Jerry."

"It's all right, Kim, it really is."

"Well," Luther said, "there's nothing we can do now. It's nearly six o'clock on a Friday afternoon, everybody's gone away for the weekend. What I suggest you do, first you should call your parents."

"Oh, my God, I have to!" Kim said, startled by the realization. "They were told I was dead, weren't they? What time is it in Chicago?"

"They're here," Luther said. "Well, not *here*, in Brisbane, but here in Australia."

Kim blinked. "They are? Why?"

"Because you're dead," Jerry told her. His voice sounded hollow, as though he were speaking from a tomb.

"I'm *really* sorry, Jerry," she said, almost reflexively by now.

Luther said, "They're down in Sydney, in a hotel there, you should phone them soon."

"Yes. I will. But then, what about George?"

"I think," Luther said, "Manville was right when he said you shouldn't go to the police yet, until he'd had legal advice. But now things are different. I think you should stay here tonight"—Jerry gave him a startled look, and Luther went smoothly on—"we'll get you a room as close to this one as we can, and then in the

morning you can telephone the place where you and Manville
were staying, to see if he's come back. If he hasn't, we'll go look
for the car in the parking lot. If it's still there, I vote we go to
the police."

"Oh, absolutely," Jerry said. "This is Richard Curtis at his
worst, his absolute worst. I know some people think I harp on
him too much, but now you get a sense of the man, you see
what it is he's capable of, what we're up against. The police,
absolutely."

"Thank you, Jerry," Luther said, and said to Kim, "Do you
want to call your parents from here, or wait till you've got your
own room?"

"You call, Luther," Kim said, "if you don't mind. Talk to them
first. Prepare them. I don't want to cause any more people to
faint."

Lying in yet another bed, in yet another room, this time with
the brightness of Brisbane beyond the curtain over the one
window, Kim felt very strange. It had been a weird rollercoaster
day, being chased by those people, losing George, finding Jerry
and Luther, talking on the phone with Mom and Dad, and then
having dinner with Jerry and Luther as though they were all
three equals together, in a way that had never been true on the
ship.

She'd also made another batch of the same small purchases:
toothbrush, toothpaste, lipstick, all the usual. And more clothing,
outer and under, enough to carry her for a few days, all bought
with money borrowed from Jerry. And a new cotton shoulder
bag to put it all in. And by now Mom would have phoned Aunt
Ellen in Chicago to go over to the house, pack up Kim's passport
and wallet, which had just arrived there today, and air express it
all back to Sydney, to arrive on Monday. So, except for George,
things seemed to be going pretty well.

George. She was tired, but she couldn't sleep, here in this strange new bed, all alone. Every time she moved, the sheets above and below her felt rough and cold. When she lay still, the big flat hard-mattressed bed seemed immense, as big as a football field. If she put her left arm out to the side, that other unused pillow over there was a big cold mound, an alien that didn't belong with her.

Last night had just been the beginning with George, and yet already being here without him seemed unnatural. She wanted the feel of him, the solidity of him, the knowledge that he was there. To have had it just begin, and then stop like this, was terrible.

She needed to sleep, because tomorrow would be another crowded day, but she remained awake, her mind skittering around recent events, and always coming back to George. To remember how he had been last night, so gentle and then so strong, did not lead her toward sleep at all, but she couldn't help the thoughts, they just kept swirling around and around, constantly there.

Is he all right? Where is he? What's happened to him?

13

There was a knock at the door.

Manville looked at it more in irritation than surprise. "You're the ones who locked it," he called. "What do you want me to do?"

The key was already turning in the lock, with a loud *snick*, before he was finished speaking, and then the door opened and a young woman entered, in a tan pantsuit, smiling apologetically, saying, "I did not want to startle you." A pile of clothing was over her arm. "If I may?"

He stepped to the side. She'd left the door open, and the hall looked empty from where he stood, but he didn't doubt one of the men who'd brought him here was out there, or some other goon of Curtis's, leaning against the wall, casual but making damn sure Manville stayed where they wanted him.

The young woman laid the clothing on the bed, neatening it, smoothing out wrinkles, then turned to smile at Manville again and say, "Mr. Curtis asks you to come to dinner in thirty minutes. You may refresh yourself in the bathroom there, and here are garments that we hope will fit you. The door will not be locked now, sir. In thirty minutes, if you would go out and to your right, and at the end of the hall turn left, that is the dining room. Thank you."

She dipped her head and left, closing the door behind her. There was no sound of the key turning in the lock.

Manville guessed he'd been in this room now no more than fifteen or twenty minutes. He hadn't looked at his watch when he'd first come in, assuming they'd be leaving him in here overnight.

They'd driven directly into the garage inside this building, and as they'd gotten out of the Daimler, all of them stiff, stretching, a young man in the same kind of tan pantsuit as this woman had opened an interior door at the left end of the garage, stepped forward through it, and called, "This way, please."

Manville had paused to note the other two vehicles parked there, a tan Land Rover and a kind of dune buggy made mostly out of chrome pipe, and then he'd followed the man, while the leader of the thugs who'd captured him—Morgan, he'd called himself—had followed Manville into that broad low-ceilinged hall outside, with what looked like Navajo carpets on the red tile floor and framed aboriginal art on both walls. At the first open door on the right the man in the pantsuit had turned and made a please-enter gesture.

"That means you," Morgan had said, and Manville had stepped into this room, and the door had shut behind him, with the unmistakable scrape of the key being turned in the lock.

This was normally a guestroom, apparently, with only the vertical bars outside the one window to suggest a prison; but probably all the ground floor windows were barred in a building as remote as this. The room contained a double bed, more native-looking throw rugs on the floor, a dresser and an easy chair beside a round table bearing a reading lamp. The compact bathroom next to it had an extremely small window, not barred, a telephone-booth-type shower, and more than enough towels.

Manville had expected to be left here by himself, locked in, to brood and worry and be the subject of psychological warfare. But now, to be suddenly presented with a change of clothes and a dinner invitation, threw him off; which might have been the idea.

Still, he should take what comfort he could. The shower was fine, with a clear lucite door and plenty of hot water and a big white bar of soap. Standing in there, letting the spray roll over him, easing the stiffness in his joints, he wondered again, for the thousandth time, what had happened to Kim. Those three had seen her—accidentally? somehow on purpose, following them?—and she'd escaped, and then they'd come back to the cafe to pick him up, and he'd walked right into it. So what would Kim have done next?

She might have gone to the police. Presumably there was a report somewhere that she was dead, so when she turned up alive, even without identification, it might force the authorities to take notice; though not necessarily to believe her fantastic accusations against a rich and respectable businessman.

Or she might have called the Planetwatch people, that guy Jerry Diedrich she'd mentioned a number of times.

He turned off the water, and stepped out of the shower.

The clothing he'd been given provided everything but shoes, and it all fit very well. Underwear, socks, dark gray slacks, pale blue buttoned shirt but no necktie, light gray sports jacket. The left pocket of the sports jacket contained two three-year-old tickets to *La Bohème* at the Sydney Opera House, suggesting this jacket had been left behind, forgotten by some houseguest, and never retrieved.

At the appointed time, Manville left his no-longer prison and followed the woman's directions. Down the hall he went to the right, then a left, and there was the dining room.

Low ceilings seemed to be the norm here, but otherwise the place was lavish. The dining room was actually one end of a very long room that was a parlor at the farther end, all deep sofas and chairs on animal skin rugs, with a broad gray-stone fireplace taking up much of the far wall. There was no fire lit at the moment, but the room was comfortably warm. A pair of refectory tables, dark wood, bearing muted lamps, stacks of magazines, framed photos, marked the dividing line between parlor and dining room.

Four people were seated, very low, in the sofas down there; Richard Curtis, and three others Manville didn't recognize, two women and a man. One of the women saw Manville enter and said something to Curtis, who immediately looked over, waved a hand over his head, and called, "There you are! Be right there."

Manville waited. Closer to him was a long dark wood dining table, big enough to seat twelve. Five elaborate place settings took up the left half of the table. Apparently Morgan and his friends would eat somewhere else; in the kitchen, maybe, or out back with the dogs.

The four people approached, Curtis smiling like a host. Saying, "Well, George, you look rested. Good. A hell of a long drive, isn't it?"

"Not too bad, in that car," Manville said. He was surprised at the calmness of his response, but could see nothing else to do. It's a natural instinct, apparently, to be polite to somebody who's being polite to you, return friendliness with friendliness, good manners with good manners.

Curtis went so far as to make introductions: "George Manville, may I introduce Albert and Helen Farrelly, they run Kennison for me, and Cindy Peters, an old friend visiting for the weekend. George," he told the others, "is a brilliant engineer, absolutely brilliant. We've been working together for a year and a half now, haven't we, George?"

"About that," Manville agreed. Not so long ago, he wanted to say, while everybody exchanged friendly greetings, you were sending people to kill me, then to kidnap me, imprison me. Has one of us lost his mind? But dinner party politeness was just too strong a force; he couldn't say a word.

Curtis even rubbed it in, saying, "It's too bad your friend Kim couldn't be with you, George, we'd make an even number. Well, we'll do what we can. I'll be father at the head of the table here, George, you take that place there on the right, Helen, you between George and me, Cindy, you on my left, and Albert, if you'd sit across from George?"

Everybody did, and Manville saw Curtis extend his foot toward what must be a call button in the floor, because almost immediately two servers in the tan pantsuits came out with plates of crisp green salad.

Manville said to Helen, on his left, "Kennison?"

Surprised, she said, "The station. This place, you'd call it a ranch. And the house. This is Kennison. You didn't know that?"

"I came here unexpectedly," Manville said.

Wine was being poured. Around the server's arm, Curtis said to Manville, "Kennison's a great place, George, I wish I could be here more often myself. I'll show you around, I think you'll be surprised and pleased."

"I'm already surprised," Manville told him, and Curtis laughed.

When the five glasses had been filled with an Australian white wine, a chardonnay, Curtis proposed a toast. "To the good life, in a good place, to getting it and keeping it."

They all drank to Curtis's toast, Manville last and only a sip. It was a good clean wine, nicely cold. He would have to be alert not to drink too much of it.

As they started their salads, Manville looked more carefully at these three new people. He might be needing allies soon; would any of them fit the bill?

Albert and Helen Farrelly were a middle-aged, comfortable-looking couple, both overweight, both with the leathery cheeks of people who spend a lot of time outdoors, as they would do if they were the overseers of a large ranch. They were Australian, by their accents, and they seemed on very easy terms with their employer.

Would the Farrellys help? They came across as decent people, not criminals, but Captain Zhang was a decent man, too, and look at what he had been prepared to do. How vital was this job, this life, to the Farrellys? Helen Farrelly spoke of Kennison as though it were heaven on earth, and her husband smiled and nodded in agreement; how willing would they be to risk it, or lose it, for a stranger?

Cindy Peters was about thirty, a poised girl, pleasant, well-spoken, also Australian. An old friend of Curtis, visiting for the weekend.

There's no comfort here, Manville told himself, as the salad plates were removed, replaced by plates of a butterflied boneless chicken breast with lightly sauteed vegetables. And more wine. I have to count on nobody but myself.

Manville turned to Curtis. "How long have you had this place? Kennison."

"Seven years. It was my second wife's idea. She's Australian, she wanted a footprint in her homeland, so we bought this. She'd have liked to keep it after the divorce, but by then I was in love with it. And not with her, you know?"

"I didn't know you were ever married," Manville said. He wanted to encourage this new friendliness in Curtis, this companionship, until he could find a way to escape.

"I was married twice," Curtis told him. And sounding more grim than before: "The second one was the mistake." Then he lightened again, and turned to rest his hand on Cindy Peters's, saying, "You don't mind if I talk about my wives, do you?"

"Just so you don't bring them around," she said.

"No fear," he told her, and turned back to Manville to say, "My first wife died at thirty-nine of leukemia."

Cindy Peters looked shocked and embarrassed, as Curtis had no doubt intended, and Manville said, "I'm very sorry."

"So was I, George, so was I. Isabel was my life to me. She got me started in business, what a team we were going to be." His jaw set and his eyes looked angry, and he said, "Isabel would have known how to deal with the goddam mainlanders. She was Hong Kong born and bred, she'd have tied them in knots, not run around wasting time and money like me."

Manville said, "She was Chinese?"

"No, a Brit," Curtis said. "Her background was. Her grandfather came out, started a construction company on the island, over a hundred years ago. Called it Hoklo Construction, which was a joke, because the Hoklo were 17th-century pirates from China that settled in Hong Kong and then assimilated and disappeared, so anybody could be Hoklo. Anybody could be a pirate, you see?"

Manville said, "It's an interesting point."

"One Isabel's grandfather always kept in mind," Curtis said, "as should have his successors. Anyway, the grandfather built the business, and went back to England to marry, and had children, and his first two sons took over the business, and Isabel was a daughter of the second son. I was just a roustabout from Oklahoma, my father was in construction but in a small way, little tract houses in developments in the dirt around Tulsa, not like Hoklo. They were big, always, from the beginning, building the big godowns the Chinese used for waterfront warehouses, putting up office buildings, apartment houses. I was always interested in travel, seeing something other than the tan dirt of Tulsa, and when I got to Hong Kong I took a job for a while with Hoklo, and met Isabel, and that's where it all started."

Manville said, "You went into the firm."

"I *became* the firm," Curtis said, and his voice was harsh

again, but then it softened as he said, "The difference between the first generation and the third, you see, the first generation has to work for it, and the second generation at least gets to see their parents work for it, but the third generation gets it handed to them on a plate, with no idea there's any work involved. Isabel's brother and two of her cousins were supposed to take over the company, and it would have been like having the company taken over by the Pillsbury Doughboy."

"You took it away from them."

Curtis smiled. If tigers smiled, it would look like that. "I showed them what it was like to be in a fight," he said.

"And lose," Manville suggested.

"I was always the one to bet on," Curtis said. "And then, no sooner was it mine, mine and Isabel's, than it hit her."

Cindy Peters put a sympathetic hand on his forearm. "That must have been horrible."

He nodded at her, "It killed me, Cindy. I was dead before she was, and she was dead in five months."

"Oh, Dick. I don't know what to say."

"Thank you, Cindy."

Manville noticed, but thought that Cindy did not, that his smile to her was patronizing, that it said, thank you for your sympathy, but you're too shallow to know what I *really* went through. He holds himself aloof from the human race, Manville thought, and that's why he can be so dangerous.

Curtis turned back to Manville to say, "It was because I missed Isabel so much that I married again, which was probably the biggest mistake of my life, and I know you know I've made a number of mistakes."

"We all do," Manville said.

"But I don't get mad at other people's mistakes," Curtis said. "Not the way I get mad at my own. The thing is, George, it's too goddam easy for a man to be an idiot. I married Rita because she looked like Isabel. *Looked* like. They couldn't have been more different, they— I'll let it go at that. When I realized— Well. I'll let it go at that."

Manville said, "Is Rita still alive?"

Curtis laughed. He seemed genuinely amused. He said, "I'm not Henry the Eighth, George. Rita and I divorced, seven months into the marriage. She got a damn good settlement. *She* doesn't think so, of course, but she did."

Curtis turned away, the veneer of friendliness gone, his attention back on the food on his plate, and Manville picked up his knife and fork as well; it was time to quit, while he was ahead.

At the end of the meal, as though a sudden gong had gone off, though in fact there had been no signal at all that Manville could see, both Farrellys thanked their employer, told Manville and Cindy how lovely it had been to meet them both, patted their mouths with their napkins, rose, said good night, and left the room, through a wide doorway down at the living room end.

Manville, starting to rise, said, "I should go, too. Thank you—"

"Wait, George," Curtis said. "Cindy, George and I have a little boring business to talk over, and then I'll be up."

"Fine," she said. "I'll be reading." And she too on her way out assured Manville it had been a pleasure to meet him.

Once they were alone, Curtis gestured toward the living room. "Let's get comfortable over there, let them clear this away."

"All right."

As they walked across the long room, Curtis said, "Brandy? A cordial? After-dinner drink?"

"Thanks, but no thanks."

Curtis patted Manville's shoulder. "Come on, George, you don't have to be wary with me."

Manville looked at him, astonished. "Of course I do."

Curtis shrugged and shook his head, as though abashed. "Well, I suppose you do," he said. "Or you have reason to think you do, which is the same thing. Take that chair, it's comfortable and it isn't impossible to get out of."

They sat at right angles, and Curtis seemed to be thinking for a minute how to phrase himself. Then he said, "I owe you an apology, George. And I offer it."

"Thank you," Manville said, wondering what on earth was coming next.

"*With* an explanation," Curtis said, and grinned at him. "Mea culpa, but with an explanation. Okay?"

"Fine," Manville said.

"You know the situation I'm in, I told you some of it."

"You told me some," Manville agreed. "I guess you thought you told me too much."

"I was running on panic, George," Curtis said, "what should have been a perfect day was completely destroyed. Your technique on Kanowit Island was perfect, it showed me I can do it again when I need to. My investors were happy, very impressed. But all of a sudden there was Jerry Diedrich, that son of a bitch, spoiling my day yet again. And I realized, the man would find some way to trip me up when I was ready to make the move, the *real* move. Don't worry, George, I'm not going to tell you any more about that move. I maybe didn't tell you too much, out there on the *Mallory*, but I almost did. It'll be better for both of us if you don't know any more than you know now."

"Fine by me."

"The thing is, I panicked," Curtis said. "And then one damn thing led to another. First, Diedrich is going to destroy me.

But no, he killed a diver and I can destroy *him*. No, the goddam girl's alive, I'm back to square one. But she *should* be dead, She's beat up enough, maybe she'll die. Maybe there's no reason for her to live. And you know, if you hadn't intervened, between us, Captain Zhang and me, we would have finished her off."

"I know you would."

"And we would have been wrong. *I* would have been wrong, completely wrong. But I didn't realize that then. And I was damn angry at you when you interfered, as you know."

"You made it pretty plain," Manville said. "The people you sent out made it plain."

"You astonished me, George," Curtis said. "I admit it, I was astonished. You're a handier man than I gave you credit for. But the point is, you *did* handle it. You handled me, and you handled the men I sent out, and now you and the girl are both still alive, and I realize I'm in no worse shape than I was before, I can still go ahead the same as ever. I can defuse Jerry Diedrich some other way, and I've got nothing to get in my way except my own damn foolishness. I didn't have to panic, I didn't have to make you an enemy, it was foolish of me, and I regret it. When I was trying to do you harm, George, you *knew* I wasn't in my right mind, didn't you?"

"I suspected," Manville said.

"All right, George," Curtis said. "I'd like us to start all over, from now. And I have a deal to offer."

"A deal?"

"I'd like you to stay here a few days," Curtis said. "A week or two at the most. Think of it as a vacation."

"Why?"

"So I can find you if I need you." Now Curtis was intense again, leaning forward in his own soft low chair, saying, "George, you know I'm going to do something big, and you know it's going to be soon, and you know I'm going to use the soliton."

"That's what you told me."

"I felt I could trust you, George. In a funny way, I still do." He gave Manville a keen look, and a rueful smile, and said, "You probably think the question of trust goes the other way."

"If it's a question," Manville said.

"Oh, it is, George, it is. But here's the thing. I *think* I can pull this off on my own, but there may be questions I can't answer. The people I'm working with aren't your caliber, George. I'd like to think, if I got stuck, I could give you a call, right here, and ask you a question in a general way, not too specific, nothing that makes you a collaborator or an accessory or any of that, and you would answer it."

"For the ten million in gold, again?"

Curtis shook his head. "I don't know why money doesn't interest you, George, that's one thing I can't figure out."

"It interests me," Manville said.

"Then there's hope. Look, George, if you stay here, no more than two weeks, I promise, probably a lot less, I'll give you whatever it is you want. Money, no money, that's all right with me. The first thing, though…" His smile this time was sly, pleased with itself. "You know about the industrial espionage?"

"I've been in a number of newspapers," Manville told him. "Yes, I know about it."

"I'll get rid of it," Curtis said. "Guaranteed. I'll explain it was my error, you weren't the guy, sorry I blackened your name, a public apology and you're cleared and as good as new. All right?"

This was important. If Curtis did this, whatever else happened, Manville would be able to get on with his life. As it now stood, no one on earth would hire him. He said, "When?"

"Tomorrow," Curtis told him. "Saturday isn't a problem, with news. I'll get it on CNN International by tomorrow night."

Pointing generally away at the interior of the house, he said, "We've got dish reception here, you'll see it for yourself."

"It would be good. If you did that," Manville agreed.

Curtis said, "George, you see now how easy I can knock you down, and how easy I can pick you up again."

"Yes."

"So I'm just asking you to help me, in a small way. And otherwise I'm only asking you to keep out of the way. Because believe me, I don't need Pallifer and his friends—"

"Who?"

Curtis laughed, surprised. "No formal introductions, eh? The people who brought you here."

"Pallifer. He'd be the one I met on the ship. Morgan?"

"The same. And you don't ever have to meet him again, George. And you don't have to read about yourself in the newspaper, either. Just take a little vacation, right here at Kennison. Do you ride?"

"Horses? No, I never have."

"We have horses here, you could learn," Curtis offered. "Albert taught me to ride, and if he could teach somebody like me, he can teach anybody. It's a relaxing place, George, a beautiful time out from the cares of the world. I envy you, I honestly do, ten days or two weeks in this place, no worries, no problems."

Manville said, "And Kim?"

Curtis looked blank. "What about her?" Then he suddenly seemed to understand. "Oh, what am I going to do about her!"

"Yes."

"Nothing, George, why should I? If she was dead on the ship, then she's a club I can beat Jerry Diedrich with. Now she doesn't mean a thing, and I'll get at Diedrich some other way."

"But what if she went to the police?"

"And said what, George? That I did something to her? I saved her life, that's all, rescued her from the sea, carried her safe to shore in my own yacht. If somebody tried to harm her in any way, what does that have to do with me?" Curtis leaned closer to say, "George, if I could swat *you* down without half-trying, what sort of threat is this girl?"

"You're not afraid she'll raise questions."

"About what? No, George, I'm safe from her, and therefore she's safe from me."

Was that true? Curtis was so devious, yet so apparently straightforward, that Manville had constant trouble figuring out what the man really wanted, what he really meant, what was lie and what was truth. "Your people were after her today," he said.

"To find you," Curtis told him. "That was the only reason. Then they did find you, so they weren't looking for her anymore."

Again, what Curtis said was plausible, without being quite persuasive. Manville brooded on it, trying to think his way through Curtis's words, while the man watched him, half-smiling. He said, "What if I don't want to stay here? What if I want to leave, tomorrow?"

Curtis sat back, but didn't lose the half smile. "I hope you won't feel that way, George. I hope we don't have to deal with it. I tell you what." He sat up again. "Sleep on it. We'll talk again tomorrow morning, Cindy and I aren't leaving until after lunch. Think it over, and we'll talk, and as soon as we've reached an agreement you can sit there and watch me get on the phone to get rid of that espionage story. Immediately. All right?"

There was nothing to be gained by arguing. "All right," Manville said.

"Fine." Curtis got to his feet, and so did Manville. "We've worked well together, George," Curtis said. "I'm sorry it turned bad for a while."

"So am I."

Curtis put his hand out. Hiding his surprise, Manville took it, and Curtis shook his hand with self-conscious pomp, as though some important international treaty had just been signed. "I'm glad we had this talk, George," he said.

"Yes."

"Good night."

"Good night," Manville said, and turned away.

As he walked back down the long room toward the dining area, its table now cleared, headed back toward his no-longer prison, or possibly prison again, Manville was very aware of Curtis behind him, standing as Manville had left him, unmoving amid the low sofas, the great gray stone wall of fireplace behind him, watching Manville recede. He's wondering if he's pulled it off, Manville knew. He's wondering if he has me fixed in place, or if I'm going to go on being a pest. And I'm wondering the same thing myself.

If I tell him no tomorrow, I've thought it over, and I don't want to stay here, beautiful and restful though Kennison might be, what then? Will he just allow me to leave, like that? Unlikely. If I don't give him my parole, what else would he do but simply make me a prisoner?

What was it that Curtis was going to attempt, sometime in the next ten days or two weeks? If Manville did nothing about it, would he regret that? Would people be hurt, or even killed? What is Richard Curtis up to?

Should he try to escape tonight? Assuming the door to his room was left unlocked, should he try to get out of here? It was impossible to believe they would have left any of the vehicles where he could get at them, but even if they did, which way would he drive? The road into here was barely a track in the dirt, difficult enough for Curtis's own chauffeur to find at night, and constantly blocked by stray cattle. Kennison was

who knew how many thousands of acres in size. There was no
way to get off it tonight.

Tomorrow? Were Pallifer and the other two still around?
Manville for a giddy second visualized Albert Farrelly teaching
him to ride a horse and then, magically, Manville atop the horse,
racing over the downs to freedom.

He left the dining room, and started down the empty hall
toward his room. Curtis had been ingratiating tonight, persuasive, reasonable, plausible; but Manville wanted none of it. He
wanted nothing but to leave this place. For now, he entered the
small neat guestroom and shut the door. Richard Curtis is at his
most dangerous, he thought, when he seems the most sane.

14

Jerry was amazed and delighted at how seriously the police were taking their story, which they'd now told three times. The first time was to a detective in the police station where he and Luther and Kim had gone to report the disappearance of George Manville, the second was to his superior at the same station, and now the third time was to an extremely senior inspector in his office here in police headquarters.

The inspector was a very tall, large-framed tweedy man with thick gray brushlike hair and astonishingly dainty granny glasses perched on his hawk nose. His name, he said, was Tony Fairchild, which seemed too diminutive for such a large man, and as he listened he made many notes on a legal pad on his desk in tiny crabbed writing that surely no one else would ever be able to read.

Other plainclothes detectives were in and out of the small but sunny office, going on mysterious errands at nods and hand gestures from Fairchild, returning with equally mysterious nods or headshakes of their own. Sometimes they returned with small slips of paper, which they put on his desk and at which he barely glanced.

Saturday morning. Before breakfast, Kim had come to their room, where she'd phoned the motel in Surfers Paradise, to be told that George Manville had not as yet returned. After breakfast at the hotel, she'd led them to the parking lot where the red car was still where Manville had left it. So then they'd gone to the police.

By now, it was nearly eleven o'clock, and Jerry was beginning to feel talked out. Kim had described the events on the ship at length, Jerry and Luther had described their own activities, Kim's parents' whereabouts in Sydney were given, the parents' unprofitable meeting with Captain Zhang related, Jerry and Luther's own encounter with Zhang told, and finally the disappearance of George Manville.

Oddly, Fairchild seemed for a while most interested in Captain Zhang, wanting to know every detail of the encounter between him and Jerry and Luther, asking if they'd been in Zhang's hotel room for even a second. "I would have," Jerry told him, "I'd have gone right on in and *insisted* he tell us the truth, but Luther wouldn't let me."

"Hard to know if that would have made a difference," Fairchild said, and at last left that issue to say to Kim, "The lawyer Manville was going to see. His office was in the Mansions in George Street?"

"I think so," Kim said. "I think that's what he said."

"And he told you the name, but you don't remember it."

"I'm sorry," Kim said. "I didn't know I was going to have to."

"Of course not," Fairchild agreed. He was managing to be both remote and sympathetic at the same time. "There aren't that many lawyers in the Mansions," he said. "Was it a European name or an Asian name, do you remember?"

"It sounded European, I think," she said, "but it wasn't anything ordinary."

Fairchild brooded, gazing at the far wall over his granny glasses, then he frowned at Kim and said, "Just a minute. You say Manville got to this lawyer through a friend in America."

"An architect in Houston, he said. I'm sorry, I don't know his name either."

"Building trades," Fairchild said. "Manville is in that line, his Houston friend is, he would have sent him on to someone in the same sort of line here, so it's a lawyer who represents architects or developers or— Would the name be Andre Brevizin?"

"Yes!" Kim said, delighted. "That's what he said. I remember it sounded like too nice a name for a lawyer."

Fairchild laughed. "I expect we have areas of agreement, Miss Baldur," he said. "Although I doubted it at first, when I heard the story you wished to tell."

"Richard Curtis, you mean," she said.

Fairchild nodded. "Among other things. But let us look at what I began with. Two days ago, in this city, your Mr. Curtis brought a complaint to the police—not to me, I'm sorry to say, I wish I'd met the man, considering subsequent events—a complaint charging a former employee, one George Manville, with industrial espionage and theft. I've had a looksee at the complaint itself, and he did seem to have sufficient evidence for the charge."

Jerry wanted to break in here with a ringing denunciation of Richard Curtis as a polluter and a well-known liar, but he restrained himself.

"Now this morning," Fairchild went on, "an unknown young American lady, yourself, with no identification but claiming a friendly relationship with the same George Manville, presents herself to the police with a wild story of kidnapping, piracy, attempted murder and the suspicious disappearance of the man Manville himself, all pointing to Richard Curtis as the villain. I must admit. Miss Baldur, at first blush you did not bring us anything we could be expected to take seriously."

"But you do take it seriously," Kim said. "I can see you take it seriously."

"For one reason only," Fairchild told her. "It is why you were brought to this office, and not dealt with rather summarily at a lower level."

Kim, looking uncertain, possibly a little afraid, so that Jerry had the urge to grasp her hand but again restrained himself, said, "Why is that?"

Fairchild lowered his head enough to look at them all, one at a time, over his granny glasses. Jerry had to force himself to meet that steady look. "I take it," Fairchild said, "none of you has had any dealings with Captain Zhang Yung-tsien since your unsatisfactory interview with him yesterday."

Jerry felt heat rising in his cheeks. Had Zhang dared to put in his own complaint? He said, more hotly than he'd intended, "Inspector, if Captain Zhang suggests we—"

Fairchild stopped him with an upraised hand. "Not at all," he said. "Captain Zhang went out his hotel room window yesterday afternoon, very near to the time you and Mr. Rickendorf spoke with him."

Jerry could only stare, open-mouthed. His first reaction was: I did it! I pressed him too hard, I forced him, I should have found a better way, a quieter way..."Oh God. What have I done?" He covered his face with his hands.

He wasn't really aware of the charged silence in the room until Fairchild broke it by saying, "Mr. Diedrich? What *have* you done?"

Then Jerry realized what he'd said, what he'd implied, and he lowered his hands, showing his flushed face, and said, "No no no! I mean—we shouldn't have pressed him so hard, I had no idea he..." Turning, he said, "Luther, *you* know what I mean!"

Luther said to Fairchild, "Did he leave a note?"

"Hard to say," Fairchild said.

Luther gave a small smile of disbelief and said, "Inspector, how can it be hard to say if he left a note?"

"On the memo pad beside his bed," Fairchild explained, "in Chinese, was his wife's name, and 'I love you,' nothing more. If it's a suicide note, it's certainly an ambiguous one. The other possibility is that he was just starting a letter to his wife when he was interrupted by his murderer."

Jerry said, "Oh, my God! You don't think we—"

Luther, gently but firmly, said, "Stop, Jerry. The inspector doesn't think we have anything to do with it at all."

"Well, if it was suicide, you did," Fairchild said. "In a way. You made it clear to Captain Zhang that the questions would only continue, and only get worse." He tapped one of the pieces of paper that had been delivered to his desk. "Miss Baldur's parents have confirmed to the Sydney police your account of their meeting with Captain Zhang. It is clear he *did* speak English, and it is clear he pretended not to be able to, because he was afraid to be questioned on the subject of Miss Baldur. Now that Miss Baldur is alive, rather than dead, we can understand why he was afraid."

"He felt guilty," Jerry said, feeling mixed emotions himself. "He *was* guilty."

Fairchild tapped a fingernail on his desk, then said, "You may all consider yourselves lucky that Captain Zhang became as desperate as he did, or that someone else became that desperate, because the captain's death is, so far, absolutely the only confirmation we have of your story. Whether it's suicide or murder, it effectively eliminates the weakest link."

Luther said, "Inspector, you still think it might be murder?"

"We can't rule that out, not yet. There was no sign of struggle. There was that note, however ambiguous. There was the timing, immediately after you two questioned him about Miss Baldur. We would, however, prefer not to be too hasty in our conclusions. There's no need to close that issue at once."

A policeman had brought in another slip of paper while Fairchild was talking, and placed it on his desk. Fairchild looked at it, raised an eyebrow, and looked back up at Kim. "Well, we seem to have another potential corroboration of your story. Looked at a certain way."

Kim said, "What? What's happened?"

"This morning," Fairchild told her, "less than an hour ago, from an undisclosed location, Richard Curtis announced he'd been misinformed about George Manville, that Manville was innocent of the charges brought against him two days ago. All charges have been dropped and Manville is once again employed by Curtis Construction. This was a sort of press conference, a teleconferencing hookup with a number of prominent business newspapers and television outlets, including CNN, which is where we got it. George Manville is no longer charged with any crime." Fairchild tapped the piece of paper. "It would seem, Miss Baldur," he said, not without sympathy, "that your friend is Richard Curtis's friend now."

15

After lunch, Curtis went riding for an hour with Albert Farrelly. Albert showed him the new swales that had been bulldozed since he'd been here last.

"It's terrific work, Albert," Curtis said. "First-rate work."

They rode on, and Curtis said, "Albert, you know that George Manville is staying here for a week or two."

"Yes, sir, I do," Albert said. "We'll take care of him, make him feel at home."

"Do that. But the truth is, Albert," Curtis said, as they rode side by side, quartering westward now, looping toward home, "he's not actually a guest here so much as a prisoner—though he doesn't know it. Or I hope he doesn't know it."

Surprised, Albert said, "Prisoner? I thought he was a friend of yours. Isn't he who you were talking about, on the TV?"

"He is. I had to give him that, Albert," Curtis explained, "because he's in a position where he could make a lot of trouble for me, over the next few weeks, if he really wanted to. And I think he may want to."

"Good heavens, Mr. Curtis, why?"

"It's hard to know why a man turns against you," Curtis said. "I thought we worked well together. It may be he thought I was taking too much credit, or not paying him well enough, or who knows what. He knows my plans, a big construction job coming up, and he could make a great deal of trouble for me if he decided to. That's why I want him to stay here. He agreed, all right, but I have to tell you I don't entirely trust him."

Solemnly, Albert said, "Mr. Curtis, what do you want me to do?"

"Keep an eye on him. Don't let him have any of the vehicles, for any reason at all. It would be better not to let him near a phone; remove them all, except in your office and bedroom, and keep those doors locked."

"Yes, sir."

"And if you think he's planning something he shouldn't," Curtis went on, "those three fellows that brought him here, that are over in the spare barracks, they'll take care of things for you. Just talk to Morgan Pallifer. But not unless there's something you don't think you can handle by yourself."

"Those fellas," Albert said, and he couldn't entirely keep a tinge of distaste from his voice, "aren't the sort I'm used to, Mr. Curtis."

"I feel the same way about them," Curtis assured him. "But sometimes we have to use the tools at hand. One or more of them may leave for a while early next week, but most of the time they'll be here, and we'll make sure Manville knows it. Oh, and if Morgan wants to use the phone, let him use the one in the office."

"Yes, sir." Albert managed a shaky laugh. "Even in a paradise like this," he said, "life can get complex can't it?"

"It surely can," Curtis said.

Leaving the horses with Albert, Curtis walked over to the building they called the spare barracks, a long low adobe shoebox of a structure, with a verandah on one long side. Entering the building, Curtis heard the sound of the TV, followed it, and found the three men sprawled on sofas, watching an old MGM musical, the bright colors looking bruised on the screen. "Morgan," Curtis said, and gestured, and Pallifer got to his feet, glanced one last time at the girls dancing in white crinoline, and came out of the room with him.

"We're off in a few minutes," Curtis told him, as they walked together down the hall. "Now, I've got my agreement with Manville, and I think he's the kind will stick to it, but in case he does try to leave, you'll stop him."

As they went out the wide door to the verandah, Pallifer said, "How hard do I stop him?"

They stood under the verandah roof. Curtis squinted across at the adobe main house, dun-colored, disappearing into the landscape despite its two-story height. "You don't kill him," he said, "unless you absolutely have to. But if he makes trouble… let me put it this way. I don't need him to be able to walk, I just need him to be able to think."

"For two weeks maximum, you say."

Curtis looked at Pallifer, the leathery face, the cold sharp eyes, the bony brow. What a nasty son of a bitch, Curtis thought. I'm glad *I* own him, and nobody else. "When I'm finished what I'm doing," he said, "you and Manville can work out whatever problems you two might have, makes no difference to me."

Pallifer smiled his mean little smile. Those small white teeth weren't his own, but they gave him the right carnivore look. He said, "How will I know when you're finished?"

Curtis laughed. He was so full of his secret that it kept bubbling out of him, he couldn't help it. "You'll know," he promised, and patted Pallifer's rock-hard shoulder. "Don't worry, Morgan, you'll know."

"If you say so," Pallifer agreed.

Curtis looked at the main house again. Manville was in there somewhere. Fixed in place? Time would tell. "About the girl," he said.

"No change, I take it."

"No change. Monday or Tuesday, you should know where she is. As far as the world's concerned, she's already dead, somewhere else, so you shouldn't leave any bodies lying around, to confuse things."

"I got that."

Curtis nodded at the main house. "And he shouldn't know," he said. "It could make the agreement come unstuck."

"I'll play Manville like a guitar," Pallifer promised. "The way those old rock stars used to. Play it and play it, and at the end you smash it up."

The shower connected to the master bedroom was almost a room in itself, a large square space with two tiled walls and two clear lucite walls. Washing off the trail dust from his ride with Albert, Curtis felt good, better than he'd felt in months, maybe years. Revenge was coming, and profit was coming. When he was finished, he'd be the richest man he knew, one of the richest men in the world. And safe as houses. Even if there were people who suspected he'd had something to do with the disaster, nobody would be able to prove it. The evidence would be gone, destroyed, buried like the Japanese barracks on Kanowit Island. Washed clean away, like the orangey-tan dust of Kennison, swirling away down the shower drain.

Cindy was in the main room, packing her overnight bag when he came out. "Call one of the boys to take our things to the chopper," he told her, crossing the room to the closets. "I just have to say a word to George, and we're off."

He found Manville in the library, reading a history of the early days in Australia, when it was being settled by convicts from Britain. Brisbane, Curtis remembered, was settled exclusively by convicts who'd committed fresh crimes after arriving in Australia; what a beginning.

"We're off, George."

Manville closed his book and rose from his low leather chair. "I guess you'll be phoning me," he said.

Curtis noticed that, from where Manville had been sitting,

he'd had a clear view out a window to the spare barracks and the verandah. Had he watched Curtis and Morgan talk together over there? Did he guess any of what they'd been saying to one another? Curtis said, "If you need anything while you're here, ask Morgan, he'll be traveling back and forth."

"And keeping an eye on me," Manville said.

Curtis's smile was easy, relaxed. "I trust you, George," he said. "You're a man of your word, and so am I."

"It does take two," Manville agreed.

Curtis stuck out his hand. "We'll talk."

Why did Manville always seem so surprised, every time Curtis offered to shake hands? I'm accepting you as an equal, you damn fool, Curtis said inside his head, be grateful for it.

Manville did consent to the handshake, grasping Curtis's hand briefly, then letting go. "Have a good trip," he said.

Curtis was almost out of the house, following Cindy, when Helen Farrelly called to him from down the hall. "You go ahead," he told the girl, "I'll catch up."

Helen bustled up to him, but not, as he'd expected, merely to say goodbye. "We've had a phone call just a few minutes ago," she said. "Some sad news."

"Oh?"

"The captain of your yacht. Captain Zhang?"

What now? Curtis thought, and knew at once that this was fresh trouble. "Yes? Captain Zhang?"

"He's killed himself, Mr. Curtis," she said. "And no one knows why."

16

The flight from Brisbane to Sydney was full, and delayed, so that they sat on the ground for twenty minutes before takeoff. Kim didn't care. She was too full of everything else that was happening to worry about simple problems like travel delays. She was both eager and apprehensive, eager to see her parents, and apprehensive about George Manville.

Could George really have caved in to Richard Curtis, the way everybody else thought, even that police inspector, Fairchild? She couldn't believe it, and yet what other explanation was there? Why would Curtis clear George's name—as casually as he'd smeared it—if George hadn't agreed to come over to his side, to help him in whatever it was he was scheming?

But how could she have been so wrong about him?

They'd given Kim the window seat, with Jerry in the middle seat to her left, and Luther on the aisle. She sat and looked out at other planes landing and taking off, little trucks scurrying busily this way and that, and her brain scurried like the little trucks around the problem of George Manville, while beside her Luther and Jerry talked. Until something Luther said attracted her attention, and she turned away from the dreary sight of Brisbane International Airport to say, "What was that? *Where* are you going from Sydney?"

"Singapore," Jerry repeated.

"But why?"

"Curtis, of course," Jerry said, surprised at her. "If what he's up to next is so damn important, if he was actually willing to commit *murder* just to keep me from finding out what he's doing—and I must say I didn't know I was that important in his life, the bastard, and I'm glad I am—well, I have to find out what he's doing, don't I?"

"I suppose," Kim said. She hadn't been thinking about Richard Curtis at all.

Jerry said, "And his headquarters is in Singapore, and I just happen to have a friend in his offices there, *he'll* know what's going on, or he'll be able to find out."

"This is the man," Kim said, "that told you things before, about what Curtis was doing."

"Like Kanowit Island, for instance," Jerry said. "Yes. So we'll go to Singapore, Luther and I, and we'll find out what Curtis is up to, and we'll stop him *cold*."

"I'll come with you," Kim said, so quickly that the words were out of her mouth almost before the thought was in her head.

Jerry frowned at her. "Why? Kim, haven't you been kicked around enough?"

"I want to know what George is up to," she said. "If Richard Curtis is based in Singapore, and if that's where he's planning whatever it is he's going to do, then that's where George will be."

Luther, leaning forward to speak past Jerry, said, "Kim, if you'll take advice from an old campaigner in the wars of love, forget the name George Manville. Go home to Chicago with your mother and father."

Kim knew that Luther meant well, and that he felt kindly toward her, but every time he tried to say something sympathetic, it came out sounding like an order that you were almost honor-bound to disobey. "Thank you, Luther," she said. "You may be right, but I just can't walk away from all this until I know what's going on. If you and Jerry don't want me along, I'll go to Singapore on my own."

"It's not that at all," Jerry said. He put a hand on Luther's arm.

Luther shook his head. "If you're that determined to go into the lion's den, Kim," he said, "and Jerry's determined to let you, better you stick with us."

"Thank you," she said, and the plane jerked forward, on its way at last.

Tired, cranky passengers pressed against one another like cattle in a chute, getting off the plane. Kim just let the movement take her, not really caring anymore, but then she saw her dad's face back there among the people waiting, and next to him Mom, and she waved her arm high above her head and saw them start when they spotted her, and she began pushing and shoving along with everybody else.

Greetings were breathless, and incoherent at first, until they got away from the deplaning crowds, and then her dad said, "I rented a car, just follow me. Is that all your luggage?"

She held up the new string bag she'd bought this morning in Brisbane. "It's all I've got."

Dad turned to Jerry and Luther, saying, "We'll give you a lift to the hotel."

Kim's mom put her arm through Kim's, leaning in to say, "When I thought you were dead, Kim, it was the worst day of my life." Kim pulled her close. Her chest still ached, but she didn't care.

She'd tell them about Singapore later. They'd try to argue her out of it, like Luther had, and she'd stand her ground, and maybe there'd be tears or shouting. But that would be later. Right now she just felt so good to have her mom's hand in hers and to squeeze it tight.

By Sunday afternoon, Manville was edgy, tense, frustrated. He was also desperately bored. He knew his best move right now was not to move at all, to stay here at Kennison as though he intended to stick to his bargain with Curtis, but it wasn't easy. Still, if he did stay put, just for a few days, if he gave the impression he intended to make no trouble, then Curtis should have no reason to go on pursuing Kim, and the clearing of Manville's name would not be interrupted, and when the time was right he could still do his best to stop Curtis from whatever scheme the man had in mind.

But it was hard, it was very hard. Manville was active by nature, a doer, not a contemplater. There was nothing to do here at Kennison, and beyond that, he was absolutely alone now, since Curtis had clearly said something to the Farrellys; they were cold now, distant, utterly unlike the friendly couple at dinner the first night. Now he ate his meals alone, served by silent staff members in their tan pantsuits.

He had access to almost the entire house—he stayed away from what was clearly the Farrellys' quarters, and they kept the downstairs office locked when they weren't in it—and he was permitted to roam the nearby countryside as well. At times, he sat and watched television, without absorbing any of it, or he leafed through books in the library without taking in the words. And every minute was interminable.

His room wasn't locked at night, and the servants treated him as though he were an ordinary houseguest. But the vehicles in the garage had had their ignition keys removed, and whenever he went for a walk he was aware of Steve or Raf, some distance away, keeping an eye on him. And, worst of all, there were no telephones.

It had to be deliberate. There wasn't a telephone to be seen, not even in the kitchen, though there were phone outlets here and there, and it seemed to Manville he remembered a telephone on a particular end table in the living room when he'd had his first surreal conversation with Curtis.

So Curtis didn't want him making contact with the outside world, which wasn't a surprise. But he needed to. He needed to know when the time was right to get out of here, and more than that, he needed to try to reach Kim.

He'd had no contact with Kim since he'd gone to see the lawyer, Brevizin. She'd escaped from Curtis's men then, but was she safe now? Had she managed to contact her friends at Planetwatch?

Also, she probably knew by now that Curtis had taken back his charges against Manville, which would have to look as though Manville had despite everything gone back to work for Curtis, had become her enemy again. He wanted her to know that wasn't true.

But how could he reach her, how could he reach anybody in the outer world, without a telephone? Kennison was a huge sprawling estate in the middle of nowhere. The nearest neighbor, supposedly, was more than fifty miles away.

The frustration was grinding him down. What if he just gave up this whole plan? He was faking agreement with Curtis, going along with him as though their differences were settled, only to find out what the man was up to; but what if he stopped? What if he managed to escape, though he didn't yet see how he could do that, and made his way back to Brisbane? Found Kim, went with her to the lawyer, then went to the police? What would Curtis do then?

Three things, that Manville could think of. He would bury

Manville and Kim under a horde of lawyers. He would turn
Pallifer and the others loose again, to hunt Manville and Kim
down and rid himself of them forever. And he would go on with
his plan, whatever it was, with no one left to stop him.

Sunday afternoon. Manville roamed the house. In the game
room, trying to distract himself, he shot a little pool, and found
he had to resist the urge to smash something with the cuestick.
On a side wall in here stood a glass-doored gun rack; it was
unlocked, and it was empty.

No more pool. He roamed again, and came to the door of the
office, which was shut and locked, the Farrellys being away in
their own quarters or somewhere else on the grounds. Beyond
this door would be telephones, and guns, and keys to the various cars. He touched the knob, waggled it. Tonight, could he
manage to break in here?

"Oh, sir, please be careful."

He turned, and it was the woman who'd brought him the
change of clothes his first night. He said, "Yes?"

She came toward him down the hall, smiling in a friendly
way, but looking concerned. "You must be careful with that
door," she said. "There's a very loud alarm, when it's locked. If
you break the circuit, it would be terribly embarrassing."

Manville took his hand away from the knob. "Embarrassing,"
he said. "Yes, I suppose it would."

18

It was becoming a joke, but not one Curtis appreciated. Every time he tried to get to Singapore, it seemed, he wound up back in this same penthouse suite in the Heritage in Brisbane. This time, he was waiting to be interviewed by some local policeman named Fairchild, and the subject, stupidly enough, was Captain Zhang.

Killed himself. The man killed himself. Why in God's name did he have to go and do that? And at this time of all times, when the last thing Richard Curtis wanted was official attention. What he planned to do was going to be very loud and very obvious and very destructive, and half the police officers in the world would be looking for the person who'd put it together. Curtis intended to keep himself well in the clear, before, during and after. He wanted not the slightest suspicion pointed in his direction. He was a businessman, he had a solid reputation, he was already rich; who would look at Richard Curtis?

Unfortunately, there were now two people who could cause the police to at least glance in the direction of Richard Curtis. They didn't know enough to stop him ahead of time, but they could certainly finger him afterward, and Curtis had no desire to be a man in hiding the rest of his life. So those two people had to be dealt with, and then no one else could be permitted to learn anything at all about what was to come.

But at least he had a plan. Pallifer would get rid of the girl in the next couple of days, and Manville would remain on ice at Kennison, to be useful if necessary during the operation, and to be dispatched immediately after. So the situation was tricky, but it could be handled. It would be handled.

And now, in the middle of it, damn Zhang has to kill himself! The police would want to know why, of course, and Curtis would have no explanation, nothing but baffled sorrow and sympathy. Zhang had been a good employee, Curtis had had no idea anything was wrong; maybe at home? Without answers, the police would keep asking questions, but Curtis knew better than to make something up. Remain baffled, and wait for it to blow over.

Would Zhang have confided in anybody else on the crew?

It seemed unlikely, but just to be on the safe side, tomorrow morning every man of them would leave Australia. Curtis would lease another ship, hire a captain, man the new ship with the old crew, and send it any damn place; Singapore, why not?

"Probably get there before I do," he muttered, glowering at the Botanical Gardens down below, and the doorbell softly ding-donged.

Three o'clock exactly. Police Inspector Fairchild was a prompt man, apparently. Let him be impatient, too, Curtis thought, as he crossed to the door, let him not give a single shit about some dead Chinaman.

On the phone, Inspector Tony Fairchild had sounded like an older man, gruff-voiced, perhaps pedantic. In person, though, he was something else, more impressive and, if you were the kind to be intimidated, intimidating. He was considerably taller than Curtis, big-boned with very little body fat, and with large big-knuckled hands. He had a hawk head, topped by a stiff brush of gray hair, and he had turned what must be a habitual squint into something that looked more like a disapproving frown. "Mr. Curtis," he said.

"Come in, Inspector. You're prompt."

"I thought you'd appreciate that, being a businessman," Fairchild said, as they shook hands. "Time is money, isn't that it?"

"That is certainly it," Curtis agreed. "Come sit over here."

As they crossed to the sofas, Fairchild looked around in approval, saying, "The last time I was in here, it was to pick up a pair of stock swindlers. Lived high, they did, for a while. These days, to them, I'm afraid, time is only a sentence."

They sat, and from his various pockets Fairchild took a notebook, a pen, and a pair of tiny granny glasses. "Captain Zhang Yung-tsien," he said.

Curtis sighed, and shook his head. "Poor Captain Zhang. I am absolutely astounded."

"No hint this was coming?"

"None. Well, in truth, I don't know the man—I mean, I didn't know the man that well."

"Only as an employee."

"Yes."

"For how long?"

"Three years."

"You get to know a man in three years, don't you, Mr. Curtis?"

"If you're around him all the time," Curtis said. "The *Mallory* is a luxury, Inspector, that I justify by having business meetings on it. I had one last week. Before that, it was probably four months since I'd been on the ship. In three years, I suppose I've been around Captain Zhang for a total of less than two months."

"What does he do— There you are, I'm doing it, too. What did he do with himself the rest of the time?"

"Yachts are not fast," Curtis said. "If I want him in San Francisco, let us say, two weeks from today, he should leave Brisbane by Wednesday at the latest. Most of the time, Captain Zhang was moving the *Mallory* toward where I wanted it next, without me being aboard."

"And when you were aboard, it was usually business."

"Always," Curtis said. "I have a station out beyond the Darling

Downs, that's where I go to rest, when I can. That's where I was when the word came about Captain Zhang."

"You'd gone there from the ship."

"Yes."

"If you don't mind my asking," Fairchild said, peering at Curtis over the top of his little glasses, "this most recent time, what business were you doing on the ship?"

"We're planning a new destination resort," Curtis told him, "on an island out by the reef. I have partners, and we were looking at the first stage of construction."

Fairchild had opened his notebook to a page covered with cramped little writing. He gazed through his glasses at it, then over them at Curtis again, and said, "This work was in the charge of an engineer named Manville?"

"George Manville, yes," Curtis said, and laughed. "You've probably seen our names together in the news, just yesterday."

"Yes, I did," Fairchild agreed. "First, he'd stolen secrets from you, and second he hadn't."

"It's a long story," Curtis said. "I'm sure it has nothing to do with Captain Zhang."

"Still," Fairchild said. "I'm the tidy type, I like to roll all the pieces of string onto the same ball."

"Someone had stolen privileged information from me," Curtis said. "It looked as though it must have been Manville. Angry, I made too hasty an accusation. Robert Bendix is a competitor of mine, who either did or did not pay for these documents. At first, he wouldn't say anything, which is why I thought Manville must be guilty, but it was merely that Bendix didn't want to have to point to the actual thief. Bendix and I know each other, we're friendly rivals, so eventually we spoke on the phone and he cleared Manville's name, and I was happy he had. George and I have always gotten along very well."

"And where is Mr. Manville now?"

"On his way to Singapore," Curtis said. "Which is where I'm supposed to be right now, myself. My main office is there."

"So if I wanted to talk to Mr. Manville," Fairchild said, "I'd have to go through your Singapore office."

"That would be simplest," Curtis agreed. "But what do you want with George? He knew Captain Zhang even less than I did."

"Still, he might have some ideas." Fairchild frowned at his notes again. "I believe there was a young woman guest on your ship as well," he said. "One Kimberly Baldur."

Curtis didn't like this. The conversation had been ranging too far from Captain Zhang almost since they'd sat down together. And now Kim Baldur. What is this police inspector up to?

The girl has gone to the police. That has to be the answer. She told who knows what story, and at the same time Curtis and Manville are in public with accusations and then retractions, and to top it all Captain Zhang has to commit suicide. Naturally this inspector is intrigued; what's going on here?

All right, he's talked with Kim Baldur. What does she know? Nothing that matters, not if this police inspector can be dealt with here and now. Tread carefully, and all will be all right.

Curtis chuckled. "Kimberly Baldur. Kim. Yes. Not exactly a guest."

"Tell me about her."

Curtis did, from the explosions on Kanowit Island to her unconscious in a cabin when he and his business partners helicoptered back to Townsville. And through it all, Fairchild took no notes; meaning he already knew all this.

At the end, Fairchild said, "What happened to Kimberly Baldur next?"

"I have no idea," Curtis said. "I haven't been interested enough to ask. I assume she got off the ship here in Brisbane."

"Well, no," Fairchild said. "She had no passport or other identification, as I understand it, but there's no record of her arrival at Immigration, and there would be."

Curtis did his own angry frown. "Just a second," he said. "The reason *Mallory*'s still here is because she lost a lifeboat. I was told it was just an error, carelessness when the boats were brought back aboard at Kanowit. Does Kim Baldur have something to do with that boat?"

"Ms. Baldur says," Fairchild answered, admitting his knowledge at last, "that people boarded the ship out by Moreton, intending to do her harm, and she and George Manville escaped."

Curtis displayed astonishment. "Pirates? This close to Brisbane? I've never— There are things like that hundreds of miles from here, but not in these waters."

"It is her belief," Fairchild said, "that you sent those people."

"Me? Good God!"

"She believes you wanted her dead," Fairchild went on, "to help you deal with your problems with Planetwatch."

"This is a very crazy and very paranoid young lady," Curtis said. "Inspector, I have *lawyers* to deal with the groups like Planetwatch, and they do it very well. The situation is, the environmentalists are on one side, and the developers are on the other, and we both lobby government, and compromises are worked out, so that business can go on and the planet is once again saved. That's the way it works. We're businessmen, we don't *kill* people. Inspector, I do not know of one businessman in the world who ever murdered an environmentalist. The idea is absurd."

By now, Fairchild was smiling. "I suppose it is," he said. "Put it that way, and I do see what you mean. And if it weren't for Captain Zhang's suicide, I would be most inclined to think of Ms. Baldur as a young woman with far too much imagination.

But here we have it. Captain Zhang. Why did he kill himself?
You profess not to know. Would you like to hear Ms. Baldur's
theory?"

"I'd love to," Curtis said, "though I have the feeling I should
be eating popcorn while listening to it."

Fairchild acknowledged that with the thinnest of smiles, and
said, "She is convinced you wanted her dead, in order to tie up
Planetwatch in the courts. She believes you wanted Captain
Zhang to do the job, but that when he wouldn't, or couldn't, you
arranged to have men intercept the ship, and ordered Captain
Zhang to slow down to help the villains get there. She believes
Captain Zhang was a basically good man who grew despondent
at the things you'd asked him to do, and who grew afraid there
would be too many questions directed at him. When Ms. Baldur's
parents tried to talk to him, he pretended not to speak English.
None of us can understand why he'd do that, unless he had
some guilty knowledge."

Curtis sat back in the sofa, "Inspector," he said, "you may be
right. I'd never even suspected the man."

Fairchild raised an eyebrow. "Of what?"

"I assume it's some sort of smuggling," Curtis said. "As I say,
I'm rarely on the *Mallory*. Captain Zhang had the ship to himself most of the time. He could have been smuggling who knows
what—dope? jewels? even *people*, for all we know—for years."

Fairchild now was taking notes, and his expression was intense, brow furrowed. He said, "So you're saying, these people
who came aboard—"

"They weren't from me," Curtis told him. "I'll say that flat
out, that's not the sort of thing I do. So if there *were* these
people, and if Captain Zhang slowed for them, then they must
have had something to do with *him*. And here was an unwanted
witness, Kim Baldur, so naturally they tried to kill her. But she

escaped, and Captain Zhang realized the truth would come out. No wonder he pretended he couldn't speak English. And then he saw there was no way out. Or just the one way out."

Fairchild flipped back and forth between new notes and old. "Ms. Baldur says she left the ship with George Manville."

"Well, I don't know why she'd say that. Unless— Inspector, *when* did she say that about George Manville? Was it after I'd accused him, but before I admitted I was wrong?"

"As a matter of fact," Fairchild said, "yes."

"Then there you are," Curtis said. "The enemy of my enemy is my friend. The woman had no proof, no corroboration. In her fantasy, she thought Manville would agree to her story, to get back at me."

"After you accused Mr. Manville," Fairchild said, "did he, do you know, consult a lawyer locally, named Brevizin?"

"I haven't the faintest idea," Curtis said. "I'm sure he consulted someone, but I don't know who."

"I'm wondering what he might have said to Mr. Brevizin."

"Inspector," Curtis said, "let me end this. Tomorrow I'll arrange for George Manville to phone you from Singapore."

"I'd appreciate that," Fairchild said.

"Believe me," Curtis told him, "if George had been involved in piracy and hugger-mugger on the *Mallory*, he would have mentioned it. He's not one to keep a good story to himself."

Fairchild laughed, and put away his notebook. "I'm sure you're right." Standing, he said, "I appreciate your time, Mr. Curtis."

He's converted, Curtis thought. All he has to do is hear from Manville tomorrow, and the new story is in place: Zhang was a smuggler, it was *his* associates who attacked Kim Baldur, and however she got off the ship it wasn't with Manville. A dead smuggler and a disbelieved fantasist, and I can get on with my work.

Also getting to his feet, Curtis said, "Inspector, I meant to send a note and a check to Captain Zhang's wife. I'm sorry it turned out he was betraying me, using my ship that way, but I'll still send the note and the check."

"Very good of you, Mr. Curtis," Fairchild said.

"Without saying anything about these suspicions," Curtis added. "We could still be wrong, I think. There could still be some other explanation."

"I doubt it," Fairchild said. "But we will, of course, keep an open mind."

"Of course."

"Good afternoon, Mr. Curtis."

"Good afternoon, Inspector."

The instant Fairchild was gone, Curtis crossed to the telephone, and called the station. Helen Farrelly answered, in her quarters, and Curtis said, "Helen, would you unlock the office and let Morgan Pallifer in there and tell him to call me at the Heritage in Brisbane?"

Yes, she would, and everything was fine there, no trouble, and five minutes later the phone rang.

"Curtis."

"Morgan here."

"Morgan," Curtis said, "I want you to spend some time today and tomorrow morning with Manville."

"Oh, yes?"

"I want you to listen to him, because I want you to be able to *do* him by tomorrow afternoon."

"Do him?"

"I mean talk like him. Talk enough like him on the telephone so that a man who's never met him will believe it's him."

"That shouldn't be hard. We're both American."

"Yes, but there's the sound of the voice, the tone, if one

person was going to describe it to another. Your voice is a little higher-pitched. Anyway, you can do it. And tomorrow at one you'll call my office in Singapore, and ask for Margaret."

"Margaret, yes."

"Margaret will patch you in to a call to Brisbane, to a police inspector named Tony Fairchild."

"I get it. I'm calling from Singapore."

"And you're George Manville. And on that last night on the *Mallory*, you slept like a baby, heard nothing, saw nothing, left the ship in Brisbane the ordinary way next morning. And you didn't see Kim Baldur that morning, but you didn't think about it. And you're happy to be working for Richard Curtis again, and you'll give Inspector Fairchild the number in Singapore— Margaret will tell you—where he can call you back if he needs any more."

Morgan Pallifer laughed. "I've never delivered anybody's last words before," he said.

Andre Brevizin entered the offices of Coolis, Maguire, Brevizin & Chin at exactly ten-thirty Monday morning, as was his wont, and Angela Brother, the firm's excellent receptionist, raised two fingers as she said, "Two calls."

"Good God," Brevizin said. "Before I even get to my office? My papers? I'm not sure I like the pace you're setting, Angela."

"They're both interesting," Angela promised.

"At this hour? Try me."

"The one is from a police inspector, Tony Fairchild. He rang at nine this morning, he wants to meet with you sometime today."

"A police inspector? As a client, or as a policeman?"

"As a policeman. You can help with his enquiries."

"We'll see about that. And the other?"

"Richard Curtis."

It took a second for the penny to drop, and then Brevizin said, "Angela! No!"

"Yes. He would also like an appointment. I promised to call them both."

"Yes, indeed. What do we know about this policeman? What's his name again?"

"Tony Fairchild. I've put notes on your desk. He's something high up in criminal investigation. He's the one who captured Edders and Petersen, remember? The stock fraud people."

Some of Brevizin's friends had been caught up in the Edders and Petersen swindles; Brevizin remembered it well. Had some client of his now been doing something iffy in the market? "We'll talk to him second," he decided. "This afternoon. Richard Curtis first. Let's try for eleven-thirty, after my tea."

✿

Richard Curtis was as Brevizin had imagined him; a tough man, exuding power and energy. He dressed casually but well, and his eye and handshake were firm. Brevizin, in his enquiries over the weekend, had heard a few faint hints of shakiness in the Curtis empire, but nothing drastic and nothing solid. The man himself seemed solid enough, and not at all shaken.

They sat together where on Friday Brevizin had talked with George Manville, and Curtis got immediately to the point: "I believe you had a conversation last Friday with a friend of mine, George Manville."

Brevizin smiled amiably. "A friend of yours?"

"We're friends now," Curtis said, taking no offense. "And I believe we'll stay friends. This little flurry is over."

"Flurry."

"George told you what we're doing on Kanowit Island?"

"The destination resort, yes."

"And his technique for reshaping the land."

"Yes," Brevizin said. "I won't claim I understood it, but he did tell me."

"Fine." Curtis sat back and spread his hands. "It is George's technique, more than anyone's, I've never denied it, and it's brilliant, and I've never denied *that*. And I pay well for it. George is a top man, and he gets top wages, or any one of my competitors would steal him away in a minute."

Curtis paused, as though Brevizin might want to comment on that, but Brevizin merely continued to smile at him, so he went on, saying, "I'm afraid George got greedy, decided he wanted more than top wages, he wanted to be a partner, to own a piece of *me*. I don't work that way, Mr. Brevizin. I've had operations with partners, where each shared the same financial risk, put the same amount in the pot, took equal shares out.

Expertise is not enough. Expertise does not get shares, it gets wages. You, for instance, are very well known in corporate legal circles in Australia. George chose well."

"Thank you," Brevizin said.

"You bring great expertise to your clients," Curtis said, "and in return they pay you very high fees."

"They do."

"But they do not give you pieces of their companies."

"Point taken," Brevizin said.

"That's what this whole thing has been about," Curtis said. "George made his demands, I turned them down. He didn't know how to get at me, force me to agree, and he concocted this little scheme. I told you he's brilliant, which doesn't mean he's practical. He thought he'd play hardball with me by running down my reputation, and continue to smear me until I came around. Spread rumors that I'd gone bust, for instance, I don't know if he gave you that one."

Brevizin smiled, and waited.

Curtis shook his head, waggled a hand. "I'm sorry, no," he said, "I wasn't asking you to repeat your conversations with a client. I'm merely saying this is the sort of rumor he was trying to spread within the industry, and he might have done it with you. No matter. The point is, the rumors got back to me, as they will, and as he wanted them to."

"Yes."

"Well, I can play hardball, too," Curtis said, and he looked as though he very well could. "I don't need my reputation smeared, I don't need him spreading wild stories about what a desperate man I am—you wouldn't believe the things that have come back to me—"

"I might," Brevizin said, "but as you say, no matter. You decided to play hardball as well."

"I cooked up a charge against him," Curtis said, almost defiantly, as though challenging Brevizin to say he'd been wrong. "Industrial espionage."

"Well, well," Brevizin said. "You do surprise me, Mr. Curtis. On Friday, Mr. Manville insisted the charges against him were made of whole cloth, and I said then I found it improbable that a reputable businessman like yourself would lie under oath in an affidavit about such a thing. And now you yourself tell me you did."

"Because I knew I could undo it at any time," Curtis said, "and because I knew no one would ever be able to prove I lied. Because it was the one way to bring George Manville to heel."

"I'd wondered about that announcement over the weekend," Brevizin said, "retracting the charges. I'd wondered if you'd been forced to reverse yourself, but you say no."

"George gave up his rebellion," Curtis said, "as I'd thought he would. He's back in Singapore now, at my main office, where I'm headed this afternoon. It was always more ego than greed, in any case, with George, and we've worked out a compromise. A clearer demonstration of the value I place on him. Change of title, better staffing. The truth is, Mr. Brevizin, I think I was taking George too much for granted, there was wrong on both sides, and it won't happen again."

"Then the story he told me last Friday…"

"Was a pack of lies. Well, no," Curtis amended himself, "it was half a pack of truth *plus* half a pack of lies. We were in dispute, that's true. He is the creator of the technique we used on Kanowit Island, that's true. I did knowingly falsely accuse him and deliberately put him in a very difficult position, that's also true. But the rumors of my poverty and desperation, well—what did Twain say? 'The report of my death was an exaggeration.'"

"And the girl he told me about? Kim Baldur?"

Curtis made a sour face. "Yes, I'm afraid George did hook up with those Planetwatch people for a while. Trying to get at me any way he could, of course. Those people are insane, I really believe they are. They're likely to say *anything*."

"Some of my clients have crossed their path," Brevizin said, "and I must say their reaction is much the same as yours."

"It takes a very particular kind of person, it seems to me," Curtis said, "to believe it's your job to rescue something as large as a planet."

Brevizin laughed. "I must repeat that," he said, "to one or two friends of mine." Manville, he was thinking, had been very glib and plausible last Friday, and Curtis is being very glib and plausible today, with utterly opposed stories to tell. Either could be lying, anything could be the truth, but Brevizin found himself leaning more toward Curtis's version, for two reasons. First, the fact that Manville was unquestionably back working with Curtis again, something he'd be unlikely to do if he really believed Curtis was trying to kill him. And second, the fact that Curtis's story didn't have any melodrama in it.

"But now," Curtis said, "as to why I'm here. George was very impressed by you, so that's why you're the one I've come to."

"Thank him for me."

"I will. What's happened is, we've had another problem, out of the blue. The captain of my yacht had been using it, when I wasn't around, for smuggling. We don't yet know what, or who he was dealing with, only that he thought he was about to be exposed, and last Friday he killed himself. Here, in Brisbane. The ship is here—"

"The *Mallory*."

"Of course, George would have mentioned the ship. The investigation into Captain Zhang is just getting underway; in fact, I had a conversation yesterday with the policeman in charge, Inspector Fairchild."

Brevizin smiled and nodded. "I've heard the name," he said.

"My ship has been used," Curtis said, "without my knowledge or permission. In an ongoing criminal enterprise. I don't know what legal ramifications this could hold for me or the ship, in Australia. In some countries, the ship would be impounded. Now, I *must* get back to Singapore today. I would like to retain your firm to represent my interests in connection with the *Mallory*, for so long as she remains here."

"We don't do criminal work, you know," Brevizin said.

"I hope it doesn't come to that," Curtis told him. "I should think it would mostly be negotiating with the proper authorities. If a criminal lawyer is eventually needed, I'd be happy to accept your recommendation."

"Thank you."

"So that's why I'm here," Curtis said.

Brevizin said, "Mr. Curtis, are you also here to undo the things Mr. Manville said to me on Friday?"

Curtis beamed. "Of course! He and I both went pretty public before we settled down. I've made his reputation whole again, but he can't quite do the same for me. Rumor is hard to kill. Yes, I would definitely like you to squelch the rumors anywhere you find them. If you're afraid this would be a conflict of interest, I'll have George phone you from Singapore tomorrow. We are of one mind now."

"No, I understood that from CNN," Brevizin said. "Well, you know, I must say I quite enjoyed the image of you as some sort of rampaging freebooter. But, as usual, reality, though less enjoyable, will have to do."

"Then you'll accept me as a client?"

"I had not actually accepted Mr. Manville as a client, expecting to see him back here today, so there is no conflict of interest. Yes, of course, I'll see what needs to be sorted out with the

Mallory, and if I happen across any rumors about you I'll laugh them to scorn."

"Thank you," Curtis said, and as they both stood, he said, "You might call Inspector Fairchild, see how he's coming along."

"I'm sure I'll speak with him," Brevizin said.

20

Tony Fairchild was making notes to himself, in the tiny crabbed writing he'd learned as a boy, when there'd never been enough money for food, much less for paper. These days, he wrote in small memo pads appropriate to the size of his penmanship, because he was well aware that his writing looked ridiculous on something the size of, say, a legal pad, where a lonely Tony Fairchild paragraph would be a tiny forested island in a great yellow sea.

He was writing notes to himself about Captain Zhang, and George Manville, and Kim Baldur, and Richard Curtis.

He was writing mostly questions, not because there weren't any answers but because there were far too many answers, and they didn't fit together. Usually, it was the policeman's job to get the principals in an investigation to open up and tell their stories; this time, only dead Captain Zhang had ever shown the slightest inclination to keep his mouth shut.

If only the stories jibed in some way, in any way at all. Being a self-made man from a poverty-stricken family, who'd never gotten a boost up from a bloody soul, Fairchild was naturally anti-Curtis in his sentiments, naturally assumed that the richest man in the room was always the biggest villain, and yet this time the rule didn't seem to hold true.

For Kim Baldur to be telling the truth, Curtis would have had to overreact to a truly astonishing degree at the presence of Planetwatch next to his Kanowit Island property. Fairchild had had people look into Curtis's history, and had found plenty of pugnacity there, any number of lawsuits and lawyers, but absolutely nothing extra-legal, if you didn't count the normal businessman's corner-cutting. Curtis's struggles a few years ago with the Chinese authorities, after Hong Kong had been returned by the British, had been monumental and had ultimately got him nowhere, but even then he'd limited himself to the courts. Oh, there'd probably been a bribe or two here and there along the way, but that too was only business.

So Fairchild thought it most probable that Curtis was being maligned here, though he wasn't entirely certain why, and that was one of his biggest questions. What did Kim Baldur hope to get out of all this? Why would she tell these stories if they weren't true?

Baldur was clearly under the control of that fellow Diedrich; could he be the one behind it? Fairchild hadn't taken to Diedrich at all, had found him hyperbolic and melodramatic and probably basically untrustworthy, but could it possibly be that Baldur was merely parroting stories Diedrich had fed her, with no other reason than that Diedrich, who had an acknowledged antipathy to Curtis, was hoping to make some extra trouble for the man along the way? It seemed a very strange thing to do; and yet.

Sergeant Willkie stuck his carrot-topped head in at the office door: "Sir, a Mr. George Manville on the line, from Singapore."

Fairchild looked at the small clock on his desk: eleven-fifty. That would be nine-fifty in the morning in Singapore, which would be about right. Curtis would have briefed Manville first, of course. He said, "Sergeant, tell them I'm in the loo, I'll call right back within five minutes, and get a phone number. Once you've got it, say, 'Oh, here he is,' and put me on."

"Right, sir."

Fairchild put down his pen. Much would depend on what Mr. Manville had to say for himself. *Had* he left the Mallory in mid-ocean, with Kim Baldur? Had the two of them kicked around Brisbane together for the latter half of last week?

There was just one verifiable point in the opposing stories: Baldur claimed to have left the ship with Manville, Curtis claimed that Manville had left the ship alone. One story had to be false, one storyteller a liar.

Sergeant Willkie's head appeared again: "He's on the line, sir."

"Very good." Fairchild picked up the phone: "Fairchild here."

"Good morning, Inspector." It was an American voice, of course, mid-range, but with some faint tinge of accent in it, as though the speaker had been away from home a long time. Which was probably true, Manville being an engineer whose work history was almost exclusively around the Pacific Rim. "George Manville here," the voice went on. "Mr. Curtis says you want to talk to me."

"Yes, thank you, Mr. Manville. Mostly it's about Captain Zhang Yung-tsien. You knew him on the *Mallory*, didn't you?"

"Well, I don't say I knew him. We said hello once or twice."

"Didn't you have your meals with him? I understood you'd been a few weeks on the ship, out at Kanowit Island."

"Oh, sure, I ate with the officers, but they mostly gabbed together, you know, and I don't talk any of that. I had my own people I worked with, didn't have much to do with the crew."

"Ah. You remember Kim Baldur."

"The idiot from Planetwatch. Oh, yeah, I remember her."

"Were you together with her in Brisbane at all?"

"*Together* with her?" The disgust in the man's voice certainly sounded genuine, "I was never together with that piece at all. Why would I be together with her?"

"Well, did you leave the ship together?"

"I never even saw her that morning, she wasn't around for breakfast. Still in bed, I suppose. I was up and out, soon as we docked. I had things to do."

"Such as see Mr. Brevizin."

A little pause, and, "Who?"

"The lawyer, Brevizin. You—"

"Oh, right! When Mr. Curtis and I had our little, whadaya-callit, difference of opinion. That's all over now."

"But that was one of the things you had to do, see Mr. Brevizin. Were you doing other things at the same time, having to do with Richard Curtis? Other people you were seeing?"

"That's all done," Manville said. His voice had risen half an octave, he sounded as though he might be getting irritated, or upset. "I don't have to talk about that."

"Mr. Manville, I'm not accusing you of anything, I merely—"

"Captain Zhang killed himself, that's what I heard, and that's what you're looking into. That's what you're looking into, isn't it?"

"Yes it is, but—"

"I was on his ship for a while, ate some meals at the same table with him, heard him talk Chink with his crew, and that's it. If you want to know why he did the chop on himself, you'll have to ask somebody else."

"I see," Fairchild said. Firmly holding down his own irritation, he said, "Well, I appreciate your speaking with me, in any event."

"Inspector, I'll tell you the truth," Manville said.

He was sounding more and more like a tough guy, less and less like an engineer. "I want to get along with Mr. Curtis these days," he said, "and he asked me to call you, so here I am. But I don't think he wants me to talk about me and him, so that's what I'm not gonna do."

"I understand completely," Fairchild said. "Thank you, Mr. Manville. If I want to call you again..."

"I'm here," Manville said. "Working hours."

"Fine. Thank you."

Fairchild replaced the receiver, and sat tapping his pen point against his memo pad, but wrote nothing down. Manville had not been exactly as anticipated, but on the other hand it was now easier for Fairchild to understand the battle of wills that had gone on last week between him and Curtis. He sounded like a man who could be quick to anger and quick to action. A diamond in the rough, it could be, a fellow from the wrong side of the tracks like Fairchild himself, got his education, became an engineer, highly thought of, but with the guttersnipe still there inside him, ready to be called upon.

And Manville supported Curtis, that was the important thing. So that should settle it; except that it didn't, not quite. Something faintly buzzed at Fairchild's attention, some fold in the fabric. Or it could be simply the possibility that Manville was lying now merely to cement his newly good relationship with Curtis.

But had Manville's reaction to Kim Baldur's name been a lie? Surely not. That had been real contempt in the man's voice. Baldur's description of Manville's heroics against the thugs who'd boarded the *Mallory* certainly fit with the man Fairchild had just encountered, but that man wouldn't be likely to save Kim Baldur from anything. Push her in harm's way quicker than offer a helping hand.

Five minutes had passed, by the desk clock. Time to make sure no one was pulling a fast one. Fairchild buzzed for Sergeant Willkie, and when he appeared said, "Call that Singapore number, would you? And buzz me when it starts to ring."

"Right, sir."

Fairchild sat thinking, and the buzzer sounded, and he picked up to hear the phone ring, and then a female voice: "RC Structural."

"Mr. Curtis, please."

"Oh, I'm sorry, Mr. Curtis won't be back until tomorrow."

"Who's second-in-command there at the moment?"

"Did you want Mr. Lowenthal?"

That was right, according to Fairchild's information, that was one of Curtis's vice-presidents. Fairchild said, "No, let me speak to Mr. Manville, please."

"May I tell him who's calling?"

"Inspector Fairchild."

"One moment, please."

It was in fact forty seconds by the clock, and here was Manville's tough voice again: "That was quick."

"It turned out I do have one more question," Fairchild told him. "Sorry to interrupt your work."

"Don't worry about it. What's the question?"

"During your time at Kanowit Island, did any other ships come by, make contact with Captain Zhang or anyone else on the crew?"

"Naw. We were alone out there until the very end, when those Planetwatch idiots showed up."

"Well, thank you, Mr. Manville."

"Any time."

Fairchild hung up, satisfied. That was Manville, and he was in Singapore, and that was the office number of RC Structural.

There was nothing here. It was all smoke and mirrors. The public catfight between Curtis and Manville had got caught up in a young woman's self-aggrandizing fantasies, and that was that. Captain Zhang had killed himself, for whatever reason, without a doubt. The two Planetwatch people had watched him unlock his door and enter his room. Very soon thereafter, he had leaped from the window. There was not the slightest sign that anyone else had been in the room. It was not murder, it was suicide, and the case was closed. If Zhang had been engaged in smuggling of some sort, the story would come out sooner or later. For now, there were other cases to think about. It had seemed briefly that Zhang's death would lead to some more complex situation, but it had all dissolved into nothingness.

Fairchild tapped the buzzer on his desk, and when Sergeant Willkie's head popped into view in the doorway he said, "Call that lawyer, Brevizin, thank him for making himself available, and tell him I won't need to speak to him after all."

"Right, sir."

As a result of which, Inspector Fairchild did not get to hear Andre Brevizin describe the events involving Kim Baldur, both on the *Mallory* and here in Brisbane, that George Manville had last Friday related to him.

21

The corporate jet owned by RC Structural had cost sixty-five thousand dollars U.S. per month merely to exist, with its crew and its parking slot at Hong Kong International Airport, and the expenses went even higher whenever Curtis actually used it to go anywhere, so that was the one contraction he'd permitted himself when the money started to tighten and the mainland bastards were squeezing him like an orange. He'd moved his operations to Singapore, but did not move the plane to Changi Airport there, selling it instead—at a decent price, at least—to one of the Chinese businessmen growing sleek on the carcass of the city they'd just killed.

Which meant, these days, when Curtis had to undertake a long flight, he went commercial. But that was all right; he usually took Singapore Air, they knew him, and they treated him well. In fact, he wasn't at all certain, after this current operation was finished and he was rich again, that he'd buy another jet for himself. That was, at his level, no longer a toy that impressed anybody.

Today's flight was at five in the afternoon, it would take under four hours, and arrive in Singapore before seven.

The Daimler that Curtis had loaned Pallifer, that had been used to spirit George Manville away to Kennison, was back in Curtis's possession, along with Harben, the driver, so he rode out to Brisbane International in smooth quiet, spending most of the trip on the phone with aides in his office in Singapore. He'd been away from his workaday business too long.

It would be good when this other stuff was out of the way, mission accomplished, and he could go back to being an ordinary businessman again. He thought of it that way, an oddity, one extraordinary act in the life of an ordinary businessman, who'd been driven to this extreme. But there was so much tension in this plan, and so much he was called on to do that he would never even have thought of doing before. When he'd said, with passion, to that policeman, that he'd never heard of a businessman killing an environmentalist, he'd meant it, meant that it was true, and it was true, and it was something entirely different that, in another compartment in his brain, Richard Curtis was now planning to kill many more than merely one environmentalist. They'd pushed him to it, those bastards, they'd left him no choice but this, to play the game just as hard as they did. Harder.

The airline's meet-and-greet waited for him at the curb in front of the terminal building. She was an attractive young Asian woman in a dark blue uniform, a clipboard held to her breast by her left forearm in echo of the Statue of Liberty. She'd been the one to walk Curtis through this process three or four times before. Her smile was radiantly welcoming. "Good afternoon, Mr. Curtis. So nice to see you again."

"And you." He didn't remember her name, if he'd ever known it.

She turned to speak a quick word to the skycap waiting behind her, and he nodded, and moved toward the car as Harben came around to open the trunk. "Your luggage will be taken care of," she said, "and I have your ticket, so all I need is your passport. You'd like to come to the lounge?"

"Yes. Thank you."

There was great bustle at the main doors to the terminal, down to his right, but the meet-and-greet led him away to the left, down a quiet corridor where they were almost immediately alone. This passage not only took him to the VIP lounge, it also meant he was not in the main part of the terminal three minutes later, when Kim Baldur and Jerry Diedrich and Luther Rickendorf arrived in a cab.

Curtis had a scotch and water in the lounge while the meet-and-greet took his passport and ticket away to handle the formalities for him. He read a *Wall Street Journal* he found there, and was amused to see that the paper still thought there was some story left in his little public dance with George Manville. Neither he nor George were actually mentioned, but the story, a rehash of various questionable activities by Robert Bendix and his Intertekno over the last several years, was clearly inspired by last weekend's flap. So now Bendix receives a little unwelcome publicity, while Curtis goes about his business unobserved; things couldn't get much better than that.

Half an hour later, the meet-and-greet was back, to smilingly hand him his passport and ticket, and escort him to the plane, along with two other businessmen, one a Brit, the other Japanese. Their route was back hallways, mostly empty, not emerging into the normal public area until they were almost to the gate, where the last of the other passengers were straggling aboard. Standard first-class passengers would have been boarded first, for the coach passengers then to sidle past on their way back to steerage, but the ones brought by the meet-and-greet arrived last, when the fuss and bustle were over. At the gate, the meet-and-greet wished her trio a bon voyage and went away, clipboard still shield-like at her breast, while Curtis and the other two were now greeted by equally smiling and equally attractive stewardesses, who took hand luggage (Curtis had none) and drink orders, and escorted their VIPs to their seats.

Curtis always took an aisle seat, for greater mobility; and

what is there to see out of a plane window, after all? Today, his seatmate was a purple-jowled angry-eyed American, already at work, reading what appeared to be a legal brief and making small meticulous notes on a yellow legal pad.

Curtis was immediately reminded of the policeman, Fairchild, and his own crabbed notes, even smaller than this fellow's handwriting, in that notebook of his. Well, he'd done what he could, with both Fairchild and the lawyer, Brevizin, to put out the fires Manville and Kim Baldur had started. With just a small amount of luck, the whole episode would quickly blow over and be forgotten. No crime, no criminals, nothing to investigate, no cause for suspicion. One Chinese sea officer, dead by his own hand, and one idiotic young woman with an overly rich imagination; nothing more.

He accepted his scotch and soda and silently toasted his own success. His seatmate, after one quick scowling glance to reassure himself that Curtis wasn't a beautiful woman, had gone back to work, which was also a plus. Curtis wasn't one for chitchat on airplanes.

Almost immediately, they were taxiing, and as the pilot's voice told the crew to prepare for takeoff the stewardess came by to reclaim Curtis's now empty glass, and just like that they were in the sky. Curtis pushed his seat back and his leg rest out, and dozed, smiling, thinking of how well things were going.

Half an hour later, some alteration in engine sound or plane movement brought him awake, to see his lawyer friend still busy. Time for a magazine. He would prefer *Scientific American* to *Black Enterprise*, but he'd take what was there. Rising, he walked back to the eye-level shelf where the magazines were stacked, looked through them, settled for *Newsweek*, and glanced down the aisle at the crowded coach section as he was about to turn back to his seat.

Jerry Diedrich.

Curtis stopped. He had never actually met Diedrich, but he'd seen him at a distance several times (several irritating times), and he'd seen Diedrich's self-satisfied face in newspapers at least twice. That was him, in the aisle seat of three, talking with a very animated young woman in the middle seat.

Kim Baldur.

It had to be. Curtis had never seen her conscious, but he remembered that sleeping face, and this was her.

And how very lively she was, alive.

Baldur and Diedrich, together, on their way to Singapore. And the man on the other side, the window seat, the blond Germanic-looking one; was he part of the group? Yes; he turned and spoke to the other two, then looked out his window again, at the nothing out there.

Curtis turned away, not wanting to be recognized. He went back to his seat, the forgotten magazine still in his hand, and the stewardess asked him if he was ready for his snack. Yes. And wine? White, please.

While he ate the caviar, and the shrimp, and the hearts of palm, and the other delicacies, Curtis considered the situation. Those three were on their way to Singapore.

There could only be one reason. They hadn't succeeded in obstructing him in Australia, so they would pursue him to Singapore. They had a mole somewhere in his organization, a spy, he was sure of it; they'd learned he was traveling back today and were on his trail. Diedrich would stop at nothing, would use every advantage, to interfere, to cause trouble. And this time it just couldn't be allowed.

Who is the mole? Who is the spy in my camp? How do I find him, and how do I get rid of him—and of those three back there?

This new project kept constantly moving him into areas beyond his experience as a businessman. In all his enterprises, he had nearly two thousand permanent employees, plus the thousands more hired for specific short-term jobs in construction and the like, but who among them would be useful for the tasks he now had to assign? Those three would get off the plane in Singapore. They had to be met somehow, they had to be dealt with. The spy in Curtis's bosom had to be dealt with.

In the seatback ahead of him there nested a telephone. Who could he call, and what could he say, to have these problems taken care of? He thought about his employees, the ones he knew, and he tried to pick and choose and find the right one. He had no one in Singapore like Morgan Pallifer, and it was too late now to phone Pallifer back in Australia and tell him to hurry in their wake. The three had to be intercepted somehow when this plane landed.

Who in Singapore did he know, and trust? Who could handle a thing like this?

The remains of the snack were taken away. Curtis slid his tray into its space in the armrest. He leaned forward and snapped out the telephone.

THREE

1

Colin Bennett drove his little Honda Civic out the East Coast
Parkway to Changi International Airport, followed the signs to
Terminal 2, and stopped as close as possible to the glass doors
where the arriving passengers streamed out, deploying into the
taxis and buses and limousines and private cars funneled into
orderly ranks; neat and tidy and controlled, like everything else
in Singapore.

His Timex said quarter to seven (he'd long ago pawned the
Rolex), so the Air Singapore flight from Sydney should be landing
just about now. Changi was noted for its efficiency; within fifteen minutes, that flow of incomers over there, through with
Customs and reunited with their luggage, would include the
travelers from Australia.

Bennett picked up the three pages of faxed photos from the
seat beside him, and studied them once again.

Jerry Diedrich. Always with his mouth open, always looking
aggravated and aggrieved. The perfect look for those morons at
Planetwatch.

"This is your lucky day, boyo," he told himself, and smiled
out at the endless herd of travelers, waiting for Jerry Diedrich
to appear. "You'll have no trouble pickin him out," he assured
himself, "and the next thing you know you'll be fat and happy
again, and damn well time for it, too. God bless Richard Curtis
and keep him warm and content."

Colin Bennett had started talking to himself two years ago,
after the wife and kiddies left. He didn't blame Brenda, he knew
he'd turned mean and solitary after he'd lost his job, but there

hadn't seemed to be any way to break out of the pattern. Self-destructive, nasty, he'd become someone no one wanted to be around except himself, so that's who he talked to.

He didn't blame Curtis either, for firing him. Curtis had had damn good reason. And Curtis hadn't even known the full extent of the mess Colin Bennett had made of things. He didn't know a man had died.

Bennett was a construction man by trade, or had been, a big burly fellow—too large for this Honda Civic, for instance, which he seemed to wear rather than ride in—who had worked for RC Structural for nine years before he'd made his beaut of a mistake. In that time, he'd moved up from crew foreman to works manager, running the whole damn site for the engineers. In those days, he was outgoing and popular, a cheerful rowdy sort of man who claimed he got along with everybody because he looked like everybody, which was very nearly true. His father had been half English and half Malay, while his mother was half Dutch and half Chinese, and the mixture had created a big man whose squarish face featured slightly uptilted eyes, a gently mashed nose, a broad mouth and high prominent cheek-bones. His ears lay flat to his skull, and his hair was straight and thick and black, now beginning to gray at the sides.

Bennett was Singapore born and bred, coming into this world when the island was still a British Crown Colony, and he could still remember the three moments of great national celebration during his schooldays, when he and all the other children filled the streets with tiny waving flags. Independence in June of 1959, then joining the Federation of Malaysia on September 16, 1963, and then leaving the Federation to declare itself a republic on August 9, 1965. By the time he was grown and ready to join the workforce, the desperate economic conditions of that republic in its early days had been successfully overcome, and Singapore was ready for the explosive growth that quickly made it a financial powerhouse among nations.

It was that growth which had first attracted Richard Curtis to Singapore, long before the question of the Hong Kong takeover. Thirteen years ago he'd opened the Singapore branch of RC Structural, with Colin Bennett among his first employees. A hands-on man, Curtis had met Bennett several times in the next years, and Bennett was sure Curtis had had a lot to do with his rapid advancement. Curtis had trusted him, and until Belize, Bennett had deserved and repaid that trust.

Belize. Well, it's over now. Has a page been turned? Has a new day dawned?

When the phone rang this afternoon, in his shabby little apartment off China Street, Bennett had been hopelessly studying yet again the help wanted ads in the *Straits Times*. These days, he had one part-time job as a messenger, and another unloading trucks at a lumber yard, but the work was dispiriting and the pay meager. Still, without references…

Then the phone rang. Not knowing what to expect, and not expecting very much, he'd answered, and the astonishing voice had said, "Colin, this is Richard Curtis."

"Mr. Curtis!" It was like getting a phone call from God, it was that impossible.

"I'm calling from an airplane," the astounding Mr. Curtis said, "and I want to make this fast."

"Yes, sir. Yes, sir."

"I'm wondering if you're a more controlled person these days."

"Oh, I am, sir! Honest to God."

"If you do a little job for me, Colin, it might make me think better of you."

"Oh, yes, sir. Just tell me what it is, sir."

"There's an annoying fellow from Planetwatch on this plane. Remember Planetwatch?"

"Oh, do I. Right buffoons."

"Worse than buffoons, Colin. They can make trouble. This fellow, Jerry Diedrich, is *determined* to make trouble. Write that name down."

"Yes, sir!" He already had the pen in his hand, hoping to find job offers to circle, and he wrote the name on the margin of the newspaper.

"When we hang up," Curtis went on, "call Margaret, at my office there, tell her I said she should fax you whatever photos of Diedrich we have in the files. I'm sure there's some, from newspaper pieces about us."

Bennett had no fax himself, nor much of anything else, but the chemist out on China Street did, and would handle it for him. "Yes, sir."

"Diedrich is traveling with two other people, a blonde girl in her twenties and a tall blond man of about thirty."

"Yes, sir."

"Our plane is to land at Singapore at six forty-five. Be outside the terminal. Find Diedrich and his friends and follow them, find out where they're staying. Be sure it's where they're *staying*, so you'll be able to find them again tomorrow."

"Yes, sir."

"Then come to my office at nine-thirty in the morning."

"Yes, sir, I will. And...thank you, sir."

So here he was, at crowded but efficient Changi, waiting in the little Honda Civic, watching those glass doors over there. In the sky, westward toward the city, the last of the rose daylight receded, and here, so close to the Straits, the air was softening, cooling from the day's heat and humidity. The Honda's air-conditioning had given up years ago, so Bennett sat here with the windows open, feeling the day's sweat gradually rise from his face and the back of his neck, while over there the people kept streaming out, streaming out.

It was Curtis he saw first, the well-remembered solid bulk of the man, moving forward with that determined focused stride, following a Malay chauffeur laden down with a large suitcase and a thick garment bag, both in soft-looking tan leather. They crossed not far from Bennett, toward the line of limousines, but Curtis never looked away from the direct path of his progress, making a much straighter line than most of the pedestrians around him.

"A lesser man," Bennett told himself in admiration, "would look around for me, want to know was I on the job. Not Richard Curtis. Richard Curtis *knows* what he wants to be done will be done, and that's all there is to say about it."

He looked away from Curtis, reluctantly, to concentrate again on the exit doors. Such a variety of persons came through those doors, a dozen races, speaking a hundred languages. Western clothing predominated, but there were saris and caftans and turbans and kaffiyehs as well, a great colorful sweep of people on the move.

Diedrich. Yes, that was him, and there was the blonde girl, "A damn pretty blonde girl," he commented, feeling a brief wince of longing for Brenda, and saw the other one, the tall blond man, bony and angular, and said, "Now what the hell kind of boyo is that one?"

The three traveled light, the girl with no more than one fat shoulderbag, the two men each with vaguely military-looking shoulderbags and small gym bags. They joined the taxi line, and Bennett shifted into gear as he took note of the number of the cab they climbed into.

He led them out of the airport. There was only the one road, the one destination, and it seemed to Bennett he'd be less noticeable if he wasn't behind his quarry the whole way. He had no idea, of course, if they knew about Curtis's interest in them, but it was better to mind the details, all in all. "Mind the details, boyo," he told himself, and felt another twinge of memory; the dam in Belize.

Airport Boulevard ran almost south out of Changi, and flowed smoothly into East Coast Parkway, the big new road built to service the big new airport. Now they curved westward, and the brightly lighted towers of Singapore stood out ahead of them, a crystal island on an island, shimmering with light that at times looked hot, at times looked very cold.

Bennett slowed, dawdling in the left lane, the evening breeze a noisy but welcome rush through the Honda's open windows. Two minutes, less, and that taxi rushed by, the three in lively conversation in the back seat.

"Well, they aren't suspicious of anything, are they?" Bennett commented, as he pulled in behind the taxi, three vehicles back. "Not worried, not looking around, not checking their back trail. Not concerned about a thing. Now, that makes it easier, doesn't it?"

2

In his world, Richard Curtis moved from one tower to another. Everywhere he went, it seemed, there were plate glass views of sky and land and city and sea, sprinkled with the tiny unimportant dots that were human beings; barely to be noticed.

This Tuesday morning, Curtis was in his office, with its two walls of huge windows high above Marina Bay, by ten past nine. Margaret, his long-time secretary, an efficient selfless woman who was twenty years older and thirty pounds heavier than when she'd first come to work for him back in Hong Kong, was waiting for him with a variety of briefings and updates on RC projects in half a dozen parts of the world, but they'd barely gotten underway when the internal telephone on Curtis's desk made its nasal buzz.

Margaret, standing beside the desk, answered the phone, spoke briefly, then told Curtis, "It's reception. There's a Mr. Bennett here, he says he has a nine-thirty appointment with you."

"And so he has," Curtis said.

He was pleased with himself. Yesterday on the plane, he'd gone methodically through the filing system in his brain and he'd come up with the perfect man to do what needed to be done. Colin Bennett would do anything to prove himself, redeem himself in Curtis's eye, and Curtis knew it. A blank check, that's what Colin Bennett was, for Curtis to spend as he saw fit.

"Tell them," he said, "to put him in the small conference room. I won't be long with him, and then we'll get back to all this."

"Yes, sir," she said, and relayed the order, as Curtis got up from the desk and left the office.

By the time Curtis got to the small conference room, an interior space without the usual panorama of windowed view, Bennett was already there. He didn't look good. He was hang-dog for such a big man, and shabby. The last few years hadn't been good to him.

He was eager, though. He stood next to the free-form teak conference table, and when Curtis entered he fairly leaped to attention: "Good morning, sir! Good to see you after all this time."

"And you, Colin." First, Curtis shut the door, then he extended his hand.

Clearly, Bennett hadn't known if he would be considered worthy of a handshake, and was hugely grateful that the answer was yes. He pumped Curtis's hand, not too long, not too hard, then said, "I've got them, you know. I've got them right now."

"Good man."

"They're in Little India," Bennett reported, "in a place called Race Course Court Hotel, on Race Course Lane."

"What kind of place?"

"One of these redone ones," Bennett said. In addition to all the new hotels built in Singapore the last few years, a lot of the older seedier places had been given facelifts, with new plumbing and new wiring and the luxury of air-conditioning. "It's mostly Americans there, I think. Young, not a lot of money."

That sounded right for Planetwatch people. Curtis said, "Would there be phones in the rooms?"

"Oh, I should think so."

"Good. Did they take a suite?"

"No, two rooms," Bennett said, and his large flat face wrinkled in confusion. "I thought it would be man woman in one, man in the other, but it isn't."

"They're fairies," Curtis said.

"Oh." Laughing at himself, Bennett said, "Thick, I am. And that's a pretty girl to be wasted like that."

You have no idea how she would have been wasted, Curtis thought, and said, "I'm going to send you to a shop in Sim Lim, called Vanguard Electronics."

Bennett, apparently remembering Curtis's instruction yesterday to write down Jerry Diedrich's name, now whipped out a small notepad and pen from his pockets and repeated, "Vanguard, in Sim Lim."

"You'll ask for Charlie."

"Charlie," Bennett echoed, and wrote it down.

"I'll have rung him," Curtis said. "He'll give you equipment for bugging their phone. The room where the men are, not the other one."

"Oh, sure," Bennett said.

"I'll want you to check into this hotel— What is it?"

"Race Course Court Hotel."

"Unattractive name," Curtis decided. "You'll check in there for the next few days, try to get a room near them. The phone bug is a radio, and its range isn't very far."

"Will do," Bennett said.

"I'll be paying for the bug," Curtis told him, "but you should put the hotel and other expenses on your credit card, and I'll reimburse you."

Looking sheepish, Bennett said, "Mr. Curtis, I don't have any credit cards just at this minute."

So things are that bad for you, are they? Curtis said, "We'll have to give you cash, then."

"Wouldn't it be better, sir, if I used a corporate card?"

It would not; Curtis didn't want Bennett connected to RC in any way. He said, "I know what you mean, hotels don't expect cash, but I wouldn't want it to get to Diedrich somehow that someone from RC Structural was staying in the same hotel."

"Oh, that's right," Bennett said.

"You'll have a story for them," Curtis suggested.

Bennett looked surprised, then smiled. "Well, I'm a local citizen," he said, "with a Singapore passport, so I'm moving out of my house because the entire building is being fumigated and repainted, and the owner's reimbursed us all in cash."

"That's very good."

Bennett preened under the praise. He'd kill for me, Curtis thought, surprised to realize it was true. And that he might have to.

Turning away, Curtis said, "Let me just ring Margaret."

"Yes, sir."

Curtis rang Margaret from the phone on the long sideboard, saying, "Have someone bring me five thousand dollars," meaning the Singapore dollar, worth slightly more than half the U.S. dollar. Hanging up, he said, "Colin, the situation here is this. This fellow Diedrich has a mole somewhere in these offices."

Bennett looked both astounded and offended: "How could that be?"

"Maybe we'll answer that when we find the mole. And that's your job."

"Yes, sir."

"The reason Diedrich is here," Curtis explained, "and I know the *only* reason he's here, is to find out my future plans, so he can disrupt them. That means he'll be making contact with the person here who's been feeding him information."

Bennett said, "Excuse me, Mr. Curtis, but are you sure? When I worked for you, sir, everyone I knew was loyal."

"A week ago today," Curtis told him, surprising himself by how much had happened within the last week, "I performed an experiment at an island off the Australian coast. There had been no public announcement, there was no information about that experiment released outside these offices. But Diedrich and the Planetwatch ship were there."

"Mm," Bennett said, and shook his head. "You're right, someone must have told them. Sir, I honestly can't think why anybody'd act that way."

Curtis shrugged. "As I say, I'm hoping you'll have the opportunity to ask the fellow in person."

"I'm to find him."

"Yes, you are."

Bennett said, "I'm to move into their hotel, bug their telephone, follow them when they go out. But, sir, I don't know the people working here, how would I recognize the right fellow? I mean, if I hear a conversation on the phone, all well and good, but what if it's just a meeting out on the street, or lunch, or whatever? It could be the right man, or it could be the wrong man."

"Buy yourself a Polaroid camera," Curtis told him. "You're just a tourist, snapping photos, only the photos contain anybody Diedrich talks to."

"Right, sir," Bennett said, smiling. "That's good."

"Bring the pictures here, show them to me or, if I'm not here, Margaret. We'll know if it's one of our people."

"I'll do that, Mr. Curtis," Bennett said, and there was a single knock at the door.

Curtis crossed to open the door, and it was one of the clerks, a young man named Hennessy, holding a thick white envelope, saying, "Miss Kembleby told me to bring this round, sir."

"Thank you, Hennessy."

Handing over the envelope, Hennessy gave Bennett a quick look of curiosity before Curtis closed the door. Curtis gave the envelope to Bennett and said, "If you need more, phone Margaret."

"Oh, I won't need all this much, sir."

"Colin," Curtis said, "I want you to buy yourself some fresh clothes. You know, to look a little more like an affluent tourist."

Bennett, of course, understood that Curtis was actually saying, to look less defeated and shabby. His grateful smile was as much for Curtis's tact as for his money.

"Thank you, sir," he said. "From the bottom of my heart, thank you. You can count on me."

3

Jerry couldn't help his impatience, but it would be folly to call Mark during the day, at work. So they'd have to wait till the evening.

They were staying at an acceptable hotel in Little India, and they spent the morning familiarizing themselves with the area, which was mostly Hindu temples. The Veeram Kali Amman Temple, dedicated to Kali, the goddess of death and destruction, was the most dramatic, with its garish illustration of the black-skinned four-armed goddess ripping apart a human being who'd gotten too close. She was flanked by her sons, Ganeshi the elephant god and Murugan the child god, but she didn't seem to Jerry particularly maternal.

At lunchtime they chose one of the handy vegetarian Indian restaurants. The meal was very good, in fact delicious, but it finished Jerry off. "No more," he said. "If you two want to wear yourselves out, go ahead. I'm going back to the hotel and sleep for an hour. Maybe two." Luther wanted to keep going but Kim sided with Jerry, and they separated outside the restaurant, Luther off to the local subway while Jerry and Kim limped homeward. A shower, Jerry kept thinking. That's all I want, a shower, and then lie down and wait for Luther to come back.

The hotel facade had been given a gaudy overlay on the ground floor during a recent remodeling, large rectangular panels of golden plastic around a wide pair of dark-tinted glass doors. As Jerry and Kim neared the doors, Jerry already sensing the coolness within, smelling the clean water of the shower that awaited him, he heard an odd familiar sound, a kind of ripping or crinkling, and thought, I know that sound, and turned to see a man with a Polaroid camera, standing out at the curb, facing the hotel. The picture he'd just taken extruded even now from the camera, still formless and gray.

Jerry, not liking the idea, said, "Did you take our picture?"

"No, no," the man said. "The front of the hotel." He was a big burly man in a short-sleeved white shirt and pressed tan chinos. Filipino or Samoan, maybe, in his forties.

Jerry found the man intimidating, mostly because of his size, and he didn't feel like forcing the issue. Still, privacy mattered for them right now. He said, "You're sure we aren't on that."

"Well, I don't know," the man said, and looked down at the not-yet-developed picture. "It's just for me," he said, "the hotel where I'm staying." The man shrugged. "If you're in it, I'll throw it away and take another one."

Jerry sighed and decided it was good enough.

Kim had already gone in, drawn by the hope of air conditioning, and stood waiting for him in the lobby. She said, "What was that all about?"

"I don't know, he was taking a picture of the front of the hotel, I thought we might be in it."

Jerry looked back at the street, where the man hunched again over his camera. Moving farther from the doors, he said, "Taking a picture of the front of the hotel. Can you believe it?"

"Tourists take pictures of anything," Kim assured him. "He wants to show his friends where he stayed in Singapore."

"A Polaroid?" Jerry said. "Of this place?"

"I'm going to my room, Jerry, call me later."

"Wait wait, I'm coming."

Riding up in the elevator, Jerry thought, I'll sleep until Luther comes home, and then I'll be with Luther until it's time to call Mark. Six? Yes; call Mark at six.

He'd completely forgotten the tourist with the Polaroid camera.

4

Morgan Pallifer was nearing the end of his rope. Not only was he stuck on land, extremely dry land at that, with no significant body of water for hundreds of miles in any direction, but his job had somehow been reduced to that of babysitter. No action in it at all, no movement. Nothing to do, day and bloody night, but play nanny, with assistant nannies Steve and Raf. Now, there was nothing wrong with Steve and Raf, Pallifer had chosen them because they were professional and reliable in a crisis, but if you didn't happen to have a crisis on your hands, those two were not what you might call stimulating company.

As for George Manville, Pallifer found him a disgusting disappointment. Where was the fire, the resistance, the defiance? Where were the escape attempts, the maneuverings to get at a telephone or a vehicle, the confrontations with his jailers? But no; all Manville did was sit around and read.

So Manville provided no diversion. The telly couldn't hold him long (it could apparently hold Steve and Raf forever), and there wasn't anything about ranch life that interested or amused him. He hadn't spoken with Curtis or anyone else in the outside world since the hugger-mugger about pretending to be both George Manville and in Singapore. Except for the food, this was like being in jail.

Pallifer was seated on the verandah of the spare barracks on Tuesday afternoon, squinting out at the dry brown land in all that sunlight, wondering if he dared leave Steve and Raf here on their own for a day or two, to watch over Richard Curtis's favorite engineer while Pallifer found himself a town somewhere on this continent with some action in it, and reluctantly he was acknowledging to himself that the newly richer relationship with Curtis was too valuable to risk, when the ranch manager, Farrelly, came out of the main house across the way and walked in this direction in the baking sun, little dust puffs rising around his boots at every step.

Pallifer watched him come, feeling mingled distaste and hope. He knew that both the Farrellys disapproved of him, as being some sort of unacceptable roustabout, and he returned the favor in spades; but would Farrelly be coming here with some sort of message? Something to end this damn inactivity?

Yes. "Phone for you," Farrelly said, when he was close enough. "In the office." And he turned around and headed back.

Pallifer rose to follow. He would have said a polite thank you, but the man had turned away too fast. Well, fuck you, too, Pallifer thought.

The office was actually a two-room complex, the outer one with a pair of desks for the Farrellys and a number of filing cabinets, the inner one a kind of mailroom, with fax and computers. These rooms were being kept locked when not in use so long as Manville was a guest in the house, so this was only the second time Pallifer had been in here.

Helen Farrelly sat at her desk, typing a letter on ranch stationery, but she stopped when Pallifer and her husband came in and said, "Good afternoon, Mr. Pallifer. The phone's right there."

So the woman was at least making an effort to be polite. "Thank you, ma'am," Pallifer said, and crossed to the side table where the phone waited off the hook. He picked up the receiver. "Hello?"

"Mr. Pallifer?"

"Yeah, that's right."

"This is Otis," said the dry and whispery voice, "from Unico

Bank. Mr. Richard Curtis requested that we phone you about
certain credit card information, concerning a Mr. George Manville."

Pallifer's spirits suddenly lifted. The trail! The credit card
trail that would lead to the missing girl, if she were still there.
Well, we can only hope.

A pen and notepad were by the phone. Picking up the pen,
"Yes, go on," he said.

"On Thursday last," the whispery Mr. Otis said, "Mr. Manville
made two telephone calls from the Brisbane area to the United
States, charging them to a credit card."

"Telephone calls." Pallifer had been hoping for a hotel or
some such thing, but of course hotels don't put through the
credit card slip until after the guest checks out. Hoping this
might still be useful somehow, he said, "Can you identify where
the call was made from?"

"Yes, of course," Mr. Otis said. "Both calls emanated from a
pay telephone on the property of the Lee-Zure-Lite Motel in
Surfers Paradise."

Bingo! "Surfers Paradise?" Pallifer asked, as he wrote the
name on the notepad, "is that the name of a town?"

"Oh, yes," Mr. Otis said. "On the Gold Coast, I believe."

"Well, thank you," Pallifer said. "That was Leisure Light
Motel?"

"Yes. It has a rather unusual spelling," Mr. Otis said, and
went on to spell it.

Pallifer wrote that also on the notepad, thanked Mr. Otis
again, said he wouldn't be needing any more information, and
hung up. Then he thanked Mrs. Farrelly, pointedly ignored Mr.
Farrelly, and went outside, where Raf stood in the shade of the
house, leaning against the wall. He straightened when he saw
Pallifer, and said, "Our friend was here. He listens at windows."

Pallifer stopped. "Does he." He didn't like that, it suggested

Manville might be up to something after all, not just obediently waiting, the way Mr. Curtis thought.

Pallifer reflected; what, if anything, would Manville have heard? The phone table in the office was against a wall between two windows, but the windows were shut because of the air-conditioning. But say Manville could have heard his part of the conversation, what was there in it?

The name of the motel. He'd repeated it when Otis said it.

"Well, you know," Pallifer said, "it might be a good thing to collect our pal and lock him away a while. I got to drive back to the coast, be gone overnight, that might excite Manville even if he didn't hear anything. Where is he now?"

"He went back in the house."

"You and Steve round him up, while I pack a bag."

"Sure thing."

Pallifer went back to the spare barracks and packed his smaller bag, and brought it to the main house. In the garage, he could choose between a green Land Rover and a white Honda Accord. The Land Rover appealed to him, but the Honda would be more anonymous once he got back around Brisbane, so he shrugged and tossed his bag into the trunk of the Honda. Then he went looking for Steve and Raf, to see how they were doing with Manville.

Not so good. "Can't find him," Raf said. He sounded more irritated than worried.

Pallifer felt the same way. "Well, where the hell could he be? He can't go anywhere. If he's hiding, it's because he wants to catch somebody. So if he makes a move at you, just kill him and fuck the whole event. I can't stay around here, I don't want to lose the daylight. Tell the Farrellys I'll call here tonight, find out what's going on. If fucking Manville's dead, so much the better."

"What if, when we find him, he's peaceable?"

Pallifer shook his head. "Then we go on babysitting," he said. "And you lock him away till I get back."

"Okay."

Pallifer grinned, feeling better about things. "But if it turns out the job's over," he said, "that would be okay, too."

Two hundred miles east of Kennison, with the sun low in the sky behind him, Pallifer pulled off the road—he was the only car in sight—got out of the Honda, and went around a hillock to relieve himself. When he came back to the car, Manville was seated in back, giving him a calm look.

"Well, I'll be a son of a bitch," Pallifer muttered, and went around to get behind the wheel. Staring at the irritating bastard in the rearview mirror, he said, "Now what?"

"Just keep going," Manville said. "I like the way you drive, so keep doing it."

"And where do you think you're going?"

"Same place as you. Lee-Zure-Lite Motel."

Pallifer nodded. "So you did hear things at that window."

"If you're going to that motel," Manville said, "then Curtis still wants Kim Baldur dead, no matter what he said to me."

"So the deal's off, is that it?"

"That's it. Drive, Mr. Pallifer."

He might as well; there was no point just sitting here, on an empty highway. He put the Honda in gear, and they started again to drive east.

When he'd got into the car, back at Kennison, he'd put a pistol in the glove compartment, the one he figured to use on the girl. Now he glanced at the glove compartment, thinking about it.

Manville said, "It isn't there anymore."

"I thought not," Pallifer said. He looked at that expressionless face in the rearview mirror, then watched the road. "You heard me on the phone, then you hid out till I put my bag in here, so you knew which car I'd be taking, and then you got in the trunk. Where were you, before?"

"On top of the framework for the garage doors, between that and the ceiling."

"So you could look to see which vehicle I was gonna take. But what if I just got in it and drove away?"

"At first," Manville told him, "I was going to drop on you as soon as you opened the driver's door. But then, when you came in and opened and closed the trunk, and went away again, I saw I could do it more quietly."

"Well, you're pretty cute," Pallifer said, and slammed on the brakes, sluing the wheel hard right across the empty road with his left hand while his right hand snaked inside his jacket to whip out his other pistol. Pressed against the door, he turned, whipping the pistol around, and Manville shot him in the head.

5

It was half an hour up the new dirt road through the jungle, twisting and turning up into the Mayan mountains of Belize. Colin Bennett, half asleep in his third-floor rear room in the Race Course Court Hotel, traveled in memory, however reluctantly, back to the day of the disaster. Outside the closed window here, the chattering sounds of Singapore continued as the day waned, but in the dim hotel room where Bennett sat beside the small radio receiver there was the heavy silence of the Belizean jungle, surrounding you as you drove up that yellowish white fresh dirt road, that new scar upward through the jungle to parallel the rushing cold Cobaz River. And at the end of the road was the worksite, the dam.

The Cobaz River was small but powerful, tumbling down the steep slopes out of Guatemala and down across Belize to empty into the Caribbean Sea, and the hydroelectric dam being built across it up here was as ecologically correct as it was possible for any construction of man to be. True, it would create a small lake where no lake had ever been before, but that was only an improvement. Otherwise, they would merely borrow the water to make electricity, then return it to the river, and the river would remain unchanged.

That had been the most difficult part to explain to the villagers downriver, that the dam had nothing to do with flood control, that the river would still occasionally flood as it always had, that from one-quarter mile below the dam the river would be exactly what it had been before.

The generating system couldn't have been simpler. A tunnel

was cut into the ground beside the lake, twelve feet in diameter, leading downward at a gentle angle. When it came parallel to the dam, inside the mountain, the tunnel became a vertical shaft, tapering smaller, dropping straight down three hundred feet to the blades of the turbines. The water, compressed, hasty, pulled by gravity, pushed by the weight of the lake behind it, hit the turbine with incredible force, enough to generate more electricity than this part of the world would be able to use for years to come.

A red light gleamed on the side of the radio receiver, to show it was working, but otherwise there was absolute silence. Jerry Diedrich had received one phone call earlier in the day from his partner, a man called Luther, merely saying he was on his way back, so Bennett knew the bug in the phone and this receiver were doing their job. But nothing was happening, no phone calls, nothing but the red light in the dusk inside the room, nothing to keep Bennett from reliving again the day of the disaster in Belize.

He was drinking too much in those days, it was part of what made him so genial, such a pleasant guy to be around. He wasn't a mean drunk or a sloppy drunk, he was a cheerful drunk who made other people happy by his presence. But he was a drunk.

He'd wanted to get to the test. There was to be a test run, releasing the water into the tunnel for the first time, merely a five-minute test to be certain everything was working right, and he'd been eager to get to that test, to sense the power of the water rushing down, to see it come out into the daylight far below the dam, in the new channel they'd cut for it, so that the volume of water they'd borrowed would return to the main body of the river, restoring everything as it had been before. That's what he'd wanted to see.

The engineers were supposed to be the ones to run the test, but they were taking too long about it. So far as Bennett could see, they were ready, they were at that stage, why delay? He was up at the dam, running the site, while the engineers were half an hour below, in the camp, in the mobile homes they used for offices. He was up there, and he was drunker than he seemed, and he said the hell with waiting. He said seal off the service entrance to the tunnel, and open the entry from the lake. Let's let that water go!

Some of the workmen spoke Spanish and some Mayan. They all had a little English, which was the only language Bennett had (except for some Singlish, the staccato patois of Singapore, useless in Central America), but whatever language any of the workmen used, they didn't have enough of it to make their objections plain. The boss insisted; eventually, they shrugged their shoulders and did what the boss said to do.

What he hadn't known, or possibly what he'd forgotten, was that the tunnel hadn't yet been entirely cleared out after the construction was done. There were two long folding tables in there, and several chairs, and some Coleman lanterns, and a stack of lumber, and a few other odds and ends.

Darkness fell inside the tunnel when the service entrance was closed, and then the water came thundering through. It snatched up everything that had been left behind, and hurled it all straight down three hundred feet of shaft to the turbine blades, smashing them into useless oars of twisted shining metal.

That was the disaster, or that was as much of the disaster as Richard Curtis knew about, and it had been enough to get Bennett fired that same day, and blacklisted from the entire industry ever since. And Curtis and the others didn't even know the worst. There had been one thing more left inside the tunnel when Bennett had shut that door and started the water through. A man.

Sometimes in dreams he was that man, Daniel Foster, in that terrifying instant before the water hit. Wide-eyed in the darkness, hearing the roar, the rush of air that would have preceded the water. And then the slam.

There hadn't been a trace of him, afterward.

"Hello, Mark?"

Bennett sat up straighter. Belize fell away, Singapore crowded in. A new voice said, "Yes. Who's this?"

"It's Jerry. Can you talk?"

"Ho ho ho," Bennett told himself, speaking softly, "is this it?"

Yes, it was. Mark's young voice said, "Where are you? Are you here?"

"Yes, Luther and me. Can we meet somewhere? Is it safe?"

"No, it isn't," Bennett said, and broadly smiled at that warming red light.

"Sure it is," Mark said. "Nobody suspects a thing, Jerry. Where shall we meet?"

6

Kim didn't think it was fair. She was part of this, wasn't she? She'd gone through as much as anybody on this; more. So why couldn't she come along to meet this Mark person?

She and Jerry and Luther were having dinner in one of the Indonesian restaurants on Orchard Road, and she spent the entire meal hammering this point. They were in this together, weren't they? She had as much reason to pursue Richard Curtis as they did; more. So why were they refusing to let her come with them to talk to their friend Mark?

At last, Luther gave her an answer. "Because," he said, "it's a gay bar."

"So what?" she said.

Jerry said, "Kim, you don't want to go to a gay bar."

"Why not?"

"You wouldn't like it."

"I've been in gay bars before," she said airily.

Sounding interested, Luther said, "Really? Why?"

It had been a lie, of course, quick and thoughtless, and she saw no way to either defend it or explain it, so she pushed forward instead, saying, "Why do you have to meet in a gay bar anyway? Why not somewhere else?"

"Because *we* are gay," Luther said, "and so is Mark. So it won't be suspicious if we all show up there at the same time."

"But if we showed up with you," Jerry pointed out, "that *would* be suspicious."

"Maybe I'm in drag," she said, and they laughed, and she saw she wasn't going to get anywhere. "I'll want to meet him later, then," she insisted. "Somewhere that tourists go, or something like that, so it won't be suspicious."

"We'll arrange it," Jerry promised.

It wasn't much comfort, but it was all she was going to get, and she knew it.

They insisted on putting her in a cab. "I can walk," she said. "It's a beautiful night, it isn't too far to walk."

"It is, in fact," Jerry told her, "but even if it weren't, you don't want to be wandering around the city streets after dark."

"I *like* the city streets," she objected, "and I wouldn't be 'wandering around,' I'd be walking from here to Little India, and straight to the hotel."

Luther said, "Kim, you have enemies in Singapore. You really do have to remember that."

Which brought her up short. It was true, she did have at least one enemy in Singapore, in Richard Curtis. And Richard Curtis had people everywhere.

Would some of those people be looking for her? Would they have her picture? Would that awful man, that killer from the boat who'd chased her in Brisbane, be here now in Singapore, waiting for further orders from Curtis? He'd accidentally stumbled on her once; could it happen again? Could she be walking peacefully along a well-lit city street in Singapore and suddenly have a car stop beside her, that man appear again, with his friends?

"All right," she said, "I'll take the taxi."

At the hotel, the cab was just pulling up to the curb when someone came bustling out of the gaudy entrance, waving his arm. "You have another customer," Kim told the cabby, and climbed out, leaving the door open.

It was the man with the Polaroid camera. He hurried into the cab, looked quickly over at her, then shut the door and rolled the window up before telling the cabby where he wanted to go.

Oh, for God's sake, I'm not snooping, she told him inside her head. What do I care where you're going, it's nothing to do with me. She turned away as the cab sped off, and went into the hotel, and up to her room.

The television set offered two channels in English, 5 and 12. Kim, restless, switched back and forth between the two for a while, then turned it off and went looking for the magazine she'd started reading on the airplane and never finished, a three-month-old copy of *Scientific American*.

At first, she couldn't find it. She knew she'd put it on top of the free tourist magazine that had been in the room when she'd arrived, but it was no longer there. Nothing was on top of that magazine. Had she moved it somewhere else?

She searched the room, failed to find the *Scientific American*, then decided to see if there could be anything at all to read in the tourist magazine. She picked it up, and the *Scientific American* was underneath.

That's not right, she thought. She'd never touched the tourist magazine before this second, so how could hers be *under* it? The maid hadn't been in here since they'd gone out to dinner. No one was supposed to have been in here.

She searched the room once more, carefully, the drawers and the closet, and when she was finished she was sure. There was no doubt in her mind. Someone had searched the room.

7

The White Swallow, where Jerry and Luther were to meet Mark, was off Orchard Road not far from Istana Park, a quieter, more restrained place than many of the discos in Singapore, most of them awash with light and noise. British expats came to the White Swallow, and discreet bureaucrats and traveling businessmen. Downstairs were the dark bar in front and the dance floor in back, while upstairs was a quiet dining room.

Jerry and Luther had eaten dinner here before, but not tonight. Tonight, all they needed from the White Swallow was an after-dinner drink and a conversation with Mark.

But they only got the former.

They'd arranged to meet at nine-thirty. Jerry and Luther had arrived fifteen minutes early. They sat at the bar, a long crescent moon, its facade decorated with chrome swallows in flight. The bird theme was maintained throughout the place, upstairs and down, but most completely at the bar, where the counters and shelves along the backbar were covered with representations of swallows, brought here or sent here by customers from around the world. They looked at the birds, they drank their drinks, and at ten to ten Jerry said, "Something's wrong."

"Maybe he fell asleep," Luther suggested.

"Do you think so? I'll go phone him."

Jerry did, and when he dialed Mark's number he got Mark's answering machine. He told it, "Jerry here, and where are you?"

Then he went back to Luther: "Answering machine."

"Then he's on the way."

But he wasn't. At ten-thirty Jerry said, "Maybe he thought we said ten-thirty," but by ten forty-five that was looking untenable, too. "Something's definitely gone wrong."

Luther said, "We should go back to the hotel, we'll find out tomorrow what happened."

"This is very frustrating," Jerry said.

"It is."

"And worrisome."

"That, too."

They taxied back to Race Course Court, where the desk held two messages for them. The first was from Mark, and it read: "Empress Place 12:30 tomorrow." The second was from Kim, and it read: "Whenever you get in, call me. I'm awake, and I want to hear everything."

"Oh, God," Jerry said. "*You* call her, Luther, I don't think I could go through it twice."

8

Richard Curtis had many projects afoot, in many parts of the world, but his days seemed to be increasingly filled by the one project he couldn't admit to in public. Wednesday morning was supposed to be devoted to the first consultation with the architects on the Kanowit Island construction, but there were two interruptions that morning, both having to do with this other matter, which seemed lately to be consuming more and more of his life.

Well, that was only right, in a way. Of all the projects, this was the only one that could *save* his life.

He'd been meeting with the architects, in the large conference room, for less than fifteen minutes, looking at the rough sketches, the general plans, placement of the airfield, the tennis courts, the offshore protected scuba area, when Margaret came in with a note: "Mr. Tian in your office."

"Thank you, Margaret," Curtis said, and to the architects he said, "I beg your pardon, this won't take long, but I do have to see this gentleman."

He left them huddling over the plans, muttering together, and returned to his office, where Jackie Tian stood at the windows, looking out. He nodded at Curtis and, by way of greeting, said, "You do like views."

"Some of them," Curtis said. "Sit down, Jackie, how's Hong Kong?"

"Pestering," Tian said, and joined Curtis at the L of sofas making up the conversation area.

Jackie Tian was a tough Hong Kong Chinese, a blunt short

man with a hard-muscled compact body and heavy bony forehead, who had been an official with a rather corrupt trucker's
union when he and Curtis had first met, years ago. He'd been
one of Curtis's more useful contacts in Hong Kong, part of that
web of influence and power he'd had to leave behind when the
mainland bastards took over. Though the city's new rulers had
cleaned up that union pretty well, nothing had ever been proved
against Tian, and he was still there.

When this plan had come to Curtis, he had known that Jackie
Tian was the perfect man to put together the work on the
ground. Because of various criminal convictions from his early
days, Tian couldn't get permanent residence for himself anywhere in the world outside Hong Kong (or, now, China), and he
had as much reason as Curtis to hate the city's new rulers, so
he'd been very willing to listen to Curtis's scheme, and to become
an active part of it. He was the one who'd found the crews in
Hong Kong, had put together the front corporations, had started
the construction.

Tian didn't know the whole scheme, of course. If Tian were
to find out what the end result of all this labor was meant to be
he wouldn't for a second go along with it. He wouldn't be able
to go along with it. So he knew only what he had to know; he
knew about the gold.

This was their first meeting in a month, and Curtis was anxious to know how Tian was progressing, so when they sat at
right angles to one another on the sofas he said, "How are we
coming along?"

"Slow," Tian said.

Curtis frowned. "Jackie, we have to get moving on this. The
longer it takes, the greater the chance somebody will notice
something."

"It's tough, Mr. Curtis," Tian said. "The land, the permits, all that was easy. Easier than when the Brits were in charge. But now we're in construction, and that part's slow."

"Construction doesn't have to be slow, Jackie."

"Not going up," Tian agreed. "We're doing that like normal, we've got a perfect construction site there, you can't tell a thing."

"Good."

"But going down, that's something else."

"Why?"

"We can only do it at night," Tian pointed out, "and we've got to be slow because some of those bank buildings have motion sensors. We aren't in the banks, but we're close, and we've got to be careful. Then, when we open a wall, we've got to close it again every morning. It all takes time, Mr. Curtis."

Of course it did. Curtis knew very well that too much haste could destroy this project, make somebody suspicious, alert the wrong people. But he felt such pressure on himself to get it done and finished and behind him that he found it hard not to exert that same pressure on Tian. "We have to get moving on this, Jackie," he said. "What if we hired more men?"

Tian shook his head. "Mr. Curtis, we got to keep this secret, and that means I got to hire men I already know, that I know I can trust to keep their mouths shut. I've already got them all. There's nobody else in the world that I'd want down in them tunnels."

"All right," Curtis said. "We had to make six connections. How many are done?"

"Three."

Curtis didn't like that at all. "Jackie, what are we looking at here? Another *month*?"

"Shorter than that," Tian assured him. "We'll have the fourth done this week."

"Can they work seven days?"

Tian considered that. "Well, maybe," he said. "For a lot of money."

"Not a problem." Since Curtis was spending his future anyway, risking everything on this one gamble, it hardly mattered what commitments he made.

"If we did seven days," Tian said, "we might be done in fifteen, maybe less."

"Do it," Curtis said. "And is the submarine there?"

"Got delivered last week. The box said it was a fuel storage tank, and that's what it looks like."

"It will do the job, though," Curtis said.

Tian shrugged. "If you say so. I don't know what you want it for."

"Another part of the operation," Curtis told him. "You'll see it on the day."

"Fine," Tian said. "I'd hate to ride in it, I'll tell you that."

"The submarine?" Curtis shook his head. "No one's going to ride in that. That isn't what it's for."

"Well, it's down in the finished part of the basement," Tian said. "In its box."

"I'm looking forward to seeing it."

"You're coming over?"

"Yes."

Tian nodded. "I guess you have to. When?"

"Next week."

"I don't know," Tian said, and frowned. "You know we're not gonna be ready next week."

"I can't wait," Curtis said. "Jackie, I Just can't wait any longer. I'll help dig."

Tian laughed, but Curtis meant it.

He was back with the architects for less than half an hour, after saying goodbye to Tian, who'd fly back to Hong Kong this afternoon, when the second interruption came. This time, they were discussing the cisterns under the tennis courts. Being a coral island, Kanowit had no ground water to speak of, so the resort would depend for its water on collecting rain, and the most useful surface for that purpose would be the tennis courts. They would be sloped, too minimally for any player to notice or be affected by, and rainwater would drain to a downspout into a deep cistern on which the courts would be built.

They were looking at the options for the filtration systems that would be needed, and the most efficient way to move the water to the hotel buildings, when Margaret returned with another note: "Mr. Bennett is in the small conference room."

"Damn it," Curtis said, "this is somebody else I absolutely have to see. I'm sorry, I promise this will be the last interruption."

The architects assured him they had nothing but time, and he went away to see Colin Bennett, who already looked less hangdog and more like his former self. The new clothing helped, and so did the confident smile.

Curtis shut the door behind himself, didn't bother to shake hands, and said, "Did you find him? So soon?"

"I'll have him today," Bennett said. Even his voice was more self-assured. "I thought I had him last night, but something must've gone wrong."

"Wrong? Are they alert? Do they know you're watching?" Curtis was suddenly aware he might have picked the wrong man for this job, or a man who was no longer right for this job or any other.

But Bennett smiled an easy smile and said, "They don't have one idea about me. What happened was, they talked on the phone yesterday around six to somebody named Mark."

"From here?"

"Don't know yet. Another poofter, apparently. They made an arrangement to meet at the bar at the White Swallow last night at nine-thirty. That's one of your more discreet places for fellows like that. Not for the hot young lads, you know, more for their uncles. Fellows who carry umbrellas, you know."

"You went there?"

"It wasn't exactly as easy as that, Mr. Curtis," Bennett said. "I don't look like their customers, you know. So I have this neighbor of mine, in the flats near me, he is more their style, and he's as hard up as I've been lately, or he wouldn't be living there. So I offered him twenty dollars plus drinking money to do my watching for me. We drove over, got there a few minutes before the time, and when I looked in they were already there. I pointed them out to Fan—he's the chap—and he went in and made some new friends, and I sat in the car just down the block. Fan's job was to come out and give me the high sign when this Mark showed up, so I could get his picture, but he never showed."

"Scared off?" Curtis asked. "By what?"

"Beats me," Bennett said. "Your two fellas stayed there at the bar almost two hours. Two or three times, I went to the door and looked in. Just to be sure Fan was keeping his mind on the job at hand, and there was Fan, and there was the two, and nobody else. Later on, Fan told me they looked at their watches a lot, and after a while one of them went to make a phone call, and finally they just up and left. I gave Fan money for a taxi, and scooted off back to the hotel myself, so I'd be there before them, which I was. And the first thing they did was call the girl, room to room."

Smiling, Curtis said, "Did they."

Bennett laughed and shook his head. "All they had to do was walk down the hall and talk to her face to face, and I wouldn't know a thing right now. But they phoned her instead."

"So you heard it."

"And I heard them say this Mark stood them up, and they

didn't know why, but when they got back to the hotel there was a message from Mark they should meet him today at Empress Place at twelve-thirty."

Curtis frowned. "Empress Place? That's the big hawker stand off the Fullerton Road, isn't it?"

"That's the one."

"I've never been there," Curtis said, "but you see it from the bridge. It's huge, isn't it? How does anybody find anybody there?"

"That's their problem, Mr. Curtis," Bennett said. "I've already found my pair. And when they find their friend, why, I'll find him, too."

9

Kim sat in the crowded bus, gazing at the teeming city they crept through. She'd told Jerry and Luther this morning about her discovery that her room had been searched, and was pleased when they didn't waste time doubting her. Jerry said, "Somebody's followed us, that's what it is, from Australia. Maybe that's why Mark didn't show up last night."

"We'll soon know," Luther said.

They got off the bus at Esplanade Park and crossed to Empress Place, a large open-air pedestrian area overlooking the Singapore River. The sprawling hawker center nearby was open-air, with booths and stalls for the food vendors and many tables, some in dappled shade, many in direct sun. The place was crowded and busy, but they soon found a table.

Luther looked at his watch. "Twelve-thirty exactly," he said, "I'll tell you the truth, Kim, I'd like it if he would show up this time."

"You think he might not?"

"I was sure he'd appear last night," he said, "and I was wrong."

They ate, ordering food from three different stalls, and the food was all good. But where was Mark? They'd taken their time, and here they were, finished, and here Mark wasn't. Their only choice, Jerry said, was to wait, to give him, say, an hour. Though that hadn't worked the last time.

Kim said, "I'm going to wander," choosing the word deliberately, and got up before either of the men could tell her not to. "I won't go far, I promise, and I won't be away long. And if I see your friend's here. I'll come right back."

There wasn't much they could do but look dubious, which

they did, and which she ignored. She got up and roved among the stalls and the many people eating their lunches. Beyond the hawker center, the city itself from here looked serene, the tall new glass office blocks rising smoothly among the old colonial-era buildings, the traffic sweeping by on the Anderson Bridge, the river endlessly flowing, the white Empress Place Building massive without being intimidating. She walked among the crowds for about five minutes, and was away from the hawker center entirely, over by the Empress Place Building, when a young man, Caucasian, slender, in white shirt and dark slacks, stopped in front of her, and said, "Here."

Automatically, she took the folded piece of paper, and he hurried around her and off. When she turned, astonished, to call after him, he was walking briskly away toward Cavenagh Bridge.

She looked at what he'd handed her and it was a sheet of white paper, folded twice. A note.

That was Mark! She was convinced of it. That was Mark, and in her hand was the explanation for his continuing non-appearance.

She thought, I should bring this back to Jerry and Luther. Then she corrected that thought: I should read this, and *then* bring it to Jerry and Luther.

There were benches along the pedestrian path in front of the Empress Place Building. Kim found a free spot, sat down, looked around, saw nothing unusual—what would be unusual? what should she look for?—and unfolded the paper.

It was letterhead, Richard Curtis's letterhead, which startled her. RC STRUCTURAL it said across the top, with the Singapore office address and phone numbers and fax numbers and e-mail address. Handwritten in the middle of the page in neat small script was: "Jerry, you are being followed by a man from Curtis. In fifteen minutes, take the #167 bus south. Be sure you're the last ones on the bus. M."

Her hands were trembling when she refolded the paper. She stood, feeling suddenly awkward, and stuffed the paper into her jeans pocket. It was as though she had stage fright, this sudden self-consciousness. She'd forgotten how to walk normally, and it seemed to her she lurched like some not-well-made robot as she made her way back to the hawker center and the two men at the table.

"Well, *there* you are," Jerry said, but Luther had looked at her face, and he said, "What is it, Kim? What happened?"

Wordlessly, she handed Luther the folded paper, then sat down. Luther opened it, and Jerry leaned close to his shoulder so they could both read it. "No reaction, Jerry," Luther said quietly, not looking up. He refolded the paper and pocketed it.

Kim could see that Jerry wanted to react all over the place, but all he did was look wide-eyed at Kim and say low, as though not to be overheard, "*Mark* gave you that?"

"It must have been him," she said. "He just stopped in front of me, handed me the note, and went right off. I didn't have a chance to say a word to him."

Jerry said, "I don't see what the point is in taking a *bus*. If somebody's following us, they can certainly follow a bus."

Luther said, "I'm sure Mark has something in mind."

"But what? He doesn't even say where to get off the bus."

"We'll find out," Luther said. "Come on."

The #167 bus was crowded enough to have standees, but they weren't all jammed tightly together. Kim and Jerry and Luther stood in a group, holding on as the bus swayed down Collyer Quay, and it seemed unlikely to Kim that any of the obvious tourist types on the bus could be the person who was following them. So, had they gotten away?

The bus made another stop, and among the people who got

on was the young man who'd given her the note. He looked around, not appearing to recognize them at first, and she noticed that Jerry and Luther also remained deadpan. Then he came toward them and stood near Jerry. "Why don't you all cluster around me?" he asked quietly.

They did, and Jerry said, "Where is he?"

"In a taxi, following the bus."

"Jesus, Mark," Jerry said. "So where can we meet?"

Mark grinned at him. "We are meeting, Jerry. This is it."

"Very clever," Luther said. "May I introduce Kim Baldur. Kim, this is Mark Hennessy."

They exchanged nods, and then Luther said, "How do you know it's somebody from Curtis?"

"Yesterday morning," Mark said, "Mr. Curtis's secretary had me carry five thousand dollars in cash to Mr. Curtis in the small conference room. There was a man in there with him, I just got a quick look at him and I don't think he noticed me at all. Last night, I was about to go into the bar to meet you two, and I saw the same man in a car parked just down the block. Today, I saw you arrive, and the same man was behind you."

"Hired by Curtis," Luther said.

"It would seem that way." Mark Hennessy was an American, Kim was pretty sure, but he'd been away from the United States long enough for his accent to begin to slip, to move into something more general and foreign, with traces of Britishness. He said, "It'll be easy to pick him out. He's a bulky man, Eurasian, and he's carrying a Polaroid camera."

Kim said, "A Polaroid!"

Jerry said, "Mark, he's staying at our hotel."

"Then he's probably tapped your phones," Mark said. "Which would explain why he knows what you're going to do."

The bus trundled along, now leaving Raffles Quay and starting down Shenton Way. Passengers got on and off, and Jerry kept his voice low, but Kim could hear the stress in it. "Mark, we can't keep meeting on buses all the time."

"Well, the fact is, we don't have to," Mark said. "I don't have that much to report. The main thing going on now in the office is the preparations for Kanowit Island, the construction and all that."

"Curtis is planning something else," Luther said, "something much worse. We just don't know what."

"Something to do with the ocean," Jerry said. "There's a destructive ocean wave he can make."

"Same as at Kanowit," Mark said, and shrugged. "Haven't a clue," he said. "I'll tell you, though, he had a visitor from Hong Kong this morning."

Luther said, "Really? I thought he'd burned all his bridges to Hong Kong."

"This is a labor thug called Jackie Tian," Mark told them. "He and Curtis were tight in the old days, in Hong Kong. I doubt Tian has any influence anywhere else."

Luther said, "You think Curtis is planning something around Hong Kong? He does have a grudge against them, god knows."

Jerry said, "But it has to be something to do with that wave, that soliton wave."

"Listen," Mark said, "I've got to get off here, I'm going to be late getting back to the office as it is. Jerry, here's the phone number of a friend of mine, he's somebody we can trust. I'll be at his place every day at six. You call me from a pay phone, not from your room, and I'll tell you what if anything I've learned."

"Very good," Jerry said, pocketing the small card Mark had given him. "I'll have some Planetwatch folks do some digging—quietly. Without telling them why."

Mark said, "And I'll snoop around, see if I can find anything that uses the soliton."

Luther said, "You have access to that sort of information?"

"I can get access," Mark said. "I was part of the support team for Kanowit. I didn't go out to the island, but I filled special requests. George Manville used to phone me all the time."

Kim started. "You know George Manville?"

"Of course. I like him, to tell the truth, I think he's a good guy."

Kim found she could hardly speak. "How is he these days?"

"No idea," Mark said. "Haven't seen him since he went off to Kanowit."

Kim said, "But didn't he come back to Singapore with Mr. Curtis?"

"Not that I know of," Mark said. "Haven't seen him around, anyway. Do you want me to look him up?"

"Not needed," Jerry said, putting a hand on Kim's shoulder. "We know all we need to know about George Manville."

All at once, Kim wasn't so sure about that.

10

"I don't like this," Colin Bennett told himself. "I think they're up to something."

What he didn't say out loud, because he didn't want to have to acknowledge it to himself, was that he thought they were onto him. *"Don't* queer this with Curtis," he begged himself, whispering inside the car, afraid to overhear himself.

But there was no denying there was a difference in the manner of those three people. He'd become aware of it only gradually, so he couldn't say for certain when the change had taken place, but it seemed to him it had been after their hawker center lunch on Wednesday.

So far as he could tell, at that lunch their friend Mark had once again failed to appear; at least, Bennett hadn't seen them meet or exchange words with anybody. At one point, the girl had wandered off by herself, but it was the men who knew Mark and expected to meet with him, so Bennett had stuck to the men, and he was absolutely certain that nobody had approached them.

Then the girl had come back, and they'd had some palaver, looked at a map or something—he was discreetly too far away to see exactly what that was—and then took a city bus to nowhere in particular, as though they were no more than tourists.

In fact, since then, they'd behaved as though that's really all they were, tourists. There were no more phone calls from or to Mark from their hotel room. They went out in the mornings, but not to anywhere in particular, as far as he could tell. Late in the afternoon on Thursday and Friday, Jerry Diedrich made brief phone calls from a pay phone wherever they happened to be, but no secret rendezvous followed; and on Saturday he didn't even do that.

Something had changed. They had been urgently trying to meet this fellow Mark—a disloyal employee of Richard Curtis's, that was certain—and they had failed twice to meet him, and now they acted as though they didn't care. As though they had no agenda at all.

There was only the one explanation possible. Somehow.

In some way, they'd come to realize they were being observed. And they would do nothing to make trouble for themselves or their friend Mark so long as they knew the observation was ongoing.

This was no good. Bennett had phoned Curtis on Friday, to assure the man he was still on the case but that nothing had as yet turned up, and Curtis had told him, "We can't take much longer on this."

"I'm on them, Mr. Curtis, night and day."

"I have to leave the city next week," Curtis had said. "I need this situation resolved before then, Colin. Can I count on you?"

"Absolutely, Mr. Curtis."

But it wasn't working the way it was supposed to. The less urgency Diedrich and his friends showed, the more urgency Bennett felt. Curtis wasn't paying him to sit around in hotel rooms and cars. Curtis was paying him to solve a problem called Jerry Diedrich, and he wasn't solving it.

And now here it was Sunday, and the three of them left the hotel in mid-morning and, after a brief stop at the local Planet-watch storefront, walked to where they could catch the #7 bus, westbound. Out Orchard Road they went, in the bus, Bennett unhappily trailing after in his little Honda, feeling the heat of the day, having to stop a block or so back every time the bus stopped, having no idea where they were going because they didn't talk to one another on the phone anymore. They rode the bus all the way out to the end of Orchard Road, then walked on to Holland Road and the entrance to the Botanic Gardens.

The Botanic Gardens! Bennett knew it well, it was an annual event when he was a schoolchild for a class trip out to the Botanic Gardens. The city was proud of the Gardens, and deservedly so. It was natural for schoolchildren to visit, and tourists. But it was not at all natural for a grown-up native Singaporean to be hulking around the Botanic Gardens all by himself in the hot humid middle of a Sunday, and Bennett found his frustration and unease steadily edging over toward resentment.

Would they at last meet the mythical Mark here? Unless Mark had disguised himself as a Boy Scout troop, Bennett didn't see how it was possible.

We can't have another week like this. Time to do something. Time to do something Richard Curtis will like.

11

Monday was a day of frustrations and irritations for Richard Curtis. First, when he arrived in the offices at nine-thirty that morning, Margaret presented him with a fax from Jackie Tian in Hong Kong:

"Diver unavailable. Arrested on smuggling. No substitute yet."

This was bad news. The project needed a skilled scuba diver, skilled and trustworthy, and Tian had a man who had been used in any number of dubious operations in the past, sabotage and smuggling, working for management and labor and government, whoever would pay him. This was a hell of a time for the man to be caught.

And if Tian had no substitute, what was Curtis supposed to do about it? He did use divers himself sometimes, in his construction projects around the world, but they were all legitimate employees, simple workers skilled with scuba equipment; none of them could be approached with *this* assignment.

"Margaret," Curtis said, "ask Personnel to put together a list of all scuba divers in our employ. On any of the projects."

"Yes, sir."

"I want their work history," Curtis said, "with us, of course, but also, where we know it, with others. And any personal information we might have on each of them would be good."

"Yes, sir."

She went off to take care of that, and he returned to the Kanowit architects.

This project was both fascinating and frustrating in a number of ways. To begin, with, it was a relatively small island, and they would have to pack it with a lot of different elements without giving the impression of overcrowding.

Then there was the soliton, the way the island had been recreated, which would leave a deceptively smooth and inviting surface. Down inside there, however, would be undigested chunks of the old Japanese buildings, and jagged blocks of coral. For items like cisterns, swimming pool, basements, the golf course lake, they would very literally be digging into the unknown, with always the possibility of creating a subsidence or discovering an air pocket.

The most elegant solution seemed to be to build all underground structures separately, aboveground, and then sink them into the new soil of Kanowit. It would be the most reliable way to build there, but it was full of complexities.

Curtis loved this work. He loved thinking about it, he loved finding the problems and then working on the solutions. He loved working with like-minded men and women, who could give the same kind of concentration and devotion as he to this kind of problem.

(That's why he'd so enjoyed working with George Manville, and why he'd been so reluctant to end the relationship by ending Manville. Could that still be worked out, somehow? He doubted it.)

It was twenty past eleven when Margaret interrupted: "Mr. Farrelly, from Australia, on the phone, Mr. Curtis," she said.

Why, I was just thinking about Manville, Curtis thought, and this must be something about him. Good or bad? "I'll be right there," he told Margaret, and said to the architects, "This won't take long."

No problem, they assured him, in the usual murmuring way, going back to the blueprints before he had left the room.

At his desk, he picked up the phone, said hello, and Albert Farrelly sounded worried: "This man Raf here wants to talk to you, Mr. Curtis."

Raf? That was one of Pallifer's men. Why didn't Pallifer come on himself? "Put him on," Curtis said, and a minute later the raspy voice said, "Morning, Mr. Curtis."

Curtis said, "Where's Pallifer?"

"Well, that's the thing, Mr. Curtis," Raf said. "Nobody knows."

"Nobody knows?"

"Well, sir, last Tuesday, Morgan got a phone call from some banker, I dunno what about—"

Curtis knew. The location of the Manville–Baldur hideyhole, no longer a factor. "What did Morgan do?"

"He said he had to go back to Brisbane, just for the one overnight, we should lock up Manville while he's gone."

With all the other details to think about, Curtis realized, he hadn't remembered to tell Pallifer that the search for Kim Baldur in Australia could stop now, that she was here in Singapore. He hadn't really thought about Pallifer at all since leaving Australia, had simply assumed everything was in position there, waiting for further orders from him.

He said, "You locked up Manville. And then?"

"Well, that's it," Raf said. "We couldn't find him."

"Couldn't find— For how long?"

"Ever since, Mr. Curtis."

Curtis took a second to absorb that. "Are you telling me," he said, "George Manville has been missing since last Tuesday? For a *week*?"

"Both of them, Mr. Curtis."

"Both of them? What both?"

"Morgan, too," the man said. "We looked for Manville and couldn't find him, all of us, and Morgan thought maybe Manville heard some of the phone call, so Morgan just took off before it got dark, and told us to lock up Manville when we found him, but we never did."

"A week ago."

"We kept expecting Morgan to come back," Raf said. He sounded worried, almost embarrassed, like a man who wasn't used to such emotions.

"Clearly," Curtis said, "Manville left with Pallifer."

"No, sir, I don't think so," Raf said. "Morgan put his bag in the trunk, and the fella wasn't there. And when he drove away, there wasn't anybody in the back or on the roof or like that, or we'd of seen him."

"Then Manville took off, on foot," Curtis said. "And Pallifer caught up with him."

"I've driven all around out there, Mr. Curtis," Raf said, "in the Land Rover, and I don't find anything. Not the car, not either man."

Curtis said, "Manville could not have walked anywhere from Kennison, it's not physically possible. He and Pallifer must have met up, somehow, there's no other explanation."

"Yes, sir," Raf said. "Except, if they met up, and if Morgan killed him, I'd of heard from Morgan by now. And if they met up, and Manville killed Morgan, we'd all have heard from the law by now."

Two men dead in the desert; the thought crossed Curtis's mind. They'd met somewhere out there, and neither survived.

But then, why wouldn't Raf have come across the car? Curtis said, "This makes no sense."

"Mr. Curtis," Raf said, "yesterday, I phoned Billie, you know, Pallifer's girlfriend in Townville, said have you heard from him, she said no, now *she's* worried. I'm sorry I did that, but I thought you ought to know."

"So no one has seen or heard from either man since last Tuesday."

"Yes, sir."

Curtis would be leaving Singapore in two days, on Wednesday. His travel plans showed him flying to Manila on the first leg of an inspection tour of RC Structural projects. Only Margaret would know where he was really going, and she wouldn't tell anyone.

He tried to work out the implications of this situation. Assume that both Manville and Pallifer are dead, because if one of them was alive somebody would know about it. Assume that one or both bodies would eventually turn up. Would anything lead back to Curtis? He said, "You and, er…"

"Steve."

"Yes. You and Steve stay there until Thursday. If you hear nothing from anybody by then, you should just go home and consider the job finished, and I'll get your money to you through what's-her-name? Billie?"

"Morgan's girlfriend, yes, sir."

"I have her address. If anything at all happens between now and Thursday, let me know at once."

"Yes, sir, I will. Mr. Curtis, I'm sorry I took so long to get to you, but I figured maybe, Morgan'd been stuck here a while, he might just want the weekend to himself. It's when he didn't come back today I figured there might be something up."

"Well," Curtis said, "keep me informed."

"I will, sir."

It's out of control, Curtis thought, as he hung up.

That was the one thing he wouldn't be able to stand. He had to remain in control of the whole enterprise, he couldn't let any part of it begin to spin away on its own.

Where was Pallifer, dammit? Where was Manville? What was coming at him, from what unforeseen quarter?

✢

The phone call from Bennett Monday afternoon was the last
straw on the day. He'd finished with the architects at last and
was back in his office, getting caught up on some other details,
preparing for departure on Wednesday, when Margaret buzzed
to say, "Mr. Bennett on the line, sir."

Curtis said, "Good," as he reached for the phone, thinking,
at last, perhaps, some good news.

Not at all. "Still no change, Mr. Curtis," Bennett said, by way
of hello.

The man was sounding hangdog again; Curtis didn't like that.
He said, "Colin, this doesn't make any sense. They came here
with a mission, they started on that mission, they arranged to
meet this spy in my organization, this person named Mark, they
didn't meet him, and now they're doing *nothing*. How did they
spend the weekend?"

"They went to the Botanic Gardens."

"For God's sake, Colin, there must be something else going
on, right under your eyes!"

It was first the loss of the scuba diver, and second the double
disappearance of Pallifer and Manville, and now Colin Bennett
was still failing to learn anything at all of any use. Curtis felt all
of his anger and frustration coming out in this last phone call,
and he didn't care.

Defending himself, more hangdog than ever, Bennett said,
"I swear, Mr. Curtis, they haven't been out of my sight. There
isn't a thing they do that I don't know about, and they're just
not doing anything at all about you and your business."

"You'll have to search their rooms," Curtis decided.

"I already did that, sir. When they went to dinner Friday, I
made sure they'd stay put a while, and I went and searched,
and I didn't find a thing. Mr. Curtis, could I ask you a question?"

"Go ahead," Curtis said.

"How many people named Mark work for you?"

"Probably a hundred," Curtis told him. "I employ thousands, Colin, a first name isn't enough to go on. Now, I'm leaving Singapore for a while on Wednesday. If we don't have any progress on the Jerry Diedrich front by then, we'll just drop it. Come into the office Wednesday afternoon, see Margaret, she'll have some money for you."

"Mr. Curtis, I'm doing—"

"You know what I want," Curtis snapped. "I want to know who the spy is. I want to know why Diedrich singles me out for all this attention. Those are the two questions. It really shouldn't be impossible to answer them, Colin, it really shouldn't."

Miserably, Bennett said, "No, sir, it shouldn't."

"Thank you for your efforts, Colin," Curtis said, and hung up.

12

He was always there. They caught only occasional glimpses of him, but he was nevertheless there, all the time, lurking. And they pretended not to notice.

Jerry didn't know what to think about it. The man always in their background, like something from a silent movie, a constant ominous presence, never getting any closer but also never going away. He hadn't done anything other than follow them, but the threat he implied was serious, and the man he worked for was serious.

If only they could find out what was going on. Every day at six, except on the weekend, Jerry had phoned Mark's friend, and spoken with Mark, and every day Mark had absolutely nothing new to tell. Their visits to the Planetwatch offices had yielded nothing either, partly because Jerry didn't feel he could tell them the whole story, but mostly, he believed, because Curtis was just too skilled at covering his tracks. Whatever he was up to, he was keeping it to himself—or doing a damn good job of hiding it in plain sight. Either way, no one had managed to dig anything up.

Jerry longed to be back on *Planetwatch III*, doing work he understood and was good at. But Richard Curtis was planning something horrible, the man was evil and needed to be stopped, and who else was there to stop him?

Not that they *were* stopping him. They'd been in Singapore a week, and were no closer to figuring things out than they'd been on arrival.

And then, Monday, Mark had news. They'd stopped at an

outdoor bar near a payphone. While Luther ordered beer for them all, Jerry went to make his call. "I still don't know what's going on," Mark said, "but something is, for sure."

"Why?" Jerry asked, feeling suddenly breathless. "What's happened?"

"First thing this morning, a fax came in from that guy I told you about. Jackie Tian?"

"A fax? From Hong Kong?"

"I got a look at it," Mark said, "and I wrote it down from memory, so I may have a word or two wrong, but I've certainly got the gist."

"Tell."

"It said, 'Diver unavailable. Arrested for smuggling. No sub-stitute.' That's all."

"Diver," Jerry echoed. "A scuba diver, you think?"

"That's what I'm thinking. If it has something to do with the soliton."

"In Hong Kong?" Jerry said. "Or off Hong Kong, I guess. Taiwan? That's the nearest large island."

"Then maybe that's where Curtis is going," Mark said. "That's my other news. He's leaving Wednesday. The story is he's going to Manila first, and then on to other places where we have pro-jects, as a kind of inspection tour, but I think that's fake. He isn't setting it up like a normal business trip. Usually, they'd have me phone people he knows in the various locations, give out his itinerary. He isn't doing that this time."

"Then where is he going?"

"Maybe Taiwan," Mark said. "I'll try to find out. Wherever he's going...it certainly seems he's going there to do whatever he's going to do."

"Oh, *god*, Mark, and we still don't know a thing!"

Mark said, "What if you went to the police?"

"And said what? In Singapore? Richard Curtis is one of their most respected businessmen. We don't have any proof, we don't even know what he plans to do."

"I'll see what I can find out tomorrow," Mark said. "But it isn't easy."

"Oh, I know it isn't, Mark, you're being wonderful, you really are."

"Not yet I'm not," Mark said. "Let's hope I can be."

"I'll call you tomorrow," Jerry said, and went back to the others to tell them Mark's news. "If Mark can find out where Curtis is really going," he finished, "maybe we could get there first, head him off somehow."

"If he can't," Luther said, "maybe we should just go to Hong Kong, try to find out more about this Tian person."

Kim said, "Do you know anybody in Hong Kong?"

"No," Jerry said. "But Kim, we do have to do something." He gulped beer, felt it hit his nervous stomach. He gestured toward the restrooms. "I'll be right back."

He rose from the table and headed for the gents', a small and rather smelly room at the rear of the building with (thank god) a window open onto a back alley. Not much air came in, and not much smell went out, but Jerry hoped not to be in here long.

He wasn't. He finished in the stall and when he pushed open the stall door to step outside the follower was there, standing at the sink, Jerry was so startled he almost forgot to pretend he didn't know who the man was. "Excuse me," he murmured, and started around the man, who turned and swung the piece of iron pipe hard, smashing it into Jerry's forehead.

13

"I don't want any more beer," Kim said.

Luther said, "When Jerry comes back, I'll settle up and go to the hotel."

"Where *is* Jerry?" Kim asked. "It's been a while."

Luther looked at his watch. "See if you can get our bill, I'll collect Jerry."

He went away, and Kim gestured to the waiter that they wanted the check. He nodded and went away inside and soon came out with a rectangular black plastic folder advertising American Express. Kim let it sit there.

But now, where was Luther? This was becoming a *long* time. Were they having some sort of talk in the men's room? A fight, maybe? Or had they just left without her?

Twice the waiter passed, giving her a raised-eyebrow look, and twice she merely smiled blankly at him. She was about to dig out her own limited cash when Luther sat down, abruptly, across from her, as though he'd been dropped there. He had a very strange expression on his face, like someone who has heard an inexplicable but frightening noise. He said, "He isn't there."

This made no sense. Kim looked toward the restrooms. "What's he doing?"

"He's *gone*, Kim, he isn't there."

Kim looked more closely at Luther, saw the sudden anxiety there beneath the disbelief. Instinctively she reached out to put a hand on his forearm as she said, "Luther! He can't be gone."

"No one in the men's room," Luther said. "None of the staff remembers seeing him go in or come out."

"But— He went in there, *we* saw him go in. And he didn't come out, Luther, we'd have seen him."

Luther abruptly stood, and stared hard at everything he could see up and down the street and around the tables. She thought he was looking for Jerry, but when he sat down again he said, "That man isn't here. The one who's been following us."

"Luther… What do you think happened?"

"I don't know." He had a stunned look. He said, "Did Jerry confront him? Jerry wouldn't confront him."

"You think Jerry ran away? Or that man ran away and Jerry followed him? But still, how could he come out here past us?"

"There's a window," Luther told her. "In the men's room, rather small, but you could climb out it."

"But why would he?"

"Maybe he saw something?" Luther shook his head. "If he suddenly saw something, no time to tell us, had to follow…" Another headshake. "Or did that man attack him? But why would he, after all this time, why change what he's doing? And Jerry can handle himself, he's no pushover."

She squeezed his forearm, saying, "He's all right, we know that. There's an explanation."

The waiter was hovering again, but Luther was too distracted to notice. "If he'd left a message, a note, but there's nothing."

Kim said, "Luther," and nodded at the waiter.

"What?" Luther looked up, understood, and said, "Oh, yes, of course."

While Luther got his wallet out and fished out a card, Kim said, "Something urgent happened, and he had to hurry away. He'll expect us to go back to the hotel."

"Yes, of course."

"He'll get a message to us there," Kim went on, "as soon as he can. It could be there now, for all we know."

"Yes. You're right, Kim. I'm sure you're right."

There was no message at the hotel, nor did they see the hulking follower anywhere, either outside or in the lobby. As they rode up together in the elevator, Kim said, "Do you think we should phone the police?"

"Not yet," Luther said.

She followed him into his room, his and Jerry's. It was very messy, as always. She sat in the one chair, by the window, while he paced.

He said, "We could still hear from him."

"Of course we could. How long has he been gone? Half an hour?"

"Closer to an hour," he told her.

"He'll call. Or he'll show up."

"What we'll do, Kim, we'll have dinner, we'll spend the evening here, and in the morning—"

"In the morning! Luther..."

"If we haven't heard from Jerry," Luther went on, "then we'll call the police."

"Jerry will be back long before then," she said, but it sounded stupid even as she was saying it.

14

Bennett did not dare think about the future. All he could possibly do was concentrate on the present, on the difficult tasks that faced him right *now*. Hitting the Diedrich fellow in the face with the iron pipe had been the easy part, almost the pleasurable part. But immediately after that, the job got complicated.

Quickly, before anybody else came into the men's room, he had to stuff this suddenly heavy inert body through the narrow opening of the window into the narrow stone-floored alley outside. Not a dirty alley, though, a very clean alley. The Singapore authorities demanded cleanliness everywhere, and backed up their demands with fines: one thousand dollars Singapore for littering. So even the alleys are frequently swept, rubbish is never allowed to accumulate, and though Bennett's victim was now bleeding from his cut forehead and his ears, and though he hit the alley stone hard, he didn't get dirty.

"That's good, then," Bennett told himself. "Well begun is half done." He clambered out the window after Diedrich, touched his throat for a pulse to be sure he was still alive, "You're not worth much dead, are you, not at this point," then hurried away down the alley to the side street where, fortunately, he had parked his car.

The alley was just barely wider than the Honda. Honking at the many pedestrians that jostled around him, muttering, "Can't you see a man's trying to do a piece of work here," Bennett backed the little car into place, the rear of it filling the alley mouth. Just enough room left for him to squeeze by.

The Honda was a hatchback. Raise the rear, and now the car almost completely blocked the view of anybody passing by on the street. Not that anybody cared. After one disapproving glare at this car stuck halfway into the sidewalk, everybody just kept on going by, concerned with their own affairs.

Bennett loped like a gorilla back to the body, which hadn't moved. "Hello, there, you still alive? Yes; good."

He picked Diedrich up like a sack of flour over his shoulder, and ran half-stumbling back to the car.

At the Honda, he dropped Diedrich into the well, not gently, and pulled over him some of the old blankets and tarps he kept back there. "There you are, all tucked in, eh?" Then he shut the hatchback, squeezed around the car, got behind the wheel, and drove away from there. (He saw the other two, still at the same table, as he went by, and muttered a farewell.)

Very well, what now? Richard Curtis had two questions that must be answered by Colin Bennett before Curtis would leave Singapore in two days' time. Only Jerry Diedrich knew the answers to those questions, and in trailing him Bennett had come to be convinced that he wasn't *going* to answer those questions, not willingly. It seemed to him, if he could at least find Mark, the elusive Mark, then he could go and lean very heavily on Mark, and force *him* to tell why Diedrich had such a very special antipathy toward Richard Curtis.

But in a week, a full week, Bennett hadn't even been able to accomplish step one. He *could not* fail Richard Curtis. Yet all he had left was today and tomorrow.

So the answer seemed obvious. He had to pluck Diedrich away from his friends, control him, and get the answers out of him directly, one way or another.

So he'd started, he'd begun, he'd gone this far. He had Diedrich unconscious and under control in the back of the

Honda. But he couldn't keep him in the Honda indefinitely. There had to be somewhere Bennett could deal with him at leisure, ask the questions and take the time to get the answers.

This was one of the crux points, when it was vital to concentrate exclusively on the present and think not at all about the future. There is no future, there is only this one step at a time, and the step now is to take this fellow home.

Well, that was the choice, wasn't it? Bennett had access to no other indoor area, not where he could keep a prisoner. Singapore is a nation and a city, but it's also an island, narrowly contained, heavily populated and cultivated. There were no remote lakes with seasonal lodges he could break into, no desert ghost towns, nowhere on the island that he could reach that wasn't already observed and occupied. So it was his own home, and nothing else to say about it.

At last he turned off China Street into an alley, somewhat wider than the alley behind that bar. "Home sweet home, by God," he announced, feeling grim.

On both sides of the alley, recently built but old-fashioned three-story buildings rose, neat but uninviting. Back here, the ground floors were open, parking for the residents who lived in the apartments above.

There was little pedestrian and no vehicular traffic back here. Bennett pulled Diedrich from the Honda, shouldered him with one blanket around him so that he was a bit less obviously a human body, and carried him up the two flights of narrow metal exterior stairs and along the outside concrete balcony to his door. It was hard to unlock the door, but Bennett didn't want to have to put the body down and pick it up again, so he persevered, commenting to himself along the way, while Diedrich bobbed on his shoulder, and finally he succeeded.

The apartment was as narrow as his garage space down below, but it went all the way through to the front. In the back, where he entered, was his kitchen, with a small bath beyond that. Next to the bath, a narrow hallway led to his small living room, illuminated by a square skylight in the middle of the celling. A closed door beyond that led to an even smaller room, with his bed and dresser and the window overlooking the side street below. If he leaned out his window, he could see the traffic on China Street, passing by down at the corner.

In the car, he'd decided what to do. He would keep the door between the living room and the bedroom closed, and also the door between the hall and the kitchen. That would give him and Diedrich a small suite of living room and bath, with only the living room's skylight and the bath's exhaust fan. Diedrich would have no view out any window except the sky, so he wouldn't be able to describe to anybody afterward even what neighborhood he'd been in.

Bennett considered. "Should I wear a mask, or maybe blindfold Diedrich?" He thought about it, the blindfold in particular, but he knew for sure they'd spotted him trailing them, they knew who he was. "Oh, they know it's me, no question." Curtis would simply have to—

This was one tiny chink of opening into the future, unavoidable, but not to be looked at too closely. Curtis would simply have to move Bennett out of Singapore once this was all over, get him a job far away on one of his other projects. (Not Belize, but somewhere.) If he stayed away from Singapore five or ten years, working in other parts of the world, that ought to do it. "Or I might decide never to come back."

Once he had Diedrich deposited on the bare living room floor, Bennett went away to the tool drawer in his kitchen for duct tape and the underwear drawer in his bedroom for a clean white sock. He taped Diedrich's wrists behind him, and taped his ankles, then stuffed the sock into Diedrich's mouth. As he did so, though, he noticed that Diedrich's breathing was very stuffy and labored, and shortly after he'd gagged him with the sock the man began to jerk and convulse. It was clear he'd stopped breathing, that something had damaged his nose—somehow the pipe had done some damage, perhaps to his sinuses—and he needed his mouth to breathe. Reluctant, but having no choice, Bennett pulled the sock out of his mouth again, and Diedrich gasped and panted and then settled down to his previous labored wheeze.

There was blood on the sock, just a little. Bennett didn't like that. He tossed the sock in with the dirty laundry, then scooped it out of there and threw it in with the trash under the sink. "Now, you *are* being stupid," he told himself, and got it back out of the trash and put it with the laundry again.

All this work had made him hungry. He had waffles he could heat in the toaster, and he could make tea. He had a narrow kitchen table and one chair, and he was seated there, eating his waffle, smelling the aroma from his teacup, when the hoarse voice in the living room yelled, "Help!"

In no hurry—no one in this neighborhood would answer a single cry like that, in the middle of the day, in English—Bennett got to his feet and walked into the living room, where Diedrich had twisted around to a half-seated position.

He stared wide-eyed and slack-mouthed at Bennett, then put his head back and screamed, "*Help!*"

Bennett crossed to give him a straight jab into that damaged nose. Diedrich fell back, stunned with pain, making little bird noises in his throat. Bennett stood over him and said, "If you shout out anymore, I'll do something to make you really hurt."

Diedrich stared at him. Bennett could see rationality come

slowly back into those eyes, rationality and fear and hate. That's all right, boyo, he said, almost out loud. Go ahead and hate me, I don't mind. He said, "You ready to talk to me?"

"You're *crazy*! They'll get you, don't you know they'll—" Bennett kicked him in the ribs. Diedrich shut up, breathing through his open mouth, and Bennett said, "That's then. This is now. Maybe it's all true, and some day you'll get to stand there and laugh and watch the coppers carry me off, all trussed up like a Christmas goose. But that's then. Right now, *I'm* in charge. You follow that?"

"I'm your prisoner," Diedrich said, almost challengingly, as though daring Bennett to admit to such an enormity.

"You are my prisoner," Bennett agreed. "And I'll tell you God's truth, boyo, I never had a prisoner before, so I'm not that certain sure how to take care of you. I got to control you, that's obvious, but I don't want to hurt you too much and have you die on me, do I? You'd like to help me keep you alive, now, wouldn't you?"

Diedrich stared at him, without answering.

Bennett shook his head, and poked the man's rib cage gently with his foot; not a real kick, just a reminder of the kick of a moment ago. "One thing I believe about having a prisoner," he said, "is when I speak, the prisoner answers. The prisoner talks when I want him to talk and shuts the fuck up when I want him to shut the fuck up. Now, have you got *that*?"

"Yes." The word came out strangled with hate and fear, but it came out.

"Very good."

Bennett felt he could sit down now, that the point of looming over Diedrich had been made, so he dragged his TV chair over and sat where he could always kick Diedrich if he had to, and said, "It's very simple, Mr. Jerry Diedrich. I have two questions, and you're going to give me the answers, and then we're done with one another."

"You're going to kill me," Diedrich said. Now, oddly enough, he sounded more angry than scared. Possibly he was mourning himself.

Bennett said, "Now, why would I want to do that? You'll give me my two answers and I'll be grateful, and what kind of gratitude is it kills the man that made me grateful?"

"I can identify you."

"Where? When? To who? Look around, boyo, do you even know where you *are*?"

"I can identify you," the fool stubbornly insisted.

"Only if you see me," Bennett pointed out. "You don't know my name, you don't know anything about me."

"Curtis sent you."

"Somebody named Curtis, you think." Bennett nodded, considering that. "And how many employees does this Curtis have?"

"Criminals? Killers?"

"Oh, now you're hurting my feelings," Bennett told him. He was beginning to enjoy himself. He hadn't been so relaxed and at ease with himself in ages. He said, "I'm no criminal, Mr. Jerry Diedrich, I'm less of a criminal than you are. Do you think you'll be looking at those police photos, and there I'll be, and you'll say, 'That's him, there he is, the handsome devil there!' Is that what you think?"

Diedrich looked away. Bennett's high spirits seemed to have a dampening effect on him. He said, "What do you want from me?"

"There, now," Bennett said. "Simplicity itself. To begin with, Mark's last name."

Diedrich stared at him. "Never!"

"Oh, don't talk about never, Jerry Diedrich," Bennett said. "There isn't a man in the world, not a man alive, who won't answer every question put to him if only it's put in the right way. Do you think I want to hurt you?"

"You already did. My nose, my…" He shook his head, feeling very sorry for himself.

"All right, then," Bennett said. "Do you think I want to hurt you *more*?"

"Probably," Diedrich said.

He's going into despair all of a sudden, Bennett thought, and knew despair could only strengthen Diedrich's resistance. He needed Diedrich to feel hope, to feel motivated to do as he was told.

Bennett got to his feet, and Diedrich flinched, but wouldn't look directly at him. Bennett went out to the kitchen and got his barely sipped tea and brought it back and knelt beside Diedrich. "I'll give you a bit of tea," he said, "to clear your mouth. You've a bit of blood in your throat, this'll help."

Diedrich pressed his teeth together. Through the clenched teeth, he said, "What's in it?"

For answer, Bennett took a swig, swirled it around in his mouth, and swallowed. Like a lab technician making a report, "Tea," he said, "with real sugar and imitation cream. Care for some?"

"No."

Bennett shrugged and got to his feet. "More for me, then," he said, and drank it down. Then he smiled at Diedrich and said, "What's Mark's last name?"

"No."

A kick in the ribs, same spot. "Yes, boyo."

"No."

Kick. "Yes."

"No."

He's trying to faint, the fairy bastard, Bennett thought. He's trying to goad me into doing something that'll make him pass out, so he won't have to answer my questions.

"We'll see about this," he said, and carried his teacup back to the kitchen, where he ruminated while he finished his waffle and washed it down with a glass of cold water.

Back in the living room, Diedrich hadn't moved. Bennett walked through into the bedroom and pulled that sock once more out of the laundry. Bringing it back with him, carefully shutting the bedroom door, he knelt before Diedrich and showed him the sock and said, "Do you see what this is?"

Diedrich gave the sock a dull look, then apparently remembered he was supposed to respond to questions, so he said, "Yes."

"It's a sock."

"Yes."

"I was using it to gag you, so you wouldn't be shouting for help and like that, such as you did, but when I put it in your mouth, turns out, your nose isn't working. So I had to take it out again. It was like this."

Diedrich tried to fight, but Bennett was stronger. He pried his jaws apart and stuffed the sock inside. "And now I've got to wash me hands, you see," he said, and got to his feet, and turned away from the strangling sounds Diedrich made, his legs kicking on the floor.

Bennett went into the bathroom and washed and dried his hands. When he came back out, Diedrich's eyes were popping, his face was mottled dark red, he was straining every muscle in his body. Bennett casually pulled the sock from his mouth, and Diedrich made horrible sounds, flopping like a captured fish in the bottom of the boat. Breathing seemed to be painful for him, but at least it was possible.

Bennett sat in his chair to wait for Diedrich to be recovered enough to talk. He wasn't a cruel man, he didn't do this sort of thing, had never done this sort of thing, but he had no choice, did he? In for a penny, in for a pound. And he'd always believed, if you take on a job, you do it as best you know how.

No self-satisfied smug little poofter like Jerry Diedrich was going to ruin Colin Bennett's life, and that was that. That was that. No second thoughts about it.

"Feel better, Jerry?"

"It hurts." The man spoke in barely a whisper, but he spoke.

"I think a hospital would do you a world of good, boyo," Bennett said. "I'd like to help get you to hospital, you know, just as soon as you answer my questions."

"What's—" The hoarse voice stumbled and stopped, rattled, wheezed, then tried again. "What's the other question?"

"Oh, I don't think so," Bennett said. "One question at a time, I think. So what's Mark's last name?"

"No."

"Ah, Jerry." Bennett knelt beside him with the sock.

Diedrich stared at him in terror. "You'll kill me! You'll kill me before you know!"

"Oh, no, Jerry," Bennett assured him. "I'll keep a very close eye on you. I'll be here to protect and safeguard you. Now, open wide."

"Mmm! Mmm!"

Once again Bennett forced the jaws open, and Diedrich yelled, "Sansan!"

"What was that?" Bennett released him and leaned back.

Diedrich's head hung. "Hennessy," he whispered.

"Well, thank you, Jerry," Bennett said. "Mark Hennessy, thank you."

"God forgive me," Diedrich said, and lowered his forehead to the floor.

"Don't blame yourself, Jerry," Bennett told him. "I told you, no one refuses to speak. Eventually, you know, everybody speaks."

Diedrich lay gasping, eyes closed, forehead pressed to the floor. Bennett doubted he'd need the sock again, but he left it on the floor, too far for Diedrich to kick, but plainly in his sight.

Bennett's telephone was in this same room. Through thick and thin, he'd kept the telephone, paying for it as best he could, knowing it was his only lifeline, and now at last it was paying off, wasn't it? The job offer he'd prayed for, he'd kept the phone for, was here, wasn't it? Came over the phone, as he'd thought it would.

And now the phone was useful again. It stood on the small table beside the sofa. Bennett went over there, sat, and dialed the number Curtis had given him, his home phone, for the evening. A servant of some sort answered, and Bennett said, "Colin Bennett here, for Mr. Curtis, if he's in."

Across the way, the gasping Diedrich didn't react. His forehead was still pressed to the wood floor, possibly because it was cooler there. Bennett was pretty sure the man had told the truth, but he wanted it to be very clear that any of his stories would be checked up on right away.

"Bennett."

"Good evening, sir. Do you have, sir, by any chance, a fellow working for you called Mark Hennessy?"

Diedrich, on the floor, moaned a little. Curtis was silent, a stunned silence, and then he said, he half-whispered, "My God. I never would have—" Another little pause, and then, "Of *course*. But how do they even know each other? No, that doesn't matter. Thank you, Colin, that's very good."

"I should have the other answer for you very soon, sir," Bennett said. He felt elated, he felt his chest swelling, he felt lightheaded, he felt better than he'd felt in years. "And tomorrow, sir, if I may," he said, "I'd like to come talk to you. About my future, you know."

Another little pause. Curtis knew what he meant. How would he react? It all depended on this one answer, right now.

"Of course, Colin," Curtis said, sounding frank and willing. "We *should* have a discussion. I'll be here most of the day."

I'm made, Bennett thought, and couldn't help smiling as he said, "Thank you, sir."

He hung up, and except for that one moan when he'd heard Hennessy's name, Diedrich had done nothing; no reactions, no moves. He still sprawled there, twisted, as Bennett had left him.

Bennett crossed to sit in the chair again, within reach of the man, and waited, and it must have been a good five minutes before a long shuddering breath wracked Diedrich like an internal storm, and he rolled over onto his side, his face slack, eyes dull. "You might as well," he whispered.

Bennett watched him. "Might as well?"

"Go on."

"Ah, question number two, you mean."

Diedrich closed his eyes. He was too weary, perhaps, to respond to a rhetorical question.

Well, that was all right. Bennett could cut the fellow a little slack, now that the resistance was done. He said, "You have a special kind of hate for Mr. Curtis. Not the environment stuff, all that stuff. With you, it's personal. So that's the question. What do you have against Richard Curtis in particular?"

Diedrich frowned, eyes still closed. Then his eyes opened and his head turned and he frowned at Bennett for a long time, as though trying to understand a foreign language, one that was now vital to understand. Then, calmly, as though they were merely having a conversation together here, he said, "You already know."

That was an odd answer. Bennett brushed it aside.

"Jerry Diedrich," he said, "I wouldn't ask you a question if I already knew the answer, now, would I? That ain't sensible, is it? So just tell me, and don't, you know, prolong it." ('Prolong the agony,' he was going to say, but corrected himself in mid-sentence, because he didn't want to be unnecessarily cruel.)

Something happened in Diedrich. Out of nowhere, he'd found some shred of his old defiance. Sounding angry again, astonishing Bennett, he said, "Ask *Curtis*, if that's what you want to know!"

Mildly, Bennett told him, "It was Mr. Curtis said I should ask *you*, you know that, no use beating around the bush."

"He knows, he already *knows*!"

Bennett sighed. Why this delay, why this complication? "Diedrich," he said, "look at that sock on the floor there, and pull yourself together. Never mind who knows what, or what you think in that very stupid mistaken head of yours. What do you have against Richard Curtis?"

Diedrich actually did obey orders. He stared blinking at the sock. He looked very desperate. He said, not a whisper, but a voice so low Bennett could barely hear it, "Daniel Foster."

What? Bennett felt a terrible cold knife run up his back. Was this whole thing an elaborate scheme aimed at him, not at Diedrich after all, but at Colin Bennett, to get him to confess to the awful thing he'd done? Daniel Foster, in the water tunnel, when the lights went out, and the sound of the rushing water came.

Bennett could hear the sound of the rushing water in his ears. It was so loud he could barely hear himself over it. He said, "What was that name? What about that name?"

Now Diedrich turned his bitter, despairing, hate-filled, enraged eyes on Bennett. "Curtis threw him away," he said, his voice strangled again, as though he'd just had another treatment with the sock. "He killed him, and covered it up, and made him disappear from the world as though he'd never *been*!"

"Diedr—"

"But he *did* exist! I loved him! I loved him, and we were going to—"

He'd half-risen in his agitation, and now he fell back and stared at the ceiling. "My letters came back, unknown. I phoned, Central America, oh, no, nobody of that name here. But I kept asking, and met people, and later on I found out, I found out from people on the crew, it was an *accident*! The kind of accident you get from people who don't *care* about other human beings! Greedy, inhuman! An accident! And they covered it up, and threw him away like a dead dog, and he's so *powerful*, Curtis, he's so *powerful*, that nobody can touch him! *I* can touch him! I'll get him, and I'll get him, and I'll get him, and we'll see how powerful he is."

Diedrich turned blazing eyes on Bennett. "He hires you scum, he can hire thousands of you scum, and it doesn't matter. You can kill me in this room, you're going to kill me in this room and we both know it, but it doesn't matter. Curtis is going to pay. He is going to pay."

Bennett stared at the man on the floor. What could he possibly do with this news? Mr. Curtis wants the answers to two questions, and I just gave him the answer to the first, but now what about the other? Can I give him that answer, ever?

"Mr. Curtis, this man, this organization behind this man, they've been after you for years now, they've been plaguing you for years now, because they blame you for a horrible crime you don't know anything about, that *I* did, that I hid from *you*, not from them, I'm the cause of your troubles, Mr. Curtis, there's the answer to your question, and can I have that job now, that we talked about?"

Now, for the first time, Bennett did allow the door to the future to slide fully open, allowed himself to look through. And for the first time, he saw that, in that future, there was no Jerry Diedrich.

15

Jerry felt the difference. In the air in the room. Through all of this, through the terror, and the pain, and the helpless rage, there had always been some faint hint, some touch of the possibility of belief, that he would live through this, that something would happen, some rescue, or that this man actually would believe he was safe in dumping Jerry somewhere, alive, after he'd finished with his questions.

But not anymore. Some chill had entered the room, the chill of death. Jerry didn't know why, or exactly at what point it had come in, but it was here now, and all at once his situation was a million times worse. Before, there'd been, however unrealistically, a sliver of hope. Now, it was gone.

Could he get it back? Could he return to wherever they'd been before, no matter how dreadful that had been? He looked at the hooded eyes of the other man, his slightly puffy and unhealthy cheeks, his blunt-fingered hands, the shambling strength of his body, and even though the man was the same brute he'd been before, there was also something new in him now, something implacable and unreachable.

Oh, could he get back to the way it was before? Feeling his throat close up again with pain and terror, he croaked, "Why do you do his work? Why do you do his *dirty* work?"

The man shook his head. He seemed to think about what to answer, or whether to answer at all. Then he sighed, and it was as though he felt he owed Jerry something, some return for murdering him; which scared Jerry even more.

"You're wrong, you know," the man said. "You got hold of the wrong idea. You know about the blind men and the elephant?"

This was a surprise. Was it hope again, a return to human contact? Jerry said, "Each blind man thinks it's a different animal. They touch different parts, the trunk, the tusks, the leg."

"You got hold of a part, and you got it wrong," the man said, "and that's the story, that's your whole story right there." He chuckled a little, and his meaty shoulders moved. "You're a lesson in the dangers of prejudice, that's what you are."

"I don't understand."

"Of course you don't. Richard Curtis is a rich man, and he goes his own way, and he don't give a damn about you, so all you can see is he must be an evil sort of person."

"He is."

"He doesn't know a thing about Daniel Foster, you know," the man said.

Jerry looked at him. Some sort of wound seemed to open up in his heart, something hollowing and mean. He said, he whispered, "What do you know about it?"

"I was drinking, you see," the man said. "Not justifying myself, excusing myself, you understand that. It's just I was a drinking man in those days, and it made me careless sometimes."

Barely daring to breathe, feeling that new emptiness in his heart, Jerry whispered, "You were *there*?"

"I swear to you, on my manhood," the man said, "I had no idea he was still in that tunnel. I didn't know all those planks and such were in there. Boyo, I was *fired*. I been out of work ever since, and only because what I did to the *turbines*. Do you think, if Richard Curtis knew I flung a *man* down that shaft, he'd take my side?"

Jerry could only stare at him, helpless, knowing he was hearing the truth, and knowing the truth was worse than anything he'd ever imagined.

The man said, "I've been a guilty fellow and a beaten fellow for a long time. My marriage broke up, I was blackballed everywhere. Not looking for sympathy, you know what I'm saying, but I've been punished. Oh, you can believe that. You wanted somebody punished for what happened to your friend, well, you got your wish."

"If Curtis didn't…" Jerry began, but then didn't know what it was he even wanted to ask.

The man nodded at him. "Curtis knew you were there," he said. "For a long time, Mr. Curtis, he's known you were out there, a thorn in his side. A mosquito, but a *bad* mosquito. You know, he didn't say to me to kill you, that isn't the sort of man we're talking about here. He said to me, Colin, find out who's the traitor in my camp, and for the love of God, Colin, find out what this fellow Diedrich has against me."

"Oh, Jesus," Jerry said. He couldn't look at the man anymore.

"Well, so I've done the job," the man said. "Haven't I, Jerry Diedrich?"

"Yes."

"I'm a willing worker, you know, I'm deserving of trust. I'm deserving of a second chance. Don't you think so?"

"You'll get your second chance," Jerry said, not trying to hide the bitterness he felt.

"Well, but there's the rub," the man told him. "I've given Mr. Curtis the information on this fellow Hennessy, so he's pleased with me for that. But can I answer his other question? Can I tell him why it is you've been hounding him all this while?"

Jerry looked at him, and now he understood why the temperature in the room had changed. He whispered, "I'll never tell anybody, I swear."

"Now, why would I trust you?" the man asked him. "What sort of relationship have we had, you and I, that I would trust you? You've already told your lover friend there, haven't you? The German boy."

"No! I never told anyone!"

"You? A bigmouth like you?" The man seemed almost amused by him. "And the girl with you," he said, "You couldn't resist telling her, could you, for a sympathetic smile?"

"Honest to God, no, I never told— I never told anybody, I never *will* tell anybody!"

"Oh, I know that," the man said.

"Please. Please. I swear to you, I'll never say a word, you can trust me, not a word to anybody, I'll never bother Curtis again. I'll—"

"I know all that," the man said, and stood. "I know all that, because you're going to keep your mouth shut." He went down on one knee beside Jerry. "You know the saying," he said. "When you want somebody to shut up and *keep* shut up, what is it you say?"

He waited, but Jerry didn't answer. Finally, almost gently, the man gave the answer himself: "Put a sock in it."

16

Mark Hennessy.

Being driven to the office Tuesday morning, Curtis couldn't get over how obvious it had been all along. Someone named Mark was passing along to Diedrich and Planetwatch information about Richard Curtis's affairs. And there was Mark Hennessy, all along, right there in his main office.

Was that why it had never occurred to him that *this* Mark might be *that* Mark? There were dozens, perhaps hundreds, of his employees named or nicknamed Mark, and his suspicions had always leaped over the nearest Mark to any and all of those out there, and now he thought the reason was that this *was* the nearest Mark. A young man who'd worked for Curtis for eight or nine years, who had always been capable and intelligent and willing and self-effacing. One wouldn't even *think* of this Mark as a traitor.

But he was. And now the question became, what to do about it.

The simple and obvious remedy would be to merely fire him, without a reference, telling the little turncoat why, and then to hire someone else in his place. Or, more likely, choose someone already in the firm to be moved up a step. That would be the simple and obvious way, but when Curtis thought back to all the trouble Planetwatch had caused him in the last several years, all made possible by this one little sneak inside his own company, it made him too angry for a mere firing to satisfy. No, there had to be more to it than that, when it came to Mark Hennessy, something that would give more satisfaction.

And Curtis thought he might know just what would do the trick.

He wondered how Bennett had smoked Hennessy out. Not that he doubted the truth of it, not for a second, but he was just curious to know how Bennett had done it. The man had certainly come through, exactly as Curtis had hoped. There might even be a place for him, somewhere, in the organization, later on; time would tell. And it would be a fine further boost for Bennett's prospects if he could also find out what Jerry Diedrich's goddam problem was.

The office was quieter today. The Kanowit architects had gone, with ledgers full of notes, and would return in a month, with revised sets of plans. (In a month, all this other would be behind him. In a month, he would be himself again.)

So the office was quieter today, mostly because it was winding down in preparation for the boss's departure. To Manila, most of them thought, all except the absolutely reliable Margaret. And to Manila Mark thought, too, fortunately.

Curtis told Margaret to buzz him in, and when the fellow arrived Curtis struggled to hide his disgust. "Good morning, Mark," he said, and managed his usual easy smile.

"Morning, sir." Mark seemed as open and boyish as ever, as guileless and as transparent.

But of course Mark had never been open and transparent, had he?

Well, Curtis could be a dissembler, too, when he needed to be. Offering his false smile to the false Mark, he said, "You know I'm off to Manila tomorrow."

"Yes, sir, of course," Mark said.

"You're one of the few people I can trust, Mark," Curtis said.

"Well, thank you, sir," Mark said, looking both pleased and surprised. "I appreciate that."

"I *can* trust you, can't I?" Curtis asked, and was immediately afraid he'd gone too far.

But Mark's smile redoubled, as he said, "Of course you can, sir! I hope you can *always* trust me."

"I'm sure I can." Curtis patted the rotten fellow's arm. "So I'm going to tell you something that no one else in the office knows, except Margaret."

Mark looked alert. "Sir?"

"I'm not actually going to Manila."

Even more alert. "No, sir?"

"I'm in the middle of something— Mark, if my competition found out, or those goddam tree-huggers…"

"Oh, I understand," Mark said.

"Where I'm going," Curtis told him, "and you really must keep this under your hat—"

"Absolutely, sir."

"Is Sydney."

Mark was obviously startled. "Sydney?"

"I'm actually taking a flight to Sydney, tomorrow," Curtis told him, "and the reason I'm telling you, I'll want you to come along."

"Sir! I'd be delighted."

"I need somebody I can count on, while I'm there."

"Yes, sir."

"Our flight leaves at eleven in the morning," Curtis said. "Margaret will help you with any paperwork you need, and a car will pick you up and bring you to Changi in the morning. See her, and then take the rest of the day off, to pack and get yourself ready."

"Yes, sir. Thank you, sir." Mark extended his hand, which Curtis reluctantly took. "Mr. Curtis," he said, "I do understand the faith you're showing in me, and I assure you I'll do my level best to live up to it."

And be phoning Diedrich the second you get home, Curtis thought, to give him the news. And good luck to you both. "See you at Changi," he said.

Once the little rat was out of the office, the next order of business was Bennett. Curtis called the Race Course Court Hotel, where Bennett was registered under his own name, and left a message for him to phone Richard, no number given. Then he waited, wondering where Bennett was at the moment. Finding out the truth about Jerry Diedrich, maybe. That would be good.

17

Bennett woke late, feeling languorous. It was a delicious feeling of physical contentment. He stretched and turned in the hotel bed, feeling the good sheets, the fluffy pillow, the light blanket, and the pleasant cool dryness of air-conditioned air. He felt like a man who'd just finished a long and complicated job and could now think of it as a job well done.

Of course, in truth, the job wasn't done, not yet. Diedrich would certainly have talked about Daniel Foster with his German friend, the tall blond fellow, and with the girl. So long as they were in Singapore, so long as they existed, they were a danger to Colin Bennett, because the circumstance just might arise in which they could tell that story to Richard Curtis, and Curtis would have to believe it.

What about Mark Hennessy? He certainly must know the story, too, and he was physically closer to Curtis, he could blab it at any time. But would Curtis be likely to believe Hennessy now, to believe anything Hennessy might say? Hennessy could easily already know the story of Bennett's downfall—most people in the company had heard about his destruction of the turbines—and Curtis would simply think Hennessy was making up the rest, to get even with the man who'd exposed him.

No, it was the other two who were the problem, Luther Rickendorf and Kim Baldur. They were the ones who had to be gotten rid of, before Bennett could report to Richard Curtis on the demise of Jerry Diedrich.

Bennett had decided, at last, that the way to handle the Diedrich matter with Curtis was to tell him a modified version of the truth. That he'd captured the fellow, and brought him home, and trussed him up, and forced him to reveal the name of the spy in RC Structural. But then, he would say, it turned out he hadn't been a very efficient interrogator, he hadn't realized exactly how much pressure he was putting on Diedrich, and the fellow had died before he could describe his grievance against Curtis.

Yes, that ought to do it. It wasn't a murder, it was an accidental death, done in Richard Curtis's service. Curtis hadn't asked for it, but he could only be pleased by the result. No more Jerry Diedrich to pester him, ever and ever. Who cares what his grievance was. It died with him.

Last night, when he'd finished talking with Diedrich, Bennett had gone out to a nearby Chinese noodle shop for dinner, a place where they knew him by sight. Then he'd gone to a kung fu movie in the neighborhood, and after that, when he got home, Diedrich was dead. In the darkness of night, it hadn't been too difficult to carry the body back down the stairs to his Honda and stuff it under the hatchback, the same as he'd brought him here, though this time not breathing. (He'd reclaimed his sock, and now it had definitely gone into the garbage.)

It was a long drive he'd then taken, over to the Central Expressway to get out of central Singapore, then west on the Ayer Rajah Expressway all the way to the end, and on out Jalan Ahmad Ibrahim past the Jurong Bird Park to the Jurong Industrial Estate, the new area reclaimed from swamp and filled with manufacturing and housing.

Down in here, at night, there were quiet dark streets leading south to the water's edge and the Straits of Jurong. Here is where Bennett stripped Diedrich of all identification, finally removed the lengths of duct tape from his wrists and ankles, and rolled him into the water. He would float or sink or whatever he might do, and eventually be discovered and would most likely be a natural death.

True, there wouldn't be water in his lungs, so he wouldn't be thought to have drowned. But he could have fallen into the water and hit his face against something and died that way. In any event, what was there to link this body to Colin Bennett? Nothing.

The other two would be more complicated. Lying in bed, in no hurry to rise, he thought about ways to kill them, and then smiled at his own thoughts. He'd never deliberately considered killing anybody before, and hadn't originally intended (so far as he knew) to kill Diedrich, but now that it had been done, something new had opened up inside Bennett, because now he saw what a solution this was. How easy, and how permanent. The solution to so many problems.

Well, he should get to it, shouldn't he? They'd be missing Diedrich, they might have already reported his disappearance to the police. Before they made too many waves, before they did too much talking to too many people, he should stop them. The good new permanent way.

Bennett rose and dressed. The hotel had no restaurant, but they put out a simple breakfast buffet in a corner of the lobby every morning. Bennett went down there to have coffee and a pair of pastries, then crossed to the desk, not expecting any messages, but just to be certain, so long as he was here.

"Yes, Mr. Bennett, one message, it came in this morning."

Call Richard. Bennett's pulse jumped, he squeezed the slip of paper tight. He felt like a dog who's been called by his master, but it wasn't a bad feeling, a humiliating feeling, it was good, it was positive, it meant he was wanted and useful and productive again.

What should he do first? Call Richard, or take care of the other two? He was tense with the pressure to take care of the other two, not even knowing where they were, if they were in the hotel, who they might be talking to. But how could he not respond to this call, from Richard?

He hurried back to his room, and made the call, and was immediately put through to Curtis, who said, "Colin, I'm going to want you to take a trip."

Bennett hardly heard that; his own news was so pressing. He said, "Sir, you don't have to worry about that fellow anymore."

There was a brief startled silence, and then: "Oh?"

"He's gone, sir," Bennett said. "He won't be back."

"You'll have to tell me all about it," Curtis said. "Later. What I want you to do, Colin—"

"Yes, sir."

"—is check out of that hotel, but keep your luggage in your car. You have your passport?"

"Yes, sir."

"There's a foodstall at Changi named Wok Wok, do you know it?"

"I can find it, sir."

"Good man. One o'clock. Be ready to travel."

"Yes, sir," Bennett said, thinking, it isn't even ten now. I'll have almost three hours to find them and deal with them, no problem, no problem.

"See you then."

"Thank you, sir," Bennett said, and hung up, and got to his feet. Pack first. Pack, check out, load the car, then come back in and deal with them.

He moved quickly, but not scrambling; he was very sure of himself. He packed his one large bag, carried it downstairs, paid the rest of his bill in cash, and took the bag out to the Honda, putting it where Diedrich had recently been. Then he was ready.

He wished he had a gun. The best he had was the length of iron pipe he'd used on Diedrich. Well, it had done the job with him, it would do the job with the other two. When he went back into the hotel, his shirt hung outside his pants, so that the pipe stuck under his belt would not be seen.

He'd kept his room key, and the clerk hadn't thought to ask for it. He went through the lobby, quietly, attracting no attention, and took the elevator to the fourth floor, where his room had been.

It felt a little odd, to enter a hotel room after one has quit it. As though he'd been wrested, for just a minute, out of the normal movement of time, been jogged back or to the side, like a knight's move in chess.

His former room was at the back of the building, overlooking a tumble of shed roofs and the rears of other buildings. The rooms of Rickendorf and Baldur were down one flight and also at the back. When he'd installed the listening device in the telephone, he'd come down the fire escape, a quick and simple route. The doorlocks were too good, beyond Bennett's capacity to pick, but the windows at the back of the hotel had not been changed when the place was refurbished, and were locked with merely an old-fashioned latch that Bennett could open with a tableknife stuck between the sashes. That was the way he'd done it last time, and that's the way he'd do it now.

The girl first. If she were there, Bennett would find some way to get in and kill her. If she weren't there, Bennett would go in and search, maybe find out where she was, or wait for her to come back.

He opened the window, and leaned out, and one flight up two Chinese men in white coveralls were painting the fire escape. Painting it shiny black enamel. They saw Bennett and waved and smiled at him, and Bennett waved and smiled back, then withdrew into the room and shut the window.

Damn. Painting the fire escape; who ever heard of such a thing? Yes, fire escapes must be painted, like anything else, but no one's ever *seen* a fire escape being painted.

So it meant he couldn't do it that way, that's all.

Another way. All right, let's do it.

Bennett felt increasing urgency and increasing determination. He would do it, and *now*. He left his former room, now truly for the last time, and took the stairs down one flight.

He hurried to Baldur's room, pulled the pipe out from under his shirt, and knocked on the door.

"Hello?"

Close to the door, imitating Diedrich's voice and accent as best he could, he called, "Kim? Have you seen Luther?"

"Jerry?"

The door opened, and Bennett cocked the length of pipe up by his shoulder, and in the doorway was the girl. He hesitated, just a second—but in that second, she recognized him, and saw the pipe in his hand, and understood what he planned.

They lunged at the same instant, she to shut the door, he to push it open. She almost managed to slam it shut, but he wedged his foot in the space, ignored the pain when the door hit his foot, and shoved against it with his whole body.

She was strong, surprisingly so, and she was screaming *helphelphelp!* but he was stronger, and slowly he forced the door farther open.

Noise down the corridor. The elevator door was opening down there. Bennett *heaved*, and the door sprang open, and he leaped inside.

She was still screaming. She ran across to the bathroom as he slammed the front door and followed. She got into the bathroom before he could reach her, and he heard the snick of the lock, but he didn't care. A bathroom lock?

Pounding on the door they'd just left. A male voice yelling

KimKimKim! The German fellow? Deal with him next, deal with the one in the bathroom now.

He lifted his foot and kicked the bathroom door next to the knob, and at the same time he heard the German kick at the front door. But that door was much stronger than this one. He could finish here with plenty of time to take care of the German.

He kicked the bathroom door again, and it snapped open, and he sprang forward, and she sprayed hairspray into his eyes, pressing hard with both hands on the top of the aerosol can, spray shooting into his startled eyes and into his nose and into his open mouth.

He couldn't see! It burned his eyes and he couldn't see, but she was still in the confines of the bathroom, and he moved forward, arms spread, and she kicked him between the legs.

He felt her brush past him, but could do nothing about it. Bent, the pipe dropped, he scraped at his face, turning, trying to see, wiping at his eyes, and the first thing he saw was the girl opening the door, and then some man he'd never laid eyes on in his life before came running into the room.

Bennett raced out of the bathroom to the window, flung it open, rolled over the sill and out onto the fire escape just before the man could reach him. Rolling on his back on the fire escape, he kicked up with both feet into that face as the man started out after him, and the man fell back into the room.

Bennett tore down the fire escape and in among the sheds, running the maze, finding a way out of here to the street, while the Chinese painters watched him in amazement.

18

George Manville?

Kim stared at him, this apparition, as astonished by Manville's presence as by that other man who'd suddenly attacked her with an iron pipe. She stared at him as he chased the other man across the room, the man diving out the window, George trying to go out after him, the other man kicking him back, kicking him in the face, George falling backward.

Only then did she come out of her momentary paralysis, start to move. Dropping the hairspray can on the bed, she hurried over to George, went to her knees beside him, called his name.

He was stunned, and there was a fresh scrape on his right cheek, bleeding a little, like four shallow claw scratches. He focused on her, or tried to: "Where is he?"

She moved to the window, looked out and down, and saw the man just dropping from the bottom of the fire escape into a jumble of lean-tos and sheds down there. Hearing chatter above her, she looked up and saw two painters pointing at the fleeing man. Seeing Kim, they pointed at her, and started to laugh.

What did they think was going on here, what did they think the story was? Kim smiled weakly at them and turned back to the room, to find George shakily getting to his feet, propping himself with the bed. "Sit down, George, sit down," she said, holding his arm, helping him to sit on the side of the bed. "I'll get a cloth."

She hurried back to the bathroom, now with its broken door, and ran warm water over a washcloth. Bringing that out to

George, she bent over him to dab at the scratches, to clean away any dirt there might have been on that man's shoes, and found herself meeting George's eyes, three inches away.

He smiled at her, crinkling the area of the wound.

"God, it's good to see you," he said.

In the police van, he explained some of what had been going on, and how he happened to be here. "After Curtis smeared me," he said, "I had to go along with him, at least for a little while, so he'd clear my name."

"I thought that was the reason," she told him, although in fact she hadn't been at all sure.

The police van was large and roomy, meant to carry a dozen officers at a time. In it now were only the police driver and a second policeman in front, plus Kim and George in back. They were traveling without siren or flashing lights, crossing Singapore toward Tanglin police station on Napier Road. "Your friend Luther's there," George had told her, "he was telling the police about Jerry when I came in."

Now, on the way, he said, "I was being held at a station Curtis owns in the middle of Australia, very isolated. When I found out Curtis wasn't keeping his part of the bargain, that he was still trying to send that man of his to kill you, the one who came out to the boat—"

"Him," she said, and shuddered, remembering the man. "Don't tell me *he's* in Singapore."

"He's dead," George said, the word coming out very flat. She would have asked him to explain more, but he went straight on, saying, "I got away from there and made my way back to Brisbane, and went to see the lawyer again. Brevizin. That was Wednesday. At first, he didn't want to see me at all. Curtis had been to him—"

"Curtis is everywhere," she said.

He shook his head and said, "It seems like that sometimes. Anyway, Curtis had hired him to take care of any legal problems with his yacht and with Captain Zhang killing himself. You see, the whole point was, if Curtis is his client, I can't be."

"He *is* everywhere," she repeated.

"Well," George said, "ultimately I did convince Brevizin to see me, and I told him what had been going on, everything I knew, and he finally agreed to look into it. Friday afternoon he called to tell me we were going to meet a police inspector named Tony Fairchild, which we did."

Kim said, "And had Curtis been to him, too?"

"As a matter of fact, yes," George told her. "He interviewed Curtis because of Zhang's suicide, and Curtis told him I was not only back working with him but was here in Singapore. He had somebody, God knows who, pretend to be me and talk to Fairchild from Singapore and convince him it was all a tempest in a teapot."

Kim said, "Why go through all that?"

"Because otherwise Fairchild and Brevizin were going to meet, and they would have found out right away they'd been told conflicting stories, and they'd have known there was something there to be investigated. This way, everyone just let it drop."

"With you stuck in the middle of Australia."

"Right. So Friday the three of us met, Brevizin and Inspector Fairchild and me, and we untangled some of the lies, and Fairchild said he'd look into it all very quietly, which I suppose he must have done over the weekend, because yesterday, first thing in the morning, we had another meeting, the three of us, and made some phone calls, and the end result is, Fairchild and I took a late flight here last night."

Surprised, Kim said, "Both of you?"

"Yes. Brevizin paid for it—he doesn't take kindly to being played for a fool. Fairchild has no jurisdiction here, of course, but Brevizin felt, to get the Singapore authorities to take this question seriously, Fairchild would need to be here, to give an unbiased take on events."

Kim said, "What question do you mean?"

"The basic question," George said. "What is Richard Curtis going to destroy, and when is he going to do it?"

19

Tony Fairchild thought his Singaporean opposite number was more or less an ass. Wai Fung, inspector of police, the exact identical rank to Fairchild, was a slender man of middle years who seemed determined not to let anything at all ruffle the orderly progression of his day, his life, his career. He seemed to believe that he was not in his position as police inspector to solve crimes, bring malefactors to justice and affirm the rule of law (all of which Fairchild believed in passionately), but was here merely to maintain calm, as though he were an usher at a cinema on a Saturday afternoon.

Which meant, of course, that Wai Fung was having a great deal of trouble accommodating the notion that he should go out and ruffle the existence of a prominent Singaporean businessman like Richard Curtis, nor that he should concern himself with the cares and woes of a provincial policeman from far-off Australia, nor that he should want to involve his island nation in the murk of international intrigue, particularly if it might at all have any bearing on Hong Kong, which is to say, China. So all in all, Wai Fung was being a smiling obstructionist.

On the other hand, Fairchild had to admit to himself that a part of his antipathy to Wai Fung was no doubt caused by his own unease. First, he was uneasy because he was out of the world he knew and into a world where he had neither insights nor standing. But even more importantly, he felt unease, even embarrassment, because he had already once before fallen down on this job so miserably and completely.

It had taken no more than three minutes of the first meeting among himself and the lawyer Brevizin and the real George

Manville for Fairchild to realize he'd been snookered, by the smooth-talking Curtis and by the false Manville, telephoning him from Singapore (and even that wasn't certain) to say he'd had minimal dealings with Kim Baldur and in fact actively disliked her.

If Fairchild hadn't allowed himself to be lulled into inactivity by that phone call, he'd have kept his original appointment with Brevizin and the whole plot would have unraveled right then, or at least begun to. Instead of which, they'd lost a week, more than a week, and Fairchild blamed himself.

As an overachiever from the Sydney slums, a bright boy who'd always had to provide his own impetus in life, Tony Fairchild was a stern taskmaster when it came to his own actions. He didn't like to fail, he didn't like to be sloppy, and he didn't like to be cozened, and all of those things had happened in the Richard Curtis affair. So he was (and grudgingly he knew this) taking it out on the unaccommodating Wai Fung.

Fairchild and Wai Fung and a few of Wai Fung's younger staff and the German, Luther Rickendorf, now sat together in a conference room in the station, waiting for George Manville to return with Kim Baldur. Jerry Diedrich had gone missing, presumed kidnapped, possibly dead, and that meant Kim Baldur was very likely also at risk; it had been agreed that the circumstances might now be too risky for Kim to travel by herself around Singapore, so rather than just telephoning her at the hotel and telling her to get a taxi, Manville had gone to fetch her. When Fairchild thought about the alacrity with which Manville had volunteered to be the one to go get the Baldur woman, he could only wince at his gullibility when he'd accepted the sneers of that other 'Manville' as genuine.

The hall door opened, and Manville came in, with a distraught-looking Kim Baldur, and a police escort. Kim turned to Rickendorf, seated near the door, to say, "Oh, Luther, he attacked me!"

Rickendorf and Manville both started to speak, but Wai Fung surprised Fairchild by slicing through them with a suddenly steely voice: "Who attacked you? You say you were attacked?"

She looked around briefly, but clearly understood that Wai Fung was the person of importance in this room. She said, "The man who's been following us. Didn't Luther tell you about him?"

Rickendorf said, "I told them, Kim."

"The man from Richard Curtis," Kim said, sounding contentious and bitter.

"From Richard Curtis," Wai Fung echoed. "Mr. Rickendorf made a similar assertion, but unfortunately lacked proof. May I hope you have brought the proof? The proof," he said, "may be of any sort. Fingerprints, documents, eyewitnesses—"

"George saw the man, he can describe what happened."

"Very well," Wai Fung said, and gestured at the conference table. "Why don't we all sit down?"

They did, and Fairchild pulled out his small notepad and black-ink pen.

Manville said, "When I got to the hotel, when I got out of the elevator, I saw this man forcing his way into Kim's room."

Wai Fung said, "You knew he was forcing? She was not inviting?"

"She was screaming for help," Manville said.

Wai Fung said, "Very well."

"I ran down there," Manville went on, "and pounded on the door, but he'd closed and locked it. Kim was still calling for help. Then I heard a crashing sound. I didn't know it then, but—"

"No, no, please, Mr. Manville," Wai Fung interrupted. "Tell it to us in the order in which you knew it."

"All right," Manville said. "I heard a crashing sound. I was trying to kick down the door, but it took a few tries. When I finally got it open Kim was there, looking very frightened. She was holding a can of something—"

"Hairspray," Kim said.

"The bathroom door was broken and the man was coming out of there, rubbing at his eyes."

Fairchild looked up from his notepad. "Well done," he told Kim.

Manville said, "He ran for the window. I chased him, but he got out the window and when I tried to follow him he kicked me." He touched an angry-looking scrape on his right cheek.

Wai Fung looked around at them all. "I take it that is it? You don't know this man? His name?"

Kim said, "He's been staying at our hotel. A Eurasian man, big and bulky. He carries a Polaroid camera."

Rickendorf said, "Inspector," and Fairchild automatically turned toward him, but of course it was Wai Fung he meant. "Inspector," he said, "we believe he put bugs in our telephones. They're probably still there."

"Interesting," Wai Fung said, and turned to Kim to say, "This man. When he attacked you, did he have a weapon of any kind?"

"A piece of pipe," she said, "Like an iron pipe, I don't know, six inches long?"

"And do we still have this pipe?"

"I gave it to your people downstairs," Manville said.

Wai Fung said, "Is that it? No witnesses?"

Manville, with a very slight edge, said, "*I'm* the witness."

"From the mark on your face, Mr. Manville," Wai Fung told him, "you were a participant. A witness is an outside observer. I take it there were none of those?"

"As a matter of fact," Kim said, "there were."

They all looked at her in surprise. Sounding not completely pleased, Wai Fung said, "And who was that?"

"When I looked out the window," she said, "while he was running down the fire escape, there were two painters out there, painting the fire escape."

Wai Fung said, "And what did they see, exactly?"

"They saw the man roll out of my room, kick George in the face, and run down the fire escape."

Now Wai Fung made a note, then peeled off the top sheet of his pad and gave it to one of his assistants, with quickly murmured instructions. Then Wai Fung turned back to the others. "Whatever may have happened in Ms. Baldur's room this morning —and we will investigate, I assure you—the connection between this incident and Richard Curtis remains, at least to my eyes, invisible."

Rickendorf said, "Inspector, my friend Jerry has a friend working for Curtis. That friend told us last Wednesday that he had seen a man in Richard Curtis's office who fit the description of the man who attacked Kim. He said he himself had carried an envelope containing five thousand dollars to Curtis, and that he'd seen Curtis give the envelope to this man."

Wai Fung said, "And this friend's name?"

Fairchild watched waves of indecision cross Rickendorf's face, like speeded-up cloud systems on a TV weather broadcast.

"Mr. Rickendorf," Wai Fung said, "without this person's statement, what do I have? Mere assertions. *Your* assertions."

Rickendorf said, "Would it be all right if I telephoned him?"

"Certainly," Wai Fung said.

20

Though Wok Wok was just off a main passenger corridor at Changi Airport, a broad main pedestrian thoroughfare full of foot traffic and some wheeled traffic as well, the food stall also had a section at the rear, behind the kitchen module, that was quiet and unobtrusive. Here is where Curtis placed himself, at one that afternoon, and here is where Bennett eventually found him, coming around the corner of the kitchen, lugging one huge battered suitcase, "A perfect place, sir," he said, by way of greeting, "A perfect place."

Curtis didn't know why Bennett looked so disheveled. There were stains on his shirt, his hair was spiky, and he had the general look of someone who's been trying to run through brambles. As the man sat down, across the table, Curtis said, "What's happened to you?"

"That girl," he said, and sounded bitter.

"Girl? Kim Baldur, you mean?"

"Yes, sir." Bennett slowly shook his head, seemed to think about what he wanted to say, and began, "Mr. Curtis, some things went like they should, and some didn't."

"Well, tell me about them."

"I could see they were onto me," Bennett said. "Not me, I don't think they spotted me in particular, but they knew they were being watched. It had to be. At first they were all in a hurry, making phone calls, setting up meetings, and then all of a sudden they're not, they just wander around the city, they don't make any more phone calls, they don't even call between their rooms anymore. So they're waiting me out, I could tell."

"Hennessy must have told them somebody was on their tail."

"*There's* a chap I'd like to meet," Bennett said.

"Oh, you will," Curtis told him, and smiled at the thought. "But go on. They were stalling."

"And I couldn't, because of you going to go away. So I snatched Diedrich and took him home—"

"Home!"

"That's the only place I had, Mr. Curtis. I set it up so he wouldn't know where he was, and I asked him the questions, and he told me about Hennessy, but then, I misjudged or whatever, and he was done for. It was an accident, but there it is."

"Don't worry about it, Colin," Curtis told him. "I know it was an accident, and I for one will not miss him."

"No, sir. Nor I."

The waitress, a tiny ancient woman barely taller than the table, now brought their meals, and they had to remain silent while she distributed the dishes. Curtis took the opportunity to study Bennett, this shambling messy creature across from him, and consider what he had done and what he seemed willing to do. He hadn't realized how much of a brute Bennett was, and the knowledge was both pleasing and alarming. The man could be even more useful than Curtis had thought, but he would also be more dangerous, because he clearly wasn't very smart. To take Diedrich home!

The waitress left, and Curtis said, "Where is he now? I mean, the... Not at home anymore?"

"In the Straits of Jurong."

"No bullets in him? Knife wounds?"

"No, sir. A broken nose, as might be."

"All right. But how did the girl get into this?"

"It seemed to me, sir," Bennett said, "you wanted her out of the way."

"I never said such a thing, Colin."

"No, sir, you didn't. But I read between the lines, like. And I went after her. And some boyo I never saw in my life come along and queered the pitch, and I had to scarper."

"A passerby?"

"No, he knew her, he kept calling her name, when he was trying to get into the room."

Curtis wasn't sure he wanted to know this entire story, but he couldn't help himself. "What room?"

"Her room, in the hotel," Bennett said. "I got in and it would've been all right, but this fellow come along and she managed to let him in, and that was it."

"Colin," Curtis said, and smiled thinly again, "are you ready to travel?"

"Yes, sir, I am," Bennett said.

Curtis put down his chopsticks long enough to take the envelope from the attaché case on the floor beside his chair. "This is your ticket," he said. "You're flying to Taipei at three o'clock."

"Taipei," Bennett said, sounding surprised, but he asked no questions.

"When you get there," Curtis told him, "you don't go through Customs. Can you carry that bag aboard?"

"It's a bit big, but I've done it in the past."

"Good. At the airport in Taipei, go to the transit passengers area, there'll be someone there to meet you."

"Yes, sir."

"He'll take you to a small charter plane that's got a flight plan to Okinawa, but you aren't going to Okinawa, you're going to Kaohsiung, at the southern end of the island."

"Sir, if I may," Bennett said, "why are we saying I'm going to Okinawa?"

"Because that's international, and you will never have actually entered Taiwan. You're a transit passenger, no checked luggage, there'll be no record of your having been in Taiwan at all."

"Okay, fine," Bennett said, though clearly he didn't understand why that was necessary.

Well, he didn't have to understand. In fact, it was better if Bennett were never to understand that Curtis was keeping a wall between them, that Bennett was a non-person in Curtis's life. Curtis said, "At the airport in Kaohsiung, someone else will meet you and drive you to the docks, where I've chartered a small ship. You'll board and wait for me, and I'll join you tomorrow."

"Okay, Mr. Curtis."

Curtis smiled. "And I'll have a pal of yours with me," he said.

Bennett looked puzzled.

"Mark Hennessy," Curtis said, and the big man's grin made him shiver.

21

Eating lunch at home, a salad of the perishables he'd already had in the kitchen, Mark Hennessy wondered about the trip, what it would be like and what kind of experiences he'd have there. Mark had worked for RC Structural ever since college, first in the field and the last three years here in the head office, and all he knew of the world was the places where Richard Curtis had sent him.

Mark Hennessy had nothing against Richard Curtis. In many ways, he liked and admired the man. He certainly was grateful for the job he had. As for the extracurricular activities he'd engaged in over the years, well, his goal wasn't to hurt the man seriously, just to do his part in a small way to provide some checks and balances. Left to his own devices, Curtis would do things from time to time that could to some extent be harmful to the environment, so keeping Jerry and Planetwatch on his case was probably doing the world some good. But it wouldn't actually *hurt* Curtis—it would just keep him honest, or a tiny bit more honest. The man would no doubt be angry if he ever found out, and would probably fire Mark on the spot, but his business wouldn't be crippled or anything.

But—

But Mark thought it was probably time to stop. Jerry had made himself just a little too irritatingly known to Richard Curtis, just a little too annoying all around, and coming here to Singapore was maybe not the smartest thing he'd ever done. Curtis had set that fellow on Jerry's trail, and was taking it all quite seriously, so it was surely time for Mark to hang up his espionage gloves.

Particularly with this new level of responsibility and trust that had suddenly come his way. Curtis was taking him along on this trip because he trusted Mark. Which meant, from now on, it would be a good idea if Curtis actually *could* trust Mark.

The phone rang. His immediate thought, staring across the room at where the phone was mounted on the wall beside the fridge, was that Curtis had changed his mind. He'd be taking someone else on the trip, after all.

Mark rose and crossed to pick up the phone, and was both relieved and troubled to recognize Luther's voice. Troubled, of course, because Luther was part of the conspiracy he'd just foresworn.

What Luther had to say, though, was worse than he'd anticipated: "Mark, Jerry has disappeared, and we're talking to the police."

"What? You mean he just wandered off?"

"We think he was kidnapped. We think the man you told us about did something."

"Good God, Luther, what do you mean *did* something? Kidnapped? People don't kidnap people."

"Well, they do," Luther said. "And Jerry's disappeared, yesterday, while we were having a beer, after he talked to you."

Mark didn't know what to think. This wasn't the way he'd visualized what they were doing, with disappearances and police and accusations of kidnapping. There had to be some explanation. He said, "Maybe he's following a lead."

"No, Mark."

"Well…" He didn't want this phone call, he didn't want any of this. He said, "Thank you for the warning, Luther, and I certainly hope Jerry turns up very soon."

"I need to give the police your name," Luther said.

"*My* name? For heaven's sake, why?"

"You're the only link between that man and Richard Curtis.

You saw him with Curtis, you saw Curtis give him money, you saw him following us, you told us about him."

"Oh, Luther, no," Mark said. "You've got to leave me out of this."

"I *can't*," Luther said. "The police have to find Jerry, and they can't find him unless they go to Curtis, and they won't go to Curtis just on what Kim and I tell them. You're the only link to Richard Curtis."

"Luther, no, it's just—it's just not possible. I'm going to—"

"Mark, we *have* to—"

"It's Sydney, Luther."

A stunned little silence, and then: "What?"

"Luther, the big secret trip Curtis is taking, he's going to Sydney! I just found out this morning. And he's taking *me*."

"Mark, I don't understand."

"Yes, you do," Mark insisted. "Curtis is going on this trip, you remember I told you I knew he wasn't really going to Manila, and this morning he told me the truth. He's going to Sydney, and he wants me to go with him because he *trusts* me. Don't you see? I'm going to find out what he's *doing*, Luther."

"Jerry is more important," Luther said.

"Jerry is fine," Mark assured him. "*This* is what you've been wanting to find out, all this time. I still don't know *what* he's up to, but at least now I know where. Sydney. And I'm going with him."

"Jerry—"

"Luther, if you tell the police I'm the one who's been spying for you, and if they tell Curtis, he won't take me with him. He'll fire me instead, and then where are you? Where am I? Where is anybody?"

"Where is Jerry, that's the point," Luther said.

"Jerry's *fine*." Mark felt frantic, felt it all slipping away. Everything was perfect, and now this had to happen. "Luther," he said, being very firm, "don't tell the police it was me."

"I have to—"

"Don't use my name, Luther."

"Mark, I'm very worried about Jerry."

"I understand that, I know you are, but this just ruins everything, destroys everything. *Don't* use my name."

Sounding unhappy and conflicted, Luther said, "I may have to, Mark."

"If you do," Mark told him, "I'll deny it. You won't gain anything, because I'll just deny the whole thing."

"You can't."

"I can. And I will. And if you give the police my name, and I say I have no idea who you are or what you're talking about, where's your credibility *then*? Eh? Luther?"

"You haven't listened to me, Mark."

"I have listened to you, and I—"

"Jerry is *missing*."

"He'll come back! But this chance *won't* come back! You are not going to spoil this, Luther."

"Don't you care about Jerry?"

"Of course I do. Luther, I have to hang up now, I have to pack," Mark said, and cradled the phone before Luther could say anything more.

22

Walking back to police headquarters after Luther's unsatisfactory phone call to Mark Hennessy, and after a pair of heated exchanges over a bolted lunch, Kim kept insisting they should give Mark's name to the police anyway and Luther kept explaining that that would be worse than no help, because Mark would deny it and Inspector Wai Fung was just looking for an excuse to do nothing.

Well, of course he'll do nothing, Manville thought. If Mark had been willing to come forward, it would have been a bit harder for Wai Fung to do nothing, but he still would have managed it.

What was there for the Singapore police to do, anyway? Manville and Kim had sworn out their complaints against the unknown assailant, and if the police found the man no doubt they'd be happy to put him in jail, but what would they do, or what could they do, about Richard Curtis? Unless they themselves tied Curtis to the assailant, the Singapore police would have nothing to make them at all interested in going after the man, and given Curtis's influence locally they weren't likely to try very hard to find something to make them interested.

In any event, Curtis's main crime wasn't that he was behind the assaults. His main crime he hadn't even committed yet: mass destruction of some sort while stealing a large quantity of gold.

When Luther had come back from his phone call to Mark, he'd brought one piece of news with him, which Manville still couldn't quite figure out. Curtis was going to Sydney. That was the secret behind the false destination of Manila.

But why Sydney? No doubt there was gold in the banks of
Sydney, but was he planning to use the soliton there somehow?
Sydney wasn't an island. There was water there, obviously, but
what could he possibly be planning to do? The soliton worked
in a confined space, not in open water; you needed divers,
working in tunnels, setting controlled explosions. Did he think
he could somehow use the technology to raise a tsunami off the
coast of Australia? It was preposterous. Any engineer could have
told him it wouldn't work. And even if it could have worked,
why there...?

Manville kept silent as the three of them walked back to the
police station, letting Kim and Luther argue out the problem of
Mark Hennessy. Luther finally said, "The point now is to find
Jerry. If they haven't...hurt him yet, there's still a chance."

Manville was thinking about the millions of other people
Richard Curtis hadn't hurt yet. The inhabitants of Sydney, or
wherever his target really was. But he appreciated why Luther's
main concern was Jerry. "We can press that point with Wai
Fung," he said. "He might not think he has a reason to go after
Curtis, but he certainly has a reason to look for the guy who
assaulted Kim and me—and took Jerry."

But Wai Fung was ahead of them. At first he was late, sending
one of his assistants to apologize for the delay; they sat around
the conference table for about forty minutes until the inspector
arrived. "I do apologize for having made you wait," he announced,
as he entered the room, "but I believe you will forgive me in just
a moment." He took a photograph from his jacket pocket. "Mr.
Manville, do you recognize this man?"

Manville took the picture, a squarish black and white head-
shot, for a driver's license or a passport. It was the man who'd
attacked Kim.

Manville looked up at the expectantly smiling Wai Fung. "That's him. The man in Kim's hotel room."

Wai Fung dipped his head. "Would you show the photo to Miss Baldur, please?"

"Of course."

Manville passed her the picture and she said, "Yes, that's him."

Wai Fung said, "Excellent," and extended his hand for the photo.

Giving it back, Manville said, "Congratulations, inspector. That was fast work."

"The man did not make it difficult," Wai Fung said. "His name is Colin Bennett. He is a Singaporean." Wai Fung sat. "Although he lives in Singapore, in an apartment near China Street, he has been staying at the Race Course Court Hotel for the last week."

"Since *we've* been there!" Kim said.

"He moved in the day after your arrival, and he checked out this morning, shortly before the attack on you. He used his own name, and he paid in cash. He explained to the hotel clerk that his building was being fumigated and the landlord was paying for him to stay in a hotel until the work was completed."

Fairchild said, "But his building was not being fumigated."

"No, of course not." Wai Fung looked around at them all and said, "There was a small radio device installed in the telephone in one of your rooms. As you predicted."

Luther was nodding. Kim was, too, but there was something in Luther's expression, Manville thought, that was less hopeful than in Kim's, a sort of fearful expectation. Jerry's name had not been mentioned yet.

Wai Fung said, "A squad has been sent to this man Bennett's home. We'll bring him in and see what he has to say for himself."

Kim said, "Ask him who hired him. Ask him about Richard Curtis."

"No," Luther said. "Jerry. Ask him where Jerry is."

"Oh, we'll ask him many questions," Wai Fung promised them both. "He will grow quite tired of our asking him questions, I assure you. But since you've brought up the matter of Richard Curtis once more," and his gaze shifted from Kim to Luther, "are you now prepared, Mr. Rickendorf, to produce this employee of Richard Curtis who's been supplying you with information?"

Luther gave an unhappy shake of his head. "He's afraid to lose his job. He won't come forward."

"A pity," Wai Fung said.

Fairchild spoke up in the silence that fell. "So we have a man who does exist, this Colin Bennett, who did move into that hotel for the apparent purpose of keeping an eye on these people, who lied to the hotel clerk about his reasons for staying at the hotel, and who assaulted Ms. Baldur earlier today. What else do we know about him?"

"He's a laborer of some sort," Wai Fung said. "We don't yet have his entire history, but we soon will. I would say he doesn't have the money needed to spend a week at that hotel, not out of his own pocket. So yes, someone did hire him to watch those three people." He shrugged. "When he gets here, that's one of the questions we'll ask him."

"And about Jerry," Luther insisted.

Wai Fung nodded to him and said, "Mr. Rickendorf, I do promise you we will do everything we possibly can to find your friend."

"Please," Luther said, as a uniformed policeman came in with a note, which he gave to Wai Fung, then left. Wai Fung opened the folded sheet of paper, read it, then said, "Mr. Bennett is not at home, although it looks as though he's been there recently. There are indications that he may be traveling. We're looking now to see if he's left the country."

"He could be hiding," Luther said, "where he's got Jerry."

"If so, we'll find them both," Wai Fung told him. Looking around the table, he said, "I think there's nothing more for us to do together at this point. I will telephone you all when we have further news."

23

The call came less than thirty-six hours later.

They were shown into the same conference room, where they took the same seats as last time, and a moment later Wai Fung and his assistants came in. This time, Wai Fung wasn't smiling. He looked grim and troubled.

He stopped just inside the doorway, looked around at the people at the conference table, and said, "I have news, none of it good, some of it very bad. Mr. Rickendorf, I'm sorry to have to tell you, but your friend is dead."

"No!" Kim cried, though of course they'd known it all along.

Luther said nothing, and after Kim's outburst they all seemed to be enclosed within Luther's silence. In that silence, Wai Fung made his way to his seat, laced his fingers on the table, looked at his hands, and said, "He was in the water, in the Sebarok Channel, found this morning."

Fairchild said, "Drowned?"

"No. His nose had been broken, and it would seem he strangled. Or was strangled. There are indications that duct tape had recently been on his wrists and ankles."

Luther still said nothing.

Wai Fung took a deep breath. "It is possible, though not certain, that the length of pipe you retrieved from Colin Bennett, Mr. Manville, was used to break Mr. Diedrich's nose. Tests are being done, but it will probably remain inconclusive."

Fairchild said, "Any further news about Bennett?"

"I was about to come to that," Wai Fung said. "Yesterday afternoon, just a few hours after the attack on Miss Baldur, Colin Bennett flew to Taiwan."

George, beside Kim, said, "Taiwan!"

Wai Fung gave him a sour smile, "Yes, Mr. Manville, and Richard Curtis flew to the same destination today, in the company of an employee of his named Mark Hennessy."

Kim blurted, before she could even think about it, "He's the spy!"

Startled looks from everybody. Wai Fung said, "Is he. Well, he may just wish he'd come forward, in that case."

George said, "You think Curtis knows?"

"We were told Hennessy was a last-minute addition to the trip," Wai Fung said. "His officemates were surprised Curtis took him."

George said, "All right. So the question is where in Taiwan are they and what are they doing there."

"It is complicated," Wai Fung said. "Mr. Bennett, arriving at Taipei, did not go through immigration, but transferred directly to a charter plane with a flight plan to Okinawa. But," he said, raising a hand to forestall Manville's interrupting, "in fact the flight did not go to Okinawa, it went to Kaohsiung instead, at the southern end of the island."

Fairchild said, "Still in Taiwan, in other words."

"Yes. The charter pilot has been located by the Taiwanese police and has confessed his part in the deception. Richard Curtis and Mark Hennessy took the exact same route today, with the same false flight plan to Okinawa. What happened when they reached Kaohsiung, we don't know."

George said, "He took a ship. The three of them took a ship."

Wai Fung looked interested. "You seem very sure of that," he said.

"From Kaohsiung," George told him, "it's four hundred miles across the South China Sea to Hong Kong. Hong Kong is the place he blames for his troubles. He says he's going to get gold, and the banks of Hong Kong are full of Chinese gold. I don't know how he's going to do it, but somehow he's going to use the soliton in Hong Kong. To create a great deal of destruction and make off with at least some of that gold."

Kim said, "The fax. Remember, Luther? Mark told us a fax had come to Curtis from a man in Hong Kong— Luther? What did he call him?"

"A labor thug," Luther said. His voice was low and measured and emotionless. It was terrible to hear. "Named Jackie Tian."

"Tian visited Curtis here, very recently," Kim told them. "And then he sent a fax from Hong Kong, saying they were going to have to find another diver, because their diver had been arrested on smuggling charges."

"A diver," George said. "So it is Hong Kong, and it is the soliton, and it's going to be very soon."

FOUR

I

Martin Ha loved his daily commute. There were times when he thought it was the best part of his job, particularly on the bad days, which were fortunately rare. But on all days, in all weather, he loved his commute.

For one thing, he began it later than most other workers, not having to be in his office until ten in the morning, Monday through Saturday. And for another thing, he could be leisurely, traveling by bicycle and ferry, not crowded into a tram or a careening bus or stuck in traffic jams. And finally, he could commute in casual clothes, and change into his uniform when he got to work.

And so it was this Monday morning, a sunny day, moderately humid, the moisture in the air somewhat muffling the perpetual clack of mahjong tiles from every balcony, every side street, every cafe. Dressed in tan canvas shoes and white knee socks and tan shorts and a white short-sleeved dress shirt, his cellphone hooked to his belt, Ha kissed his wife Nancy, wheeled his bicycle out of the apartment, and took the elevator down to the street.

Martin Ha lived on a comparatively quiet side street in the middle-class neighborhood called Hung Horn, southeast of Chatham Road, an area heavily populated by the city's Chinese civil servants, in which group, dressed for his commute, he seemed barely likely to belong. Mounted on his bicycle, teetering slightly as he made the turn onto Ma Tau Wai Road, this slender knobby-kneed serious-expressioned man of about 40 looked as though he might be a rickshaw driver on his day off. He didn't look like anybody important at all.

Ha rode his bike down Ma Tau Wai Road and right onto Wuhu Street and then left onto Gilles Avenue, all the while ignoring the usual press of traffic that raced and squealed and struggled all around him, the other bicyclists, the hurrying pedestrians, the taxis and trucks and double-decker buses and even, though this was off their normal grounds, the occasional bewildered tourist. Gilles Avenue led him at last to the new Hung Horn ferry pier. Until just a few years ago, where he now stood had been Hung Horn Bay, next to the main railway terminal, but the bay had been filled in just recently, to make more precious land, on which had been built the opulent new Harbour Plaza Hotel, five minutes from the railroad terminal and even closer to the ferry pier.

The ferry ran every ten minutes or so, and took only fifteen minutes to cross the harbor, and *this* was what Martin Ha loved. The view from the ferry. Out in front of him, across the sparkling water, Hong Kong Island gleamed and blazed in the sunshine, its glittering towers bunched together like the crowded upraised lancetips of some buried army. Behind him, almost as huge, almost as modern, almost as gleaming and sleek and new, clustered Kowloon, Hong Kong's mainland extension, the gateway to China. In the old days, you could take the train from that railway terminal beside the ferry dock on Kowloon and travel all the way across Czarist Russia and all of Europe to Calais in France, and then board one more ferry, and be in England. The jet plane had changed all that, of course, but the sense of it was still there, the ribbon that tied two worlds together.

Off to his right, as he stood against the side rail of the ferry, holding his bicycle with one hand and watching the great glorious harbor around him, Ha could see other ferries at work, particularly the green-and-white boats of the Star Ferry, the ferry the tourists rode, a trip half as long and half as glorious as this voyage Ha took twelve times a week.

At Wan Chai Perry Pier, Ha mounted his bike again for the short ride down Harbour Road and Fenwick Pier Street and the pedestrian walkway over broad and busy Harcourt Road down to Queensway Plaza, behind police headquarters. As he approached the building, the salutes began.

Three minutes to ten. In his blue uniform of a full Inspector in the Hong Kong Island Police, formerly the Royal Hong Kong Police, Martin Ha settled himself at his desk by the windows overlooking Arsenal Street and looked at the various papers that had been placed here by Min and Qi, his assistants. There were the overnight reports of crimes in the various districts, the reports of undercover agents, and messages from those who felt they needed to speak directly with the inspector.

The last twenty-four hours had not been bad in Hong Kong, Ha was happy to see. Pocketpicking was still the most persistent and irritating crime in the city. The Big Circle gang had not been heard from, not for several weeks now; good.

The Big Circle was a very loose association of mainland criminals, some of them former Red Army soldiers, who would sneak across the border from time to time to pull off usually pretty spectacular robberies, mostly of banks and jewelry stores. Their raids generally seemed to have been scripted by the same people who made Hong Kong's action movies, with plenty of high-speed car chases and flying bullets. Now that Hong Kong was Chinese, the mainland authorities were making more serious efforts to capture or at least control the members of the Big Circle, so that particular crime wave might be at last ebbing.

Ha got to his phone messages last, and among them was surprised to see one from Inspector Wai Fung of Singapore. Ha had never met Wai Fung in the flesh, but they had spoken a number of times on the phone and communicated even more by fax, and their departments had cooperated in a number of smuggling cases.

Was this more smuggling? Intrigued, Ha intercommed to Min to return the call from Singapore, and three minutes later he was put through.

"I apologize for having to ruffle your day," Wai Fung said.

Ha was aware that an unruffled day was Inspector Wai Fung's dearest wish in life, but he himself didn't mind a little excitement from time to time, so long as he could win at the end. He said, "Smuggling?"

"Not this time, no. In fact," Wai Fung went on, and Ha could sense the man's unease, "I can't tell you with any certainty *what* the problem is. I can only tell you a group of people are coming to see you, and that, although I would prefer not to believe their story, I'm very much afraid they may not be simple alarmists."

"Who are these people," Ha asked, "and about what do they wish to alarm me?"

"One is a police inspector from Australia," Wai Fung said, "from Brisbane there. I believe his rank is roughly equivalent to ours."

"I don't think I know any Australian police."

"This one is named Tony Fairchild."

Writing that down, Ha said, "And the others with him?"

"Three. Two men and a woman. The ones who first became aware of the problem."

"And what is the problem?"

"There is another man," Wai Fung said, "lately of Hong Kong, now of Singapore, named Richard Curtis. He is in the construction business. Very successful."

"I remember that name," Ha said. "A corner-cutter, as I recall."

"I'm sure he is," Wai Fung agreed. "But also wealthy and with some acquaintances of importance."

"Yes, of course. Is he in trouble?"

"It seems," Wai Fung said, "he might be the *cause* of the trouble. At least, these people claim he intends some massive destruction very soon, possibly in Hong Kong, and most likely in connection with the stealing of gold."

"Gold." There was a lot of gold under Hong Kong Island, of course, not in veins in the ground but in vaults within banks. It sounded like the Big Circle gang again, combining destruction with robbery. "But that doesn't sound quite right," he said. "Forgive me for saying so. A businessman has other ways to obtain gold. He doesn't run into a bank with guns blazing to steal it."

"Nevertheless," Wai Fung said, "there does seem to be sufficient evidence to suggest an investigation might be in order."

And better on my turf than yours, Ha thought. He said, "This Australian policeman and the others. They have the evidence?"

"They have very little that you or I might call evidence," Wai Fung told him, "but they have a story you ought to hear."

Ha said, "That sounds ominous. As though I'll be opening a hornet's nest."

"They are staying at the Peninsula. They are waiting for you to call," Wai Fung said. "Do please keep me informed."

"Certainly I'll let you know what happens, if anything happens."

They made courteous farewells, then Ha spent a moment in thought, brooding at the phone. Some unnamed trouble, waiting to be uncorked at the Peninsula, Hong Kong's most luxurious hotel, an unlikely venue for lurking trouble.

Phone this Australian inspector and his friends? Or perhaps learn a bit about Mr. Richard Curtis first.

Ha intercommed to Min: "A former Hong Kong resident, Richard Curtis, businessman in construction. See what we might have on file about him."

The surprising thing, Ha thought, as he sat in the air-conditioned back of his official Vauxhall, feeling the slight forward tug of the Star Ferry taking him back across to Kowloon, was how little the city had changed. Everyone had thought the transition from British rule to Chinese rule would be fraught with problems, particularly political and social problems, everything but economic problems, but everyone as usual had been wrong.

In hindsight, it was easy to see why. For one hundred fifty years, Hong Kong had been ruled by an oligarchy installed from a far-off capital, London. Then, for just a few years, there was an attempt to paste a democratic smile on this autocratic face, but the instant the pressure was released the smile fell off, and now Hong Kong was once again ruled by an oligarchy installed from a far-off capital, Beijing. Nothing had changed.

Except, of course, for some of the gweilos living in Hong Kong, the expats as they called themselves, the Europeans and Americans, but mostly the British, who had done well by serving the far-off capital of London but couldn't be expected to receive the same opportunity to batten off the far-off capital of Beijing.

The ones who belonged to the working class, the barmaids and jockeys and interior decorators, mostly took it in good part, vanished when their work permits expired—or shortly after, when they were found to be still on the premises—and were presumably now living much the same lives in Singapore or Macao or Manila or half a dozen other neon-lit centers of the Pacific Rim.

At the other end of the spectrum, a few Richard Curtises had also found the world shifting beneath their feet. The homes they'd enjoyed for so many years up on the Peaks, the steep hills in the middle of Hong Kong Island, behind and south of the main financial districts, they'd sold off to their Chinese counterparts, entrepreneurs who now made their comfortable livings in exactly the same way the Curtises used to do. Those who'd left had sold those mansions on the Peak before the real estate crash; not bad. And if they hadn't gotten *quite* as much in the sale as they'd have liked, well, how much money did any one rich person really need?

So maybe it was true that, although Ha could see that here in Hong Kong nothing had changed and nothing would change and life would go on very much as before, for a few British barmaids or American businessmen life *had* changed, in that they'd had to call the movers and buy a one-way ticket somewhere else. But none of them had been destroyed by it. No one had died or gone to jail. No one had been ruined; certainly not Richard Curtis, now living the same life as before in Singapore.

Curtis, in fact, was one of the people Hong Kong was better off without, a man who was a little too quick with a bribe or a lawsuit, a little too given to ruthlessness and sharp practice. The dossier Ha had been given on the man showed him to be a sharper who expected his contacts and his influence to keep him safely above the law. It must have been quite a bump when he'd suddenly discovered that the rules had changed.

But could the man seriously harbor a grudge? Was that even

possible? It seemed to Ha that it was not possible, though the people he was on his way to see would try to convince him otherwise.

Well, he thought, either they will convince me after all or I will have at the very least had an excellent lunch at the Peninsula.

2

Kim found the Peninsula Hotel astonishing, and she'd found it so even before she'd first seen it. When the four of them arrived yesterday at Hong Kong International Airport, a uniformed chauffeur had been there, holding up a sign with FAIRCHILD printed on it. He had led them to a white Rolls Royce sent by the hotel to pick them up. The hotel, it seemed, kept a fleet of these white Rolls Royces for the use of its guests. That was the first astonishment.

Then there was the hotel itself, an imposing C-shaped structure, ten stories tall, with a newer twenty-story addition above the central part. Fountains splashed in front, the doormen wore white uniforms, and the lobby was huge, all gold and white, colonnaded, columned and corniced. A string quartet played Mozart, and clumps of package-tour travelers with nametags and identical shoulderbags and harried expressions, who would have cluttered and dominated most settings, here seemed to be swallowed and muted by these vast dignified spaces.

And now the suites. It had been decided, mostly by Andre Brevizin, consulted via long-distance telephone call, but with Inspector Fairchild in full agreement, that a show of luxury would make them more credible to the Hong Kong police. "It is a city centered on the acquisition of money," Brevizin had said. "You'll never be listened to there if you look poor."

So here they were in suites, the inspector in one, Luther and George and Kim in another, across the hall. Brevizin was covering the cost of the inspector's suite, while Luther had made one more international phone call and then told George and Kim, "It's all right. My father will pay." George had tried to argue, but Luther had smiled his now-sad smile and said, "No, don't worry. It's good for him sometimes to pay."

Their suites were in the new tall addition, so they had views out over the nearby buildings. Inspector Fairchild had what was considered the better view, south toward Hong Kong Island across the harbor, but Kim found the northern view over Kowloon and the New Territories endlessly fascinating, a colorful gaudy jumble like a really complex jigsaw puzzle in which you had to study every piece for a good long time.

When, that is, she could bear to look away from the suite itself. The wide central room was luxuriously furnished in deep blue, gold and ivory, and contained a full bar. One part of the room was a kind of office, with a fax machine and an elaborately furnished desk. Chinese prints on the walls and some Chinese pieces of furniture reminded you where you were. Off the main room, to left and right, were large bedrooms, also with spectacular views, and marble bathrooms with Jacuzzis. Kim moved between these rooms in a happy daze. She was a long way from *Planetwatch III*.

Luther's father, whether he knew it or not, had also treated them all to a wonderful dinner last night, downstairs at Gaddi's, one of the hotel's three terrific restaurants, and she and George had then slept in cool quiet on their giant bed, the jeweled lights of Kowloon outside making a muted rainbow of the room, and they inside it. Her ribs felt almost healed by now; making love was no longer a problem in engineering.

When the phone rang, the ornate clock over the bar in the living room read exactly one o'clock. "He's prompt, this inspector," George said.

The three of them had been sitting here in the living room waiting, George reading another of his paperback thrillers, Kim looking out at the colorful city below, Luther just staring at his hands and quietly thinking.

And then the phone rang. Luther answered, murmured a bit, then hung up and said, "It's time."

Kim had decided to dress for maturity at this meeting, so this morning she'd gone to one of the hotel shops and bought a very plain just-above-the-knee dark blue skirt, black pumps, and a short-sleeved white blouse with a ruffle at the throat, charging it all to the room, which was to say, Luther's father once more. She felt more than her usual self-confidence as the three of them trooped across the hall to the other suite. They had invited the inspector to meet them here to avoid the distractions and lack of security of a restaurant and also to emphasize the luxury just a bit.

Hotel staff had set up an elaborate round table for them by the windows, with Hong Kong Island gleaming over there like cutlery in a drainboard. The table was covered in white linen, the service was all white and gold, and two white-uniformed, white-gloved waiters seated them, with Inspector Ha facing the view most directly.

The inspector was a little man who seemed to Kim quite wrong for the part. Inside a very serious and distinguished dark blue uniform decorated with much insignia and braid was someone who looked like he might be a messenger or a pushcart vendor. I wonder, Kim thought, if he can see past *our* appearances, our uniforms. And whether he'll see past Richard Curtis's.

Wine was poured, sparkling water was poured, small plates of delicious food were presented, and the two waiters retired behind the bar, handy if needed but out of earshot of the conversation at the table.

Inspector Ha said, "My friend Wai Fung in Singapore tells me you intend to alarm me."

Fairchild said, "It seems only fair. You shouldn't be the only one in the room not alarmed. The danger is to your city, after all."

Inspector Ha said, "Wai Fung was vague about the threat, but promised you would all be more specific."

Fairchild said, "You explain it, George," and George did, describing briefly the work he'd done for Richard Curtis on Kanowit Island, and that Curtis had told George he would be using the method, the soliton, again in a larger way, in a dangerous and illegal way, and that he would get a lot of gold by doing it. When he finished, Fairchild said, "We don't know exactly *where* he intends to pull this off, but when last heard from, he seemed to be headed in this direction."

"There's no record of his having entered Hong Kong recently," Inspector Ha said, "I checked on that this morning."

Luther said, "There wouldn't be. He's trying to keep his skirts clean."

With a gesture at the windows, Fairchild said, "We think he's probably on one of those boats out there. One yacht out of a hundred, five hundred."

George said, "As for where he'll do it, this is a very specific technique, it isn't something that can be done just anywhere. It needs a combination of landfill and tunnels."

Inspector Ha put down his fork and leaned back in his chair. To Kim, he looked grayer.

Fairchild said, "You know his target."

Inspector Ha nodded at the windows. "Hong Kong Island has been added to and added to. The island used to end far back at Queens Road. Just about everything you're looking at on the flats is reclaimed land."

They all looked at the gleaming towers, and Kim remembered the great bruise of water thundering at her from Kanowit. She suddenly felt cold.

George said, very quietly, "Inspector, you're using the wrong word."

"What word?"

"Reclaimed," George said. "Everyone likes to talk about reclaimed land. 'The new airport is on reclaimed land.' It's a wonderfully solid word, but it is a distraction."

Ha said, "From what?"

"The Dutch reclaim land," George said. "They build dikes, and force the sea back, and the lands they find are called polders. They're solid and real, the same lands they always were except they used to have water on them."

He waved a hand toward the window. "That isn't reclaimed. It's landfill."

Inspector Ha said, "Reclaimed is more...dignified."

"But landfill is what it is," George insisted. "Inherently unstable, never quite solid. And now I suppose you'll tell me there are tunnels under there."

"Yes, of course," the inspector said.

Fairchild said, "What are they? A subway line, something like that?"

"No no," Inspector Ha said, "many tunnels. In Hong Kong, as you know, air-conditioning is a necessity. The most efficient and inexpensive way to cool those buildings over there is with water from the harbor. There's a tunnel from the seawall in to almost every one of those buildings. The longest is to the Bank of Hong Kong, at three hundred yards."

"Three football fields," George said. "But those would be pipes, not tunnels."

"Pipes in tunnels," Inspector Ha said. "The pipes have to be maintained. There are design differences from building to building, but the basic structure is a tunnel of concrete ten to fifteen feet in diameter, with three separate foot-wide pipes in it, one to bring water in, one to bring it out, and the third as standby." Frowning at George, he said, "But you suggested these tunnels, for this soliton thing to work, have to be interconnected. The air-conditioning tunnels are sealed from one another, going only from the seawall to one specific building."

"But," George said, "they won't be far from one another. At night, a crew could make side tunnels, and then conceal them again."

Fairchild said, "Inspector, how deep underground are these tunnels?"

"Fifty feet."

"And the bank vaults, how deep are they?"

"Usually, about the same."

Fairchild said, "That's what he plans to do, then. Steal as much gold as he can lay his hands on, probably out of the Bank of China, open up the cross tunnels, flood them, set off the soliton."

Inspector Ha said, "But that would be— That isn't theft, that's mass murder!"

George said, "At the end of it there won't be any evidence." He gestured again at the windows. "Everything you see out there," he said, "will fall into the harbor, turn into mud and debris. No one will know what if anything was stolen. No one will know what happened or how it happened, or who was responsible."

Inspector Ha digested this. "I am not convinced."

Fairchild said, "I understand how you feel. But we know Curtis plans to use this thing, we know he's killed at least one person to cover his tracks and tried to kill these two here, and we know his anger is aimed at Hong Kong."

"Oh, I don't doubt Mr. Curtis's intent," Inspector Ha said. "I can see that he has the motive and I accept that he has the means. But what of the opportunity? Strangers can't merely wander around in those tunnels, you know. The construction job you're suggesting, digging cross tunnels, breaking into bank vaults, couldn't be done without somebody noticing."

"We don't know *how* he plans to do it," Fairchild said, "but we are certain sure he does intend to."

"There's one way I can think of he might do it," George said. "Curtis is in construction, that's his primary business. In Hong Kong, there's so little space, even with all the landfill—all the *reclaimed* land—that buildings are constantly being torn down so new ones can be built. Fifteen-, twenty-year-old buildings are demolished. Right now, there are probably twenty construction sites over there."

"More," Inspector Ha said.

"What if one of them belongs to Curtis?" George asked him. "Through a dummy corporation, a dummy name. It would look as though he's building upward, like everybody else, but secretly he'd be burrowing down."

Luther said, "Maybe he has Jackie Tian fronting him."

Inspector Ha looked alert. "Jackie Tian? What does he have to do with Richard Curtis?"

"Two weeks ago," Luther told him, "he visited Curtis in Singapore. A friend of ours—now disappeared—who works for Curtis, saw a fax from Tian to Curtis saying a diver they were going to use had been arrested and they'd have to find another."

Martin Ha got to his feet and walked around the table to stand and look out the window. Kim was surprised to see that he stood straighter now, he seemed to fit the uniform better. Looking away from them, out toward the view, he said, "I must tell Wai Fung you've succeeded. I am alarmed."

3

For Luther, the last few days had been muffled, without resonance, like a pistol shot in a padded room. Or as though his brain and all his senses were in that padded room. Nothing came through to him with much impact or clarity. It was as though he watched the world now on a television monitor, listened to it through a not-very-good sound system.

He still went through the motions. He thought about the problem of Richard Curtis, he took care of his own needs, he responded quite normally to Kim and George and the others, but it was all simple momentum, nothing else. He went through these motions because there was no way to stop them, short of death, and he didn't much feel like death right now; it would simply be the state he was already in, intensified.

He supposed he grieved for Jerry, but even that was muffled. He couldn't find in himself much enthusiasm for revenge or justice, though he continued to trudge along with the others in Curtis's wake. What he was realizing, and even that slowly and without much force, was that in grieving for Jerry he was grieving for a part of himself. Jerry had been his id, the outward expression of all those emotions and instant reactions that Luther had never quite managed to feel or express on his own. Without Jerry, he was merely the cool and amiable somnambulist he used to be, but now with the added memory of there having been once a Jerry.

He wondered what would become of him now. He was done with Planetwatch, of course, that had merely been the place Jerry had led him. None of the previous scenes of his life seemed worth repeating, but what else was there? He might even go back to Germany, ignore his father, live one way or another on his own. Not that it mattered.

It might be interesting, in fact, to stay here in Hong Kong, particularly if they didn't after all manage to thwart Curtis. To stay at the Peninsula—switching to a Hong Kong view room, of course—to sit in a comfortable chair by the window, and to watch the towers across the way begin to tremble, to shudder, then to fall to their knees, window panes snapping out into the air like frightened hawks, walls dropping away, floors tilting, desks and filing cabinets and people sliding out into the world, then to feel the power ripple in this direction across the harbor, to see it come like a ghost in the water, to feel it tug at the land-fill on this side, the buildings swaying, the yachts and junks and huge cargo ships all foundering and failing and staring with one last despairing gaze at the sky, then the harbor boiling, this very building bending down to kiss the sea...

What a spectacular sight. Who would want to look at anything else after that?

Well, yes, that was possible. In the meantime, though, the effort was still being made to save that city over there, and all its people, and all its gold, and all the many ships in the harbor. Inspector Ha was on the telephone, talking to assistants, making plans. Soon, they would all go inspect one of the air-conditioning tunnels.

That would be interesting.

The last part was a metal staircase down through a conical concrete tube slanting through the earth beneath the bank. The elevator only descended so far.

Luther was at the back of the pack of seven descending toward the tunnel. The bank building's head of security was first, in his

tan uniform and Sam Browne belt, then the building's operations manager in white shirt and hardhat, then Inspector Ha,
Tony Fairchild, Kim, and George. Luther preferred being last,
it meant he didn't have to wonder what expression, if any, was
on his face.

The tunnel was a roughly circular concrete tube, twelve feet
across, with a flat metal floor. The three water pipes, gray plastic,
a foot in diameter each, were above their heads, filling the upper
curve. Electric lights in translucent white plastic shields were
spaced at long intervals on the walls, alternating left and right
and giving just enough illumination to move around.

To the right, the tunnel ended in seven or eight feet at a
blank concrete wall, just beyond where the three pipes bent
upward and out of sight. To the left, the tunnel was absolutely
straight, the distance vague and difficult to see.

The security chief and building manager and Inspector Ha
all had flashlights, and they now played them on the walls to
both sides as the group moved slowly forward, toward the seawall. Inspector Ha had told the building people only that information had been received that a potential breach of the tunnel
was being planned by people whose ultimate goal was the bank
vault, which was just a foot or so through the wall to their left at
the point where they started their inspection. The security
chief had said that kind of attack was impossible, they had
motion sensors, not for the tunnel but certainly for the vault,
but Inspector Ha had explained that all tips from normally
credible sources had to be looked into, and he personally would
at least like to know what the tunnel looked like, so here they
all were.

There wasn't much conversation once they began, moving
forward very slowly, playing the light over the curve of the
walls, one or another of them occasionally moving closer to

study a section. The wall was pitted concrete, and took the light with many tiny black shadows, like a moonscape, so it had to be stared at very closely before you could be sure exactly what you were seeing.

Luther trailed the others. The air was cool but slightly dank, probably because of the water streaming through two of the pipes overhead. It made him think of the family's tomb in the cemetery outside Dusseldorf, where five generations of Rickendorfs and their spouses were stowed away in stone drawers, or the cremated ones in urns on an ornate stone shelf. There had been family occasions, mostly church-related, when the whole family had driven out to visit the cemetery, when Luther was much younger and his grandparents still alive, but those customs had fallen into disuse now. It used to amuse him to think of presenting Jerry's body to the family for storage in the tomb in the drawer beneath the one reserved for himself; now, when he remembered that, he could only think: No, no one will visit Jerry's grave, ever.

They walked ten minutes before they reached the seawall, where the building manager explained that the blank end wall they saw was three courses of brick behind the visible sheathing of concrete. Where the pipes vanished into the wall there were thin black grommets.

They hadn't spotted anything out of the ordinary, but they repeated the flashlight inspection on the return trip, moving even more slowly than before. Luther still trailed, not really with the group, following them but not a part of them, not studying the wall as the others did, his thoughts far away.

Then he heard a sound. A faint scraping sound. He moved on another step before the sound registered, and the fact that it had come from behind him. Behind him. But the others were all in front.

Luther turned to frown at the empty tunnel behind him. Would they have rats in this place? No, it was all kept very clean, and the whole tunnel was sealed, no way in or out except that door down there that the group was converging on, and then the flight of metal stairs leading upward.

But he had heard something, he knew that. He took a step back the way he'd come, seeing only the converging lines of the pipes overhead, the dim lights at regular intervals, the pools of darkness between, the seawall now only a vague blur, far away. He took a second step back, trying to see, trying to hear.

Again. The tiny brushing sound of someone trying not to move, but unable to stay forever still.

Luther looked up, and the man hurtled onto him from on top of the left side pipe. He'd been hiding up there, on that too-narrow space, out of direct light, above the area they'd been searching with the flashlights. He hadn't expected anybody to come in here, and had only managed to hide just barely out of the way, but the pipe was narrow and it had been difficult to maintain his balance, so he had made that sound.

And now he was committed. Luther looked up, and had only time to register with blank astonishment that it was the man Bennett from Singapore, the man who'd killed Jerry, when the weight of him knocked Luther back and down, hitting his head against the curved-in concrete wall just above the metal floor. Bennett's weight stayed on him, Luther dazed from the hit on the head, Bennett's hand clamping down hard over Luther's nose and mouth, his other hand closing on Luther's windpipe.

The others were too far away, they were almost to the door. Luther had been behind them, and then he'd stopped, and then he'd turned back, and by now they were too far away, they couldn't have heard the small thud of the bodies falling, the small scrapes and grunts of the struggle.

Luther was tall and slender, strong but not as powerful as this big man bearing down on him, his weight pressing down, his hand squeezing shut Luther's throat, Luther feebly struggling, not really conscious.

Far away, they started through the doorway. Even if one of them were to look back, what would they see? Shadows, between the dim lights.

Luther's hands pulled helplessly at the man's hand on his throat, he tried to kick the floor but Bennett's legs held his legs down, he tried to twist his head this way or that way, but the other hand stayed clamped on his nose and mouth.

The door down there shut. The lights switched off.

4

Mark had been terrified for so long that it had become dull, like an old wound that wouldn't heal. It was dulled by fatigue, and by hunger, and by physical pain, and the despair that comes from knowing they are going to kill you, when they please, how they please, and that by the time it happens you'll be relieved that at last it's over. So the terror was dulled, and familiar, and no longer struck at him with such sharp pangs of agony and disbelief, but it was still there, inside his head, every waking second and every second of exhausted sleep; absolute unrelenting terror.

It had begun—it felt as though it had begun years ago, that he'd been a slave in this underground place most of his life, but it had begun less than a week ago, when he left Singapore with Richard Curtis. Curtis had told him they would fly to Sydney, but when he got to Changi Airport Curtis handed him a first-class ticket to Taipei instead.

Mark expressed surprise, naturally, and Curtis said, "This is to throw the competition off the track." And he never thought a thing about it.

He'd trusted Curtis, he'd believed in Curtis, and more than that, he'd believed in himself, in his own decision to be loyal to Curtis from now on. Having made that decision, everything should have been all right.

He still hadn't been worried when they got to Taipei and the plans changed again. They took the transit passenger route through the terminal, as though to pick up their Sydney flight, neither having checked any luggage, but then they were met by a pilot from a small charter company, and Curtis had explained to Mark they would be making a small sidetrip to Okinawa to see someone there who was a part of the new secret enterprise. Tomorrow they would fly from there on to Sydney. And still Mark had believed him.

This was a night flight, so it had taken him longer to realize they weren't traveling over water. If they were on the way to Okinawa, shouldn't there be water below? Clearly, they were on their way to some other part of Taiwan.

That was when doubt first touched at Mark, and a little shiver of fear. What was going on? He was alone in this small plane with Richard Curtis and the pilot. Had Curtis found out that Mark had been spying on him? Was he going to open the plane's door and hurl Mark out into the jungle below?

But then he would rather throw Mark into the ocean, wouldn't he? To be sure no body was ever found. So it had to be something else. But what?

As they were about to land—somewhere—Curtis had given him another explanation: "I like it that you don't ask a lot of questions, Mark," he'd said. "That shows you can keep quiet, keep discreet."

"Thank you, sir."

"You've probably noticed we're flying over land."

"Yes, sir, I did."

"We'll be landing at Kaohsiung, it's a port on the southern coast of Taiwan."

"Are we taking a ship, sir?"

"Good man," Curtis had said, and smiled at him, and patted his arm. "This thing I'm doing is absolutely hush-hush, Mark," he'd explained, "but you can't keep your movements private when you travel by commercial air. A boat it is."

And a boat it was. A black Daimler met them at Kaohsiung

airport and drove them to the port, where a cabin cruiser waited for them. Not as big as Curtis's yacht, it probably slept six, had a very small galley kitchen, and a crew of two, husband and wife, both Chinese. The ship was called *Granjya*, it flew the Chinese flag, and it was aboard her that the terror began.

The instant they were aboard, the wife cast off and the husband steered them away from the dock and toward the harbor mouth. Curtis led the way through the small common room to the cabins aft, saying, "I'm in the cabin on the right, and that's yours on the left. You might as well unpack, we'll be aboard for nearly twenty-four hours."

"Yes, sir."

Curtis closed his cabin door behind himself, so Mark did the same, noticing the clean simplicity of the cabin, with its bunk-beds, built-in drawers and minimal floor space. Out the round porthole, the lights of Kaohsiung swiftly receded, black night rushing in, and he felt the difference underfoot when they cleared the harbor and moved out onto the open sea.

He was in the cabin only a minute or two, laying out his possessions on the top bunk, deciding he'd sleep on the lower, when there was a sharp rap at the door. Expecting Curtis, he crossed to pull the door open, and the man from that day in Curtis's office shouldered in, shoving the door out of the way, punching Mark very hard in the stomach.

Reeling, doubled over, bile in his throat, Mark felt panic and blank astonishment. The man he'd delivered the money for, the one who'd been following Jerry and Luther, who'd done something to Jerry, was *here*! In this room, shutting the door behind himself. And when Mark stared upward at him, mouth strained open, air all shoved out of him, the man punched him in the face.

Oh, Luther, tell them! Tell the police, force me to change

my mind, convince me, make me stay in Singapore and tell the police what I know, make me stay, anywhere but here! Luther, let me not be here!

The second punch had knocked him to the floor, and now the man kicked him, time after time, wherever there was an opening. Mark curled into the corner between the bunk and the porthole wall, trying to protect himself with arms and legs, but the kicks kept on and kept on; and then stopped.

Dazed, Mark lifted his head, blinking through tears, and the hulking man was just going, carrying Mark's luggage with him. The door snapped shut behind him. A lock snapped into a hasp out there.

He was bleeding, cuts and bruises on his face and head and hands and arms. Every movement hurt, and he thought certain he'd throw up, but it never quite happened. He lured me here, Mark thought, really afraid now, really afraid, he lured me here to get revenge. And there's nothing I can do.

They didn't feed him at all on the trip, and for a while it seemed as though they wouldn't let him sleep either. Twice he fell asleep, and both times his tormentor came in and woke him again, with fists and feet. Mark was shaking, he was babbling, he was begging a chance to speak to Curtis, see Curtis, just a word with Curtis, but the man ignored him as though he hadn't spoken at all.

They didn't let him out to use the ship's only toilet, though he begged and pleaded, and finally there was nothing to do but use the lowest of the built-in drawers, closing the drawer afterward but still aware of the stench, still aware of how they were destroying him, making him less than human. And fear had loosened his bowels, so he had to keep opening the drawer, even though he wasn't being fed.

But then they did at last at least let him sleep, the next afternoon, and it must have been so he'd be unconscious when they made their way into the new harbor, so he wouldn't raise any alarm, attract any attention. The ship was at anchor in the harbor and it was night again when they came back, the big man kicking him awake, dragging him to his feet, shoving him out of the cabin. He was pushed and prodded to the common room, where Curtis, dressed in black pullover and slacks, turned away, saying, "Bring him along, Bennett."

Mark started to speak, to beg, to explain, to *talk*, but a heavy hand cracked him across the right ear, and Bennett said, low and menacing, "Not a sound."

There was ringing inside his ear, pain everywhere.

Not a sound. Mark went out on deck, after Curtis, and there was a motorboat there, with a dark figure at the wheel. All around them was a city, huge, towering, great glass walls reflecting back the stars and the city lights and the thousand movements of the water.

Where was he? While he was trying to make sense of it, Bennett casually cuffed him to the bottom of this new boat, and he lay there, defeated, finished, knowing it didn't matter what city this was. He'd die in it, that's all.

He hardly knew how or where they went. The motorboat thudded across the harbor, the hard ride of it increasing all of his pains, and then it stopped at some unlit pier and Bennett leaned down to squeeze Mark's jaw and whisper again, "Not a sound."

Mark knew he didn't need an answer, didn't want an answer, already knew the answer. Bennett dragged him up onto his feet, and again he followed Curtis.

They went up a wooden flight of stairs and along a dark passageway between buildings and out onto a dim-lit street of warehouses or factories. A black van was there, with Chinese characters in white on the side. As Curtis went up front to sit beside the driver, Bennett opened the van's rear door, picked Mark up by the shoulder and the belt, and tossed him into the van. There were coils of rope in there, large plastic cans. Mark lay on them, stunned, and Bennett climbed in, shutting the door behind himself.

Mark could see almost nothing. They drove through dim streets, and then more brightly lit streets, and then paused, and then bumped over some barrier and into somewhere, and Mark heard what sounded like a large gate being closed. Bennett got up as the van stopped, opened its rear door, and clambered out. Mark, not wanting to be thrown around again, scurried after him, but Bennett slapped him on the head anyway, to knock him down on the dirt behind the van.

The van drove off, spurting stones and dirt onto Mark's face, and then Curtis came back and said, "Put him on his feet."

There was no point trying to do it himself, they wouldn't let him. Bennett yanked him upright, and Curtis said, "Look at me."

Mark looked at him. Everything else was blurry, but Curtis's eyes were clear, and very cold.

Curtis said, "You're still working for me, Mark, but now your job will be a little different."

"Mis—"

Bennett hit him openhanded but hard, across the ear. Mark flinched and whimpered, and stayed silent.

Curtis went on as though there'd been no interruption. "I have a lot of work to be done here," he said, "and I'm short-handed. I *would* have enough people, if I had enough time, but because of you I don't have all the time I need, so I'm short-handed. Naturally, you want to make up for the trouble you've made—"

Mark opened his mouth, but then caught himself and shut his mouth again.

"—and happily you can." To Bennett, he said, "Take him where I showed you on the map, give him to Li. At least you two can speak the same lingo with each other."

Curtis went away, and Bennett pointed. "Walk over there."

Mark took a step, and another, and managed to walk.

And now he saw that he was in some sort of large construction site. The thing must take up half or more of a city block, with wooden fence all around the perimeter, blue plastic sheathing on the three or four stories already built, many construction vehicles parked here and there, but only the sparse worklights left gleaming.

Put me to work, he thought, put me to work? Where?

Bennett prodded him to the building under construction and through the blue tarpaulin. It was darker inside, only a few bare bulbs lit on the meager superstructure of the lower part of the building. Bennett shoved Mark over to the big square vertical tube of a cage where the construction elevator would be, and pushed the button.

Is he going to take me to the top, Mark wondered, and throw me off? He hadn't the strength to resist.

The elevator came up, not down, rising from some basement level. Bennett pulled back the accordion gate, shoved Mark aboard, followed him, and started them down again. The elevator, a cage in a cage, moved slowly downward, through an excavation only minimally built on, beams and posts to support the work above. Then it ran through a kind of floor, which should have been the bottom of the excavation but was not, and descended through darkness, and then into a different kind of light, an interior dim light, as the elevator descended into a tunnel.

The tunnel was very rough, the earth walls and floor uncovered, the plywood sheets of the ceiling crudely shored up. Temporary electric wire sagged from light fixture to light fixture along one side. The tunnel started here at the elevator and continued for about twenty-five feet into darkness. At the other end was a massive bulldozer with a deep scoop mouth, faced this way and filling the tunnel, looking impossible here.

A side tunnel led off from this one, and that's where Bennett moved Mark, with pokes and prods. In the smaller tunnel stood a low rubber-wheeled tram. Two men with shovels were filling the tram with dirt and rubble thrown back to them by four other men digging at the face of the tunnel. The men wore only shorts and shoes; it was hot down here.

Bennett spoke in an Asian dialect to one of the men filling the tram, who stopped, nodded, and looked at Mark with pleased interest. He was thin and harsh-eyed, and the sweat ran down his face and chest.

Bennett turned away without a look at Mark, and the worker came over to push his shovel into Mark's hands and point at the pile of dirt. Mark understood; this is my new job with Curtis Construction.

He stepped over to the dirt pile, which kept growing from the work of the men at the tunnel face, and started to dig, throwing the dirt into the tram. The dirt was surprisingly heavy, the job an immediate strain on his back and shoulders. He watched the other man working here, and tried to imitate his moves; stand where he could throw the dirt to the side, which used only the arms, instead of to the front, which strained the back.

The man, Li, waved a hand to attract Mark's attention, and then did a little hand-running gesture: work faster. All right. Mark worked faster, and Li went off to get another shovel.

❖

There was no day or night. There was no time passing, it was all the same; dig and dig and dig. The crew he'd been working with went away, replaced by another, but they didn't let him stop working. He was exhausted, he fell down sometimes, but they would merely give him angry kicks and make him get back to it.

From time to time there was food, and they let him join them, and it was always cooked rice and bowls of lukewarm water. He was starving, he ate everything they gave him, and it was never enough. They aren't feeding me as though I'm a prisoner, he thought, they're feeding me as though I'm a work animal that must be kept in fuel for a little while, until it dies.

Back in the main tunnel there was a portable toilet, so at last he could go to the bathroom like a human being, but if he stayed in there more than a minute they pounded on the door, and cuffed him on the side of the head when he came out.

Sometimes he would fall and simply be too weak to rise, no matter what they did, so then they would let him sleep where he was, for a while; never for long enough. His body, not used to this kind of labor, screamed with pain. His hands were bloody shreds, but he had to keep holding the shovel, bending, lifting, throwing. The pain was awful, but when he stopped the pain they gave him to force him to go on was worse.

The tunnel they were digging was almost as large around as the main one behind them, but even more primitive, as though no one intended to use it for long. While the men at the face dug, burrowing downward and forward from the top, and Mark and one other man filled the tram, other men removed and replaced and emptied the tram, and other men worked with the beams and the plywood to shore up the ceiling and hold back the bulging walls.

After a while, the men digging at the face came to something solid, which pleased them. Mark didn't dare spend too much time looking, but it seemed to be some sort of underground wall, possibly of concrete, convex, curving toward them. Excited, the men cleared more of it, working their way down the wall across a narrow band, not bothering to clear to left and right. They threw dirt back more quickly than ever, and Mark worked and worked.

Then everyone stopped while another man arrived, a more important man, in shirt and long pants, and carrying something that looked at first like a space-age machine gun. Everyone stepped out of his way, and Mark leaned, grateful, against the tram, and the man stepped over to the newly reached wall. He aimed his machine at it, and it was some sort of high-powered laser, shooting a thread-thin beam too bright to look at directly.

The man was very skilled. He scored the concrete wall with a kind of long narrow vertical oval, perhaps four feet high, a foot and a half wide, just large enough for a man to slide through. He scored several times on the same line, cutting at an angle inward, until he'd sliced all the way through. Then Li came forward with two metal handles, which were fastened with screws to the concrete. Grasping the handles, two of the men lifted the cut section out and away, and Mark saw there was some sort of dim-lit room beyond it. A cool breeze came in from that room, like the sympathetic touch of an angel. Mark cried, feeling that touch, but no one noticed or cared.

Bennett appeared, from the main tunnel. Mark looked at him like a beaten dog, but Bennett paid him no attention. He went through the new opening into that distant room, spoke back into the tunnel, and the man with the laser and four other men went through, carrying shovels and a rolled-up length of canvas. The cut-away piece of wall was put back snugly into place, and the nice cool breeze stopped, and work began again.

It was some time later that the laser man was there once more. More of the wall had been exposed, completely clearing it on the left, and the laser man scored a vertical line down that side, as though to open the wall completely to the same size as the tunnel. This time, though, he didn't cut all the way through, just drew that line partly into the concrete, to make it weak.

Then it was another time. The plug in the concrete wall was sometimes open, sometimes shut. Men brought back heavy loads of dirt wrapped in the length of canvas. Men went through with their tools, and later they came back.

The clearing of the wall on this side was nearly done.

Mark looked up and Luther went by. He stumbled, he seemed dazed, he looked at Mark without recognition and moved on, shoved by Bennett.

Luther? Mark tried to think. Was Luther here? Had he forgotten? Was Jerry here? He tried to think, but it was very hard to think.

A hand smacked him across the back of the head. He bent over the shovel, and worked.

5

No one noticed that Luther was missing until they were in the elevator on the way back up to lobby level. Kim was thinking how strangely ordinary the tunnel had seemed, like somebody's wine cellar, only longer, or the basement under a very old house, and then she found herself thinking about poor Luther, how remote he seemed these days, how he didn't seem to react to or even much notice anything around him. And then she realized he wasn't there. "Luther!" she said.

Everybody looked at her, not knowing what she meant, and then they all made the same discovery. Mr. Hang, the building manager, gave them a look more exasperated than accusing, and said, "There was one more of you!"

"Luther," George said. "We left him behind."

Captain Sahling, the rather impatient chief of the building's security, snapped, "The man didn't stay with us? Why did no one keep an eye on him?"

Mr. Hang said, "We'll have to send someone down for him."

Kim said, "Can't he just get the elevator?"

"The door to the tunnel," Captain Sahling said, in the iciest of tones, "is kept locked. In fact, both doors, at the head and the foot of the staircase, are kept locked. Someone will have to go down to release him."

The elevator took them up to the lobby, a high echoing place of glass and chrome, with a marble floor that made footsteps ring out as though everybody were suddenly more important. Captain Sahling spoke in irritable Chinese into his walkie-talkie, then the six of them stood around waiting, to one side, away from the traffic to and from the elevators. George and Tony Fairchild took turns trying to placate the captain, assuring him that Luther had been under a strain lately, that they all appreciated that this was taking up more of the captain's time than he'd bargained for, and they were certain Luther would be completely chagrined when he came up. The captain reacted to all this with stiff impatience, and Kim noticed that Inspector Ha and Mr. Hang didn't bother trying to soothe the captain's ruffled feelings at all.

Two slim young security men in tan uniforms hurried into view, saluted their captain, and took an elevator down. Captain Sahling assured them all once more that he was a busy man. Mr. Hang said he was sorry Luther hadn't managed to call out to them or knock on the door to attract their attention, because he would be in darkness down there. "Poor Luther," Kim said.

Captain Sahling's walkie-talkie made its sputter. The reactions of Inspector Ha and Mr. Hang to the transmission in rapid Chinese suggested some sort of bad news.

Captain Sahling, more irritable than ever, snapped something angry into his walkie-talkie, and it rasped a response. One more exchange, and he glared at them with fury compounded by doubt. "They say," he reported, "he isn't there."

George said, "That's impossible."

"Nevertheless."

Mr. Hang said, "We must go back down."

"I will go," Captain Sahling said.

George said, "We'll all go, Captain."

The captain was going to argue, but then decided not to, and they all rode the elevator back down to the lowest basement and the small bare concrete room where the two young security men stood, looking awkward and embarrassed, afraid they were about to be blamed for something.

In addition to the door to the stairwell, there was one metal door from this room to the rest of the sub-basement, but it was locked and had not been disturbed. Captain Sahling spoke with the security men and then, more calmly, Inspector Ha spoke with them, and then everybody trooped down the stairs again and into the tunnel.

There was no one there. Luther was gone. They spent ten minutes searching the place, and there was no sign of Luther, no sign of any other way in or out. At last they gathered again at the door to the stairwell, not knowing what to do next. Their flashlights bobbed uncertainly, pointing this way and that. Captain Sahling, who clearly resented situations he couldn't control, said, "I don't know what your friend has done."

George said, "Our friend? Captain, it's your tunnel."

Sahling stared at him, then looked away, down the length of the tunnel. "Is it?" he asked.

6

Mr. Curtis was furious, and Bennett understood why, but what else could he have done? If he'd killed the German and left the body there, that would have been worse, wouldn't it? There was no time or way to invent an accident. So those people had a disappearance on their hands, that's all, no way to be absolutely certain what had happened. Maybe the German had even walked off on his own. After all, the others had forgotten all about him, they'd walked off themselves and left him there.

"All right, all right," Curtis said, at last calming down a little. "You did what you had to do."

"Thank you, sir."

The three of them stood in Curtis's quarters on the site, a small construction trailer kept strictly for his use, the rare times he was here. Half of it was an office, simple but complete, with Internet access and fax machine, where they now talked. The other half was a bedroom and bath, which Curtis had never used.

Bennett had brought the German directly here, because what else was there to do with him? Curtis had been seated at his desk, computer screen open before him, and when he'd seen the German he'd jumped to his feet, yelled at Bennett to shut the door, and had demanded to know where the German had come from and what was going on. Now, the first shock of it done, he was a bit calmer. "All right," he said. "The damn fellow can do some work for us."

"Oh, good, sir, like the other one."

The German was recovered now from his tussle with Bennett,

but merely looked at them both with a vague expression on his face, as though they were speaking a language he didn't understand. Gesturing at him, Bennett said, "Should I give him to Li too?"

"No, I don't want them together," Curtis said. "Take him to the other side, there's a dig supervisor named Chin."

"Good, sir."

"And come back."

"Yes, sir."

Bennett took the German by the arm and led him outside. Halfway across to the building, the German made a sudden dash toward the main gate, and Bennett had to grab him and hit him several times to calm him down. But then he went along quietly.

They were digging cross-tunnels in two directions from here, trying to reach as many water tunnels as possible, so Bennett delivered the German to the work crew on the second side, then returned to Curtis, now at the large table, with construction plans laid out. Looking up at Bennett, he said, "Any trouble?"

"No, sir."

"Good. Come over here."

Bennett went over to stand beside Curtis and study the plans. God, it was good to be back in construction again! To be standing in a site office, shoulder to shoulder with the boss, looking over the plans. This, Bennett thought, is where I've been supposed to be, lo, these many years. "Yes, sir," he said.

Looking at the plans, Curtis said, "We don't have as much time as I'd hoped, Colin."

"No, sir."

"Them being here in Hong Kong, *and* in one of the tunnels, suggests they know far too much."

"It's that Mark Hennessy, sir," Bennett said, meaning, *there's* a bad employee, and here, sir, right here at your side, is a good employee.

Curtis said, "I suppose part of it is Mark, but not all of it, he didn't know that much. I think it's mostly George Manville, figuring things out. Why I didn't get rid of him when I had my hands on him I'll never know."

"You thought he could still help you, sir."

"Well, I was wrong about that," Curtis said. "But it isn't going to stop us, Colin."

Us. "No, sir!"

Bending over the plans, Curtis said, "We've linked seven of the tunnels. I'd hoped for ten, and more profit, too." He tapped the plans. "There's some gold out there we won't be getting, Colin."

"We'll be getting a lot, sir."

"Oh, yes, I know we will. But we're going to have to do the job right now."

Surprised, Colin said, "Now, sir?"

"Tonight." Curtis looked away, at the flat rectangle of window framing the sunlit construction site. Within, the air-conditioning faintly hummed, "In a way," Curtis said, and Bennett knew he was talking mostly to himself, "it's better to have them here. Deals with everything at once."

"Yes, sir."

"You're going to be my eyes and ears, Colin," Curtis said, and there was a knock at the door. Curtis said, "That'll be Jackie, I just called him to come over. Let him in."

"Yes, sir."

Bennett didn't much like Jackie Tian, his manner of being on the inside track here in Hong Kong, but he'd never let either Tian or Curtis know it. He crossed to open the door, and smiled a big smile at Tian, saying, "How are you?"

"Good," Tian said, curtly, as though Bennett were too unimportant to care about. Entering, he said, "Afternoon, Mr. Curtis."

"Hello, Jackie, we've had a little problem here."

Tian looked at Bennett as though assuming he was the cause of the problem, and said, "What's that?"

"The people who've been bothering me are here in Hong Kong. Colin found them in one of the bank tunnels, but they didn't see him."

Surprised, Tian said, "In the tunnel? You mean, they know what we're doing?"

"They can't know everything," Curtis said, "or they'd be in this room with us right now, and a number of policemen as well. But they know *something*, they know too much to risk waiting anymore. As I just told Colin, we'll have to change our plans, cut back on what we hoped to accomplish, and run the operation tonight."

Tian frowned down at the construction plans on the table, though Bennett doubted the man could read them. "Will that work?" he asked. "We aren't everywhere we wanted to be, are we?"

"We're close enough," Curtis told him. "There'll still be plenty of profit for all of us, Jackie."

"Good," Tian said. "I'm ready to go live somewhere else for a while."

Curtis laughed, sounding a bit shrill. "I think we all are, Jackie," he said. "Now take a look at this."

The three men bent over the table as Curtis moved a finger along the various tunnels. "Jackie," he said, "your job is the bulldozer and the vaults. Is the submarine hooked to the bulldozer?"

"It'll trail me like a geisha," Tian said, "everywhere I go. It's on the wheeled carriage."

"All right. Once we start, we'll have to move very fast. They'll know something's happening, their alarms will be going mad, but they won't know where we've come from and they won't know where we're going and they won't be able to come down to interfere with us." Turning, he said, "Colin, that's where you start. The first set of explosives are in position—"

"Yes, sir."

"—and you'll set them off when Jackie says he's ready. He'll radio you as he moves, and you'll be in here with the controls."

"Yes, sir."

"When the submarine's full," Curtis said, "Jackie, you'll come up out of there, with your crew. But moving fast, Jackie."

"Count on me," Tian said.

"When Jackie radios you that he's clear," Curtis said to Bennett, "you fire the explosives, to breach the seawall at the ends of the tunnels."

"Right, sir."

Curtis said to Tian, "Is the new diver here?"

"He'll be here tonight," Tian promised.

"He stays in the tunnel with the submarine," Curtis said. "Once the tunnel fills with water, he uses the external controls to guide it down the tunnel and into the harbor. Then he switches it to radio control, and I guide it from there."

"Right."

"Then he comes back through the tunnel and up here."

Tian said, "Why doesn't he just go out across the harbor, come out anywhere?"

"And be questioned?" Curtis shook his head. "The only safe way in and out, Jackie," he said, "is this construction site. That's what it's here for."

"Fine," Tian said.

Curtis turned back to Bennett. "Now, the second set of explosives," he said, and tapped the plans here and there, "we're going to have to move. We're in fewer tunnels, the physics changes, and to be honest, I'd feel more comfortable if I had George here to look at my figures. But I've done it, and I *know* I'm right."

Bennett hadn't the first idea what Curtis was talking about, but that didn't matter. "Yes, sir."

Curtis said, "I've marked the new positions. They all move, all six of them, slightly. But the *exact* position is important, all right, Colin?"

"Absolutely, sir," Bennett said. He frowned at the plans as though to memorize the new positions of the explosives, though in fact he'd be carrying a set of the plans with him when he made the changes.

"Once the tunnels are flooded," Curtis said, "you trigger the second explosives with the radio."

"Yes, sir."

"You will then have thirty minutes."

"Yes, sir."

"When those explosives go," Curtis said, and turned his bland eyes on Bennett, "they will destroy every bit of evidence of what we've done. I think it possible there'll be some damage even here."

"Yes, sir."

"Don't try to leave the island," Curtis said, "but do get away from this neighborhood. Maybe east, over toward Wan Chai. I want you all safe," Curtis assured them.

"Yes, sir," they both said.

7

They were all gathered around Inspector Ha's table. After the inspection of the tunnel under the bank building, and the disappearance of Luther Rickendorf, they'd come back here to police headquarters and this conference room, where they sat around the long oval pale-wood table on gray swivel chairs with black plastic arms.

Inspector Ha shook his head ruefully. "I have always been proud of how large and important our city is, how dense, how many people we have put together on this small island. More here than in Manhattan. But now, to find one man in it, one wealthy man, here illegally, with who knows how many people working for him, paid to keep him hidden…" He spread his hands, to show the complexity of the task.

"An army," Tony said, feeling glum. "That's what Curtis has, an army at his disposal. Of course, we have an army, too, or you do, Inspector, but Curtis also has time on his side."

"That's what I'm afraid of," George said. "If he has Luther, and I guess he must, then he knows we're here. He knows we're close. So if he can speed up what he's doing, he will, even if it means he loses some of the loot he's after."

Ha said, "Mr. Manville, I agree with you that he must be using one of the current construction projects to cover his activities. He's probably staying on the site when he comes to the city, and when he leaves he'll do so late at night in a small boat. If he does that, we'll never find him, and never prove anything against him. So we are trying now to learn which construction site is the front for Richard Curtis."

Tony said, "There can't be that many. And they're controlled by the city, aren't they?"

"Yes, of course," Ha agreed. "The buildings department must give permits, do inspections. The trouble is, none of these large construction projects are done by one company, it's always a consortium, some of the same people but not all, shifting groups becoming involved. The corporate names are always new. We have to search through the records, track down every principal on every site, make sure the developers are who they're supposed to be. The buildings department is working on that right now."

Tony said, "How long to complete the search?"

"They estimate they'll have gone through everything by Thursday."

George, looking ready to jump out of his skin, cried, "Thursday!"

"That's what they tell me," Ha said, and spread his hands. "I don't like it either."

Tony said, "Inspector, they aren't doing clerks' hours, are they? Nine to five? We need them at work round the clock."

Ha looked dubious. "The civil service…"

"Will also drown," George said.

Troubled, Ha said, "It's difficult to explain that without telling too many people too much about the circumstances. We don't want to cause panic."

"If this isn't a good time for panic," George said, "when is?"

Tony felt the need to assist his fellow inspector. He said, "George, I understand what the inspector is saying. We don't want a panic because in fact a panic *would* be worse. A million people trying to leave this island all at once would be a disaster."

"I appreciate that," George said. "But we're not talking about somebody who's going to blow up a building. Curtis means to take the *city* down." To Ha, he said, "Inspector, I've worked on this process, I've seen it in action on Kanowit Island. If he's gotten through to enough tunnels, and if we don't stop him before he sets off the charges, every bit of reclaimed land on this island, including where we are right now, is going to be reclaimed sea. Curtis isn't going to give us until Thursday. I'll be surprised if he gives us till tomorrow."

Ha said, "But what if he isn't ready to invade the bank vaults? He might still have to wait."

"What it comes down to," George said, "is which he wants worse, revenge or profit. If he's afraid he won't have time to take the profit, because we're breathing down his neck, I'm certain he'll settle for revenge."

"Another thing," Kim said, "is that if he's stopped, there's evidence against him. But if he destroys this city and everybody in it, there won't be any evidence, people won't even know what happened."

Ha looked very worried. He said, "I'll speak to my opposite number in the buildings department. I'll call him now, and I'll tell him as much as is needed to make him as frightened as I am, and I'll ask him not to spread the news any more than he has to."

"Good," George said.

"In the meantime," Ha told them, "is there anything any of you can think of that might help point us in the direction of one construction company rather than another? Anything Curtis might have said or done?"

George thought about it. It seemed to him that there was something, something nagging at the back of his mind. He thought back to the dinner at the ranch in Australia, to Curtis's stories of getting started in the business. "I think I may have an idea," George said, "about what name Curtis could be using. For whatever corporation he set up."

Kim said, "He could call it anything, George."

"But I think he'd like to stamp it with his personality somehow," George said. "He's a man who puts his initials on his dinner plates."

Tony, intrigued, said, "What do you think he's going to do? Not RC, surely."

"No, that would be too obvious," George said. "But he told me, at that ranch of his, that station in Australia, he married into the construction business, and his first wife's grandfather started the business, here in Hong Kong. The old man called it Hoklo Construction. After the boat people who first came here as pirates. Curtis said his wife's grandfather called his company Hoklo because he wanted always to remember that the Hoklo had blended in with everybody else, so anybody could be a pirate. A pirate can hide in plain sight."

Tony said, "But would he name *this* company Hoklo? Wouldn't that point right at him?"

"Some variant on it," George said. "Some version of it that only Curtis, maybe, would understand."

Inspector Ha was already standing, had walked over to a phone mounted on the wall and was talking into it, and he now held up two fingers for quiet. They all waited.

"Thank you," Ha said into the receiver after another few minutes had passed, and he hung it up with a click that echoed through the now-silent room. He returned to the table. "Your instinct may have been right this time, Mr. Manville."

"Really?" Tony said. He was a bit surprised. He hadn't really believed Curtis would have the time or the inclination to play catch-me games. "Hoklo Construction?"

"No, Xian Bing Shu," Ha told him. And when he saw that

none of them had any idea what this meant: "Xian Bing means a pie, the sort you eat. He's hiding in plain sight, don't you see?"

"And what does 'Shu' mean?" George asked.

"Rat," Ha said.

8

By midnight, Curtis was back aboard *Granjya*, with everything in position. Tian and Bennett and the diver would do their jobs, and by three in the morning the operation would be under way. The attacks on the bank vaults would be swift and massive, and soon done. From the beginning of the operation until the drone submarine full of gold came out of the breached seawall should be less than an hour. And thirty minutes later, it would all be over.

He was still just a little troubled by that last half hour, but it shouldn't be a problem. He would have preferred to set off the soliton the instant the submarine was clear of the seawall, but then the submarine too would be caught up in the wave and the destruction. Thirty minutes was long enough for the submarine to cross the harbor, following *Granjya* out to sea, but it shouldn't be long enough for Bennett or Tian or anyone else to get clear. Wherever they were on the island's flats, they would die.

Of course, not everyone on Hong Kong Island would die. Some people living on the peaks, the steep heights behind the main city to its south, would survive tonight. But Jackie Tian and Colin Bennett and the rest of the crew were not likely to find their way to the peaks in that final half hour. Real money lived up there—Curtis himself had lived up there, in the old days—and he doubted any of the people working now for Xian Bing Shu had ever even *been* to the peaks, unless it was for the purpose of burglary.

No, they would all stay in the city, and they would all die.

And with them Rickendorf and Mark Hennessy and George Manville. Manville no doubt had brought the girl Kim along, so she would go, too. And there would be no one on the face of the earth who would have any reason to believe that Richard Curtis had had anything to do with the cataclysm that struck Hong Kong.

They wouldn't even know, in all that chaos, that the gold was gone.

He knew he should sleep for a while, and had actually set the alarm for two-thirty, but he was too keyed up to lie down. The months of preparation, the tension, the mistakes with Manville and the girl, the constant risk of being exposed, the doubt that at the end he'd be man enough to go through with it, all were coming to a head tonight.

Had he left anything undone, any threads that could lead to him? He didn't think so. The Farrellys were prepared, if necessary, to swear to the world that Curtis had been at Kennison constantly this last week. The drone submarine, a standard model used in undersea exploration by everybody from fisheries scientists to oil companies, had been bought by Xian Bing Shu, and Xian Bing Shu was absolutely untraceable to Richard Curtis.

The Hsus, operators of the *Granjya*, knew only what they needed to know, and were not curious by nature. If, in future, they were to realize they'd been party to the destruction of Hong Kong, they would be too implicated themselves to dare come forward. Besides, they were being paid well, and knew they would be paid well for more work in the future.

In the meantime, the *Granjya* stood at the western end of Victoria Harbor. Once the submarine was out of the tunnels and trailing them, the *Granjya* would head west and then south around the end of Hong Kong Island, through Sulphur Channel, between Kennedy Town and Green and Little Green Islands. They would stay well west of the new airport off Lamma Island, then at last turn east and south toward Kaohsiung, four hundred miles away.

Throughout the trip back to Taiwan, the submarine would run half a mile behind them, close enough to monitor but far enough away so there would be no obvious link between them. And in Kaohsiung he owned a waterfront godown where submarine and contents could be stored while gradually he moved the gold into his bank accounts, slowly converting it from heavy cumbersome yellow metal to impulses in cyberspace.

The radio and phone were set up in the main cabin, amidships, between the helm up forward and the sleeping cabins aft. Curtis paced in and out of the main cabin, first to the port deck and then to the starboard, out to the soft night air and the distant city lights, then back inside, pacing like an animal in the zoo, unable to stop himself.

This was the tense moment, the final moment. If something were to go wrong, what then? Over there on Hong Kong Island, if Bennett and Tian and the others were to fail, or if the soliton failed, or if the submarine for some reason failed, what then?

He would flee. If he had the submarine but the soliton failed, he would cut loose of the submarine, give up the gold, because they would know it was gone. He would take the same route as originally planned, use the same subterfuges, finish his journey at Kennison the same as before, ready to try again when circumstances improved. He would hold off his creditors, somehow, just a little longer.

But nothing would fail. Everything was prepared, and everything would work, and tomorrow he would become again what he had never stopped being all along: a businessman, a construction expert, a solid man in a solid world, no better or worse than the men around him. Once this was done, he would be Richard Curtis again.

It was nearly two in the morning when the call came from Bennett. That was too early, and worrisome. Curtis said, "What is it?"

Bennett said, "Our German guest has gone out."

Startled, Curtis said, "Left the property?"

"Oh, no," Bennett said, "he won't be leaving the property." He sounded grim and determined, a man out to prove himself.

"Well, that's good."

"What it is, I think," Bennett said, "I didn't prepare him as well as I prepared Mark."

He hadn't been beaten into despair, in other words. So he'd fought back somehow, escaped from them, was somewhere on the construction site. But the gates and the tall fences would hold him in, and the crew would find him, sooner or later. Or the soliton would get him. "Colin," Curtis said, "I'll leave all that to your judgment."

"Thank you, sir. You see, what it is, sir, he's just like gone for a walk around the property. When he comes back. I'll talk to him like I talked to Mark, get him to understand the situation here."

"You do that," Curtis said.

"I'll speak to you later, sir," Bennett said.

The next call came ten minutes later; still too early. It was Bennett's voice again, sounding tense and worried. "Policemen at the gate, sir."

"Don't let them in!"

"Oh, no, sir, I know that."

"Is Jackie there?"

Mulish, Bennett said, "Right here, sir." At times, Bennett's resentment of Jackie Tian as a co-worker could be amusing; at the moment, it was only irrelevant.

Jackie's voice, no-nonsense, tough, came on: "Yes, sir?"

"Start now," Curtis said.

9

Martin Ha did not like gunfire. In the first place, most people weren't very good at it, especially when excited, and having bullets miscellaneously in the air meant no one was safe anywhere. In the second place, it made it more difficult to interrogate people afterward, since they tended either to be distracted by wounds or dead. In the third place, it tended to create a terrible mess, hard to conduct an investigation in and nasty to clean up. There were more places, but those would do.

And they were why Ha continued to speak reasonably through the chain-link gate at the Xian Bing Shu construction site even when he was convinced that the two hard-hatted crew members inside the gate were merely stalling for time, and time was the one thing he simply could not give them.

Ha had arrived here five minutes ago with a sizable force, three police cars and a police bus, for a total of twenty-three men, with more on the way. (Tony Fairchild was also on the way, with his group, but Ha was sure Tony was professional enough to keep the civilians well away from the operation.)

The site looked perfectly ordinary from the outside, half a city block enclosed in a high chain-link fence supplemented by board fence here and there, with a deep excavation within and a shrouded building armature starting upward. Work was clearly going on despite the hour, but this wouldn't be the first time in Hong Kong that construction worked three shifts, the owners as anxious to get into their new building as, ten or fifteen years from now, they would be to tear it down again.

Ha had arrived, had left his force at the curb, and had proceeded alone to the gate, where he'd been met by these two

mulish workmen refusing to open up. Since then, he had repeatedly explained the situation, calmly and reasonably. That he
was a police officer, that they came within his jurisdiction, and
that they were required by law to do what he ordered them to
do, which at this moment was to open the gate.

They responded, sullenly and doggedly, that they'd been
ordered by their boss not to open the gate at night for anybody
at all, and they had no intention of risking their jobs for somebody they didn't know; people in the office were trying to call
the boss right now, that's what they claimed, but their lack of
urgency was as palpable as Ha's sense of urgency.

Still, he hadn't contented himself with nothing but talk. He'd
already ordered the armored personnel carrier from the police
garage, and when it got here, they'd do what they had to do. In
the meantime, he continued to try to convince these people
that the results of their actions, if they interfered with the
police in the performance of their duty, would be much worse
than the potential of making their boss angry.

Sergeant Noh called from the curb. He stood beside the car he
and Ha had arrived in, and now he called, "Inspector!" and when
Ha turned to look at him he made a quick beckoning gesture. He
looked worried.

"I'll be right back," Ha promised the workmen, and went
over to Noh, who said, "The Cathay Bank building has just lost
power."

That was two blocks west of here. "They've started," Ha said,
and here came the personnel carrier, rumbling down the street.
"Sergeant, move the vehicles out of the way."

"Sir!"

He went out to the street, to talk with the driver of the personnel carrier, which was a beefed-up panel truck with bullet-
resistant metal sides and a reinforced grill that made it a fine
battering ram. The driver, a young uniformed police officer,

saluted and Ha said, "I'll tell those people one last time we're coming in whether they like it or not. If I signal to you, go through the gate."

"Yes, sir." The driver smiled, looking forward to it.

When Ha approached the gate again, the two workmen had been supplemented by at least a dozen more, all of them looking tough and ready for anything. He kept his attention on the first two, saying, "Have you reached your boss yet?"

"No."

"Well, we're coming in."

A large bulldozer started up the slope of the excavation, moving rapidly this way. To block the gate?

One of the new men said, "We got our orders. We won't let you through the gate."

"I'm afraid you will," Ha said, and turned to signal the driver of the personnel carrier. As he lifted his hand, the windshield of the personnel carrier starred and crazed and went opaque, and a sudden loud report boomed from behind him.

He turned back, astonished, thinking this was not an occasion that called for gunfire, didn't they realize that, and the rifleman shifted aim to shoot Ha in the chest. As he staggered back, seeing the rifleman aim at the personnel carrier again, half a dozen of the workmen produced pistols and started firing.

Ha was dead before he hit the ground.

10

Jackie Tian steered the bulldozer directly at the rough-coated bulging concrete wall. The man with the borer had earlier scored around the four sides of the cleared area, making a line like that between postage stamps; when Tian hit it, at twenty miles an hour, the wall popped away from the broad iron bulldozer blade, splintering into a thousand jagged rocks, all scattered ahead of him. Directly across the Interbank Building water tunnel he drove and through the scored wall on the opposite side and the next connecting tunnel.

Bumping along behind him like a dachshund on a leash was the submarine, lashed to a four-wheeled trailer and chained to the rear of the bulldozer. The sub, fifteen feet long, tapered fore and aft, had rudder and exterior propeller at the rear but no conning tower. Compressed air between its inner and outer bulls would keep it buoyant, even with two or three tons of gold aboard. Its electronic gear was all in a thickly shielded cone in its nose. Three screw-shut hatches along the flat top gave access to the cargo area.

Behind the sub came thirty men, carrying shovels, wearing workgloves and headlamps beside their shorts and shoes. They cleared the rubble Tian created, to quicken the return journey, and kept moving, their lights casting quick narrow smoky beams in the temporary cross tunnels.

Third tunnel. The gold was to the left. Tian moved the levers to turn the treads and drew back the blade. The bulldozer swiveled on its treads, huge in this space. The right corner of the blade gouged out a chunk of the far wall as he made the turn.

As he started down the tunnel, nearly filling it from side to side, his head just beneath the water pipes, submarine and workmen trailing behind, the tunnel's lights abruptly flicked out. So everything was on schedule.

Bennett sat at Richard Curtis's desk in Richard Curtis's trailer and felt like a captain on the bridge of a giant ship. Seated here, he could keep in touch with Jackie in the tunnels and with Mr. Curtis himself, on his ship in the harbor. When the time came, he would be the one to detonate the explosives in the seawall, flooding the tunnels. When the diver came back after releasing the submarine into the harbor, it was Bennett who would arm the final set of explosives in the tunnel, to remove all evidence of what they'd done, and it was then Bennett who would lead Jackie Tian's work crew through the construction site, the false building seemingly under construction there, and out the concealed exit into Partition Street, away from the main gate and all the police.

He could hear the occasional gunfire, and didn't much like it. That was Jackie Tian's way to do things, loud and violent and tough. Bennett was an engineer, a construction man. He wished there'd been some other way to keep the police out while the bank vault was being breached. He wished he'd dealt properly with those people in Singapore, because then there would be no police outside to deal with now.

Well, but here they were, and there was no other way to deal with them. The Jackie Tians and their willing workers were useful at times. Half an hour, no more, was all they needed, and then the gold would be gone, and so would Bennett and Tian and the diver and all the workmen. All who survived.

❧

The diver was a Malay named Sharom, who had come late to the project. He did not know his predecessor, but he understood the man had been arrested on some sort of smuggling charge not related to this job here.

Sharom had known Jackie Tian for years, not well, but trusted him to be competent and professional, and he knew Tian felt the same way about him. His specialty was industrial sabotage. If you wanted a competitor's offshore oil-drilling operation to run into expensive difficulties; if you wanted your aging freighter to sink in such a way the insurance company could never prove it had been scuppered; if your operation needed an illegal dead-of-night explosion in a coral reef or other protected waters, Sharom was your man.

Tonight's operation was a simple one, for which he was being well paid, the first half of his fee already in his account in Jakarta. He trailed the bulldozer and the sub and the workcrew through the tunnels, dressed in his wetsuit. Scuba tank on his back, goggles pushed down around his throat, headlamp gleaming. He carried his flippers, and wore thin-soled rubber thongs he'd store inside the wetsuit when the time came.

On his utility belt he carried a small radio, which would switch on the submarine's engine once the tunnels were full of water, and which he could use to direct the sub down the straight run of the tunnel to what would then be a gaping hole in the seawall. He would swim just beside or above the sub, shepherding it along the way. Once the sub was clear of the seawall, the radio would also alert the other operator, who would take over control.

Sharom understood the other operator was also the employer in this operation, but didn't know himself who the man was, had never met him, didn't need to. Jackie Tian was all he needed to know.

Ahead, in the darkness criss-crossed by headlamp beams, the bulldozer crashed into the vault wall.

✻

Tony Fairchild couldn't believe what had happened. Inspector Ha was dead. Tony had liked Inspector Ha, had found him congenial and knowledgeable. He could certainly not be faulted for having put himself in harm's way, because who could have expected this level of violence? Four police dead, including Inspector Ha and the driver of an armored personnel carrier and two other officers. And undoubtedly there were some dead or wounded among the people inside.

Both sides had now pulled back from the fence, the people on the inside having driven a large bulldozer smack up against the gate on their side, so it couldn't be forced. Anyone attempting to get to the fence with wire-cutters could expect to be shot down before they could accomplish a thing; thus, one of the police dead.

Tony and George and Kim sat in the van that had brought them here, parked now a safe distance from the site entrance. In one way or another, they'd all expressed their shock at the death of Inspector Ha and their frustration at the stalemate, and now there was nothing to do but wait.

George was having the worst problem with that. Twice now, Tony had had to restrain him from leaving the van, saying, "You aren't going to do any good out there, George, leave it to the professionals."

"We don't have the *time!*"

"I'm well aware of that. But they're bringing up reinforcements, we'll soon be through the gate."

"If not," George said, "we're all going to die. Right here."

The workmen formed a kind of bucket brigade, moving the heavy gold ingots from their pallets in the vault out through the breached wall and into the submarine. A little farther down the tunnel, some security people had emerged from a door and been shot down by Tian's people, who now guarded the staircase there, to see to it they were not disturbed.

Steadily, the submarine filled with gold. Sharom sat on the rear bar of the trailer to remove his thongs and put on the flippers.

The walkie-talkie on the desk in front of Bennett crackled twice, then spoke in Jackie Tian's voice. "Coming out."

Bennett's hand strayed to the button that would detonate the seawall explosives, but then all at once he was in Belize again, visualizing another man in another tunnel, the sudden onrush of water. He closed his eyes, and his hand moved back from that button to pick up the walkie-talkie. "Let me know when it's safe to set off the charge."

"Naturally."

Sharom was alone. His headlamp was the only light, shining on the abandoned bulldozer, the submarine on its trailer, the new ragged hole in the wall to the vault. He could hear the radio talk, knew when they meant to blow the seawall, and stepped into the vault to be out of the direct line of it.

Fortunately, he'd thought to put in ear plugs. The sound of the blast, in this long tubular enclosed space, was like a physical punch, booming down the tunnel, an invisible landslide. Sharom closed eyes and mouth, covered nostrils, and waited. When the vibrations eased, he looked out, leaning through the hole in the wall, aiming his headlamp down the tunnel.

Here it came. The water had side-channels to fill, long tunnels to inundate, so it came on strongly but not in an overpowering rush.

As water rose around him, Sharom removed the ropes holding the sub to the trailer. Now the water was above the sub's propellers, so Sharom started its engine and felt the sudden surge in the water as the propellers spun. Slowly he moved the submarine forward, swimming along behind it.

The water filled the tunnel, and the side tunnels, and six other water tunnels. Power failed in several of the buildings. The submarine arrowed out into the harbor, a slender black metal fish. Sharom released control, and turned back.

11

It was when the man hit Luther on the back of the head with a fist-size stone, when he felt the pain and a runnel of blood trickling down his neck, that he finally snapped out of the stupor he'd been in ever since Bennett had dropped on top of him in the water tunnel. He turned to look at the man who'd hit him, a short compact pugnacious Chinese, who gestured angrily at the pile of rubble in front of them, making it clear Luther was working too slowly. The man tossed the bloodied stone into the tram and glared at Luther, hands on hips. Luther lifted the shovel, turned, and hit him in the face with it.

That time he used the flat of the shovel, but in the melee that followed he used the edge; it made a very adequate lance, producing quite satisfactory gashes in arms and foreheads.

They were working in one of the temporary side tunnels, and Luther retreated as he fought, out of the tunnel, then saw the construction elevator off to his left, one man there, waiting for it, the elevator descending. Luther ran for the elevator, clutching the shovel, and swung it at the man as the elevator stopped at the bottom.

Yank open the accordion gate, jump in, find the buttons, push Up, jam the gate shut with the shovel handle. Workmen tried to get at him through the gate, but had to drop away as the elevator jolted upward. The last he saw was the supervisor who'd hit him, shouting urgently into a walkie-talkie.

He didn't ride all the way to the surface, but got off at a sub-basement, then sent the elevator on up toward the top of the shaft without him. This was a storage area, with only one worklight, that one near the elevator shaft cage. Stacks of lumber, rolls of wire and plastic, barrels of nails, were all jumbled any which way. Luther moved into the darkness away from the elevator, certain he could find hiding places in here until he could figure out his escape.

It took him a little while to realize there was no pursuit. He was hiding here, in the middle of a collection of barrels, and no one was chasing him.

Why not? Rising from his hiding place, he roamed the darkness in here, moving slowly, not wanting to fall through some invisible hole in the floor, and eventually came across a ladder leading upward. In the next quarter hour, he managed to zigzag his way to the surface, where the lights were, and the structures, and men moving around.

And now he saw why they felt they needn't waste time and manpower searching for one runaway. The construction site was completely enclosed by high fences, some wooden, some chain link, razor wire running in a coil along the top. If he tried to climb that to escape, forget the razor wire, he'd be spotted before he was halfway to the top and shot dead.

Giving up the thought of escape, at least for the moment, he moved back into the shadows, hunkered down, and waited to see what would develop.

This was not long before the actual shooting began, and when it did it startled him, because he'd been thinking about shooting, and at first he couldn't tell who was shooting, or why, or at whom. Then he saw the bulldozer race up the road slope from the bottom of the excavation, saw it placed to block the gate, and realized what must be going on.

What could he do? He was seated now on a stack of pipes meant for scaffolding, just inside the blue plastic sheathing of the building under construction. Ahead of him was the muddy floor of the excavation, spotted with construction vehicles, but now empty of workmen or anybody else. Fifteen or twenty feet from where he sat the steep slope of the dirt access road angled up to where the bulldozer blocked the entrance. To both sides, the excavation fell away steeply just inside the fence.

The police would only be able to come in through that gate, and the bulldozer would probably have to be blown out of the way with dynamite. How much time did the authorities have, to come to that conclusion and then to act on it?

Not enough, Luther thought, not enough time at all.

He had never driven a bulldozer, but he had driven similar machines in the Alps, when he worked for the ski lodge. He remembered that they didn't operate at all like an automobile, didn't even have a steering wheel, but separate levers to manage the right and left treads.

Wait. Think this through, don't be hasty. What was it about acceleration? There are floor pedals; which is the accelerator?

Neither. That's another lever, on the left or the right. Which? One on one side controls speed, the other on the other side controls the blade. What do the pedals do? Brake.

Well, that's all I can remember, he thought. When I get there, it will come to me right away or somebody will shoot me while I'm thinking about it. So I hope it comes to me right away.

The nearest vehicle to where he now sat was a small flatbed truck with two stacks of Sheetrock on it, covered by clear plastic tarps. Would the key be in the ignition? Almost certainly yes; several people would drive each of these vehicles, none of which would be leaving the site. So all he had to do was get up on his feet and walk over there.

Still he hesitated, people had been shooting, though the shooting had stopped now. But they had been shooting, and if they saw someone in motion they might start to shoot again.

Should he run, or walk? If he ran they would know he was their enemy and they might start shooting at him at once. If he walked, they might at first think he was one of them. On the other hand, he was taller than any of them, and much more blond, so if he walked they would have more time to study him and realize he could not be one of their crew.

There isn't time to waste here, you know. And yet he continued to sit on the stack of pipes, leaning forward slightly, looking out from his concealment at that flatbed truck. Am I a coward? he asked himself. He didn't think he was a coward. He'd braved the mountains, he'd braved the ocean, he'd braved his father's scorn. And yet, there was something about people shooting at you, something different about that.

For God's sake, let's do it, he told himself. There's no one else to do it, so let's do it. Stop thinking about it and just stand up and do it.

He stood up. He walked out of his protected shadow and across the open dirt to the flatbed truck. He saw no one, heard no one cry out, heard no shooting.

There were no doors on the truck, and the bench seat was covered by a tattered rattan throw. A key ring dangled from the ignition.

Luther slid behind the wheel and somebody shouted.

He bent low, turning the key, and the engine coughed into life, very loud, so he couldn't hear if the shout was repeated. He shifted into low, and drove abruptly up the access road.

The bulldozer loomed ahead. He jerked the truck to a stop without bothering to shut off the engine, jumped out onto the dirt, and the truck rolled slowly backward, down the slope. He ran up beside the bulldozer, climbed the tread, grabbed the vertical metal post holding up the canopy, and swung himself into the seat.

Something *pinged* off the muffler, that thick vertical black pipe in front of him, rising from the engine. They *are* shooting at me!

Where was the starter switch? Oh, God, that was the part he hadn't thought out ahead of time.

It's outside! It's on the canopy support post I grabbed coming up!

He leaned down low to the right, feeling for the starter switch, hearing another *ping* somewhere, then being aware of shooting out in front of him, and thinking, don't shoot at me, I'm on *your* side!

Starter switch. Yes; the big engine roared into life.

Blade control, which was the blade control? Here on the right. The instructions for everything in this cab were very clearly laid out, in Chinese.

The blade was down on the ground, almost touching the chain-link gate. Luther moved the blade control, and the blade tried to press lower, nearly lifting the bulldozer.

He moved it the other way, and the blade lifted, scraping the gate.

He would never figure out reverse. Could he just make it move forward? Transmission and engine-speed controls here on the left.

Yes! The machine strained forward, treads slipping on the loose dirt, the gate bending but not breaking.

More *pings* all around him. He had to get out of here. Hunkered low, feeling bullets punch into the seat behind him, he pushed the right-hand steering lever forward, the left-hand steering lever back. The bulldozer swiveled leftward, and as it did the blade yanked the right side of the gate out of its hinges, metal snapping and flying everywhere.

Reverse, reverse, right lever back, left lever forward, swivel the other way, feel a beebite on the left side of the head, just above the ear, no time to think about it.

Sprong! The gate gave way, and Luther brought both levers straight, and the bulldozer shot out onto the road, pushing the wrecked gate ahead of it. He was too excited and confused, and couldn't figure out how to stop the thing until it ran into a police bus on the other side of the road.

Fortunately, the bus was empty.

12

The diver's voice spoke from one of the walkie-talkies: "Job done. Coming back."

"Yes," Bennett said in response. He put that walkie-talkie down and grabbed the other one to say into it, "Jackie? Where are you?"

"Coming out," Tian's voice said. "We can only do ten in the elevator at a time."

"There's more shooting up here, Jackie," Bennett said, and he knew his nervousness could be heard in his voice, and he envied the tough calm that Tian still showed.

"Hold them off," Tian said, "we're coming out as fast as we can. The diver isn't back yet, either."

"He's on his way," Bennett said, and the phone rang, which must be Curtis.

Yes. What was in Curtis's voice was triumph: "We've done it, Colin!"

"Yes, sir."

"Did you set the last timers?"

"Not yet, sir. Jackie's crew and the diver are still coming out."

"Well, set them, man. They still have thirty minutes."

"Yes, sir."

"Do it now, Colin."

"Yes, sir, I will."

"And, Colin?"

"Sir?"

"Leave the phone off the hook. I'll be listening to what happens there, and you'll be able to talk to me any time you have to."

"Very good, sir."

"And start those timers."

"Yes, sir."

When Jackie Tian rode the elevator from the level above the flooding up to the surface, traveling with the last of his work-crew, he found the rest of his men milling around inside the area swathed in the blue plastic tarps.

"Bulldozer's gone," one of them said.

Tian looked around an edge of plastic. He saw an armored personnel carrier, windshield shattered, slowly driving down the access road from the smashed-open gate. A couple of men sniped at the personnel carrier from behind parked trucks, but he could see it was all over.

"We go now," he decided, and signaled to his men, and they trotted after him in a long line away from the battle, toward the passage to the alley leading to Partition Street.

"I have to leave here now, sir," Bennett said into the phone, knowing how panicky he sounded but unable to stop it. "The police broke through, they're coming this way."

"Did you set the timers?"

"Yes, sir."

"Leave the phone off the hook."

"But I have to go now, sir, I—"

"Leave it off the hook!"

"Yes, sir," Bennett said, and dropped the phone onto the desk. Standing, he ran around the desk, and pulled open the door, and blue-uniformed policemen swarmed in.

Sharom swam through the flooded tunnels, his headlamp showing the way. At the end, there was a ladder, and he climbed it to the level above the water. He pushed the button there to summon the elevator, and while waiting for it he changed out of his flippers and back into the rubber thongs.

Then the elevator came, and he rode upward, flippers under his left arm. When he got to the surface level and stopped, the elevator cage was surrounded by uniformed policemen, most of them pointing pistols or rifles at him. When he raised his arms, the flippers fell to the floor of the cage.

In six places in the flooded tunnels, carefully positioned by Colin Bennett following Richard Curtis's precise instructions, tucked against side walls in the pitch blackness, were rectangular metal boxes, each about the size of a child's coffin. The boxes had hinged tops and padlocks, and inside, in waterproof plastic bags, were the timers, the radio receivers, the detonators and the slim tubes of TNT.

Water had already seeped into the boxes, but that didn't matter. The timers chittered quietly to themselves, unreeling the seconds. When they judged the instant was right, one after the other, they would detonate.

No one explosion would be very severe, but every one of them would agitate the water in these confined tunnels, every additional one increasing the agitation, until the sixth explosion would be like attaining free-fall. The energy would now renew itself, the water shoulder more space for itself, pressing outward, crumbling the concrete, eating the landfill, turning all the island below the clustered tall buildings into porridge.

Curtis sat at the table in the main cabin of *Granjya*, telephone to his ear, his eye on the radio and sonar that controlled the submarine. *Granjya* plowed steadily through the night, south and west, and the submarine obediently followed.

Through the phone, he could hear a confusion of people milling around in his office at the construction site. Voices spoke, too far away from the receiver for him to make out what they were saying, but from the sound of it he believed they'd captured Colin.

What would he tell them? Would he implicate Curtis? Not that it mattered. Nothing that anyone in that room could say would matter, before long.

All those lights, he thought, looking out at Hong Kong Island as it receded in the night, all those lights will soon switch off. Forever. I won't see it, he thought, but I'll hear it, the beginning of it. In just...twenty-seven minutes.

13

The shooting seemed to be over. Manville followed Tony Fairchild down the steep gradient of the access road, Kim beside him. Fairchild walked beside the new inspector, the overweight man who'd been rushed in to take Inspector Ha's place, whose name Manville hadn't caught. Fairchild was trying to establish some rapport with this new man, but Manville didn't think he was getting very far.

Well, the new man had a lot on his plate. Some sort of insurrection in the center of the city, and apparently a nearby theft of a lot of gold. Also, vandalism in the water tunnels. And he was coming to it all from a standing start.

As they walked down the slope, Manville saw a small sullen cluster of prisoners off to the left, two bodies on the ground nearby awaiting transportation, and uniformed policemen everywhere. More lights were being brought in, the blue plastic sheathing was being stripped from the shell of the building-that-wasn't, and the construction vehicles were being moved out of the way.

Unfortunately, Luther had been taken off to the hospital because of a graze wound on the side of his head before Manville could ask him about circumstances inside here. Where was Bennett, that was the question. The tunnels had been flooded, they knew that much. Was the soliton set?

As they neared the bottom of the slope, Manville called to Fairchild, "Do they have Bennett? Do they know where he is?"

Fairchild paused for Manville to catch up, as the new inspector strode on. "They have someone in the site office," he said, "and a diver. We'll go see."

As they started across the cleared excavation toward the trailer containing the office, Manville said, "We don't know how much time Curtis has given us."

"Bennett may know," Fairchild said. "I gather they may have used a submarine to take the loot away. If it's in the harbor now, Curtis won't want to do anything that might sink it."

"If it's in the harbor now, it's leaving the harbor fast," Manville said.

The site office was crammed with people. Bennett and a short olive-skinned man in a wetsuit sat on a bench to one side. A dozen policemen milled around the room, searching drawers, testing walkie-talkies, getting in each other's way.

Manville crossed to Bennett.

"You," Bennett said.

Manville unconsciously raised two fingers to the scar on his cheek. "Did you set the explosives?"

Bennett gave him a dull look, and a policeman angrily snapped at Manville in Cantonese to get away from the prisoners. Ignoring him, Manville said, "Bennett! Do you want to die?"

The policeman tugged at Manville's arm, and the new inspector called, "Inspector Fairchild! Get that man away from the prisoner!"

"Inspector," Fairchild said, "we have to stop the next round of explosions."

"We're in control here now," the new inspector said. "There will be no more explosions."

Manville said, "You don't understand—"

The new inspector said, "Inspector Fairchild, you cannot bring these civilians in here. I must demand they return to the street, to the other side of the barricade."

Manville said to Fairchild, "He doesn't know about it. Inspector Ha was trying to avoid panic, remember? He told as few people as possible what was happening here. This man hasn't the first idea what's going on."

"Inspector Fairchild," the new inspector announced, "I don't know what lenience my predecessor demonstrated for you, but I must insist on my orders being carried out. If you don't have these people removed, my men will remove them."

"We need them here," Fairchild began, and Manville turned back to Bennett: "Did you or did you not set the explosives?"

Again the Chinese policeman yanked at Manville's arm, yelling at him, but this time, with sudden ferocity. Fairchild spun on him, towering, red-faced, and roared, "Let the man ask his questions!"

The policeman, stunned, looked to his inspector for guidance. Tony turned his glower on the new inspector. A long silent moment went by, when no one spoke or moved.

They just got out from under the British thumb, Manville thought. They aren't going to like being yelled at by this big overbearing Australian.

But then the new inspector's professionalism broke through, and he snapped something at his policeman, who nodded, though grudgingly, and backed off. The new inspector made an imperious come-closer gesture at Fairchild and said, "Come here, sir, and explain yourself."

"I will, Inspector."

While Tony did, Manville turned back to Bennett. "If you didn't set the charges yet," he said, "for God's sake, tell me so. If you did, let's undo it before we're all killed."

"We'll be all right," Bennett muttered, not looking at him.

"We'll be all *right*?"

"Maybe get a block or two away."

"Man, don't you know what Curtis has set up?"

"It's a robbery," Bennett said. "I expect I'll do time."

"It's a massacre! Bennett, have you heard about the soliton?"

Before Bennett could answer, a ragged creature crashed into the office, crying, "Help me! Help me! I'm an American! Help me!"

Everybody stared at the man in bewilderment. He wore tattered grubby shorts and the remnants of shoes. He was unshaven, filthy, hair matted, wounds and scars all over his body. "My name," he moaned, "is Hennessy."

Kim, in awe, whispered, "Mark?"

"Kim!" Mark lurched toward her across the office. He dropped to his knees in front of her, staring up at her. "Don't let them," he begged. "Kim, don't let them."

"Mark." She went to her knees beside him, starting to touch him but then clearly afraid that any touch would only increase his pain.

"Mark Hennessy," Manville said. And then, turning to Bennett: "You recognize this man? You know he worked for Curtis?" Manville leaned down toward the quivering man. "You have to tell Bennett about the soliton."

Mark shook his head, confused. "But you...*you* know what it is. You built it."

"But if he hears it from you, he'll know I'm not making it up, trying to fool him. Tell him, Mark. What is the soliton?"

"You used it at the island, Kanowit Island."

"Tell him what it does."

"Turns land—landfill—turns it into mud."

"How?"

"Water in tunnels, explosives in water."

Wheeling on Bennett, Manville said, "He told you it would just remove the evidence, didn't he? But *you're* the evidence,

Bennett, we're *all* the evidence. There'll be probably six explosive devices, am I right?"

Bennett frowned at him. "Well, what do they do, then?"

"Every part of this island that has been added to," Manville told him, "will be gone. And the buildings on it, all of them. And us."

"He told me—"

"You believed him? You believed he'd let you live, to hold *this* over his head?"

Bennett shook his heavy head, back and forth, back and forth.

"You set them."

"Yes."

"How long ago?"

"I don't know, ten minutes, maybe less."

"For how long?"

"Thirty minutes." Bennett looked up at Manville. "Couldn't we get away in time?"

"From the *city*? How do you switch it off?"

"You don't," Bennett said, sounding surprised. "No one ever said anything about switching it off."

Manville laughed, without mirth. "No fail-safe, once again. Naturally."

Tony Fairchild said, "Can we get to the explosives, switch them off manually?" Beside him, the new inspector was looking ashen-faced and terrified.

Manville said, "They're underwater, in the tunnels. We'd need divers, we'd never get divers here in time."

One of the policemen in the office suddenly noticed something and spoke up. "That telephone," he said, "is off the hook."

They all stared at it. Tony strode to the table, picked up the receiver, listened, reacted, and turned to say, "I heard him hang up."

Manville said to Bennett, "Curtis?"

Bennett nodded.

Fairchild said, "George? Is there really no way to stop it?"

Kim said, "I can go."

14

Kim had never been so frightened in her life. All she could see in her mind's eye was that great boulder of hard gray water rolling at her from Kanowit Island, surrounding her, submerging her, beating her into a rag doll.

She was now wearing the other diver's wetsuit and goggles and headlamp and flippers and air tank, thanking heaven he was a small man so it more or less fit. She moved strongly through the black tunnels. The water filling the tunnels was clouded, already beginning to mix with dirt from the temporary cross-tunnels. In a little while, you wouldn't be able to see down here at all. Of course, in a little while, there would be no down here.

The more she thought about the urgency of the job, the need for speed and efficiency, the more anxious she became. And she knew that could be fatal. She'd almost fallen down the ladder into the water, unable to control her feet in flippers on the ladder rungs. And she didn't want to dive or fall into that water, because who knew what debris might be in there, to cut her or knock her out.

And now, when she should be concentrating on swimming forward, finding the bombs, defusing them, all she could think about was the destroyer wave off Kanowit Island, all she could do was feed her fear.

George hadn't wanted her to come down here. None of them had wanted her to do it, none of them would have asked her to risk her life to save theirs—to save everyone's. But who else was there?

For about two seconds there had been the idea of convincing

the other diver of the peril of the situation, and having *him* come down here, but everybody agreed he wouldn't understand the danger and would most likely just swim through the tunnels and out the breached seawall and away.

So it had to be her. George had said it wouldn't be necessary to disarm all six bombs, even if there'd been time, and there surely was not that much time. "These three," he'd said, pointing them out on the construction plans, and Kim concentrated on what she had to do when she got down below.

It was simple, if she could only remember it. Through the first cross-tunnel, then down that water tunnel a little way to the right, and that would be number one. Back, find the next cross-tunnel, take it, pass through the next main tunnel to go to the *next* main tunnel, and to the left, and that would be number two. Then back the way she'd come, all the way back, past the ladder, down a different tunnel, another left into a cross-tunnel, another right, and there would be number three. And then, as quickly as possible, scoot back to the ladder and up.

"The other three," George had said, "will do some damage, but there won't be enough pressure to build up the soliton wave. As long as you're out of the water once they start to go off, you'll be all right."

Be all right. She didn't see how she could possibly be all right, she didn't see how any of them could be all right.

There. In the increasingly murky water, there it was, on the floor, next to the wall, looking like a flattened footlocker. On an elastic loop around her wrist was the padlock key Bennett had dug out of the desk drawer, and when she hunkered beside the box to try the key, it worked.

How much time was left now? Ten minutes? Less?

Her hands fumbled when she pulled the wire-clippers from her belt. "Just cut the wires between the timer and the detonator,"

George had told her. "It's a very simple device. Cut the wires, and move on."

The wires. She squeezed the wire clippers, and the wires were tougher than she'd expected. *More* time wasted. She had to cut the wires one at a time. At least that worked.

Clippers back into utility belt; *don't* drop them!

The headlamp glow reflected back at her more and more from the dirty water. She slid along the right side of the water tunnel, finding the cross tunnel mostly by feel, moving on.

What if the water becomes too dirty to see in at all? How can I move fast if I'm blind?

It took more swimming than it felt to her like it should have, more than she could afford, but then her fingers brushed something hard against the wall and she felt along its outline. The second box. Knowing how to do it now, she moved more quickly, but reminded herself not to hurry, not to make any mistakes. Her heart pounded inside the wetsuit as she manipulated the clippers, then slid them back into her belt and kicked out and away, reversing course, swimming as strongly as she could back the way she'd come.

Oh, how she wanted to climb that ladder when it came dimly into view, but no, not yet, there was more to be done. One more. Without disabling one more, she'd only have weakened the soliton, not prevented it. Maybe only a hundred thousand would die rather than millions—that was some victory, she supposed. But not an entirely satisfying one. Especially given that the dead would include her. And George.

She swam past the ladder and on down the dark tunnel, only able to see the side of the tunnel she was nearest to. Her own movements agitated the water, mixing it more quickly with the dirt in the side tunnels. It was like swimming in a sewer. Like swimming in a nightmare.

She kept her head down, kicked harder, took the turns George had shown her. Box number three was there where it was supposed to be, but she couldn't see it at all, had to open the padlock by feel, grope around inside it for the wires. She found them and braced the clippers against them, shifted her grip for greater leverage—and the clippers slipped from her hand.

She fumbled for them, grabbed at them, and missed.

For a second she couldn't breathe. Just a second, but it was the most painful second of her life, physically painful, like she was being crushed from all sides at once. She forced herself to take air in, forced herself to focus. *You're going to die down here*, she told herself, and strangely it succeeded in calming her down.

She stretched her arm out, groped along the bottom of the open box, praying, and when her fingers made contact with the rubber-sheathed grips of the clippers she seized them.

No more time. The wires had to be cut, and no time to do it one by one. Grimacing, she forced the jaws of the clippers together around the wires, squeezed hard with both hands. She'd have sworn she could hear the clippers bite shut as the wires split. It was done. She'd done it.

But the relief she felt was short-lived. For even if the explosives that were left wouldn't create a soliton wave, they would be more than enough to snuff out the life of one unfortunate diver caught in their path. She'd miraculously survived one underwater explosion already—no one beat the odds twice.

She let the clippers fall and tore back through the tunnel, scraping her hands painfully as she went because she couldn't see, had to do it all by feel.

She almost went past the ladder. It brushed her left leg as she went by, and she realized what she'd been about to do, to swim endlessly down this tunnel, directly into the explosions.

She reversed, felt around, couldn't find it, couldn't find it, couldn't find it, *there!*

Get these damn flippers off, get them *off*. She kicked them away, her shaking hands clutching at the ladder rungs, and she started to climb.

Her head had just broken the surface, seeing the floor another eight feet above her, the ladder extending upward to that platform there, when all at once the water around her vibrated, and then lifted, and she was underwater again, clinging to the ladder, the water reaching for her with a million fingers, trying to pluck her off the ladder, drag her away. The water surged upward around her, powerful, lifting her, then drained back, bearing strongly downward, still trying to carry her with it, she still clutching hard to the rungs, stupid with fright.

The first bomb has gone off. *I really am going to die here.*

The water receded, foaming, her head was in air again, and a hand was there, reaching down for her. She looked up, gaping through the goggles, and it was George, holding onto the ladder just above her, reaching down for her.

She put one shaking hand in his, and he pulled upward, and they both rose out of the water to collapse onto the floor, the water boiling eight feet below. She lay there gasping, on her side, the air tank still cumbersome on her back, the goggles still on, looking blearily out and down at the water heaving in the darkness below.

Distant thunder boomed. The water heaved upward as though to recapture them. They clung to each other and watched it rise, and then it fell back, quiet again.

Solemnly, "I don't ever want to dive again," Kim said.

George laughed, and kissed her, and they didn't care about the third and last explosion.

15

Curtis paced the narrow portside deck of *Granjya*, staring north-ward, watching the glittery lights of the island city far away, willing it to happen. Thirty-two minutes. Thirty-three.

Could they possibly have stopped it, defeated the soliton? He *knew* the charges were located where they should be. How could they have stopped him? They'd have to send divers into the tunnels, the water in the tunnels would be filthy, they wouldn't have the time or the people to do all that. And there's no other way to stop the soliton.

Thirty-four minutes.

It's George, somehow. George Manville has done this to me. He should be dead, the man should be dead, and in any case he's nothing but an unimaginative engineer, how can he stop *me*?

Curtis had always known this was a possibility, but he'd had to go forward anyway. His position was untenable and getting worse. He had to get out from under or *go* under, ruined, disgraced. So he'd had to make this gamble, and now he'd lost.

Thirty-seven minutes.

It wasn't going to blow. George Manville, of all people, had beaten him. (He never even thought of Kim.)

But was this any worse than to fail the other way? To be sued, hounded, taken through bankruptcy courts, reviled by everyone who used to shake his hand and drink his liquor. If things had worked out…

If things had worked out, he would have had all the money he needed to solve his problems, and he would not have had one breath of scandal to touch upon him. He would have had his revenge on the city that had tried to destroy him, and he would have continued to be Richard Curtis, owner of Curtis Construction and RC Structural, respected, accepted everywhere in the world.

Well, he had failed, and now that failure was behind him, and it was time to start again. He still had a very few trusted people—the Farrellys at Kennison, for instance—he could rely on. Richard Curtis would have to disappear forever, and gradually he would have to build up a new identity. He had lost a battle, that's all, not the war.

To disappear meant totally, and that meant he had to start now. Defeat had made him tougher, more decisive. He knew what had to be done, and he wouldn't shrink from doing it.

There was a pistol in his cabin, an Iver Johnson Trailsman .32. He went there and got it, and walked forward to where the Hsus stood together, he at the wheel, she seated in the bolted-down chair beside him, chatting. Curtis shot her first, in the head, and then her husband, quickly, before he could think about it. Then he rolled the bodies over the side.

This was the first thing. No one must know how he left Hong Kong, where he went. Before, he'd been in a position where he could trust the Hsus to keep silent, because they would want more of his work in the future. But now, they would know he was a fugitive, and they would not want to be linked to him, and they would go to the police at the very first opportunity. So they wouldn't get an opportunity.

He could operate this ship alone. The thing to do now was choose a new destination, because the authorities would surely know by now he'd come to Hong Kong from Taiwan, so he could not go back to Taiwan.

There are other places in this world, some not even as far away as Taiwan. There was Macao, for instance. Farther off, but possibly even more useful, there was Vietnam. Or the Philippines.

He could decide all that later. The main thing now was to deal with the submarine, get farther away from the Chinese coast, and at last get some sleep, an hour or two of sleep before daylight.

It would be very good if he could keep the submarine, but he didn't dare. If he were stopped, he was Mark Hennessy, with a partly burned passport, due to an accident on board. (All of Mark's travel goods were still aboard, and he would arrange a small fire in the main cabin to back up his story.) But he could not be Mark Hennessy, an innocent traveler, if he were leashed to a submarine carrying a full load of gold ingots, so unfortunately the submarine would have to go.

But not the gold, or at least not all of it. He would bring, say, a dozen ingots aboard *Granjya*, hide them, and have that as the base for his next fortune. So, once the Hsus were out of the way, he throttled back the *Granjya* engines to their slowest forward speed, just making enough headway into the chop so the ship wouldn't begin dangerously to roll. Delicately, with the radio controls, he brought the submarine to the surface and then forward, to hover beside *Granjya*, maintaining the same speed, while he got a rope around the rudder, just forward of the propeller.

There was nothing else on the sleek machine to tie onto, but he had both vessels moving at the same speed, in the same direction, so everything would be fine so long as they were tethered together in at least one spot. And this transfer wouldn't take long.

The top of the submarine, when it rode on the surface, was below the side deck of *Granjya*. Curtis had to lie on his stomach on the deck and reach down to the central hatch cover of the submarine, a round metal wafer three feet across, with crescent indentations for handholds. Tugging on two of these indentations, he was resisted at first, and then the cover turned easily. So easily that all at once it was free, and sliding off the metal hull to fall away into the water. Not a problem; the whole submarine would be scuttled soon.

The interior was not full. The top two feet of stowage space was empty, so Curtis couldn't reach the nearest ingots from the deck of *Granjya*. He had to slide under the rail out over the submarine and lower himself through the hatch.

Now it was easy. He bent down, grabbed an ingot, was surprised by how heavy it was, but lifted it up and turned to push it onto the deck of *Granjya*, under the lower bar of the rail. Then he transferred a second ingot, and then he paused; they were really very heavy.

When he lifted the third ingot and turned, the deck of *Granjya* was too far away. Some wave had slightly altered the two vessels' courses.

No matter. They were still tied together. What Curtis had to do now was get to the rear of the submarine, grab the rope, bring the two boats back in line.

It seemed to him too dangerous to try to crawl over the top of the submarine. It was probably too slippery, and he didn't want to wind up in the water, even with *Granjya* right there next to him. So he slid down into the submarine, lay on his back on the lumpy ingots of gold, and opened the aft hatch cover from inside. All of this was taking longer than he'd expected.

This cover also slid away into the sea. Curtis slithered along the gold, raised himself through the aft hatch, and by the running lights of Granjya he could see that the two vessels had now yawed widely from one another, like an alligator's mouth opening very wide. Both ships tried to move steadily forward, but each was hampered by the other, and they were turning almost disdainfully away from one another, the submarine attached by the rope around its rudder at the rear now facing almost directly away from the prow of *Granjya*.

The rope! Curtis saw it was going to happen, and lunged, but too late. The ships made one more incremental turn away from one another, and the rope tying them together met the spinning propeller of the submarine, and the propeller neatly sliced through.

Immediately the ships lunged away from one another. Curtis saw the lights of *Granjya* rapidly recede. There were no lights on the submarine.

Dive into the sea? He couldn't possibly hope to swim fast enough to catch up with *Granjya*. But if he stayed in the submarine, what then?

Granjya's lights were fainter, they disappeared. Curtis was getting wet. As the waves ran over the submarine, water ran inside through the two open hatches.

He was in pitch blackness, in this small heaving boat on the surface of the sea. It was riding lower, taking on water faster.

There was no light anywhere in the world, except far away to the north, far away, the cold white sheen of Hong Kong against the night sky. Curtis, standing in the hatchway on his gold ingots, his body moving with the roll of the submarine, kept his eyes on that far-off pale glow.

After a while, the lights were still there, but he was not.

Afterword
by Jeff Kleeman

I discovered the joys of James Bond in 1973, when I was nine years old and my stepfather took me to see *Live and Let Die*. Two years later I discovered Donald Westlake. While wandering in a bookstore I came upon a novel by Tony Kenrick. One reviewer compared Kenrick to Westlake. Who is this Westlake guy who's supposed to be so great, I wondered.

So I went hunting, like a heist artist in a Westlake plot. But trying to find a Westlake book in a sleepy California suburb, long before the days of Internet searches, wasn't so easy. Eventually, I unearthed a trove of them in the public library and once I overcame the final obstacle (a librarian concerned the books were inappropriate for a child), I was hooked for life.

Twenty years later, a veteran fan of all things Westlake and Bond, I joined United Artists, where I found a way to unite them for the first time. Or so I thought. While I was unaware at the time, it turns out that watching *Live and Let Die* in 1973 was actually the first moment I laid eyes on both Bond and Don. Here's Don divulging it to me in 1995:

> *Dear Jeff,*
>
> *In LIVE AND LET DIE, I am the passenger in the red car in the stunt driving sequence on the FDR Drive in New York. When I saw the movie, back then, I was astonished at how much that black silhouette (moi) inside that car was being thrown around. At the time, it had just seemed like a little sideswipe, not such a much at all.*

One car didn't make it into the shot; a flashy pimpmobile with a black stunt driver in outrageous togs. After a rehearsal, he told the director he was almost out of gas and drove away and didn't come back. Hours later, we learned what had happened. Being, like all the stunt drivers on that job, from Pennsylvania, he hadn't known he couldn't make a right turn on a red light in New York City. Wall Street area, Sunday, zero traffic. He turns, a police car appears out of nowhere, he's stopped, he's asked for license and registration. There's no registration in the glove compartment of this rented specialty car. His wallet is in his regular clothes, not his costume. He has nothing. He said, "You see, I'm a stunt driver in a James Bond movie." "And I," said the cop, "am Minnie Mouse. Outta the car." It was five hours before he got his phone call.

Show biz.

The tale of reviving the James Bond franchise is too lengthy to be unspooled here, but this you need to know: when we made *GoldenEye*, the film industry didn't believe it would succeed. They had good reason. Marketing surveys revealed that the majority of teenage boys in 1995 had no idea who James Bond was. The few who were aware described him as "that guy my father likes." There was a good reason for this: a Bond film hadn't done substantial business since *Octopussy* in 1983. The Dalton Bonds never found a large audience. Fifteen-year-olds in 1995 had been only two years old the last time James Bond had been culturally significant.

The massive doubts about *GoldenEye* were accentuated by several factors: Pierce Brosnan was an ex-TV actor whose biggest recent role was a supporting turn in the Robin Williams comedy *Mrs. Doubtfire*. Martin Campbell had done some wonderful television but had never directed a successful feature film.

Barbara Broccoli and Michael Wilson had grown up working on the Bond films, but they had never before been lead producers.

The first hint that *GoldenEye* would explode conventional Hollywood wisdom came during production, when Martin Campbell did something I'd never seen another director do: even though we were in the middle of a complex shoot, Martin managed to cut together the opening sequence and then showed it to the cast, crew and all of us at the studio. This was his way of keeping morale high. Boy, did he succeed.

The next indicator came when we released a teaser trailer that displayed everything we believed a Bond film should be. In theaters across the country the response was ecstatic.

By the time we saw a first cut in early 1995, the feeling at MGM/UA had shifted from doubt to hope that Bond might be the savior the studio needed.

In 1993, when I joined United Artists, I rewatched every Bond film, reread every book, dove into the archives and learned everything I could about the history of the franchise. I was struck by the unusual connections between the movies and novelists. Roald Dahl wrote the screenplay for *You Only Live Twice* and the finished film has a unique, rebellious wit I suspect comes directly from Dahl. Anthony Burgess wrote the first draft of the *Spy Who Loved Me* screenplay.

I began to fantasize about what a Donald Westlake version of Bond would be. Don struck me as having it all—intricate plotting, Dahl and Burgess's anarchic wit, plus an ability neither of them had: writing ingenious, tough, gritty action.

It's normal for a studio to hire a writer for a potential sequel even before a film is released. If the film works then the next installment in the franchise is already on a fast track; if the film flops the money spent on a first draft is inconsequential to the studio's bottom line.

In March of 1995, with *GoldenEye*'s release still eight months away, I proposed reaching out to Donald Westlake to see if he would be interested in writing the next Bond film—assuming there was going to be a next Bond film.

The studio was game for anything. And Barbara and Michael were intrigued by the idea. They've always supported bringing fresh voices to Bond as long as we protect the particular qualities that make Bond singular in the action genre. So they gave me their blessing to reach out to Don.

Now, while Don had written the occasional screenplay (and had even been nominated for an Academy Award for *The Grifters* in 1990), he'd never courted Hollywood. He had a rule that he would never adapt of one of his own novels, so the frequent options on his books never led to direct involvement with the filmmaking community. But I had to try—I couldn't pass up the chance to get him involved with this.

How many people get the opportunity to do something that would thrill their childhood self beyond all imagining? Working on a James Bond movie was just such an opportunity for me, and working with Donald Westlake on a Bond film would be even more so. When I reached out to Don through his agent, I had the incredible feeling that I was fulfilling a promise to that eleven-year-old boy who is still very much a part of me. Of course, I had no idea what Don's response would be.

3/29/95

Dear Jeff,

I have looked at the 3 Bonds, and am now more interested than ever. Here are some thoughts.

A continuing motif, I see, is birth through water; I have no problem with that. And another theme, which I take it got

*lost later on, was always somehow to top the previous work;
he dies __and__ he's buried at sea, so do something even more
over the top next time.*

*May I ask for one more of the earlier Bonds? I'd like to see
LIVE AND LET DIE again, because I'm in it.*

Don was interested! We exchanged faxes—email had not yet
become the norm. Don immediately had an idea involving a
computer hacker who'd been stealing information from British
Intelligence and the CIA. Because he's in their systems, the
U.K. and U.S. can't use any of their wired tech, they have to go
old school and thus, they turn to Bond to take on this very
modern villain. The villain's in league with some Third World
financiers and their big scheme is to create chaos in the stock
exchanges, destroying the entire economic system of the premier
nations. As Don summed his thinking up:

*This could be too cerebral a threat, but I believe it could be
made the equivalent of a bomb going off.*

*I have not seen all 16 of the previous Bonds, nor all sixteen
thousand of the imitation Bonds (I did see TRUE LIES, though),
so for all I know the computer genius who will bring society to
its economic knees has already been met. If not, I think he
could be fun. Every day now, the newspapers have another
story about how vulnerable that vast interconnected web of
computer technology is, so if it's that vulnerable, why don't
we go get it?*

Don's idea was prescient. Except for *WarGames* back in
1983, movies hadn't tackled our newly wired world. *Hackers*
(which we were in production on at UA when Don made his
pitch), *The Net*, and all the other films that would soon explore
the issues Don was intrigued by hadn't yet been released. But
there was one intractable problem with Don's pitch (though it

was also the most reassuring thing about it): clearly he had already mind-melded with our thinking about Bond because his idea was integral to the premise of *GoldenEye*, a villain planning to take down the world's stock exchanges via the Internet. I filled Don in on *GoldenEye*'s plot and three days later I received a fax from him that began, "Okay, Plan B. Round two. The second coming. Hello again."

This time he proposed a story about a villain in Southeast Asia who is planning to use weather satellites to destroy all the grain in North and South America, effectively killing all the livestock, resulting in the elimination of the entire food supply for the Western Hemisphere.

That idea didn't feel quite right for us. But Don's excitement wasn't dampened. He was committed to rising to the challenge of creating a new Bond story.

We arranged a trip to London so Don could meet with Barbara and Michael. I'd idolized Don for twenty years and now, suddenly, I was taking a trip to Europe with him in order to work together on building a story from the ground up. I was ecstatic, and oh-so-nervous.

The London trip was perfect. Don loved travel and he did it well. And, having had a little more time to ruminate, what ideas he had conjured up by the time we arrived!

Bond movies always begin with a pre-credit sequence, often in an exotic foreign locale. Don suggested we open on Bond running through moonlit woods. It would feel very real, very dangerous. A chyron would flash on the screen displaying the location: Transylvania. Since Transylvania is a part of Eastern Europe, it's perfectly reasonable that Bond might have a mission there. And yet...Transylvania. It was a brilliant idea in the same vein as the brilliance Dahl brought to *You Only Live Twice*. It's unexpected, attention-getting (immediately you're leaning forward because this is and yet isn't a typical Bond opening), funny while still grounded.

Then Don unveiled his biggest idea: if *GoldenEye* succeeded —a necessity for the 18th Bond film to be greenlit—then we knew the studio would want the film currently known only as *Bond 18* to be released in theaters by 1997. This was a certainty because MGM/UA was going be sold in 1997, and to attract the highest bids it would need a slate that promised bankable films. Another certainty was that one of the biggest events of 1997 would be the handover of Hong Kong from the United Kingdom (Bond's employer) to China. What if *Bond 18* was the first James Bond movie that correlated with a real historic event, one that happened simultaneously with the film's release?

It was bold and exciting. We were thrilled by the possibilities and locale (Bond hadn't spent real time in Hong Kong since *The Man With the Golden Gun*). A deal was quickly made and Don went to work writing a treatment.

I'm fascinated by how ideas take shape and how writers write. Some writers outline extensively, some start with an ending and work backward, some write a bunch of scenes in no particular order and with no obvious connection and then eventually pick a few of the best and build a story around them. None of these were Don's method. He relied on what he called "narrative push."

Don would get an idea, usually for a beginning, an opening scene, something like, *What if there's a bank robbery in progress and the getaway car can't find a parking space in front of the bank?* (This was the idea Don said was the spark for writing the first of his Dortmunder novels.) Don would start from a premise like that and just write, without any plan for where he was going, trusting that eventually he'd end up with a story. He told me there was only one story he ever started that he couldn't puzzle out a way to finish. It involved insurance fraud and after six weeks Don realized he'd written his characters into such a tight corner he was unable to keep them moving all the way to a resolution. I hope one day Hard Case Crime will unearth the manuscript and we'll get to see Don's version of an impossible story.

But the method worked for him the rest of the time, and as a consequence, Don didn't outline.

Bond films work differently. For those, a treatment—basically an outline—that represents a blueprint for the story is required before we send the writer off to draft a screenplay.

When a writer who doesn't naturally outline is asked to do so, the result is often either dry, like a mathematical proof—B follows from A; C from B—or cartoonish because the real voice of the characters and the tone hasn't yet been found through the writing. As far as I know, *Bond 18* was the first time Don had ever been required to perform the interim step of fully plotting out an original story in a relatively schematic fashion. Not his natural process, but he gave it his all.

In September 1995, Don delivered a thirty-five page treatment for *Bond 18*.

It was a delight to read. Every page brimmed with ideas and fun. But not all of it worked, or at least worked for us. For example, Don had come up with an intriguing new pre-credits sequence, but Bond was absent from it. We needed one with Bond in it. Don had also placed most of the action in Australia, and while amusing—Q equips Bond with a boomerang "that goes boom"—the *Crocodile Dundee* movies were still pretty fresh in people's minds, creating a risk that the overlay would tilt us toward unintentional comedy.

Fortunately, because *GoldenEye*'s release date was still two months away and we didn't yet know if it would be successful enough to trigger pre-production on the next film, we had some time to work on *Bond 18*. So we sent Don off to write a new treatment that satisfied our Bond parameters.

There were elements from Don's work to date we wanted to retain: the Carpathians (Transylvania), the handover of Hong Kong to China as central to the villain's plot, and Bond partnering with a female Chinese agent. Don went to work and in October, a few weeks before *GoldenEye* hit the theaters, he delivered a new outline.

This treatment was substantially shorter—nine pages. Once again it had wonderful moments, but it now hewed so closely to traditional Bonds that it didn't clothe the expected beats with enough fresh surprises.

As we pondered what to do, *GoldenEye* opened to immediate success. Barbara, Michael, Pierce, Martin, Bruce Feirstein and the rest of our cast and crew delivered a Bond film that reminded the world why Bond, since the 1960s, has been the most beloved action hero of the western world. The ripple effect expanded far beyond the box office. The entire library of Bond films gained new value. Nintendo launched a tie-in videogame that took the gaming world by storm. Almost overnight, *GoldenEye* created an entire Bond industry.

Within a month of *GoldenEye*'s release, MGM/UA realized that producing the next Bond film as quickly as possible was the top priority.

As Don, Barbara, Michael and I had predicted, MGM/UA demanded that *Bond 18* be released in 1997. The fate of the studio was riding on it.

So: what to do.

Don's treatments had all the wonderful ideas he'd pitched in London, but neither was fully convincing as a Bond movie. I know Don would have found the right balance if he could have written the script and discovered the story's details as he wrote, but *GoldenEye*'s enormous success now imposed on us a full-speed-ahead production time-frame.

If you're making a movie as complex as a Bond film and you're rushing toward a release date, then an outline is a necessity. The schedule for *Bond 18* necessitated that locations be scouted, stunts planned, actors cast long before a shooting script would ever be completed (as it turned out, the actual shooting script wasn't completed until three weeks before production *ended*). If Don continued, he'd have to change out most of what he'd created, going back to the drawing board yet again, while continuing to do the thing that wasn't his natural writing method—creating an outline before he wrote the script.

This issue was compounded by a growing concern from the studio over centering the story around the transfer of Hong Kong to China. Nobody knew what would happen when Hong Kong changed hands and some people were predicting violent, bloody outcomes. What if we made the most expensive movie in the history of MGM/UA, the movie that the studio was relying on to keep it in business, and it took a lighthearted approach to something that emerged as the biggest global horror-show of 1997?

It was analogous to what would happen in 1999 with Y2K: there were just enough smart people who predicted disaster that even though disaster appeared unlikely, it was still wise to make sure you had a good emergency kit stashed away for the new year. While MGM/UA knew the odds were in favor of a peaceful handover, was it worth taking a risk on when some experts were predicting carnage?

China also turned out not to be a fan of *GoldenEye*. The Chinese blocked the film's release due to the opening credit sequence, which the Chinese deemed anti-communist. China was an emerging film market and if things didn't go well with the transfer of Hong Kong, MGM/UA didn't want to be unable to release yet another Bond film there.

Heartbreakingly, all of this meant parting ways with Don. Don was disappointed, but not angry. He'd become attached to his idea of robbing Hong Kong's banks and then destroying the city. Now that MGM/UA didn't want Bond anywhere near Hong Kong during 1997, Don saw it as a practical matter— the conceit he'd fallen in love with collided with the studio's anxieties.

Don, his wife Abby, and I remained friends. Whenever I went to New York the three of us would meet for dinner at the most interesting restaurant of the moment—along with a love of travel, the three of us shared a love of good food. And watching the two of them together was such a pleasure. They delighted in each other and that made them always delightful to be with. Abby's sense of humor, and her curiosity about the world and about people, fully equaled Don's. It would not surprise me if when he wrote, it wasn't to please all of us, it was to please her.

Over the years I learned a vast amount from Don about writing and storytelling. I turned to him for advice while working on *The Thomas Crown Affair*. A few years later, when I received an urgent a call for help from John McTiernan who was in pre-production on a movie called *Basic*—John was having difficulty planting subtle but memorable clues in a way that would leave the audience feeling the film had played evenhandedly with them when a surprise twist occurred near the end—I asked Don if he'd help John out. Don agreed, so John and I spent a wonderful afternoon at Don's house, where Don applied his theories of storytelling to John's problem (my favorite: if you want the audience to feel a clue was laid in fairly, you need to show it to them in three different ways). All the while, Don and I continued to try and figure out a movie we could make together.

When Don died there was every reason to think I'd read my last Westlake novel. Don's lifelong narrative push had come to a halt. This was a painful loss for all of Don's readers and fans, but doubly so for me, because as massive a body of work as Don left behind, it was still missing one entry: the movie we were going to make.

I never imagined Don still had one more trick up his sleeve—that he'd taken the underlying McGuffin in his *Bond 18* treatments and fashioned an original thriller around it. In retrospect it makes complete sense—when you've come up with something as interesting as using Hong Kong's unique geography to destroy it, how can you let such a good scheme go to waste? But in all our conversations and meals since 1995, he'd kept it secret.

There's a history of repurposing storylines in Hollywood which, as far as I know, begins appropriately with James Bond. Ian Fleming, Kevin McClory and Jack Whittingham wrote *Thunderball* as a screenplay for an original Bond movie, but they failed to sell it. So Fleming turned the script into the novel *Thunderball*. After the novel's success, it was then transformed back into a screenplay and made into the fourth James Bond film.

I had a brush with plot repurposing on the remake of *The Thomas Crown Affair*. One of the first writers we discussed the project with, and who then pitched us an approach, was Ron Bass. Ron's a wonderful writer and his approach was intriguing, but it didn't deliver what we were looking for so we passed.

Ron, not wanting to abandon a clever idea, immediately re-worked it into the movie *Entrapment*. In 1999, two Bonds, Sean Connery and Pierce Brosnan, both starred in romantic cat-and-mouse heist movies inspired by the 1968 *Thomas Crown Affair*.

Charles Ardai told me about Westlake's clandestine reworking of his *Bond 18* premise a few months ago and I was giddy. The pleasure of reading several hundred more pages of Don's writing, the wonder of seeing the idea I'd watched him come up with made into a fully wrought story…it was even better than making a movie together, it was knowing that an author I'd loved for forty years had written a book I'd played a part in inspiring.

Authors often imagine their readers, and readers imagine conversations with authors, but rarely do they result in a book.

John le Carré sent a one-line telegram to George Roy Hill after seeing a screening of *The Little Drummer Girl*. It said, "You've taken my ox and turned it into a bouillon cube." Don, however, slyly reversed the process.

Forever and a Death is not to be confused with a novelization, which is a fleshing out of a movie's screenplay without traveling too far from any of its elements. Don has taken a place, an event and a McGuffin and created an entirely new story and characters around them. His treatments and this book share the same germ of inspiration, but they take it in completely different directions. It's a wonderful exercise in seeing how the same core idea can be imagined two different ways.

It's impossible for me not to wonder if there are certain aspects of the book—beyond the central device—that are Bond-influenced. For example, Manville bears an uncanny resemblance to Michael Wilson, the Bond producer. Michael physically resembles Westlake's descriptions of Manville, and Michael has an engineering background, something every

Bond writer is aware of because Michael takes an engineer's approach to dissecting story and action sequences, in the same way that Manville approaches solving the problem of the gun's safety mechanism when facing down deadly enemies on Richard Curtis's yacht. Then again, I can also see Manville as an alter ego for Don, who also had an engineer's head for plot, whether it be the conception of the soliton device or any number of his exceptional heist ideas. Either way, how wonderful to have a pulpy action novel where engineering solves both guns and sex.

So, what do the book and Don's treatments have in common? In both, the villain is a wealthy and powerful businessman with a worldwide construction company who had earlier married into a Hong Kong family. He's created a device that can produce a destructive soliton wave, which he first tests on an island in the Coral Sea that had been a Japanese observation post in WWII. The test is in service of being able to rebuild the island as a resort.

There's an environmental watch group boat that tries to stop the test and one of its members (a female Chinese agent in the treatments, an impetuous American girl in the book) dives into the water, is knocked unconscious by the blast, and is brought aboard the villain's boat. Though it's only in Don's treatment you'll get to find Bond murmuring as he witnesses the soliton reshaping the island, "Shaken not stirred."

The villain has a compound in a remote part of Australia where Bond and Manville are treated as both guests and prisoners. As part of their escape, both end up hanging on to the metal framework of the garage door (an idea Don lifted from one of his own Richard Stark novels!).

The villain's plot is to rob Hong Kong's banks and then level the city as an act of revenge (in the treatments it's a revenge against China as they are about to receive Hong Kong in the handover, whereas the book takes place after the handover).

Figuring out which Hong Kong construction site is being used; the workers barricading it against the police, resulting in a ' giant firefight; a radio-operated submarine to carry looted gold out through flooded tunnels; these elements can all be found in both the novel and at least some of Don's work on the film.

In Don's final treatment, the submarine isn't used; rather Don came up with a method where the gold is ground up, turned into a slurry with seawater and pumped out into a waiting barge where it piles up like sand. There's a climactic fight between Bond and the villain with the hill of gold sand rising around them. In a moment thematically reminiscent of the book's final pages, the villain is buried by the still-descending gold as Bond says, "Too rich for him, I think."

For a Westlake fan, *Forever and a Death* is a rewarding book. And that's true whether you know about the Bond connection or not. Westlake's quiet craftsmanship is on display with every sentence. Ten degrees to the right and any given sequence could be in a Parker book, ten degrees to the left and it could be in a Dortmunder story. (Take the set piece on the yacht where Manville and Kim have to escape three killers. The killers could be from a Parker story; Manville having to defend himself with a pepper mill could easily be a Dortmunder moment.) It's a beautiful illustration of how carefully Don calibrated language and tone, and how he found humor in his plots without sacrificing suspense.

There are wonderful inside jokes for Westlake aficionados, like Manville learning how to be tough by reading a novel titled *Payback* (the title of Mel Gibson's film adaptation of Westlake's first Parker novel, *The Hunter*). And of course Don's love of food and travel is evident throughout. It's a novel in which much of the joy is in how wonderfully Don's thought through the small details.

Which is not to say that there aren't frustrations. The reader begins by expecting that Manville is going to drive the story and then he's suddenly offstage for a large fraction of it, emerging as no more than an ensemble player by the end. The book switches from a traditional action-hero story to a fragmented structure more akin to Don's *Dancing Aztecs*.

I can understand why Don abandoned Manville as his lead midway through the book. While I love Manville's evolution from meek to hard-boiled engineer, as characters go, well, he's no James Bond. (No doubt deliberately so—Don clearly wanted the novel to be its own work, not a "Bond novel" or a pastiche of one, and in that he succeeded.)

And I wonder whether Don might never have felt fully in his element writing a do-gooder hero, whether Manville or Bond. If you think about it, in Don's most memorable novels his protagonists, whether it be Parker, Dortmunder or the leads of standalone novels like *The Ax*, are all on the wrong side of the law. They initiate actions whose reverberations propel the story. With this in mind, it's no surprise, perhaps, that it's the villain of *Forever and a Death*, Richard Curtis, who emerges as the book's most interesting and richly developed character, and whose devastating end gives the book its unforgettable final scene.

There are wonderful things in Don's treatments I wish I could have seen on screen. For example, when Bond first meets with M he's discomforted to learn there's a new 003. *They recycle the numbers?!?* M explains that since 00s never live for long, it's simplest to recycle the nine digits. Bond reflects on how strange it is to realize that one day there will be another 007 and, of course, another M too. It's a tour de force moment that underlines the danger of what Bond is about to do, makes a meta-reference to all the actors past and future who will be

Bond, and generates a melancholy emotion during a scene that's usually very dry.

But if he'd gone to script Don would have been writing a story that would then have been tossed around and reshaped by many others. It would have become more conventional Bond and less Westlake. As an executive, conventional Bond enlivened by Westlake is a dream. But as a Westlake fan, pure Westlake is still the best Westlake. So, while I still wonder what a Donald Westlake Bond screenplay might have yielded, I cherish the book.

With the publication of *Forever and a Death* my quest is complete. As a teenager I'd been in search of a Westlake book, then the man, then a film collaboration; and now he's brought me full circle, back to finding a Westlake book, and one I never imagined could have existed. A book that is filled with uniquely Westlake-ian pleasures and makes me appreciate and understand his work in ways I never had before.

In our attempts to make a movie together, I worked with Don one more time after *Bond 18*. I convinced him to adapt a series of detective novels by Steven Saylor set in ancient Rome. Don did a superb job and the movie would have been made if not for *Gladiator* coming along first and stealing its thunder.

In Don's script, the detective, Gordianus, exonerates a group of slaves for a murder they didn't commit. On the final page of the script he learns that though he's proven them innocent, all he's accomplished is exchanging one bad fate for them for another: they're being shipped to Egypt, where they'll wind up in worse bondage than before.

The final bittersweet lines Don wrote sum up both his philosophy of life and my feelings reading *Forever and a Death*. "We can only do what we can," Marcus Mummius counsels Gordianus, who replies, "And hold to beauty where we find it."

**Don't Let the Mystery End Here.
Try More Great Books From
HARD CASE CRIME!**

Hard Case Crime brings you gripping, award-winning crime fiction
by best-selling authors and the hottest new writers in the field.
Find out what you've been missing:

The COMEDY
Is FINISHED
by DONALD E. WESTLAKE

The year is 1977, and America is finally getting over the nightmares of Watergate and Vietnam and the national hangover that was the 1960s.

But not everyone is ready to let it go. Not aging comedian Koo Davis, friend to generals and presidents and veteran of countless USO tours to buck up American troops in the field. And not the five remaining members of the self-proclaimed People's Revolutionary Army, who've decided that kidnapping Koo Davis would be the perfect way to bring their cause back to life...

RAVES FOR DONALD E. WESTLAKE:

"One of the great writers of the 20th Century."
— Newsweek

*"[A] book by this guy
is cause for happiness."*
— Stephen King

**Available now at your favorite bookstore.
For more information, visit
www.HardCaseCrime.com**

M
Westlake, Donald
Forever and a death

DATE DUE		
SE 15 '2		

HERITAGE VILLAGE
LIBRARY

WITHDRAWN